SW. GA. REG. LIB. P9-BYB-358
DECATUR • MILLER • SEMINOLE
BAINBRIDGE, GEORGIA

SWGRL-DEC LG-PRNT
31052005483726
LP MCC 2001
McCrumb, Sharyn.
The songcatcher /

WITHDRAWN

The Songcatcher

SHARYN MCCRUMB

The Songcatcher

A Ballad Novel

WHEELER
PUBLISHING, INC.
ROCKLAND, MA

★ AN AMERICAN COMPANY ★

Copyright © 2001 by Sharyn McCrumb
All rights reserved.

Published in Large Print by arrangement with Dutton, a member of
Penguin Putnam, Inc., in the United States and Canada.

Wheeler Large Print Book Series.

Set in 16 pt Plantin.

Library of Congress Cataloging-in-Publication Data

McCrumb, Sharyn, 1948-.
    The songcatcher / Sharyn McCrumb.
        p. (large print) cm.(Wheeler large print book series)
    ISBN 1-58724-047-5 (hardcover)
    1. Scottish Americans—Fiction. 2. North Carolina—Fiction.
3. Mountain life—Fiction. 4. Women singers—Fiction.
5. Folk singers—Fiction. 6. Ballads—Fiction. 7. Large type books.
    I. Title. II. Series

[PS3563.C3527 S66   2001b]
813'.54—dc21   2001035199
                                                              CIP

For My Friends of Song

Betty Smith
Sweetwater (Shelley Stevens,
Shari Wolf, and Cindy Funk)
Jack Hinshelwood

Prologue

The old man in the lawn chair had visitors already.

He sat near the railing of the redwood deck, leaning forward in his aluminum chair, nodding and smiling, deeply engrossed in his conversation. To everything else he was oblivious: to the patchwork of fields and forest stretching away from the deck toward a haze of mountains in the distance; to the sound of the dog, chained in the yard below, now howling its sudden displeasure; and to the two women in the doorway who watched him in strained silence.

"There ain't nobody there but him," Becky Tilden whispered. She jerked her head toward the old man in the chair.

Nora Bonesteel stood beside her on the threshold of the small frame house, watching the man on the deck. Her hair was the same silver color as her woolen shawl, but for all her seventy-odd years, she still stood tall and straight. The years had been kinder to her than they had been to her old friend in the lawn chair.

1

He sat there hunched and shrunken in the baggy blue sweater that had once fit him, oblivious to their presence by his deafness and perhaps for other reasons as well.

"He's been this way for a week now," Becky said. "He'll sit out there or else in the front room for an hour or more, talking up a storm, and then he'll call me in and ask me to bring coffee for him and his guests. But there's never anybody there but him."

"Yes," said Nora Bonesteel. "I see."

"Well, look at him! He's a-talking to thin air. Nothing wrong with him. Physically, I mean. Except that he's old. Eighty-three last September. His hearing is almost gone, and his eyes aren't what they used to be, but his mind seems clear enough when he talks to me. Judge knows who he is, and where he is, and all. It's just this one notion he's got that scares me. He insists he's having company, and nothing I say makes a whit of difference."

Nora Bonesteel nodded. "It does happen."

"And Judge just can't understand why I can't see them, too." Her voice quavered. "He won't go into a home, mind you. He was always dead set against that. I just don't want him to forget who folks are. I can get extra nurses in if he starts to wander, or if his health fails. If Medicare won't pay for it, he can afford it himself, but he seems fine except for this one thing."

Nora Bonesteel laid her hand on Becky Tilden's arm. "Don't you worry about a nursing home," she said. "It won't come to

2

that." Her eyes never left the old man, still unaware of their presence, still smiling and nodding as if he were not alone on the deck.

He seemed shrunken now. The cardigan sweater hung loosely from his bony shoulders, and the skin of his face and hands were mottled parchment, stretched taut across bone. He bore little resemblance to the jaunty, black-haired boy who had once chased a young Nora Bonesteel through a mountain briar patch, waving a black snake for a bullwhip. He would be too small now to fit in the second lieutenant's uniform that he had worn when he came home on leave in World War II.

"I thought maybe he was lonely," his housekeeper was saying. "I thought that if he had a real visitor, it would help take his mind off the imaginary ones, but he doesn't have many friends left."

Nora Bonesteel nodded. Never did have, she thought. Most people at eighty have outlived the majority of their acquaintances, but even in his youth John Walker had never had the knack for keeping friends. She reckoned it was the McCourry blood on his mother's side. The McCourry clan was known for keeping to themselves. To the world in general they were genial enough, invariably pleasant if you made an effort to befriend them, but indifferent to whether you stayed around or not. People came and went. It was all one to the McCourrys.

"I'm grateful to you for coming." The sentence trailed off because Becky Tilden wasn't

3

sure what to call this old woman that she'd known all her life. At fifty she would feel foolish saying "Aunt Nora," as she had in her teens, and "Miz Bonesteel" seemed too formal for so long an acquaintance. Still, Becky could not imagine being on a first-name basis with this ramrod of a woman, who had seemed old to her forever.

"I'm glad to come," said Nora Bonesteel. "John and I have known each other for more years than I care to count."

Becky Tilden nodded, wondering if she should say any more. She'd learned to cite Scripture in Miz Bonesteel's Sunday school class, and she still had the Jerusalem quilt that Nora had made for her parents when they got married back in 1951, but like everybody else in Wake County, Becky Tilden knew what people said about Nora Bonesteel. That she knew things. The Sight, they called it. They said that when she was a child she would see black crepe ribbons on the beehives, or ask about funeral wreaths that weren't there yet, and sure enough, within a week of her saying such a thing, there would be a death in the family where she'd seen the signs. Nora Bonesteel never talked about it herself, and Lord knows she never volunteered to tell anybody what lay in store for them, but still it made people uneasy, wondering what she knew about them that they'd rather not know themselves.

Becky Tilden stood there in the doorway twisting her apron, still watching the old man.

4

Nora Bonesteel touched her arm. "I'll go and have a word with him," she said.

His visitors are gone now.

Nora Bonesteel squared her shoulders and walked out onto the deck to visit her old friend.

Chapter One

Nora Bonesteel had not seen him for years.

More than a decade ago John Walker quit his one-man law practice, and he and his wife Luanne had left the Tennessee mountains to retire in a tiny lakeside cottage in western North Carolina, where John had declared his intention to divide the rest of his days between fishing and playing bridge. Since he didn't like people much, his ties to the community did not particularly concern him. His fellow bridge players and other new acquaintances saw John as a genial old fellow with an endless supply of funny stories, but that amiable facade was just a trick to keep people from getting too close. John Walker realized long ago that if you make people laugh, they never realize that they don't know you at all.

The Walkers had a few good years of retirement, and then Luanne's health began to fail. When the housekeeping became too much for one old fellow to handle, John had hired Becky Tilden from the trailer park down the road to serve as a housekeeper and practical nurse. She had moved to the lake after an early and disastrous marriage, but originally she had been a Harkryder from Wake County, Tennessee, where John and Luanne had spent most of their lives. John helped her with the paperwork on her divorce, and he saw to it that Olan hadn't made off with their Christmas club money or the wedding present silver plate.

Becky had been with the Walkers ever since, more than ten years now. After Luanne died of a stroke, Becky looked in on John a couple of times a week, and he stayed on there in the lake house, fighting old age and the infirmity which takes first one's dignity, and then takes everything.

Since Becky was as plain as pea turkey and had never finished high school, not even the most fanciful local gossips ever assumed there was anything going on between John Walker and his housekeeper, and there never was. John came from a generation that liked pretty women who knew their place; a generation that, lacking in all domestic skills, needed women to look after them. Maybe if John hadn't found Becky, he'd have had to let some likely looking widow snare him, just for the house-keeping. After Luanne's death, more than one local biddy had tried to get her hooks into him at the bridge club, but the aging Clairol blonde who always passed after his two no-trump opening bid had no chance of becoming the second Mrs. Walker.

It was easier just to pay Becky minimum wage and not have to deal with courting and new kinfolks, grown stepchildren maybe, and all the rest of the social nonsense that John never

8

could stand even when he had good health and more patience.

Perhaps Becky's greatest skill was the ability to put up with John Walker. Becky called the old man "Judge," because he had once been a magistrate back in Tennessee, and, while she felt too close to him to call him "Mr. Walker," it didn't seem right to her to call him "John" at his age and her just working for him. So to Becky, and by extension to everyone else in his new community, the old man became known as "Judge." He spent his seventies in a comfortable haze of fishing trips punctuated by bridge games, in an isolation that he thought of as independence, but this last Indian summer of health and middle age could not go on forever.

At last, after a winter bout with bronchial pneumonia, the judge had lost the battle for self-sufficiency, and, despite his bitter objections, Becky Tilden had brought him back to Tennessee, where she wouldn't be so alone in caring for the old man. Hamelin was near to her kin and to the local hospital she trusted more than the "fancy country club one" near the lake in North Carolina. The lake folks were polite enough, but they treated her like the "help," and the high-priced doctors at that hospital acted like she didn't have good sense, so she told John that it was time they went home. He was too feeble now for fishing, and too set in his ways to find new help, so back they went to Hamelin, just one mountain over the Tennessee line. Becky saw to the packing, and the closing of the last good times of Judge's life. With the power of attorney he had given her in case of a medical emergency, Becky sold the lake cottage through an ad in the paper, because she'd heard—somewhere—that real estate agents charged a twenty percent commission. The judge didn't seem to care what she did as long as he was kept out of it.

The cottage sold in a week, for far less than it was worth, but they were pleased with the transaction, because Becky didn't know any better and John was past caring. They used the money from the sale to buy a small frame house on five acres of hillside near town. The house was put in both their names, with the understanding that Becky would inherit it when Judge died. The old man was ending where he had begun, no more than a dozen miles from the farmhouse he had been born in.

They had settled in well enough, and Becky managed to fit in most of the lake house furniture, though some of the rooms were so cluttered they were hard to walk through. Judge didn't want to throw anything away, though. That old furniture was all of the past he had left, she supposed. He seemed to be happy enough in the new place until just recently, when he started having these conversations with people who just flat weren't there. He seemed fine, otherwise, but Becky was afraid that things were going to get worse, and she cast about for somebody who could tell her how much worse and how soon it was likely to happen.

At first Becky had not even thought to call Nora Bonesteel, who was known in these parts for having the Sight. The Judge was past eighty, so the future was not exactly hard to predict. It was just a question of when, and that didn't matter very much. He could go whenever he was ready, as far as Becky was concerned. He had lived a full life, and there didn't seem to be anything to look forward to on his part. As for Becky herself, she was fifty, and she reckoned that was old enough to be on her own when the time came. She still had family back in one of the hollers a few miles from town, but she didn't talk about her folks, and Judge had never known her to visit them. She reckoned Judge was family to her, after all these years, but the old man's death didn't worry her much. The prospect of a prolonged and expensive illness was another matter, however. She was afraid they might lose the house if he needed too much intensive care.

When Judge started acting peculiar and hearing voices, Becky had sent straight away for Dr. Banner, who had been everybody's doctor when she was growing up in these parts. The doctor was nearly as old as Judge, and semiretired now, but he was alert and spry enough to be twenty years younger, and he still made house calls for old friends.

John Walker had treated the doctor's visit as a social call, greeting him as calmly and pleasantly as he did the other callers that helped him pass the time these days—the ones that

11

Becky couldn't see. When Alton Banner pulled out his stethoscope and said, "Well, John, it's good to visit with you, but I came to work," Judge had not protested, except to say that he felt as well as could be expected for a man over eighty. When Becky saw that Judge was going to cooperate with the examination, she left the two of them alone in the den to get on with it.

Half an hour later, when she returned with mugs of coffee and a plate of Little Debbie brownies, carefully unwrapped and put on a Melmac plate, the medical part of the visit was over. The two old friends were sitting in companionable silence watching the Sports Channel on television. A while later, when John Walker had nodded off to sleep in his armchair, Becky walked Alton Banner to the door.

"What do you reckon?" she asked. "Is it... old-timers disease?" Alzheimer's, she meant. Alton Banner didn't correct her. Many of his less educated patients called it that, and he supposed it was as good a name as any. Whatever you called the ailment, it was a terrifying prospect. Poor Becky—she'd had to take a deep breath before she could even bring herself to say the words. He knew she was worried about her own future when John Walker passed on, and he supposed she hated the thought of Judge going that way, dying a little bit at a time, and taking all the good memories with him as he lost his own.

The doctor shook his head. "I see no sign of senile dementia. John is lucid. We talked about everything from Tennessee football to his blood pressure medication—which, incidentally, seems to be working. We can be thankful for that. He's as healthy as a person can be and still be in his eighties. His hearing isn't what it once was. Neither is mine, come to that. But as for the quality of the conversation, John was holding his own as well as he ever did. I saw no deterioration."

"Did he tell you about his visitors?"

"None of them showed up while I was with him. John knew who I was. He wasn't disoriented or delusional in conversation. He seems all right to me."

"I'm glad you think so." The tone of her voice made it clear that she wasn't convinced.

Alton Banner smiled. "Well, if you're still worried, Becky, we can haul John into the medical center in Johnson City and do a thousand dollars' worth of tests, but after they finish with him, I don't think we'll know a bit more than we do right now. Knowing John, I don't think we could get him into that hospital for tests with a cattle prod, but if you want me to order it, I will, and you can try to make him go."

"But...he's seeing things."

"Yes, he told me about the visitors. Just mentioned them in passing. It doesn't seem to worry him, though."

"What should I do about it? Can you give him something?"

Alton Banner shook his head. "John isn't the problem, Becky," he said at last. "You are.

You're the one that's worrying herself sick over the situation. John is fine. But I think you ought to call Nora Bonesteel. Ask her to come by and visit John."

"Nora Bonesteel? But why?"

Alton Banner hesitated for a moment before he answered. "John might be lonely," he said at last. "It would do him good to have some real live visitors every now and again. Nora Bonesteel has known him all her life, so they will have things to talk about, memories to share. Nora Bonesteel is patient with folks who are ailing. You send for her. Tell her I advised it. She'll come." All that was true enough. If there was more to it than that, Alton Banner saw no need to explain it to Becky Tilden.

Now that Nora Bonesteel had come, Becky wondered what good her visit was going to do. Judge was having strange visions these days, but Nora Bonesteel had "seen" things all her life. What consolation could she be on the subject of hallucinations?

"I hate to see him like this," said Becky, still watching John Walker from the doorway. "Judge was always such a tartar. If you didn't fix just exactly what he wanted for lunch, or if you forgot to pick up something when he sent you to town, he'd tear a strip off you with his harsh words. Now Miss Luanne wasn't put off at all by his domineering moods. She knew how to get around him, and he thought the world of her. She would just laugh at him when he got into one of his conniptions, but he always scared me green, even though I knew he wouldn't do nothing but fuss. He's never even threatened to fire me. Judge could say the most cruel things, though. You'd do anything to make him stop." She stared at the old man in the chair, searching for some trace of the bearlike tyrant he had once been.

"Judge can be funny when he wants to be. People used to say he was more like Andy Griffith than Andy hisself, but he has a side to him, too. Sometimes I felt about eight years old when I was around Judge, and I used to wonder if that would have changed if I'd had an education and an outside job to make money that didn't come from him."

"It's hard to say."

"Well, he was my boss, and I let him have the last word, every time, right or wrong. He liked being in charge, that's for sure. And, you know, I could never imagine him losing that power. I never could picture Judge old and weak...wasting away. I always thought he'd just keel over one day from sheer rage. You know, caught behind a farm truck on the no-passing stretch of Route 107? Oh, he hates slow drivers! I thought one day Judge would boil over in fury and burst an artery, and it would all be over in two seconds. One minute he'd be his fierce old self, and the next minute he'd be gone—instantaneous darkness, like a power outage in a thunderstorm. That is the one thing about Judge I was sure of."

Nora Bonesteel nodded, but she was still

looking out at the old man in the lawn chair. She had never seen the tyrannical side of John Walker, but then she didn't have to live with him. The dark side of mountain politeness is that an angry man sometimes swallows his rage against the world at large, and lets it out only in the privacy of his home. She'd known of more than one genial and witty man who was a terror in private.

Whatever John Walker's anger had been about, it was gone now. All that was left was the McCourry indifference, the hunkering down into the sufficiency of self that was the McCourrys' strength and their refuge—and ultimately the source of their loneliness. There was nothing she could do to change that, and even if she could it was likely that John wouldn't want her to try.

"It would have been easier on everybody, wouldn't it?" said Becky. "If Judge had just died in a heartbeat during one of his rages?"

Nora Bonesteel considered it. "Hardly any way is easy," she said. "When people are taken sudden, their families grieve because there wasn't time to resolve things, to make peace, and say good-bye. Oftentimes they are left with guilt. At least you've been given time to settle things."

"Well...I guess..." Becky didn't see any point in trying to make peace with a deaf old man who had probably forgotten most of the injuries he had inflicted—cruel words and slights that still hurt her to the heart when she let herself dwell on them. What could he possibly say that would make up for the past, and how much sincerity would there be in any profession of forgiveness she made?

"Speaking of resolving things: You've called his daughter, haven't you?"

Becky Tilden's eyes widened, and she darted a glance at John Walker to see if he had heard them. "No!" she whispered. "I can't! He'd never let me!"

Nora Bonesteel's face hardened into the scowl reserved for irreverent boys in Sunday school class. "And why not?"

"He wouldn't let me. He never wants her to know when he's took sick. He'd say it's on account of Lark being so famous and busy and all, and him not wanting to bother her with his aches and pains, but that's not the real reason. They didn't get along, you know. Never did. He doesn't want her to come."

"Never mind what he wants, Becky Tilden. And don't try to tell me that an eighty-three-year-old man could stop you from making a phone call. Dying in peace is a fine thing, I'm sure, but leaving your family in peace is just as important, and if that man goes without letting his only child come to say good-bye, it will be the cruelest thing he's ever done to her—and to my mind, that's saying something."

Becky's face took on the mulish expression that meant that she would try to get out of the chore without making an outright refusal. "Even if I call her, she may not want to come back."

"She ought to be given the chance, though. It's her that has to go on living with memories, so I say it's more her decision than his. Will you tell him that or shall I?"

Becky's clouded face cleared with relief. "Oh, Miz Nora, would you tell him? Ever' time I try to talk about Lark, he just sets his face like a stone idol and turns away muttering. Would you like me to take you out to him now? So you can tell him?"

Nora Bonesteel sighed. "I've known John a long time, but we're not close. This would be better coming from you, but if I have to do it I will. John Walker never scared me any. Not even waving a black snake over his head, and I'm not about to start being afraid of him now."

"Well...try not to upset him."

"It will be all right, Becky. I won't leave until he's back in a good mood. You go in and call his daughter. Tell her she may not have long to dither about this."

Becky gasped. "You think...I mean...do you *know*?"

Nora Bonesteel would not be drawn. "Never mind what I know," she said. "You make that call right now."

The music soared on fiddle strings and thundered in drumbeats in her head. The tour bus had just reached a break in the trees on a Colorado mountainside, sending shafts of sunlight down on a patchwork of green rectangles hemstitched by white-trunked trees and lines of narrow creeks. Sometimes she liked to look out at the scenery, if only to measure their progress in the changing landscape, but today her mind was on other things and she was content to let the world slide by beneath her, unnoticed. Right now the sounds in her head were more compelling than the wonder of seeing the valley below from a telescopic distance. When you traveled enough—and lord knows she did—then beautiful scenery was nothing to get excited about anymore. Nothing worth seeing out the window. She spent a lot of the time sleeping in her little bedroom in the back of the bus. After ten years in show business, road trips were just downtime to be used productively, as long as the twists and turns didn't remind you that your "office" was hurtling along at sixty miles an hour.

Lark McCourry clasped the earphones against her ears, listening not only to melody but to rhythm, and chord changes, and what she called the *song path*, by which she meant that she could hear where the song was going. Most people could tell generalities about a song in the music of their own culture. There was a pattern that songs followed. Each mode had its own rules, but after a while you learned to know what to expect in each one. Often a song played on the guitar would bring the tune back to the dominant chord to complete the verse where it began, and then the listener could hear that an ending had been reached. Lark's song path went beyond that, though. When she closed her eyes, she could see the notes as colors. She could watch them swirl around each other in swaths of pastel harmony as the notes intertwined to make chords.

She felt a gentle tapping on her arm, and in her mind the colors faded. She switched off the CD player. "Yes?"

"You're missing some pretty scenery out there."

She managed a weak smile. Stevie Wolfe was a genius with catgut, and he could play anything anybody could hum, but he never could keep his mouth shut on road trips. She'd never seen him pick up a book. Here in the Meadowlark, a customized Greyhound that had cost as much as her first house, Stevie paced the aisles so much that he might as well have walked to the performance. On planes he kept his seat belt on, with the aid of constant reminders from everybody else, but he never sat still. Airborne pacing became foot-tapping or the drumming of his fingers on the armrest. Lark thought he struck up conversations just to let his mouth move. He was on the wagon, though, and that was something. Better a sober nuisance than a dead drunk lead guitar, she thought.

"Guess these mountains are bigger than those molehills of yours back home."

She rolled her eyes. Jamie Raeburn, taking an outing from his corporate job with the record label, had finally decided to say something, and wouldn't you know it would be a

20

condescending remark. *Save us from the urban bureaucrats,* Lark thought.

Aloud she said, "Our mountains are older. The Appalachians probably looked like this when dinosaurs walked the earth, when these mountains really *were* molehills."

"Couple of trailers here and there," Stevie Wolfe said innocently. "Look, Lark! Don't it might remind you of your Tennessee mountain home."

He was teasing. The Dolly Parton song title was part of the joke, but the corporate guy didn't get it. He thought Stevie was serious, for god's sake. Lark sighed. "You guys are baiting me, hoping I'll get on my soapbox about east Tennessee, because you've got the fidgets. You can't stand stillness and you can't stand silence. Well, lay off. It won't work."

Raeburn smiled indulgently at her. Celebrities were like children, really. You had to take that into account. "Let's hear your soapbox speech about east Tennessee. I'm interested. Honest."

Remembering forbearance, Lark changed her scowl to a sigh. "Trailers my ass," she said. "We weren't all poor back in east Tennessee, Jamie. My father was a lawyer."

Made a lawyer, the farm cousins used to say: *John Walker made a lawyer,* as if children were born as formless as clay and could be molded into their adult identities like model people in toy villages, discernible by their tools of office: the doctor with his stethoscope, the policeman

21

with his badge. Lark looked down at the guitar that rested on a stand beside her stool. *I made a musician,* she thought.

Made a musician. It was true enough that musicians are born, not made, in the sense that the ability to carry a tune and the quality of one's voice was a gift. Those things could not be taught, and maybe in the old days they would have been enough to make a musician of their possessor, but by the time Lark McCourry came along, with a head full of old songs and a voice to sing them with, voice and memory were no longer enough. Now the music business was more business than music. Now it took movie star looks and a dancer's body to keep you in the game. And sometimes even the voice was optional, now that studio magic and backup singers could smooth over any imperfections in an otherwise perfect package. Lark sometimes wondered if plump little Patsy Cline would have made it past the demo tape in the contemporary music world of size-four divas. The fat lady doesn't sing anymore.

Jamie pointed to the tape player in her lap, "So how do you like the song?"

Lark had not worked with Jamie Raeburn before. He had just been assigned to help her choose songs for a new album, and he had come on the road trip to get a sense of her music and her audience. She hoped he knew what he was doing. You could never tell with corporate.

She pressed the rewind key on the tape

player. "It's pretty good, Jamie. I'm impressed. Not bad for your first effort."

"So how does it strike you?"

She considered it. "Well, when you listen to it for a while, the rhythm just becomes your heartbeat. It made me want to sway in time to the music, which is good. It's Scottish, isn't it?"

Jamie Raeburn shrugged. "Close enough. From the Gaelic-speaking end of Britain anyhow. Did you recognize the tune, or was it just the shape of the melody that tipped you off about its origin?"

"Well, between that and the percussion it could hardly be anything else. Those drums in the background are bodhrans, aren't they?"

"Sound like it to me."

"I didn't recognize it, though. It isn't new, is it? Not with a sound like that it isn't."

He shook his head. "Traditional. I just thought you might know it."

"Don't think so. I never heard it played back home. I thought the recording might be the Chieftains. Is the tune old enough to have come over with the pioneers?"

"I'd have to look it up to be sure, but offhand I'd say it's as old as the Mountains of Mourne. That version you're listening to is by one of my favorite musicians—Mike Cross, who's from North Carolina, not Ireland, which is why I thought you might know it."

She shook her head. "I like it, though."

"Good. It's traditional—so no copyright problem. I thought that including it would add a grace note to the next album."

"Does it have words?"

"None that I ever heard. We'd have to do it as an instrumental—or take a crack at writing the lyrics ourselves."

She nodded thoughtfully. "That might work. I have written songs for other albums."

"I know. You wrote 'Prayers the Devil Answers,' didn't you?"

"Yeah. Title song on my first album. It came from a saying in our family. When you wish for something and it comes true in a bad way that you weren't expecting, we used to say that it was a prayer the devil answered."

Raeburn smiled. "Great line."

"I thought so. It got a lot of attention. Won some awards. I guess I owe my career to that song." She looked around at the shabby old bus and smiled. "Maybe *that* was a prayer the devil answered. So...what's the name of this tune on the tape?"

He looked pleased with himself. "Well, see, that's why I thought you'd know. But I couldn't resist it. It's called 'Lark in the Morning'."

She stared at him. "You're serious?"

"I am. So if you like the melody, I think we have our title song, don't you?"

"Sure. Perfect. But is it obscure enough? I don't want to compete with half a dozen other versions of it when the album comes out."

"I don't think that will be a problem. I'll check to make sure, of course."

"Good. Then all we need are a few more songs to record. Tunes that haven't been

24

done to death. Remember when Dolly Parton and Kurt Cobain both did 'In the Pines' on albums in the same month?"

Jamie Raeburn shrugged. "Go figure," he said. He had been in high school when Kurt Cobain died, but it wouldn't be prudent to mention that to the talent here; might make her feel old. Depression was bad for performance. "Now, as to other tunes, I can suggest one or two, but that's not really my thing. I thought that finding obscure folk melodies might be more in your line, given your Tennessee down-home roots. Surely there are old songs floating around those mountain hollers that have never been recorded. Something obscure that you heard as a child on somebody's front porch?"

She wrinkled her nose. Hillbilly jokes were her least favorite part of the job. It was hard to tell if people were kidding or if they really were that stupid. Lark decided that her role, being the cultural ambassador for Appalachia, mostly meant informing city types that *The Dukes of Hazzard* was not a documentary. Sometimes, though, even the documentaries weren't what you'd call true. In one recent case a socialite filmmaker made a "documentary" about the poor people of a small community in Appalachia and got on all the networks as the authority on the mountain South. Her film showed gaunt poor people living in shacks and trailers, and people everywhere tut-tutted about how sad it was that everybody in that area was so pitiful. What they didn't know was

25

that in order to reach those few shanty houses, the film crew had to drive past two miles of well-kept, middle-class brick houses and an expensive new stone-and-glass community center. None of those positive images appeared in the film, of course. It would have spoiled the effect. Everything was image these days. Nobody cared what was real.

"Songs in the holler." She sighed. "You're most of a century too late for quaint, Jamie. If you wanted to hear traditional songs, you should have asked my grandmother. When I was growing up, we were listening to Kris Kristofferson and Dolly Parton. Besides, the song catchers came in between the world wars, and they collected every song anybody would sing for them."

"Well, that's good. Preserving the heritage."

Lark shook her head. "Nothing is ever that easy. I'll tell you about it some time. It'll be right up your alley."

A song. Singers gathered on a porch. She closed her eyes, remembering a still summer evening on a dark front porch. A group of men in work boots sat in straight-backed kitchen chairs, handing a guitar back and forth. She pictured the glow of a lit cigarette wavering on somebody's lips as he sang harmony in a quavering tenor voice.

She pushed harder at the memory, trying to add sound to the images running in her head, but the audio portion of the scene would not be summoned. She couldn't have been more than eight years old at the time, because not long after that, little girls aren't allowed to hang around anymore when the men folk get together. When they are little, all youngsters are puppies, free to tag along if they don't make nuisances of themselves. Then children of either sex can be invisible listeners when the songs are sung and the tales are told by the menfolk in the family, but when little girls become big girls, the spell is broken. After that, without a harsh word being said, a wall as insubstantial as a spiderweb blocked the girl child away forever from the company of the men. She had become "the other," and now her place was in the kitchen and parlor where different songs were sung and different stories told, this time punctuated by women's work with darning needle or paring knife.

There had been a song, though. She had heard it on one of those last magical summer evenings before she had been banished from the men's world. What was that song? An old sad melody. She couldn't remember an instrument. Just sung, then, without accompaniment. Something about a woman and a ghost. She had only heard it once, but who had sung it? One of her great-uncles? The memory eluded her.

"Couldn't you take a couple of days and go home?" Jamie was saying. "Maybe your family could come up with some old songs."

She sighed. "I don't think so. My father is too old now to be much help. His hearing is shot. But even when he was younger, he was fairly hopeless. In high school, when I first got interested in folk music, I tried to get him to sing me some old songs, because it was cool to come up with tunes that nobody else knew. I got 'Little Margaret' from him, which is a Child Ballad, and he said it had been handed down in the family, so I thought I was really on to a storehouse of cultural riches." She laughed at the memory. "Daddy's next 'ancient folk ballad' turned out to have been written in 1959. And the one after that was Roy Acuff's 'Wreck on the Highway,' which anybody ought to know is not an eighteenth-century folk ballad. It turns out that my father cannot tell authentic ballads from forties jukebox tunes. And even when he manages to get the words right, his melodies are pretty shaky. Picture Francis Child possessed by Ernest Tubb. That's my father doing English folk tunes. By the time he's done with her, Barbry Ellen has morphed into Minnie Pearl."

"Barbara Allen morphing into Minnie Pearl." Jamie nodded approvingly. "You know, that's the best definition of country music I ever heard."

"Well, I just don't think it would do any good for me to go back to Wake County in search of material. Not without a time machine."

"Maybe not."

She shrugged. "But that isn't the real reason I don't want to go back. My father lives there. He and I don't get along."

"Well, aren't there other people back there that might know the song?"

She considered it. "Maybe. Maybe I will go. There's people back there I wouldn't mind seeing. It's just that my dad isn't one of them."

In her white frame house on Ashe Mountain, Nora Bonesteel was closing the day. She had finished her cup of tea, and washed the silver teaspoon and the china cup. Her sewing was laid aside in its basket with her reading glasses close by. She was tired.

Every evening just past ten, she would begin the ritual of readying the house for the night: making sure that the outside doors were locked and the curtains closed, then shutting off the lights one by one. First she checked the kitchen to see that it was tidied, and that the stove burners had not been left on. Then, with a last look, she put out the light. Next she came to her parlor, with its stone fireplace and the braided rag rug over the plank floor—a tidy room, smelling of lemon oil and beeswax. Then the overhead light in the hallway that led to her bedroom. After the white embroidered counterpane had been turned down to the foot of the bed, and the curtains securely drawn, she would turn on the lamp on her bedside table, shut off the ceiling light, and close the bedroom door.

For nearly half a century now Nora Bonesteel had lived alone on Ashe Mountain, and this evening ritual had stretched into decades, unchanged. Now that she had grown old, she decided that the closing of life involved much the same process as ending the day. Over the years of your life span you moved from bright lights and many rooms into a series of ever-diminishing spaces, until at last your world was a circle of lamplight only as large as your bed. And then you put out the light.

She lay in bed, but sleep would not come. Something was troubling her, but she wasn't sure what it was. She had no more aches and pains than usual, the garden was all right for this time of year, and no one else's sorrow came to mind that could keep her from sleeping.

There was no use lying in bed and trying to force sleep to come, so she got up, went to the kitchen, and put the kettle on for a cup of tea. While she waited for the water to boil, she sat down at the table and began to lay out a game of solitaire. Patience, some people called it, and she could see why. Playing cards alone, game after game, was a good way to lull your mind into that drifting state when thoughts rose up to the surface, and if you were lucky you could spot what it was that really troubled you. The game itself ceased to matter by the time the drifting state arrived, which was just as well, because Nora found that then she would often know what a card would be before she turned it over. She continued to lay out the cards without much interest in the outcome as she searched for the thorn of her sleeplessness.

John Walker was going to die soon, but surely that was not what troubled her. She regretted losing a part of her own history in the passing of an old friend, but death was a natural facet of existence, and not something that she could change. She had lost dearer friends than John as the years went by, and she reckoned she was used to parting with folks by now.

She thought back to her conversation with him that afternoon. He had turned to look up at her, and after a moment while his failing eyesight registered recognition, he gave her a smile that stretched back forty years. "Well, Miss Nora Bonesteel! The belle of Dark Hollow." He paused for a moment, peering at her with narrowed eyes. "Did Becky let you in?"

"She did."

"Good. She can see you then."

Nora Bonesteel nodded. "Becky can see me just fine, John."

"Glad to hear it. It's been like old home week around here lately. I don't know when I've had so much company. My uncle Henry was here just a little while ago. You know what a fiddle player he was."

"I remember," said Nora. "How do you feel, John?"

"I had beans and cornbread for lunch. And fresh tomatoes. You can't beat that. Ate by myself, though. Becky wouldn't bring but one plate."

"I don't reckon your company was hungry, John. You know, Henry died back in...well, '74, I believe it was."

"No, he was here today. Looking fit as

ever. You just missed him. And Greg McElroy. You remember him?"

Nora nodded. Greg McElroy had gone to school with them in a little one-room schoolhouse between the river and the railroad tracks. He had been the brightest of the bunch. The first day of school the young teacher had caught Greg reading a Zane Gray novel tucked inside his third-grade reader, and by the end of the day, he had joined John and Nora in the fifth-grade reading circle. Greg McElroy had gone down in a Flying Fortress over Belgium in 1944.

"Who else comes to see you, John?" she asked gently. "Luanne?"

"No. Not Luanne." He frowned with the effort of remembering. "Not Luanne. Some old friends, and then some old folks I don't know," he said at last. "I think maybe they're relatives of mine, but I don't recall just who they are."

"It's good that you're having visitors, John."

"Becky claims she can't see them," he said plaintively.

Nora put her hand on his shoulder. "I can see them, John."

"Figured you could."

"I think they've come to take you off on a journey with them."

The old man considered this. Nora Bonesteel waited. "That might be all right," he said at last.

"Yes, I think it will, John. I think that you can trust Greg and your uncle Henry to...to see you safely home...but before you head off with them, there's somebody else you need to ask to come and visit you. And that somebody is Lark."

John Walker set his jaw. "*Lark* she calls herself. And taking her grandmother's last name. Linda Walker wasn't fancy enough, I reckon. She doesn't care about us. Never has. She's a rich girl now. She has got above her raising."

Nora sighed. She knew that young Linda Walker had grown up in a large brick home on the best street in Hamelin, with a lawyer father, a bridge-playing mother, and a maid to do the housework. Her success in music might have moved her up a class, but John's old age and his antisocial obstinance had moved him much farther down. She thought the gulf between them was of John's making, not his daughter's, but she decided to answer him with a milder comment so as to be truthful but not hurtful.

" 'Above her raising.' " Nora Bonesteel smiled gently. "Well, John, if some of us hadn't got above our raising every now and then, the rest of us would still be living in caves and eating raw meat, don't you reckon?"

But he had set his jaw and was no longer listening. He didn't want to talk about Lark, and he had always hated for a woman to tell him he was wrong, no matter how tactfully. Even a friend of more than sixty years was expected to know her place and keep her distance. Luanne had thought her lawyer husband had hung the moon, and whatever Becky Tilden thought, she had sense enough not to argue with her employer. Someone had to set John straight, though. Nora could face harsh words if she had to, and there wasn't time enough left to be humoring John Walker in his masculine vanity.

"Lark has to come home, John," she said quietly. "Get used to the idea."

The old man set his jaw. "Over my dead body."

Malcolm McCourry—1751

Long after the dark shape of Scotland had faded into the mist, I held on to that white pebble, clutching it in my fist and willing its long-promised magic to save me.

I could hear the roar of the cold sea heaving against the ship's hull, lashing the deck with waves, and my stomach pitched with every lurch of the vessel, but I was walled away in darkness, and I could see nothing.

The men who had taken me off the beach had locked me below deck in the brig. Maybe they meant it as a kindness so that I would not be washed overboard, or it may be that they thought a kidnapped boy might throw himself into the waves and try to swim for shore. They need not have worried on that account, for I knew what little chance a swimmer had in the cold waters off Scotland. I had seen more than one drowned man washed up on the beach of our island and brought back to the village on a plank, when the sea chose to give up its dead. For all my mother's fears, I had no wish to end my life so early, and I did not quite trust that pebble of mine to save me.

For the whole of my life—all nine years of it—I had carried that bit of sacred white rock, mostly to humor my mother, I suppose, for no child ever really believes in the possibility of his own death. A beating, though—now that was a certainty if my mother ever caught me without that stone in my pocket. Then she would either weep or flail me again, depending on her mood, and so I carried it to preserve myself, not from the sea's wrath, but from hers.

Not a week of my life had gone by without someone in the village hectoring me to keep that talisman with me always, for when the time came, it was to be my salvation. As I hunkered down below deck in the darkness of that brig, I was thinking that the blessed rock had done little enough to save me so far.

The waves pounded the hull, making the ship pitch so sharply that the deck must have stood straight up above the churning sea. Anything not battened down would tumble overboard and be lost in an instant. I could feel my heart pounding in rhythm to the waves, and in my narrow prison I shivered, thinking that though my captors had done me a good turn shutting me up here, so that I would not be swept away, they might well forget to release me if the ship began to founder. Best not to think of the ship going down, for then I might cry, and no good would come of that.

I flattened myself against the door of the brig, my stomach rumbling from hunger. For once I was glad enough that there was nothing in it to be lost in seasickness. I was much afraid of the storm and of the foreign-speaking out-landers who had taken me, but I think I remember a cold joy, too, knowing that adventure had come at last, and I faced my captivity with a heart lightened by knowing that the prophecy hanging over me all my life was coming to pass, so that, dead or alive, I would be free of it.

I had never sailed on so large a vessel, but, despite my mother's protests, I had been taken out on the fishing boats often enough, for the sea was both mother and master in our village. We lived on a dot of land called only "island"—*Islay* on the sea charts. I knew the pitch and toss of seafaring. I knew, too, that the sea was cruel. It would take me if it could.

Tangled in the skein of my earliest memories was my mother's fear of the sea. In a land of fishermen and seafarers, all our women-folk hated the ocean, for every one of them had lost a man to it: father, husband, brother, son. The sea was the enemy, and if the men felt the spell of its magic, no Highland woman ever did. But my mother feared more than most, because of the prophecy.

The sea will take him.

The midwife foretold it on the day of my birth, and who on the island ever doubted her? She was a stern silent woman, who tended to the sick more from duty than from kindness, but for all her dour ways, she had the healing touch, and people with sickness in the house were glad to see her come—but glad to see her go as well. She knew things.

The tale tellers said that she had drunk two drams from the *Banrigh's* cup, an act that had given her great wisdom, but perhaps the old woman was not magic at all, but had only lived long enough to learn a great many things. In our village the tale tellers have a fanciful explanation for everything, all spoken so solemnly that you cannot know if they believe it themselves or not, for they never smile. The old men say that our island, which in Gaelic is *ile,* was named in olden times for a Viking princess called Ila, who walked over the sea from Ireland, using the wee islands for stepping stones. They say that she died on our island, and that her grave is marked by the standing stone above Knock Bay. It is an unlucky place, but it is on the other side of the island, and for all the mischief my friends and I got up to, we never ventured there.

My village is on the Rinns of Islay, a wing of land that juts westward off the main body of the island, separated from the other half by Loch Indaal, which is more of a great long bay than a lake, for it is connected to the sea and deep enough for tall ships to navigate. They go past our village on the way to Port Charlotte, where our landlord Great Daniel Campbell lives. The boys watch the tall ships sail past, and we wish ourselves aboard, with a chance to see more of the world than we are ever likely to. I wished it as hard as anyone, despite the prophecy that hung over me.

The sea will take him.

The midwife who birthed me had the Sight, and if it ever steered her wrong, I never heard tell of it. No one could remember a time when she was not old. She kept to herself, and people had no desire for her company, nor she for theirs, except when necessity made them ask for her help. At those times they were careful to pay her with an egg or a hunk of cheese, so that they would not be beholden to her. She had the gift of knowing what was to come, or of seeing things that happened far away, and most of what she had to tell folk was news they'd as soon not hear, so it was only human nature to keep clear of her, except when the need for her skill was too great to ignore.

Many times I'd heard the women talk of how the old one had helped my mother with the birthing when she was called to straw. She did as much for all the women in the parish. As the wise woman she knew what herbs to give to stop the bleeding, when a dram of whiskey was better for the sufferer than water, and how to take the pain away with soft words and a candle flame. My mother's voice always trembled when she told the part about when the birthing was over, and myself the newborn had been washed and wrapped in homespun wool, with a pinch of salt put in my mouth for protection. Then the old woman looked into my wobbly blue eyes, and pronounced my destiny.

The sea will take him, she had said, and she stared into the peat fire with a faraway look as if she were watching things happen in some distant place and time. My mother wept then, and asked the old woman to tell her more, but that was all she would say. At last the drugged sleep overtook my mother, and when she awoke to my cries the midwife was gone.

After the birth prophecy was uttered, they say my mother grieved for many days and would not be comforted, but when the first shock of hearing the prophecy wore off, her obstinance set in, and she began to think of a way around the prediction. She would not give up her firstborn without a fight. *Believing is one thing, but accepting is another,* my mother often said. Though she never doubted the truth of the wise woman's words, she chose to see them as a warning and not a death sentence, for, she said, *why else would we be given to know what's to come?* My mother could not read or cipher, but she was bold and shrewd. I think it is from her that I got the steel in my spine and the will to fight back against whatever Fate has dealt me. Early on I learned that the world is no friend to anyone, and that you must fight for what you get, and fight harder yet to keep it. It will not be a fair fight. Fate cheats.

In mid-January 1742 I was christened in the

village kirk, and given the name Malcolm MacCourry, a fine name on our tiny isle. The honor of my name was my father's story, and all he had to be proud of by way of a legacy, I suppose. We had neither land nor money now, but long ago, my father said, when the chiefs of Clan Donald were lords of the isles of Scotland, the MacCourrys had been set up as rulers—*thanes,* they called them—of this island. That my forefathers were leaders long ago is a fine thing, for all that it was a small island and only a backwater to the history of Scotland, but we MacCourrys did not boast about our history, since even that flicker of glory was long past by the time I came into the world. The clan ways were dying by then, and in my childhood they would be sent to ruin by the Rising of '45, intended to put Charles Stuart back on the throne of Scotland. Since Islay had been Campbell land for centuries and was Protestant to boot, we were spared the ravages of that war. For more than twenty years Islay had been the property of Great Daniel Campbell, a rich man from over Glasgow way. His ownership was not unlike the way of the clan, in that one powerful man owned the land and ruled the tenants, but the difference was that this landlord was no kinsman of ours, and did not care what became of his charges, so long as his purse was untouched. We ordinary folk saw little enough of Great Daniel, and he could not have conversed with us if he did come to call, for we spoke Gaelic and he braid Scots. He could not more communicate with us than he could his flocks of sheep, and perhaps he saw little difference between the two populations he owned, except that the sheep were a better bet to bring him money.

Politics was a thing I knew little about. With the defeat of Charles Edward Stuart (he was never "Bonnie Prince Charlie" to our folk) scarcely five years past, and some of the highland clan chiefs still in hiding or in exile, the schoolmaster thought it best not to dwell on the troubled present. He kept safely to the distant past in our history lessons, so that the Romans were more clear to me than the ruling Parliament in London. Anyway, our village was too poor to care who ran the country; nothing was likely to change for us. We were ordinary folk: the people who did not speak, but were spoken for.

All my parents cared of worldly danger was whether the year's harvest and the fishing would be good, and that their newborn son should live to grow up, for boys were useful to fishermen and farmers. The boys themselves longed for adventure, and often we wished that we had been born in time to fight in the '45, not for the politics of the thing, but just for the glory of tasting war. I was not to live long anyway, I reasoned, so I might as well make an adventure of it.

The holy water had been scarcely dry upon my forehead before my mother was asking all and sundry for ways to forestall my doom. The minister, a Whig and a Lowlander, was a stranger to our ways, and he did not hold with such pagan beliefs as the Sight, but he said that he could see no harm in offering up prayers for my deliverance. My mother doubted that Whig prayers counted for much in heaven, and she resolved to fight the prophecy with Highlander's weapons: charm against curse.

Every woman in the village had a thought about how to ward off the doom: a cross of rowan wood for protection, or a bit of iron to keep away the Shining Folk on the Great Hill. Those who suggested such charms claimed no belief in such things themselves, but where was the harm in it, they said. Put a bit of iron beneath the bairn's bedsack of chaff, they told her. Lay your man's old trousers over the blanket to keep the fairies at bay. Most of those doing the advising had lost a child themselves, my father said. From such pain as that comes the belief in charms and omens.

My parents did all that was suggested to protect me, but still my mother did not feel easy in her mind about my safety. Her people were fishermen, and at last it was the fishermen who decided her. She remembered the old family stories about charms to prevent drowning, though I wonder she had any faith in them, seeing how many folk were lost to the sea. Still, it was a chance. As soon as the spring weather was fair, off she sent my father in a borrowed boat on a long day's journey, north past Colonsay and around the Ross of Mull to the Holy Isle to bring her a talisman.

It was only a rounded nugget of green-mottled marble stone that my father had picked up from the ground, and it was indistinguishable from a thousand other sea-smoothed pebbles that dotted the western isles. But this bit of rock was a talisman because it had come from the Holy Isle—Iona—where ten centuries ago *Colum Cille*—St. Columba—had come over from Ireland, beached his wee leather coracle, and built a great church, and from there he set about converting Scotland to Christianity, just as Patrick did for Ireland. For five centuries the grounds of Columba's church had been the burying place of the kings of Scotland. That alone would make the island sacred, but as it was the home of a great saint as well every inch of Iona was holy ground, and the stones themselves had power.

My father did not set much store by it, but if pagan ways would bring a bit of peace to my mother, as prayer did not, he would let her have her way.

So he brought back a smooth stone, no bigger than the nail on his little finger, and my mother put it at first in a wee leather pouch about my neck. When she told people about the stone and where it had come from, everyone said what a fine, shrewd thing she had done, and that now I was safe for sure. My mother was so proud of herself for having procured a talisman to outwit the fates that she boasted about it to the wise woman the next time she saw her creeping about the village.

"My son has the saints' protection!" she said, lifting up the wee leather pouch from within the swaddling cloths. "He will be kept safe now. *That* to your prophecy!" And she spit in the dirt.

I did not hear this part of the story from my parents. They never spoke of it, but the one who witnessed it and later told me said that the old woman stood stock-still for a long moment, returning my mother's mocking smile with a leaden stare. At last she picked up another pebble, just an ordinary bit of rock lying in the road. She peered into it as if it were hollow, and then she looked up again at my mother and said, "You are too fond of your firstborn, cheating death to keep him as you have. Maybe the stone will save him and maybe it won't. But here's what you have brought down upon yourselves: *No McCourry from this day forth shall ever love best his first-born child. Another will always supplant it.*"

I have had cause to remember those words. I think my parents took little heed of it, though. The drowning prophecy was all that mattered to them.

I do not remember my parents with any warmth. Surely they loved me, their only child, yet sometimes when my mood is dark, I wonder if they fought the prophecy out of love for me, or simply because they did not wish to be cheated by fate out of property that was rightfully theirs, and an extra pair of hands to work. I remember no embraces from my mother, and no happy moments of companionship with my father. Only the scolding comes to me in dreams, and a memory of cold.

It might have strengthened the charm to have dipped the stone in holy water, and had it blessed in the church, but it was no use asking our Whig minister for such as that, and perhaps my mother thought that the protection of St. Columba was worth more than the prayers of a Glasgow preacher.

From the time I was a toddling child, I had been made to keep the pebble with me always. When I grew older, I was allowed to keep it loose in my pocket. Each time I crossed the threshold of our whitewashed cottage, even if I were only going out to play a few feet from the door, I must have it with me. Carrying the stone had become second nature to me now, and I would have felt lost without it.

The stone lay in my pocket, taken for granted and forgotten, that morning when I made my way down to the beach. I had wanted to watch for seals. Last evening when I was playing by the fishing boats with Tam and Jamie, we overheard one of the fishermen say that as he was heading in for the night, he had seen seals at play in the waters off the western shore.

It was a blazing day in high summer, when there's hardly any night at all, and the dew is gone from the grass before cock crow. I had risen early to do my chores and to have a bit of time to myself before the schoolmaster's bell rang for lessons. I knew that time was short, and I had counted on meeting my friends behind the church, but I was impatient to have my adventures, so that when ten

45

minutes had passed and they had not appeared, I left without them, making my way up the hill past the two standing stones, because it was a good climb, and the most direct route to the shore. From the crest of the hill where the stone circle stood you could see for many miles—all the way to Ireland on the clearest of days.

The circle of tall stones set at the highest point of the hill was so ancient and massive that we could not imagine who had put it there or why. Old stories about giants and enchanted heroes were easy to believe in the face of such a wonder. Surely mere mortals did not transport those great slabs to the highest hill and set them upright? What purpose would they serve ordinary folk?

We children were told never to play there, and also to stay away from the great hill, said by the old folk to be the home of the *Banrigh,* the Fairy Queen herself. "Why should we stay away?" we asked our parents. "Didn't the *Banrigh* give wisdom to the women of the island with her magic cup?" Such was the story the fishermen told. "She's yet away on the hill," they would say of a foolish woman, meaning that she had missed her turn at the cup of wisdom. We children thought a meeting with the Fairy Queen would be a fine thing. We would much rather drink our learning in one gulp than have to waste fine weather in the schoolroom, learning our sums and our grammar by rote.

"You'll get your wisdom from the schoolmaster," our mothers would tell us. "And you'll leave the hill alone."

Were they afraid of the old stories of fairies kidnapping children, or were the slick, sharp rocks of the hillside danger enough in themselves to make them invent reasons to keep us away?

Stories gave our lives a shape. Now that I have been taken away, perhaps the tale tellers have already fashioned a legend about me—the boy who was last seen walking toward the stone circle of Cultoon and then was seen no more. I wonder where they think I have gone.

My mother will know, though. She will look out to sea and grieve for me. She has dreaded this day all my life.

On that bright morning I stood on the hill of standing stones and looked down at the glistening sea. I saw no seals on the sunlit water, but a little way out from shore a ship was anchored. I studied it with interest, but not with fear. Tall-masted sailing ships were not uncommon around our island, but the sighting of one was a noteworthy event to the boys of the village, for there was little else to provide a novelty. Whenever we saw one, we would speculate about the great world beyond our swath of ocean, and we professed to long for adventure, though I don't suppose any of us really imagined a life anywhere but on Ile.

The ship before me was a small brig, surely a merchant vessel, just out from Oban, perhaps, though I wondered why it had dropped anchor at our island in such fine sailing weather. The likeliest answer was for fresh water, or perhaps someone on board had been taken ill. Oban was no great distance away for a sailing ship. In truth I knew so little about the ways of merchant ships that I could not begin to guess what one would do or why.

I stood for a moment, watching the glint of the white canvas sails, caught between the glare of sunlit water and the luminous blue of the summer sky. Then I began to thread my way down the rocks of the cliff to reach the water's edge, where I might get a closer look at the vessel. Perhaps I would be able to read her name, or make out the details of a figure-head on the prow. One of our island sheep can scramble from the cliff top to a rocky beach in a matter of minutes, and it is their narrow trails that have made the path that leads there, but since a sheep trail is barely the width of a hoof, and the fall to sharp rocks below is a hundred feet or more, I made no haste in my descent. One foot in front of the other, I inched my way along the cliff, and then down to the shore. I kept my eyes on the ship, bob-bing in the swells offshore, for it made my stomach lurch to look down at the narrow strip of earth no wider than my foot. Those hand-fuls of hoof-trodden earth were all that sep-arated me from a long drop onto the upthrust rocks far below.

I scurried down the last ten feet of the rocky incline, breathless with excitement from my climb, and perhaps with relief that I was safely down. I had scarcely set foot on the level ground when four men stepped out from behind the boulders and began moving slowly toward me. I had not seen them before, because in my descent down the cliff, I had been looking out to sea instead of down at the rocks below. They must have had a small boat beached behind the tall rocks that lined the shore, but I did not see it.

Stricken with fear, I saw their faces as one jumbled blur of scars and beards and grinning mouths with brown stumps of teeth. Some of them wore short jackets, with pistols bulging in their pockets, and one man in a stained shirt, a blue handkerchief at his throat, came slowly toward me with his case knife pointed at my belly. For an instant I froze, trying to decide what action to take, but there was none. It would be useless to shout for help. No fishing boats lay within sight of the beach, and the nearest cottages were well away from the cliff—not within hailing distance. I could not expect help to come from my neighbors. Useless now to wish that I had waited for the other boys before I left the village. My heart pounded and my muscles ached to run, but I knew that I was caught between the sea and the sheer rock face of the fairy hill. Perhaps I could put a few paces of distance between myself and them, but I would probably get a bullet in the back for my trouble.

I struggled when they took hold of me, for by then I was past any rational thought, but I had no chance against four grown men. The encounter must have taken only minutes, though it seemed much longer to me then. When I was being taken, I cried out, I think, but I never heard the strangers speak a single word. After a few moments, when my flailing caught one of them in the jaw, the bearded man brought the butt of his pistol down against the side of my head, and I knew no more. I awoke in darkness many hours later in a ship caught in a storm at sea, and I had no way of knowing how far we had come or in what direction.

I wonder why they took me. Was it simply my bad luck to be in the wrong place that morning? Compared to the others boys on the island, I was big for my age, so perhaps the sailors thought me old enough to serve aboard their vessel. Or were they protecting someone? Had one of the renegade clan chiefs from the Rebellion been hiding in a cave on that side of the island, and had I ventured too near his lair? Perhaps my family had some enemy who wished my father ill or coveted his land, and struck at him through me.

I would never know. Now the reason for my abduction had ceased to matter. In that instant on the beach, I passed out of one life and into another. Later I would realize that I must learn to survive in the new existence, without burdening myself with thoughts of what I had left behind.

The Iona stone that was my talisman was with me still. I gripped it tight, knowing that I had carried it all my life in anticipation of this day, this storm, this journey. The prophecy had hung over my head since the day of my birth, and now it was coming to pass.

I wondered which way the ship was headed. The storm clouds would shut out the stars, so that even if I had been allowed on deck, I would not be able to get my bearings. Would we be sailing north as the mind leads, south as the heart turns, east toward the sunrise, or west, the way of the dead? I could not determine our direction, and I understood almost nothing of the language spoken by the sailors. I supposed it was English, from the sound of it. When the sailors had taken me on the beach, I shouted at them in Gaelic, but they gave no sign that they understood.

I knew what my parents would think when I did not come home. My mother would know that the prophecy had come true at last, but she would not weep for me. She would stare into the peat fire with cold eyes, saying nothing. She would think me dead, and go on hating the sea. Perhaps she would go down to the beach herself and keep a walking vigil, as I had seen other women do when there had been a drowning in the family. As they waited for the bodies of their menfolk to wash up on the shore, the mothers and wives would walk along the tide line, their eyes searching among the rocks and seaweed for the white gleam of a hand or a bloodless face, and they would sing, sad, rhythmic chants as they went. Hour after hour, from one day to the next, the searching and the singing went on, until at last the ocean gave up its dead.

Perhaps my mother would pace along the shore, looking into the sorrowful eyes of the seals, and wonder if the soul of her lost son now resided in a sleek dark body. She would think that the death foretold had come to pass, and grudgingly, but knowing it to be God's will, she would let me go.

It came to me then that the midwife's prophecy had indeed come true. *The sea will take him.* And so it had, by way of this ship, for in all my life I would never see the island or my kinfolk again. But the promise of Iona's saints would be kept as well. I would not drown.

Chapter Two

"Strange way to spend your birthday," said Martha Ayers. She pulled the patrol car over to the red clay shoulder of the road and let the engine idle. "Out in the woods, all by yourself, all weekend."

Joe LeDonne shrugged. "It's a milestone birthday," he said, perhaps the tenth time he'd reminded her of that. "New millennium and all. I want to think."

Martha was in the brown uniform of a Tennessee deputy sheriff. After she dropped him off at the head of the trail, she would drive back to town, ready to go on patrol duty at four.

LeDonne felt uncomfortable, seeing her at the wheel, wearing the uniform, while he was in the passenger seat, in jeans, an old UT sweatshirt, and a plaid flannel jacket. He was sweating, not from nervousness, but because the afternoon was too warm to be wearing a jacket. Still, it would be cold on the mountain by nightfall, and by then he knew he'd be glad of the extra covering. It wasn't that he felt odd being out of uniform. It was just the contrast between Martha's outfit, a display of authority and therefore of power, and his own shabby apparel, which conferred an anonymity he was unaccustomed to. He felt outranked, and his uneasiness about it made him that much more anxious to dispense with the civilities and get on with his plans. He wanted to disappear into the woods, and now he had the feeling that the process had already begun.

Martha had driven the few miles to the North Carolina line in silence, as if sensing his discomfort. She probably *could* sense it. Six years they'd been together. She knew him by now. The moods, the silences, the nightmares, the bouts of depression and anger. She even went to counseling sessions with him at the VA hospital in Johnson City. He wasn't an easy man to live with, and he knew it. The wonder was that she put up with him at all. If she were younger, or prettier, or if her ex-husband hadn't been such bad news, maybe she would realize that LeDonne was no prize. She said she loved him, though, and sometimes he believed her.

She should have been glad to be rid of him for the days surrounding his birthday. He was doing her a favor. Really. Surely she must know that the fallout from his misery would make the next couple of days unbearable for anyone in the vicinity of Joe LeDonne. The dark mood had been coming on for weeks. With each passing day his sleep grew more fitful, his silences became longer and his temper shorter. He hardly listened anymore when she spoke to him at home. He was already somewhere else. The act of taking himself off into the wilderness was just a token formality. Anyone would think she'd breathe a sigh of relief to see him stalk off into the woods alone, taking his misery with him.

Why had she driven so slowly? She knew this road by heart. The first few miles of it, lined with houses and mom-and-pop stores, were on the patrol route for the sheriff's department. By prolonging the trip she was buying time to talk, hoping that he would reconsider. Trying not to show his impatience, LeDonne had turned away to watch the scenery. The car had left the town limits of Hamelin a few miles back. There the neat brick houses on postage stamp lawns stopped. In another mile or so the older frame houses with truck tire flower gardens had given way to wire-fenced cow pastures, and then to scrub pines and underbrush in an unfenced no-man's-land that signaled the border of the Cherokee National Forest. There the road paralleled a shallow, rocky creek bed and became a tunnel through ancient hardwood trees that shaded the road into perpetual twilight. Tall thickets of rhododendron grew in shadows, their intricate branches forming a vast tangled maze in which small animals sometimes became trapped, and struggled until they died of exhaustion, or starved. New millennium or not, he thought, the Tennessee mountains were still a wilderness, and dying was always an option here.

It was Martha who broke the silence. It always was.

She glanced at him, a look full of concern. "Look, Joe, are you sure you want to do this? I know you hate parties, but we could go out to dinner, you know. Maybe take in a movie. You shouldn't be alone on your birthday."

"I'll be fine," he told her. "I want it this way." It never occurred to him that maybe she didn't. Or that a relationship of some years' standing made even one's own birthday an occasion for joint decisions. Martha was not in his thoughts now. The next three days belonged to him.

After a few more miles of green darkness the road veered away from the path of the creek bed and began to climb out of the valley. Here the tall poplars gave way once more to scrub pines and locust trees, evidence of the meager soil of an eroded mountainside. After another mile or so of turns and switchbacks they emerged into sunlight once more, astraddle a rocky ridge with a precipice overlooking miles of field and forest below them, lit by the sparkle of spring sunlight in a blue canopy over-head. The turnoff was only a few hundred yards ahead; a little way beyond that lay the North Carolina state line. A sign marked the change of jurisdictions; so did the condition of the two-lane blacktop, newly repaved and graded only on the Tennessee side of the line.

"It's that next cutoff on the left." he told her.

"I know." She eased the car off the road and into the small paved parking area which marked the intersection of the highway and the hiking trail. Martha shifted into park, the engine idling. "Are you sure you've got everything?"

He leaned over into the backseat and lifted the green canvas knapsack. "It's only three days," he said, keeping his voice light. "I don't even need what I've got here."

Martha looked skeptical. "You probably don't have enough water," she said. "Drinking from streams is a bad idea these days, what with acid rain and lord knows what else in the runoffs."

"I have a canteen." It didn't contain water, though.

"And I think you ought to take along a cell phone."

He smiled, unswayed in his resolve, but touched by her concern in spite of himself. "What's the range of a cell phone in these moun-tains, Martha? Twenty yards?" He smiled to soften his criticism of her logic. He had learned to do that. "And even if I did manage to call for help, how would I give directions to the rescue squad?"

"Well, I just think you ought to take some sensible precautions. You're not..." He gave her a sharp look, and she lapsed into silence. *Not what?* he thought. *Not as young as you used to be? Not in combat anymore?* Or—her greatest fear—*Not carrying your pistol?* Perhaps she wondered if he meant to kill himself out there alone in the woods.

Whatever it was, she had thought better of saying it. She merely shrugged and looked at her watch. "I have to be heading back," she said.

LeDonne nodded. "Yeah. You go on at four. You should make it, though. Thanks for the ride. See you Monday."

"Back here?"

"Right." He looked at his watch. "Same time okay?"

"Sure."

Now that he was standing at the foot of the gravel slope, he felt reluctant to see her go. "Maybe we'll do the dinner out on Monday. If you still want to, that is."

Martha smiled. "Monday then. But you're buying. It won't be your birthday anymore." Before he could reply, she put the car back in gear and made a U-turn back down the mountain toward town. She did not look back.

LeDonne stood alone for a minute on the deserted mountain road, waiting for the sound of her car engine to be swallowed by the forest, and then he turned and headed up the graveled hill to a clearing, where he would pick up the trail that led into the National Forest.

A week before, when Martha had asked him what he wanted to do for his birthday, the first words that came into his mind were *I want to go home*. He did not say them, because he would not have been able to tell her what he meant by that. Home... He had been born and raised in Gallipolis, Ohio, a small community on the Ohio River, but he had left there to go into the army, and except for the occasional perfunctory appearance at family funerals, he had never gone back. Now he had no family left there, and any acquaintances from school days had either moved away or turned into middle-aged strangers. The town that stood on the riverbank today with its motels and its fast-food restaurants bore little resemblance to the place he knew in his boyhood. He had no reason ever to go back. The word *home* did not conjure up visions of Gallipolis in his mind, past or present.

From a backpacking trip along the Appalachian Trail, he had drifted into Hamelin, liked the scenery, felt at home with the people, and ended up taking a deputy's job with the sheriff's department, thinking that he could always hit the Trail when the spirit moved him. He never had made it to Trail's end at Mount Katahdin, Maine, and if anyone had asked him where home was, he would have said Hamelin readily enough, but just now he was feeling like a stranger once again.

He had few friends in Hamelin, where relationships grow out of family connections or church membership, neither of which he could claim. He supposed part of his isolation came with the job. Cops are loners, either by choice or from the necessity of odd hours and a need for objectivity. Still he wished he knew people that he could talk to without talking being a chore requiring conscious effort. He wished he could believe that someone besides Martha would care if he went into the woods and never came back. Most of all he wished he could shake the feeling that if a community of bright and caring people did exist somewhere out there, he would be unworthy of membership and uncomfortable in their midst. He had no home because he was a willing exile.

LeDonne doubted that he would find what he was looking for in the wilderness, but at least out here he would not have to pretend that he belonged.

Ah, the glamor of a life in show business, thought Lark McCourry: hunched over the john in an interstate highway rest area, trying to hear a voice through the static on her cell phone.

"I said: you might want to come home!"

For all of two heartbeats she wondered what the caller meant by "home": the rented place on the West Coast, or the faux colonial in the Nashville suburb of Brentwood, the fancy house she'd bought with the money from the first platinum album sale? The one her dad had never set foot in.

"Linda! Can you hear me on this thing? Linda?"

Ah, *that* home, she thought, Wake County, Tennessee, where no matter how many times they saw her picture on a magazine cover or heard her voice on the radio, she'd still be *Linda Ann Walker,* not *Lark McCourry.* People who had known her forever would still write to ask if she could sing at the high school band concert, or the church revival service, or the county fair. Maybe if she'd let her publicist send out the form letter in reply, they might finally realize that she was famous, but she could never summon the arrogance to do that. She didn't want them to think she was "uppity," so she penned handwritten regrets on hotel stationery, pleading conflicts or scheduling problems, and the requests from the home folks kept coming.

She recognized the voice now, and the realization made her scowl. It was Becky Tilden, sounding breathless and harried, as she always did. Lark pictured her, red-faced and tomato-shaped, standing at the wall phone in a kitchen with garish vegetable-themed wallpaper, staring at the funeral home scenic calendar picture and twisting the cord while she talked. Idly, Lark wondered if Becky always sounded anxious, or if it just seemed so because Becky called only when there was an emergency, usually some medical crisis that involved her father and required a certified check from Lark.

She wondered how much it was going to be this time—not that she minded footing the bill for Daddy's illnesses. As far as she was concerned, it was Becky who did the hard part: putting up with the old tartar on a day-to-day basis, and having to play the dutiful handmaiden when she was old enough to be a grandmother herself, considering the age at which people of her class got married. Of course, Becky never seemed to enrage John Walker the way his daughter Lark did.

In the early days of her success as a singer, she had always invited her father to her concerts, even sending him plane tickets a time or two, but he never came. He would call to tell her how ill he was. He couldn't possibly travel. Then, in a later conversation, Becky would let it slip that they had gone on an outing to Dollywood that weekend over in Gatlinburg, or on a picnic to Warrior State Park.

She kept trying, though. As her success grew, Lark phoned her father regularly with the news of her little triumphs. *Hey, Dad, I'm going to be singing a duet with... Hey, Dad, I won the... My record is on the* Billboard *chart at number...* The response from John Walker was always the same. *Well, that's nice, Linda,* followed by a two-second pause, and then he would say, *You know, Becky made a blackberry pie today that was the best thing I ever ate...* or *Becky put new linoleum in the bathroom all by herself...* or *You know that garden plot out by the deck? Well, Becky grew a beefsteak tomato out there that must have weighed two pounds...* The final straw came when Lark's CMA Music Award was trumped by Becky's winning a hundred dollars in the Virginia

61

lottery. Lark gave up then. She offered to share no more triumphs. After that when she made herself call home, which was once every three weeks or so, she would ask her father how he felt, and then listen patiently to his litany of aches and pains and recent dinner menus. He always tried to make his adventures with the doctors sound amusing, so that he could tell himself he wasn't complaining, but he never talked about anything but himself. He never asked about her life, and she stopped wanting to tell him anything about it at all.

She knew that if she had died first, suddenly—in a plane crash, say—her father would have had no idea what friends of hers to notify, what colors she liked, or which flowers she would want at her funeral. They were more profoundly distanced than strangers—they were *estrangers,* entitled to be close, and yet mutually rejected, each fueling the separation with the anger and shame of having been found wanting.

So Daddy was ailing again. So what? It was easier to write the check and move on than to go back and be hurt.

"Yes, Becky, I'm here," she said into the phone, willing herself to sound brisk and pleasant. "I'm on the road right now, though. Can you just tell me how much money you're going to need, and let me call you back later for the details?"

"We *need* for you to come home, Linda." Becky's exasperation was tinged with fear. "Judge is losing touch with reality, and Dr.

Banner thinks that this time we ought to be prepared for the worst."

"What do you mean *losing touch with reality*?" Not Alzheimer's, thought Lark. Her life might become a living hell if that happened, because he'd never let them put him in an institution. The old man had instilled enough guilt about that concept to terrify a whole roomful of well-meaning daughters. She might have to choose between putting her career on hold to care for him, or spending most of what she made on private nursing care.

"How bad is it?" she asked. "He hasn't talked about killing himself, or anything, has he?"

"Naw." Becky's tone was wry. "Judge is too mountain for that. Mountain folk don't go where they ain't been invited."

"Well, what's the matter, then?"

"Your phone is beeping," said Becky. "I'll bet you forgot to charge it up. Just come. I'll tell you everything when you get here."

The line went dead then, and Lark stared at the receiver, marveling at the gumption she had seldom seen in her father's dogsbody: ordering her around as if everything in the world revolved around Judge's little ailments. What about her career—commitments made months in advance, contracts signed, booking agency...

There was nothing for it. Now she would have to go home. Except that nothing in her life proceeded in a straight line anymore, so first she would do tonight's concert, and then she

63

would stop off in Brentwood to make sure that things were taken care of for a few days, and then she would fly to east Tennessee for the ordeal of a visit with Daddy. That wasn't a pleasant prospect even at the best of times. She would sit around the house feeling like a visiting social worker while her Daddy fawned over Becky as if *she* were the daughter of the house instead of the housekeeper. Lark got through those visits to the white frame house in Hamelin by the grace of God and the power of Pepto-Bismol.

Well, she was lucky this time. She had a four-day break coming up in her schedule, only instead of resting, she supposed that she would have to spend it going home. But she wasn't going alone if she could help it.

Malcolm McCourry—1751

Back on the island my mother will never say of me, "He has died": *Bhasaich e.* It is not our custom to speak so bluntly about the passing of a human soul. *Bhasaich e* is said at the death of an animal, not a person. When one of our own has perished, folk always say: *Shiubhail.* "He has traveled." How ironic that my mother will speak the truth about my fate and never realize it. Perhaps it is a jest of God to put the answer to my disappearance

64

in the words out of her own mouth, and then to keep her from hearing the truth of it.

I have traveled. Yes. Surely I have passed out of one life and into another as much as if death has taken me. As surely as if I had drowned and my soul had been trapped within the thick wet fur of a seal.

I had seen no seals for many days now. I looked for them each morning when I came up on deck, my belly still cramping with hunger after my one allotted bowl of *sowans,* salt porridge boiled with water. To distract my thoughts from the hollow space under my ribs, I would first gauge the position of the morning sun, then I would lean over the side as far as I could to look for a bobbing black head among the waves, but I never saw one. The ship was heading south into warmer waters, where the seals do not go. I had lost my last link with home.

Now the sea stretched away in every direction without a speck of land to break the horizon. At first I marveled at the sight of so much emptiness, for in our waters back home, there are always bits of land to steer by wherever you look. On clear days the coast of Antrim is a dark shape to the south. Here, though, there was no sign of land, and the sea lay flat against the edge of the sky without a break between them. I would gaze down into the depths, trying to imagine what it would be like to live as a seal, floating armless in the cold darkness, remembering perhaps some other life, but drifting in the haze of this one, with only the sad human eyes remaining from another existence.

At first I stared at the boundless ocean, searching for a bit of land or even the mast of another vessel—anything to fill the blue void. I would look west, wondering if the land of Tir Nan Og was out there, as the old folk said it was, and whether it could be seen by mortal eyes. Tir Nan Og meant the land of the young—a place without age or sickness or hunger. It was where the dead went, or so we hoped, to be resurrected forever young and beautiful and to live among the old gods in peace and plenty. I yearned for a glimpse of it in the light of sunset, but since it was the island of the dead, perhaps to see it would mean that the ship had brought us to our deaths, and I confess that I looked westward with dread in my heart, half fearing to see the dark shape of that land.

Before many days had passed, though, I tired of the featureless expanse of gray-green water, and I scarcely glanced over the side anymore. By now we had traveled so far from where I was taken that the sailors no longer thought of me as a captive. Two nights into the voyage they ceased to keep me locked away in the hold. Now I was expected to work for my keep. A scowling man gave me a mop and pail, and, with gestures and sharp words meaningless to me, he motioned for me to swab the deck. Before long I began to learn a word or two, enough to scurry up the masts when I was told to, or to fetch a shriveled apple from the wooden barrel for one of the crew. I could not ask anyone where we were bound, for I still could not understand enough of the language of my captors, but I knew by the warm winds and by the sunrise that the ship was heading south—as the heart goes, people said, and my heart did feel joy in the novelty of sailing and in the warmth of this new latitude. The ship was an unending adventure for me, and now that I knew that my captors did not mean to kill me, but only intended to make me work, I lost much of my dread of the journey. For a boy of nine it is a heady thing to be treated like a man instead of a child. Here I was not a puppy underfoot, as I had been in my village, but a crew member with a job to do. I was cuffed now and again for inattention or shoddy work, but that was not new to me, either, and I settled in without complaint.

Later in the colonies I heard stories about children taken prisoner by the Indians, who, when rescued, did not want to go home. Their new lives appealed to them more than the family they left behind. I suppose I came to feel the same, partly out of necessity to survive, and partly because I was as anxious as any lad to pass into manhood.

Every gust in the sails took me farther from my home island, and I felt my homesickness ebb with each passing hour. Already the faces of the villagers were fading in my memory to an indistinct blur, as if the island had sunk into the mist when I left it. For the first few nights after I was taken, I lay on my blanket and wept for my lost family, but I took care that my tears should be soundless ones, knowing that if my sobs disturbed the rest of any of man sleeping nearby, I would be given good cause to weep with a sound thrashing or the crunch of a boot in my ribs.

Still, I could not be sad for every waking moment, because I was only ten, an age when even the soul heals quickly, and the brave part of myself knew that I had embarked on a great adventure. Already I had seen more of the world than my father ever had, and if I ever did manage to make my way back home, I would have tales to tell that would last a lifetime.

I knew that my mother had lost me forever, though, whether I went home or not. In the weeks that I had been on board the ship, I had ceased to be a child. Hard work and hunger, beatings and loneliness had all aged me without adding a pound to my frame or an inch to my height. My days with the schoolmaster were over now, but my education had begun in earnest. Now I knew enough of this new language and enough about being a sailor to do what was asked of me without a clout on my shoulders to drive in the meaning. I had my sea legs, so that I could walk about the ship without falling with each toss of a wave, and sickness from the endless lurching no longer hurled the food from my shriveled stomach.

The first thing I had learned was that a ship is different from what you may imagine it to be when you stand on the crest of a hill and see her far out to sea, gliding silently on the waves like a great seabird. Once aboard her, you realize that the silence was an illusion, and your senses will reel from the noise of her: the thundering of the great canvas sails overhead, the roar of rushing water against the hull, like a mountain stream tumbling in a long fall over rocks, and the shouting of the men, who must make themselves heard above all the rest. Certainly I added little to the noise on board, for there was no one to understand my words, and nothing to be gained by crying out.

After the first fear of the strange place left me, I learned to sit in the darkness near the lamp-lit circle of crewmen not on watch, listening to the rhythm of their voices and trying to find the thread of meaning in their words. By now they had ceased to be faceless monsters to me, and I saw that some of them were only a few years older than I. First I took care to note which ones were quickest with their fists, so that I could give them a wide berth, and from among the rest I chose to listen closest to a familiar voice, one speaking braid Scots, not the Gaelic tongue that I understood, but at least a language I had heard before. The other men, I had decided, were mostly English, for although their words were pronounced in many different ways, they all seemed to understand one another well enough.

I thought that if I could learn some English from the sailors' talk together, I could discover the destination of the ship. I had begun to enjoy my newfound independence as a young crewman on this vessel, but at times I did wonder what they meant to do with me when we reached landfall.

As the weeks passed, my stomach ceased to rebel at the taste of salt-soaked meat and whiskey-colored water, and the strange sounds of the crew began to sort themselves out into words in my head. It was my good fortune to be young enough for my mind to be an empty slate upon which new things, like skills and languages, could be written with ease. I only had to listen to make sense of the talking, and since the men ignored me except to shout commands, I was as free as the ship's cat to linger unheeded in their company.

As we ate, the men told tales of their voyages, bragging about the dangers they had lived through or boasting of the wonders they had seen. They talked most about the West Indies, which were like saints' gardens, they said, bright islands set in a sea as warm as blood, with birds like rainbows and flowers the size of cabbages. *The Caribbean.* The word was strange to my tongue, but the tropical islands sounded like paradise to me, and I longed to visit them, until the men began to tell tales of the plantations there, where captive men worked the cane fields in an eternal blazing summer and died in delirium of strange fevers. They said that for all its beauty, the Caribbean was treacherous. It harbored pirates who lurked between the islands, waiting to steal a ship and its cargo, casting her crew overboard to drown in the warm sea.

The sailors swore there were fish the size of horses that could cut a swimmer in half with one bite, and that a patch of sea choked with seaweed would becalm a ship, entangling it in a green web, so that the stranded crew died of thirst and hunger, unable to break free. Those tales I did not believe, but even so the Indies did not sound like such a fine place to settle. Still I thought I would like to see them once for the adventure of it.

Sooner or later the talk would turn to the American colonies. That was a land I had heard a bit about. Back home some of the old people in the village had talked about the group who set out from Islay to settle a land grant in a colony of the Americas, but if they ever said the name of the place they went, I had forgotten it.

The sailors spoke often of the Carolinas, a land of plantations in need of slaves to work the fields, where the owners would pay well for new laborers. From the way they talked, I thought they had seen more than one ship's passenger sold at journey's end to make extra pocket money for the crew. Most of the workers were brought from Africa, they said, but Englishmen, too, could be sold by the ship that transported them. The English could get free after seven years, they thought, but the Africans stayed slaves forever.

The prospect of slavery in a hot, strange land so frightened me that I resolved to be the best sailor on board, so that I should be more valuable to the ship as a crewman than as a body to be sold. By now I had learned from listening to the tale tellers that ten is thought a proper age to be sent to sea, and more than one of my shipmates had come aboard at just my age, although most perhaps more willingly than I. Some of the sailors, whom I had thought so old and hardened on first acquaintance, turned out to be no more than sixteen years old themselves.

"Young boys are teachable at any rate," said one of the mates, after I had done well on the rigging. "These grown landsmen who think to run away to sea past their twentieth year are as useless as teats on a bull. Nothing ever comes naturally to them. They must always be trying to remember what they've been told. They can't keep their balance, and they're always afraid of what the sea will do. But give me a boy of ten, and inside of six months he'll be seafaring with no more thought than he gives to breathing."

I learned to do it well enough, for the old fellow was right about ten being a malleable age, but no amount of praise or caning could make me love the sea—not while the stone in my pocket reminded me of my destiny.

I did like the strength that came from learning, though, and being treated like a man instead of a child. At night the singing could make me happy for a little while. Sometimes late after dark one or another of the crew would take up a song, and this was even better than the tales of far-off lands. They never sang any of the songs that I knew from back home, but those tunes were slipping away from me now, as the Gaelic language faded from my thoughts. At first these new songs sounded strange to me, because their tunes did not fit the pattern of the singing I was used to, the high nasal drone of notes that seemed to hang in the air like a rainbow long after the singer had sung his piece. These songs moved to a steady rhythm with tunes like none I had heard before, and each song told a story. I longed to hear more of them, for in a featureless ocean, these tunes were my windows on all creation.

I can remember no happy stories in the songs of the crew, but I thought nothing of that. I remembered the keening women walking the shores of Ile, waiting for the bodies of their drowned men to be returned to them. All of us sing more from sorrow than from joy. It is tragedy that leaves a mark on the mind and calls for the tribute of a song. Happiness is its own gift, and needs no other.

There may have been some hymns sung by one or two of the pious sailors, but I do not recall any, nor do I think they would have been popular with the others, for the nighttime singing was meant to be entertainment, not a worship service. Some songs told of ghosts and killings, and those bewitched me with their hints of magical possibility, though for the first time or two that I heard them they troubled my sleep. I dreaded hearing the ballad of the house carpenter. When Ellick Boone began to sing it, they told me it was a love story, but they were only having a game with me. The house carpenter in the song comes back from the sea and persuades his lost love to leave her husband and babies and return to sea with him. When the lovers are aboard his ship, and the lady asks where they are headed, the house carpenter tells her that for their sins they must go to hell. With that he stamps his cloven foot, splitting the ship in two like a cockleshell, and they both sink with it into the deep. I never cared to learn that song—or any song about shipwrecks—and whenever someone sang that tune, I would find myself wondering if one of my own shipmates might be the devil himself in disguise. For solace I always asked to hear "The False Knight on the Road" immediately thereafter, for in that song a clever schoolboy outwits the devil on the high road and he goes on his way unharmed.

Some of the men liked to tease the younger lads with the song of "The Gallant Argosy," and I pretended not to mind, but I liked that song even less than "The House Carpenter." The sailors swore to me that the tale was true, but I hope it was not. They said that the *Gallant Argosy* was an English warship sent out to fight the Spanish navy off the coast of Holland. The crew is afraid of being captured by the Spanish enemy, and the captain promises great rewards to the cabin boy—who is "the age of twelve and three," the song says—if the lad will go into the water, swim alongside the enemy vessel, drill a hole into its side, and sink it. The boy does as he was bid, and when he has sunk the Spanish galleon, the captain refuses to rescue him—in order to keep from paying the boy his reward, I suppose, though I could never make sense of that part of it.

> *The crew they hauled him up, but upon
>   the deck he died,*
> *so they wrapped him in his blanket so very
>   soft and wide,*
> *and cast him overboard to drift upon the
>   tide,*
> *and he sank in the Lowland, Lowland,
>   low...*
> *he sank in the Lowland Sea.*

I knew that this would be my fate if for whatever reason I died on board ship. The men would wrap me in the dirty blanket from my hammock and slide me down a plank into the dark water... *The sea will take him...* I would drift into the cold depths, slowly dissolving into an eyeless log, fodder for the fish and sea worms, unmourned and forgotten... The song made me shiver. It reminded me not only of the terrors of death, but of how alone I was, and how little the life of a cabin boy mattered to anyone at sea.

Among the singers I found my first friend at sea: Robert Bell, one of the oldest sailors. He, too, was a Scot, a Lowland one from the Borders, and although he did not speak my old language beyond a word or two, I soon learned his. He had a voice that lived up to his name, and a way of imparting the words of a tune as if it were his own story he was telling the listeners and not just a song about strangers he'd learned somewhere from other strangers. It was his singing I liked best of anyone's. One night when the singing had gone on for a bit, I plucked up the courage to ask him to sing a particular song.

"Give us the one about the open grave," I said.

He looked puzzled. "What, 'The Unquiet Grave,' young Malcolm? Didn't Tom just sing that one a bit ago? Were you sleeping through it?"

I shook my head. "Not that one. That one is too sad to hear again. I mean the one where the dead leave the churchyard until cock crow."

" 'The Rowan Stave'?" He smiled. "So you're partial to that one, are you?"

I nodded, glad that he would not tease me for liking the tune, and shy from the enormity of asking a favor. I did not like to be in anyone's debt, even for so small a request as this, but Robert was the only one I trusted even so far as that, and I thought it might be all right to owe a small debt to a kind man. I would soon find a way to repay him, with extra work or part of my rations. Robert Bell was thin, and he coughed too much. I did not think he would make many more voyages.

Of all the songs I had heard anyone sing I liked that one best. The tune haunted me when I worked, and its mournful notes called to my mind the songs back home, so similar in melody and measure. It was the strange and terrible story, though, that made me long to hear it over and over, though by now I knew it by heart. I caught my breath as his hammock swayed gently, and he took up the tune in the dark.

"Upon the hill above the kirk at moon rise
   she did stand
To tend her sheep that Samhain eve, with
   rowan stave in hand.
And where she's been and what she's seen,
   no living soul may know,
And when she's come back home, she will
   be changed—oh!

"Midnight came, the owls cried out, the
   shepherd girl did hide;
She saw the churchyard dead come forth,
   from graves laid open wide.
And where she's been and what she's seen,
   no living soul may know,
And when she's come back home, she will
   be changed—oh!

"When all the dead but one returned she
   neared the empty grave,
And 'cross its narrow earthen sides she
   laid her rowan stave,
And where she's been and what she's seen,
   no living soul may know,
And when she's come back home, she will
   be changed—oh!"

Robert peered at me in the darkness. "Is that the one? Do you know what the song is about, then?"

"I do," I said, eager to show how well I was learning this new tongue. "There is a woman tending her sheep near the churchyard on Samhain eve. At moonrise she sees the graves begin to open, and one by one the ghosts come out of the earth, and take human form again for that one night. By and by, as dawn comes, the ghosts all go back into their graves, but one large fine grave remains empty. So the shepherdess puts her rowan staff down across the open grave."

"So the song says," he agreed, and I could tell by his voice that he was teasing me. "Though why the shepherd woman should do such a thing is beyond me."

"Why, rowan wood has the power of protection," I told him. Surely everyone knew that. "People plant a rowan tree near the threshold of their cottages to keep the evil ones at bay. So right enough, if she put her rowan staff across the grave, no ghost could pass through it to get back in."

Robert laughed. "And what business was it of the shepherdess I'd like to know!"

I was puzzled over his words, trying to decide if he was teasing me. "Sing the rest!"

*"Oh, who has barred me from this grave I
  left for Samhain tide,
I've journeyed far to Denmark's shore; I
  left there as a bride;*

And where I've been and what I've seen,
*   no living soul may know,*
And when I've come back home, I will be
*   changed—oh!*

"If you will let me gain my grave before
*   the end of night*
I'll gie your babe a magic stane that he
*   may have the Sight*
And where he'll go and what he'll see, no
*   living soul may know,*
And when he's come back home, he will be
*   changed—oh!"*

He stopped singing and shook himself, as if he were waking up from a dream. "Do you have it by heart yet? You've heard it twice now, and that should be enough. Now you must sing it back to me."

I cleared my throat, and took up the song in a quavering voice, "Upon the hill above the kirk at moonrise she did stand, to tend her sheep that Samhain eve with rowan staff in hand..."

He touched my arm and motioned for me to stop singing. "You said 'staff.' It's not staff. 'Tis *stave.*"

"It's the same thing, isn't it? A long stick?"

"It doesn't matter. *Stave* is what was sung to you, and *stave* you must say. When you are given a song that has been handed along from singer to singer over the years, you are entrusted with it, for it is the work of folk who are gone now. Their song. Not yours. It is not your place to change it. You must pass it along to others,

79

and keep it as good as you found it. Sing it as you got it or not at all. Go again."

This time I finished the words to his satisfaction, and he nodded. "You've no voice for a minstrel, Malcolm, but you've a good head for remembering words."

"It's a grand tale," I said.

"Oh, it's a true story, that song. Or so they say in the Highlands. Are you yourself now any part of a Mackenzie?"

I shook my head. "I'm only fond of the tune, because I have a magic stone myself."

"A magic stone, is it?" He laughed at that. "And what charms can you call up, then, young Malcolm? Can you give us calm seas and a good west wind?"

"I cannot do anything," I sighed. "But the stone I carry is from the Holy Isle, and it keeps me safe from drowning." I told him about the prophecy at my birth, and how my father had fetched the stone from Iona to keep me safe.

He laughed. "Well, that will make you a prize worth keeping on board, won't it? I don't suppose the ship will sink out from under you with the saints themselves protecting you." He lowered his voice. "Only don't tell too many aboard about this lucky stone of yours, though, or you'll find yourself robbed of it one night. Even an honest man might try to steal a bit of luck, and a knave will steal anything."

"I keep it hidden," I told him. "Thank you for the gift of the song. Is it really true? I'm thinking of the ghost lady who goes over the sea to her home in Denmark of a night. Who was she, do you know?"

He shrugged. "A Viking maid, a princess some say. If I ever knew her name I've forgotten it. There have been a fair few in Scotland down through the years."

"Perhaps she was our one," I said. "A princess called Ile. Folk say that my home island is named for her and that she walked to it from the coast of Ireland."

He smiled a little, and I could tell he thought it unlikely. "Well, let her be your princess then, if it pleases you," he said indifferently. "Though I think she may have been buried on an island well to the north of where you come from, because I do know the name of the other lass. The shepherd maiden in the song. Now *she* was an islander, same as you, and a Mackenzie. You'll have heard of her son, though—Kenneth, called the Brahan Seer?"

I shook my head.

His eyes widened in astonishment. "Have you never heard of the Brahan Seer? And you a *gaeltacht* lad?"

I hesitated. "We spoke the language, but we did not speak much about Highland matters. We had a Campbell for a landlord, you ken."

"Rubbish. The Seer had naught to do with the troubles of the '45, though he may have had a word or two to say about them, now that I think on it. He had the Sight, boy. They say his power to prophesy came from the stone that his mother was given in the churchyard that Samhain night. When he grew older, Kenneth

81

would put the white stone up against his eye, and he'd fall into a trance, as if he were seeing things happening far away, and then he would tell what he saw. He spoke in riddles though, most times. Or perhaps he couldn't always make sense of what he saw."

"Did his prophecies all come true?"

"Not yet. But it's early days. The Seer looked far into the future, they say. We'll not live long enough to see them all come to pass. But a fair few have proved true."

I thought it would be a fine thing to meet such a man one day. I wondered if he could tell me what I should do with my life, since as foretold the sea had taken me, but yet I lived on. What came next? I resolved that if the ship ever put in port to Scotland again, I would seek out this Brahan Seer and ask for his advice. "Where does he live then?"

"Oh, he doesn't. He was burnt at the stake by a laird's wife who didn't care for the prediction he gave her, but it came true all the same. The Seer has been dead a century or so now, but they say that he prophesied what was to befall Scotland in the years to come. He told about the rising—about Charles Edward Stuart—and he predicted disaster." He grunted. "Not that it would take a prophet to have foreseen that calamity."

"Is there another song about him?"

"Bound to be, boy. Bound to be. I never heard it sung, though I have known one or two folk who had some of the prophecies down by heart."

"Can you say one for me?"

"I reckon I could call one to mind if I thought about it long enough, but what use would it be to you, Malcolm, for all the Seer's prophecies foretell only the fate of Scotland, and you and I are done with that. What we all need is a wise man who will tell us about the New World."

"But perhaps I will go home someday," I mused.

He laughed and struck playfully at my arm with his fist. "I think you have seen the last of Scotland, boy," he said. "I am no Mackenzie and no prophet, but I'll wager that I can assure you of that."

Chapter Three

Sharp shadows...rustling sounds in the distant underbrush. He felt his muscles tense, and he took a long slow breath to combat the feeling.

Sometimes just walking in the woods was enough to bring back the waking dreams. If the shadows lengthened in the dense forest and the monotony of walking lulled him into a fugue state, LeDonne could forget just where he was, and suddenly the pines and poplars of the Tennessee mountains would transform in his imaginings into jungle foliage, and he would be back in southeast Asia again, still fighting the war. The intervals between nightmares had become greater as time went on, but he was never entirely free of them. He might be all right, though, if it didn't rain.

Rain. That was the one ordinary sound that could send him back. *The sound of rain on big leaves.* The deliberate plop of water dropping slowly on a wide, slick leaf made his heart pound and his muscles tense, recalling the terror of walking through a quiet, green place and knowing that in an instant the world could explode around you. Johnny Cash wrote a song in which he called the war "a slow walk in a sad rain..." It was the best description LeDonne had ever heard to describe his memories of combat.

For the fifth time he looked up at the sky. Above a stand of tall poplars, the sky was deep blue, streaked with high wisps of cirrus clouds that wouldn't bring rain. It was going to be all right, he told himself. Perhaps he had chosen the right year after all.

LeDonne's decision to spend his birthday alone on the mountain had not been a matter of sudden impulse. He had been planning it for decades. At least he had managed to postpone his sojourn for three years. He had always planned to make this solitary pilgrimage when—*if*—he turned forty-five, but his birthday fell in midweek that year, and Martha made dinner reservations at the Parson's Table, so, what with one thing and another, he couldn't get away. So now, a few years deferred, he was using the millennium as an excuse for the journey.

The big forty-five.

As a teenaged soldier in Vietnam, the thought of reaching such an advanced age as forty-five had struck him as absurd. In those days he thought he could measure his life span in months. Surely it was only a question of what would kill him first: the booze, the cigarettes, the war, or himself. At other times during his year of combat, he thought he must have reached forty-five already. When you are in a line company *in country* during the rainy season, a day seems to stretch on into a sunless gray limbo in which months could pass unfelt. He would sometimes think, *Surely I have been here forever. Surely I have been walking this path, hearing this tap of rain on big leaves for ten years, instead of ten months.*

He would imagine himself emerging from the jungle one day to learn that decades had passed in the world outside, and that he was an old man whose chance at life was over. Hadn't he heard about a Japanese soldier on some remote Pacific island who kept fighting World War II well into the fifties? Maybe that soldier thought only months had passed, too. Maybe time was different out here.

Perhaps because he had been so young at the time, LeDonne's year of war seemed to last forever. He had survived it, though. Mostly. He had stayed in counseling for years after his return from the war, and the dreams never quite seemed to go away. Sometimes he could go months without a nightmare, and then some annoyance, some trick of stress and chemistry would pull him back into the past, and he would find himself under the bed, shouting, sometimes sobbing. It was no good telling himself then that he had escaped. The booze, the cigarettes, and his own pistol were still ever-present, and the danger of war had been replaced by the stress of law enforcement, his drug of choice to simulate the combat high. He could have chosen fire fighting, he could have become an emergency medical technician, but cop work was better. At least you could fight back.

So now he was looking down the barrel of a never-never birthday.

The age of forty-five had always seemed remote and improbable to someone who valued only the virtues of youth, but he had thought that if he got there at all, he would reach forty-five encumbered with a wife, children, the house with the big lawn and the picket fence, and a meaningless but respectable job.

He had thought of the number in ballistic terms: forty-five, a loaded forty-five, pointing straight at him, with nothing past it but death. But when it came, it was an anticlimax. Nothing happened. He just went on eating and sleeping and working, and waiting for something he couldn't quite put a name to. He had passed his milestone birthday three years ago, without the wife, the children, or the picket fence, and he was still alive. Still drifting. Now he had actually survived into a new millennium.

It was time to take stock of his life.

Becky Tilden wondered if she ought to knock before she went into the den. She knew that Judge had no visitors today, but that didn't mean that *he* thought so. He was still having those delusions about his invisible friends. Nora Bonesteel, who was at least a real person, even if she was pretty strange herself, had visited, and that little reunion had cheered Judge up, but it hadn't helped his condition any, as far as Becky could tell. He had just gone right back to entertaining his imaginary friends. Why, he could be in there shooting the breeze with Elvis for all she knew. Well, he wasn't, of course, but maybe *he'd* think he was. And if he did, Becky certainly wasn't going to argue with him. Judge used to say that if he wanted your opinion, he'd give you one.

She dithered for a few moments outside the closed door, wondering if she'd get bawled out for going in—or worse. Suppose she flung open the door one day and a ghost really was standing there? She'd fall flat out on the floor, that's all there was to it. She had begun to look out of the corner of her eye each time she entered a room, and she'd taken to leaving the lights on all over the house. Now she pressed her ear to the door to see if she could hear Judge talking to anybody, but the only sounds coming from within were television voices—those mindlessly cheerful drones with flat California accents and the rhythm that tells you the speaker is selling something even if you can't make out the words. She pushed open the door and peeked inside.

At first she thought he was asleep, but his head jerked back, and then he gave her his broad just-plain-folks smile, the one he used when he was humoring people or trying to pretend he didn't think you were stupid.

"Becky, come in! It's about time for *Jeopardy*, isn't it?" he said. He pointed to the overstuffed chair facing the television, as an invitation for her to join him. As the opening credits flashed upon the screen, Judge reached for the remote and turned up the sound.

Becky sighed and took her seat in the big chair. Judge enjoyed his evening quiz show. He read a lot; he had a good memory and a law degree; and he had lived through more than eighty years of current events, which meant that in most categories—except, of course, opera and gourmet cooking—he could answer the questions before the contestants did. He thought of himself as an expert, and he was sure that he could have been a five-day undefeated champion if only he had bothered to try out for the program. Whether he could have done as well under hot studio lights in front of a large audience as he did at home, and whether he had the reflexes to be the first to ring the contestant's buzzer were not factors he ever considered, and Becky certainly wasn't going to bring them up. Her role in the nightly quiz show ritual was to be an audience of one, to cheer him on, and to marvel at the scope of his knowledge.

Becky didn't much care for quiz shows. She hadn't read a book since high school, and she had no particular curiosity about history or science, so the featured categories never interested her. She was lucky if she knew two answers in the whole show—usually movie star trivia—but then she wasn't expected to know the answers. That was the whole point. Judge knew them all, and he wanted someone to be impressed with his brilliance. Becky didn't mind. She would put her mind into neutral, and every now and then she'd marvel dutifully at one of his unlikely triumphs, an obscure question, missed by the three studio contestants, but answered correctly by Judge. *(The last prisoner kept in the Tower of London.)* He got it right, and then grinned triumphantly at her, *For you to get that one right, Becky, I guess the question would have to be "Where is the Tower of London?"* She nodded amiably at him, and the show went on.

Mostly, Becky used the *Jeopardy* half hour to figure out what groceries they needed, or whether it was time to change the towels and bed linens again. She didn't mind the background noise, and it always put Judge in a good mood. It didn't take much to keep him happy. Just play along, that's all.

Becky wondered why the famous Lark McCourry couldn't see that. Or maybe she did see it, and was just too stubborn to play dumb. That could be it. Father and daughter were alike in that way. You could sharpen knives on their pride.

Lark had been visiting her father back in February, just after Judge and Becky left the lake house and moved back to Tennessee. She was only staying two days, just to see her father settled in, she said, and to make sure everything was all right. She bustled about, buying house plants at Wal-Mart and trying to talk him into letting her hire a decorator from Knoxville to fix up the inside. You could tell she thought the little frame house was just one step up from the dog pound, but that was why Becky liked it. Fancy houses made her feel awkward. This house came cheap, and Judge wasn't unhappy about that, either. He grew up in the Depression, so spending money wasn't one of his favorite pastimes either. He vetoed the interior decorator idea even after she told him twice that she'd be happy to pay for it.

"We don't need fancy furnishings," he said with his coldest smile. "We don't entertain much, and Lord knows we're not pretentious, are we, Becky?"

Meaning that Lark was, of course. She had shut her lips like a drawstring purse after that, but she didn't answer him back, because if you ever called Judge on one of his little insults, he would always look surprised and hurt and then claim that he hadn't meant the remark the way you took it. That way he hurt you twice. It was always best just to let it go.

The conversation between Judge and his famous daughter was heavy going, with Lark bragging about her career and Judge making stiff smiles and polite noises so she'd be sure to know he wasn't impressed by any of it. Judge said that he saw in the evening paper that the twenty-sixth was Johnny Cash's birthday, and why didn't Lark call him up so they could wish him many happy returns. She stammered a bit, and said she maybe could get the number, but it would take a couple of phone calls, and maybe a day or so to wait for a reply. Judge looked real surprised at that, and said, "But I thought you and he were neighbors out there in Nashville."

He knew full well that Lark didn't have Johnny Cash's home phone number, so that put her in her place good and proper. It seemed like the more famous she got, the harder he tried to show her that she wasn't important enough. It reminded Becky of a 4-H horse show she'd seen one time. The young riders were doing a jumping exhibition, running their ponies at a wooden pole set between two posts. Every time the pony cleared the hurdle, somebody would run out and raise the bar. That was how Judge treated Lark. He used to try it on Becky, too, but she wouldn't jump. Becky wondered why Lark never quit trying to make it over the bar.

By the third day of Lark's visit it felt to all of them like she'd been there a month.

Finally that evening when the conversation between father and daughter had just frozen over, Judge glanced at his watch and then snatched up the remote to turn on the television in time for his quiz show. Becky thought he probably wanted to show his daughter how smart he was—not as rich as Lark, but smarter. It was something, anyhow.

Becky had been standing in the doorway, not eavesdropping exactly, but just working up to asking if either of them wanted apple pie and coffee, and she could tell that the old man had put on the television because he wanted Lark to be his cheerleader for this evening's session of *Jeopardy*. After all, he had listened to her jabber on about her career for at least as long as the show would last. Fair was fair: his turn to show off.

Now you're home free, Girl, Becky thought. *All you've got to do is act amazed when he yells out the capital of Cuba, and then tell him how wonderful he is, and he'll thaw right out toward you.*

Lark didn't get it, though. She had been to college, too, and she came from a generation that didn't think a woman should have to simper in order to be liked. She thought she could please Judge by being smart, like the people on the quiz show. She thought this was another test for her to pass to prove to the old man that she was worth something, even if she didn't have Johnny Cash's phone number memorized.

The categories were revealed, the rules explained, and the game began. Halfway through the first category Lark started answering the questions faster than Judge did.

You could tell he didn't like that. He kept darting glances at her between questions. When she answered the third question in a row,

Judge glowered at her and pursed his lips in that put-out way of his that meant somebody was in contempt of court for sure.

That wasn't the worst of it, though. In the second half of the program, when the values of the questions were doubled, one of the featured categories turned out to be country music. Well, the old man had listened to country music all his life—at least up until the last ten years or so, when his hearing started going, and the radio began to sound like noise. He could have handled country music questions all night if they'd asked about the music from the golden age. Roy Acuff. Hank-Williams-the-First. Patsy Cline. But they didn't. The program's researchers, who were all probably younger than day-old bread, had come up with questions about the country singers of today, which, as Judge said later, hardly anybody can keep track of anyhow on account of they all look and sound alike.

On the two-hundred-dollar country music question, something about youngest female singer ever to do something-or-other, *he* had said "Brenda Lee," and *she* had said, "LeAnn Rimes," and of course she had been right. It was just about then that Judge sat very still and started looking like he was weaned on a pickle.

Quit now, Becky thought. *Let him win. You're leaving tomorrow, but I'll have to put up with his foul mood all week.*

Lark didn't quit, though. Instead she went and did the worst thing she could possibly have done. She started coming up with the answers

93

before the cards slid up to reveal the questions. "The next one will be about Shania Twain," Lark would say. And, sure enough, when the blue card went up, it said, "Canadian singer whose real name is Eileen," and the returning champion buzzed in and shouted, "Who is Shania Twain?" and his score went up another thousand dollars.

Judge sat there for a minute or so until the commercial break, letting his daughter think she was pleasing him by showing how smart she was. Guessing the answers without seeing the questions. He had never done that. Finally he said—just as casual as a band saw coming down on your bare hand—"Oh, how come they didn't have any questions in that country music category about *you*, Lark?"

That shut her up. But not for long. She swallowed whatever it was she was feeling, forced on a plastic smile, and said, "Why, Daddy, I guess I'm just too obscure to be an answer to a *Jeopardy* question. You know, these shows have to make things so easy that any idiot can get them right."

Lark left the next afternoon, claiming she had to be at the recording studio in Nashville the next day—though she hadn't mentioned it before—and Judge had said snide things about his daughter every chance he got for the next month. Becky stayed out of the crossfire. The way she saw it, she owed Judge a lot for looking out for her and giving her a steady job and a place to live—not easy things to come by if you can barely read and write. She thought he treated his daughter like dirt, all right, but she wasn't about to put her job on the line by telling him so. The truth was: She didn't care all that much for Lark herself. Miss High and Mighty—always looking down her nose at Becky, and making little suggestions about what meals to cook and how to fix up the house, as if Becky was white trash who didn't know how to take care of Judge properly. Lark getting her feelings hurt would just about even the score, Becky figured. So let her come.

Morristown—1759

I seldom speak anymore about my life at sea.

Though I was a long time believing it, my first friend of the new life, old Robert Bell, was right in his prediction that I was done with Scotland. I stayed aboard ship, and before many months were out, the sea had become so completely my home that I nearly lost the memory of that earlier life, and it seemed to me that I had been tarred at birth. As the images of my Scottish island faded from my thoughts, I began to think more of the future than the past, and I became eager to see what there was of the world at the end of this ocean. I heard that New York and Boston were great bustling cities, like calves of London, growing and prospering in the colonies across the sea. I meant to see them both before I was done with sailing.

I grew accustomed to a sailor's lot, and I spent nearly ten years aboard sailing vessels, inscribing the great nautical circle down from France or England to the Canaries, and from there across the Atlantic to the West Indies, to change one cargo for another. Then we would sail north, up the coast of the American colonies, to catch the easterly currents at Newfoundland and thus return again to the shores of Europe.

Once I even found myself back in Scotland, when the brig I served on put into port in Edinburgh, but as we had only a few days to stay ashore, there was not enough time for me to cross the country and make the crossing to Islay, or so I told myself. In truth I was afraid to see my old home, for fear that the reality of it would taint my childhood memories. My parents would either be indifferent to my resurrection or else they would demand that I stay and take care of them in their old age—neither prospect made the idea of a reunion appealing. Since I could think of no reason to go back, and a great many reasons not to, I let the moment slip away. The opportunity never came again.

As months and then years went by, spent in pursuit of favorable winds and profitable cargoes, the awkward boy prisoner grew into an able-bodied seaman, advancing in rank and power as my strength and prowess grew. A ship is a small kingdom but an absolute one, and I gloried in a power that belied my youth. Eight years I spent learning my trade and leaving childhood in my wake, but the day came when I knew I'd had enough.

I lost the rock.

I wish I could say that my talisman was taken from me in some grand and glorious catastrophe: a shipwreck, perhaps, or an attack by pirates in Jamaican waters. Someday I probably *will* say something of the sort, playing with the saga until I find the chain of events that best pleases my audience, but the truth is a sorry tale.

As I grew older and more burdened with responsibility, I had less time to think about the past, of which the green-flecked pebble was my only tangible reminder. When carrying it in my pocket began to feel like a remnant of childish cowardice, I put it away somewhere— stashed it in my trunk, I thought, or in a drawstring bag of coins, perhaps. The talisman did not cross my mind from one year to the next, as I took it for granted, just as my awe of the ocean's power became dulled by the monotony of many uneventful sea voyages.

One day I happened to be sifting through my belongings in search of stray coins for a dice game I wanted to join, and it came to me that my wee Iona stone might bring me luck in the gambling. I opened my leather pouch to draw it out, and found that it was not there. For the next quarter hour, while shouts from the circle of men in the galley told me that the game went on without me, I searched every inch of my trunk, and then every cranny of all the clothing I owned, but there was no sign of my talisman.

We were five days out of port that night, bound for New York harbor, and I do not think I slept another hour for the rest of the voyage. Now that I had discovered the loss of my charm, I was without protection. The old fears came back redoubled in strength. Every swell of a wave drew an answering lurch from my stomach, and I vomited over the side so many times that my mates began to swear the meat was tainted.

Surely, the prophecy is coming true at last, I thought. *Eight years at sea, and now I must pay the price of my pride and my carelessness.* Worse yet, a ship full of men would go down with me, never knowing that I was the cause of their destruction. I wondered if I should confess to my mates what a danger I had become, and urge them to fling me over the side to save themselves, as the sailors in the Scriptures had done to Jonah. If I warned them, the vessel might be spared my fate.

I told no one, though.

Much as I feared being cast overboard to drown, I dreaded even more the possibility that I was wrong and that my announcement would be met only with shouts of laughter: *The Scotch savage has lost his magic rock, and he thinks the fairies will scuttle the ship!* I could well imagine the taunts that would come from this godless bunch of Englishmen. It was a badge of honor for most of them to have faith in nothing. Some of the crew might believe me, but they would not dare to speak out against the jeering of the rest. And if I did tell and then the vessel did not founder, I would be the laughingstock of every port in the Atlantic for the rest of my days: the *Iona Jonah*. No, I thought, I would rather drown than face the ridicule of the crew. Well, I was only eighteen. Every time I pictured my own funeral, I would imagine my spectral self standing behind the mourners, watching as my blanket-draped corpse slid off the plank and into the sea. In my youth I could not quite get my mind around the idea that the world could sail on without me.

I did pray, though, for deliverance from the curse, and I read my Bible until it was too dark to see my hand on the page. Whether the Almighty chose to spare our ship as He spared the sinners warned by Jonah in Ninevah, or whether the old wise woman on Islay had misread my fate, I neither know nor care. By the time we sighted the wooded shores of Long Island, I was ready to swim ashore, so glad was I to see dry land. I knew then that I would never go to sea again. I had promised as much to God for the salvation of me and my ship, and for good measure I had promised the Shining Folk as well. I was spared, but I knew that I had better keep my word and go to sea no more.

When the ship put into port at New York, I left her there, and with no more than an hour's misgivings, I made my way inland. I said good-bye to no one, and I did not look back. Having made my vow to give up the sea, I had no heart for explanations. I wanted to put a good many miles between me and the waves before nightfall. I did not intend to live near the sea.

On the docks of every port we put into I had seen aging sailors—old, maimed, toothless—worn out from a life at sea, but still lingering about the harbor, so caught up in the spell of seafaring that they were unable to move any farther inland than the water's edge. These doddering old salts did a bit of work when they could get it, for pay enough to get them drunk as like as not, and they spent the rest of the time lazing about like old dogs in the sun, full of tales about their years before the mast. I did not want to end my days like that.

It was time to become someone else.

Having missed the dice game, I had my pay from the last voyage and a bit of money saved up besides, but not enough to take me far. I had not even the price of a horse, much less enough for a farm, and though I knew no trade but sailing, I was determined to make my way in the world on dry land. I had this in my favor, though: I was young and strong, quick to learn, and willing to work. I could read and write, both English and a bit of Latin, and I could cipher as well as anybody. In a young country without too many gentry, and with more land and jobs than people, I reckoned those skills would take me far enough. I could dig ditches if I had to, but I reckoned to aim my sights a good bit higher before I resorted to menial labor.

With a whispered prayer of thanksgiving for my deliverance, I turned my back on the great ocean whose only kindness to me over the years had been not to kill me, and I set out to choose a new home. New York was the first city in my path, but I knew I wanted no part of it, for it was a port, and, besides, it put me in mind of that description of accursed Ninevah given in the book of Jonah: "...that great city, wherein are more than sixscore thousand persons that cannot discern between their right hand and their left hand; and also much cattle."

I was born in a village with fewer than a hundred souls, and I spent eight years in a ship's crew which is a smaller village yet, so I had become accustomed to less raucous and sprawling places, but I still needed somewhere large enough to offer me a chance in life. I went in search of a town of manageable size, where a likely lad, old beyond his years, might make his mark on the world.

A great, crowded pike led away to the west, and as I walked along it, I saw low rolling hills rising up in the distance, and I resolved to cross them before I stopped for the night, for these hills would make a comforting barrier between myself and the Atlantic. As I traveled, I found that the road had a current of its own. I was pulled along by a steady stream of passing carters, amiable herdsmen, and fellow wanderers, a tide of commerce that floated me from inn to tavern as I drifted along. By the second day of my journey, I had talked to many people along the way, both villagers and travelers, and I had learned that the hills I had crossed over are called the Wachung Mountains, though to one born in Scotland they are scarcely deserving of the name. *Well,* I thought, *if they make mountains out of molehills in this new land, perhaps they can make a gentleman out of a penniless lad.*

By talking to folk along the road, I had concluded that a place called Morristown was the likeliest port for a lad of modest ambition and no love of farm work.

A garrulous silversmith who gave me a ride in his wagon provided good advice and pleasant company for a few miles of my journey. When I told him where I was headed, he remarked that Morristown was a "clever little village." It sat in a rich valley at the foot of five hills, encircled by farms, he said, and there were iron mines and a forge close by. The town was fortunately situated to receive travelers heading west from New York. Besides its inns and merchants' establishments, the community boasted a courthouse and other trappings of local government, for it was the county town of Morris County. I had some misgivings about the size of the place upon hearing all this, but the silversmith assured me that Morristown was a small and insignificant place indeed compared to the great city of New York that I had just come from, and I was satisfied.

"But what about Indians?" I asked my traveling companion, for I had heard my share of tales about the savages in the colonies. "Is there any danger of attack so far inland?"

He smiled at my foolishness. "You are a good half a century too late for such worries as that here," he said. "The Indians sold Morris County's land forty years ago for guns, powder, and other trade goods. Anyhow, there aren't so many of them about anymore. They took sick, you see. Pox and measles carried them off by the score. I'll warrant you'll find the county as safe as any port you've visited."

That was not very reassuring, but I could see that he meant well and knew little of a sailor's life, so I smiled my thanks.

"Have you kinfolk that bring you to Morristown?"

I told him about my life at sea, and my newfound ambition to learn a trade away from the ocean. "I thought to stay here in New Jersey, for I have no wish to become a slave in the plantation colonies down south."

He gave me a puzzled look. "A slave, boy? *You?*"

I was embarrassed to be so ignorant of life ashore. "Well," I stammered, "I have heard that even a man who is not an African can be sold to the farmers down there, and that he is made to serve in bondage for seven years. Like Joseph in the Book of Exodus."

The silversmith nodded with a trace of a smile. "I am no Bible scholar," he said, "So remind me, boy—did not Joseph thereafter become a man of great wealth and power in Egypt?"

I stared at him openmouthed. I had not thought of that aspect of the Bible story. As I stammered my assent, he said gently, "For a young man like yourself there is such a thing as an apprenticeship. You sign a contract with a tradesman, agreeing to seven years' labor, and in exchange the master teaches you his craft. When your term ends, you are free to set yourself up in business with the skills you have learned from him. Some tradesmen are kinder than others, of course, but it is a good way for an ambitious lad to get a start in life. I never thought myself a slave in my own apprenticeship, and I hope the lads in my service do not think it of themselves, either."

I stared at him. "You were an apprentice?"

He smiled. "A man is not born knowing how to work silver."

At length, when he came to the farm he was to visit, I got out to begin my journey on foot again. I thanked the smith for all he had given me to think about, and pressed money on him, but he would not take a penny, and wished me well. I walked on, so full of thoughts about what sort of trade I wished to learn that for a few more miles I scarcely noticed my blistered feet.

By the time I reached Morristown, I was so footsore from the unaccustomed hiking on dry land that I think I would have stopped there even if the devil himself had been elected mayor and the cobbles smelled of smoke, but fortunately this was not the case, and the aspect of the little village pleased me greatly. There was a village green in the center of town with a great bower of trees making a peaceful park. This common, bordered by a tavern, two churches, the jail, and the court-house, anchored the town to a rigging of wide cobbled streets containing shops and well-kept white frame residences. Of course Morristown had a river nearby to supply water to its people and their livestock, but it was not a navigable river for such ships as I was used to—another point in Morristown's favor.

I resolved to stay if I could find work, but I knew no one, and what money I had would only keep me for a month, I thought. In truth, except for a few days' shore leave now and again, I had never been required to pay for food or lodging, so I was not sure that my resources would stretch as far as my pride. I arrived late on Saturday afternoon, dreading what I knew must come next: a long round of meetings with strangers, as I went hat in hand from one tradesman to the next, asking for the charity of employment. I found the thought of asking such a favor so distasteful that, but for the thought of another painful thirty-mile walk, I might have retraced my steps and gone back to a life at sea. I took the cheapest lodgings I could find and tried to get my money's worth by actually sleeping, but with little success. My spirits rose in the morning with the sound of church bells.

Church.

In church I could meet men of substance without going hat in hand as a beggar to their place of business. I hastened to put on my cleanest clothes and to scrub the road dust from the rest of me. When I looked as fit as I was going to, I went out into the street to choose a church.

When I say that I chose the Presbyterian Church because as a good Scots Protestant it was the one that best suited my faith, I hope in part that is true, but I know, too, that the church sat in regal prominence on the village green, an imposing white structure with a steeple at one end and arched windows cut into the shingled roof. Its rival, the Baptist Church, looked squat and simple, and more like a barn than a church, from what little I had seen of either. *If I were a man of substance,* I thought, *I would cast my lot with the Presbyterians,* and as I meant to be just that one day, I joined the throng of people trooping toward the vestibule of the sanctuary, ready to take my place in the pew as a God-fearing New Jersey Presbyterian.

I had not seen the inside of too many houses of worship since my boyhood, though I'll warrant I prayed enough at sea for two churches. I stood there in the aisle, trying to fathom if the pews were private property or if I should be told by some churchman where I was to sit, when someone tapped me on the hand. "Come along, silly. The latecomers can't get past you!"

I looked down into the mischievous green eyes of a freckled young miss, not more than eight years of age. She wore a starched linen cap and a blue dress of a fine material that belied its simplicity just as her lively face was at odds with her prim attire. I bent down to the level of her ear and whispered, "I don't know where I'm to sit."

She nodded. "I thought so. You must come with me then. I know all about churching. What's your name?"

"Malcolm McCourry. What's yours?"

"Elizabeth Freeman. Come on. We mustn't tarry!"

I allowed myself to be led into a pew midway along the aisle, and soon I found myself ensconced among the members of the Freeman family, feeling rather like a lost puppy who has just been dragged home. Young Elizabeth, on my left, insisted upon prompting me through the service as if I were a visiting headhunter who had no notion of Christian ritual. She nudged me to close my eyes for prayer, elbowed me in the ribs when we were required to stand, and sang the first stanzas of each hymn into my ear so that I might pick up the tune and follow along. On the other side of me sat the young miss's father, a portly, dignified man of middle age. Throughout the service this worthy gentleman contrived to ignore me, but a time or two I thought I saw his lips twitch as if he were suppressing a smile.

When the sermon wound down at last, with the minister wishing us the peace and protection of God for yet another week of living, I nodded my thanks to my young guide and turned to pay my respects to her father. "I am Malcolm McCourry, sir, and I beg your pardon for my intrusion upon your pew, sir," I said. "I am a stranger here."

The man offered me his hand. "I judged you to be more of a hostage than an intruder," he said dryly. "I am Benjamin Freeman, lawyer of this parish and father of that young imp who waylaid you in the aisle. Let me bid you welcome to Morristown. Have you come to settle?"

"I hope to, sir, if I can find a way to earn my living."

He studied me for a moment, and then as we filed out of the pew, he said, "Well, you are a likely looking fellow, and kind to children—whether they deserve it or not." Here he cast a stern look at his offspring, and she made a gargoyle face at him in reply. Then they both laughed.

"I believe we owe you a dinner at least in return for your ordeal at my daughter's hands," he said, turning his attention to me once again. "Let us go to my house, and after the meal, we will talk. I may be able to offer some advice to you about prospects in these parts. But now you must meet the rest of my family— you will find them better behaved than the one you have thus far encountered. Malcolm, may I present my wife and my elder daughter, Rachel."

I bowed politely to Mistress Freeman and to Miss Rachel Freeman. The elder daughter was a prim young lady of fifteen, whose green eyes and chestnut hair gave her some resemblance to her sister, but this lass was stiff and formal, lacking the spark of gaiety that lit the features of young Elizabeth. As we all set forth from the church, I found myself walking between the two sisters, trailing the elder Freemans at a respectful pace. Elizabeth was still talking nineteen to the dozen—about barn kittens, I think—which Rachel interspersed with polite questions about my origins and my intentions to settle in Morristown.

When I told them that I had been at sea since boyhood, they were both thrilled and horrified that I should have lived a life of such adventure, but so bereft of family.

"But how can you bear to be alone?" Elizabeth demanded. "Don't you miss your father and mother?"

I could bear to be alone very well, I thought, but this did not appear to be the civil answer to give to my self-appointed benefactors, so I said, "My parents are surely dead by now, and my homeland is very far away. All I can hope for is to fashion a family of my own to replace what I have lost."

It was not Elizabeth who replied, but Rachel, who said softly, "I hope that you find a family here."

I had not been an hour in the Freeman household before I made up my mind that if I had any power over it, this should be my family. Benjamin Freeman was not a wealthy man, perhaps, by London standards, but he would pass for a lord in Morristown. The silver gleamed in the candlelight upon the polished mahogany table, and the dinner, brought in by a bustling servant, was rich and plentiful. Thick soup was followed by a joint of pork, with root vegetables, all circling the table in heaping bowls, while I tried to earn my dinner by regaling them with tales of my adventures at sea. I added somewhat to the luster of my accomplishments in the interests of storytelling, and while the elder Freemans listened with polite interest and curiosity about the exotic ports of the world, young Elizabeth peppered me with questions about whaling voyages, mermaids, and cannibals in the South Seas—things I knew nothing about from experience, though I endeavored to entertain her by passing along tales that others had told about them. Through my recital her older sister Miss Rachel blushed and favored me with shy glances, though her eyes shone when she looked at me.

At length Benjamin Freeman set down his glass and regarded me with raised eyebrows and the speculative gaze that no doubt he used upon people in the witness box. "And yet you are giving up this glorious life for the backwater of our humble village?"

I was ready for this, however. Meeting his gaze, I replied, "Well, sir, I cannot help but feel that my God-given wit and learning could be put to better use than on the deck of a ship."

He would not be drawn. "In what way?" he said, as coolly as one might discuss the purchase of a fish for one's supper.

I looked down at my reflection in the pewter plate and answered softly: "Well, sir, I read Latin, and I am used to a bit of authority over my fellow men. I learn quickly, and memorize easily, and I have no fear of hard work or painstaking detail. What profession would you think me best suited for?"

"Why, the pulpit," he replied. "You could convert the devil himself, I'll warrant."

The others all burst into laughter at this spark of wit, and I joined in, for I knew that before I again crossed the Freeman threshold, I would have secured a patron to pilot me to the bar, as it were. I would become a lawyer, and I would take care to keep the goodwill of the man who could help me accomplish it.

When at last the agreement was made between Lawyer Freeman and myself on the terms of my apprenticeship, I learned that a genial soul who is charitable toward hungry strangers may also drive a hard bargain in the way of business. I grant that he did me a great favor by agreeing to teach me the profession of law, but by heaven he saw that he lost nothing by it, for in return for his teaching, Benjamin Freeman would receive from me the services of a clerk and scribe. In addition to this free labor of a clerk, I would also do whatever errands or chores were required by my master for board and keep—tending the fires, cleaning the office, and so on—but without additional pay, for a period of seven years, at which time I should be free to set myself up as a brother attorney and begin to make my fortune.

We signed the legal contract, witnessed by another gentleman in the law, and the consequences of that document were explained to me. I could not change my mind, and if I should attempt to evade my responsibilities—to escape, in short—I would be brought back and treated as any other lawbreaker. I felt some trepidation about committing myself to seven years of servitude, but Benjamin Freeman seemed a kindlier man than many a captain I'd sailed with, and I thought that if I could endure the confinement of shipboard, I could manage this captivity for the rewards it would later bring. I signed.

As the paper was being put away, Benjamin Freeman clapped me on the shoulder and said something about Jacob's profiting by a similar agreement with Laban. His words were lost on me then, so dazed was I at the prospect of signing away the rest of my youth. It was only later that I realized what he must have meant by that remark: Jacob in the Book of Genesis, who worked seven years—and then seven more—for...Rachel.

Legem pone mihi, Domine, viam justificationum tuarum... Latin runs through my head by day, and thunders through my dreams at night. I believe that, except for a few stray barnacles, the language I was born to has been scoured completely away from the keel of my brain, replaced first by English and now by my expanded vocabulary and constant practice in Latin. It is just as well that my Gaelic is gone, though, for folk here in Morris County are disdainful of "Irish" ways. It is an attitude they picked up from the Englishmen, who see their neighbors to the west as pale Indians: savages or, at best, servants.

I did not mean to be either.

The Freemans treated me well, and it was clear that the goodwill of Benjamin Freeman's daughters kept me from being treated as a hired boy. I took most of my meals with the family, and I endeavored to entrench myself within the family circle by being an agreeable guest and an amusing conversationalist. The task was easy enough with young Elizabeth, for she was as lively as a hornets' nest, and always ready for a song or a bit of a jest. I found myself calculating how old she would be in seven years' time when my apprenticeship should be over, for I much preferred the lively little firebrand to her prim and awkward elder sister. Elizabeth was a child still, but in her features and

113

her character I could see the glimmerings of the woman to come, and I knew that she would be a prize well worth the winning. I worked all the harder, thinking that I must distinguish myself to convince her father that I was worthy of her.

Three years into my apprenticeship I had come to think of myself as part of the family, no longer needing an invitation to pass an evening in the Freemans' parlor, and relied upon not as a servant but as a family friend to carry parcels or give an opinion of a dress fabric, or squire the Misses Freeman on errands about the village.

One November evening we sat together in the parlor, as Rachel got on with her needlework in the candle glow, and Elizabeth attempted to teach me to play a few chords upon the rosewood pianoforte. I tried a few of the simpler songs to please her, but in truth I did not care for her music master's taste in tunes, though perhaps they might have improved with a more adept student striking the keys.

"Would you like me to teach you a song?" I asked her.

She tossed her head and gave me a playful look. "Oh, what songs a sailor knows would get me in Coventry for sure!" she said, laughing. "You will put swear words in the chorus, I'll warrant, to devil me."

"Not while your father draws breath," I shot back, laughing as well. That worthy gentleman looked up from his reading then and gave us the vacant smile of one who has over-heard no more than the mention of his name. "I promise you," I told Elizabeth, "I shall deliver a real song for your approval. One I learned when I was no older than you."

She studied my face to see if the shadow of a smile played in my countenance, but finding me in perfect earnestness for once, she relented. "Very well," she said. "Play it for me."

I looked at the instrument with dismay. "That I cannot do. I have no skill with playing, but I can sing it for you. If you wish to play it on the pianoforte, you must work out the notes for yourself."

"Now, there's a gift," she said. "Promise a brick and instead give mud and straw. Make your own, indeed! Well, then, let us hear this song of yours."

I have no voice to boast of. I can hear the notes well enough in my head, and I can sound them faithfully with my throat, but I have not that gift of resonance that makes an instrument of the voice, so that sounds roll forth from the singer's throat like the rounded notes from an organ. My pipes are not so grand as that, but I can deliver the sense of a tune without the artistry to make a show of it. In truth Elizabeth sang little better than I, but she had such spirit and charm that it was a pleasure to hear her anyhow; at least, for me it was. Her sister often told her that she made a noise like a scalded cat, and begged her to leave off.

I gathered my wits about me, and searched

in my mind for the right place to begin—on a note neither too high nor too low to allow my voice to continue the melody. *"On the hill above the kirk at moon rise she did stand...*"

The song about the ghost girl had stayed with me all those years, from the time Robert Bell had sung it for me on my first voyage. I sang it alone on deck the night we slid his body into the sea on an oak plank, and from time to time as I worked or studied, I found its melody dancing in my head. I wonder if I kept it in my memory out of fondness for it, or if it haunted me. When I sang it this time, I thought not of the shepherd girl hiding in the kirkyard, but of the poor lost Viking princess, who could only go home on the low road of death. I wondered if I might someday lie in a New Jersey grave, and fly out to seek my home in Scotland on the night of the walking spirits. I did not miss it in my conscious thoughts, but sometimes in dreams I would find myself back on Islay, watching the gray sea from a windswept hill.

When I had completed the last verse, Elizabeth looked at me with shining eyes and said, "Sing it again!"

Rachel heaved a sigh. "*Must* he?" she groaned. "It is so odd a tune. Not at all the sort of song people sing nowadays."

But I sang it again, though softer this time, and at last Elizabeth ran to get a bit of paper so that she might write down the words and work out the notes to play them. We spent the better part of an hour trying this chord and that, attempting to work out the melody, but

116

we could not find all the right notes, and by the time Elizabeth declared that she had mastered it, the tune had changed a bit, though I did not tell her so.

The fire had burned low, and the yawns and stretching of the Freemans gave me to understand that it was time I took my leave, and so I said my good nights and started for the door. Elizabeth walked with me to the hall. "It is a beautiful song, Malcolm," she whispered. "I hope I shall remember it all my life."

It was a prayer the devil answered, for within a few weeks, my dear Elizabeth had taken ill with pneumonia, and though she fought her illness with all the courage of a soldier, she was dead before the new year.

Chapter Four

Joe LeDonne hadn't lasted more than a couple of hours on the Appalachian Trail. *You might as well try to hike in the Johnson City Mall*, he thought. This was the busy season for the long-haul hikers, whose strategy was to cover the southern part of the journey in the spring months before it got too hot and to reach the trail's end in Maine before the weather in New England turned cold again early in the fall. LeDonne's sense of isolation was broken at regular intervals by chattering groups of Gen-

Xers, wearing designer sunglasses and swilling bottled water. Without missing a beat in their conversation these day-trippers would edge past him, and he would be left in the diminishing wake of their chatter until another hiker overtook him. He finally decided to leave the path altogether when a camera was thrust into his hands, and a ponytailed youth asked him to take his picture with his hiking companion: a Labrador retriever with a bandana for a collar. LeDonne snapped the shutter, thrust the camera back at its owner, and fled.

Fortunately there were other paths he could take. The Appalachian Trail was the longest and best-known path, but the mountains were crisscrossed by other trails. Long before the twentieth century, when the United States government had blazed the Appalachian Trail from Maine to Georgia, the Cherokee had followed their own trace through these mountains: the Warriors Path, used to pursue war and commerce with neighboring tribes to the north and south. The settlers and their descendants had cut their own routes throughout the area, adding narrow dirt lanes that had once led to now-abandoned farmsteads, and old logging roads dating from the early 1900s when the timber industry had nearly clear-cut the entire mountain region to provide valuable hardwoods for the furniture manufacturers. It was partly in reaction to that devastation that the national parks were formed in a conservation effort to preserve the beauty of the land. LeDonne wished he had been around to see the mountains before the loggers destroyed the old growth forest. Some of those oaks and chestnuts must have been around even before Columbus reached the new world.

LeDonne was looking for a way out. He kept walking until he found the next divide in the path: The Appalachian Trail went one way, and another trace, this one overgrown with weeds, led off to the south. Hearing another gaggle of hikers approaching in the distance made up his mind for him, and he swerved onto the overgrown path, heedless of the briars tugging at the legs of his trousers. Before the other hikers could overtake him, he was around the bend and out of sight.

"I have to go home," said Lark McCourry through clenched teeth. She sat curled up on her seat in the bus, striking the arm of it gently with her fist. "Damn!"

Jamie Raeburn closed the copy of *Sing Out!* magazine and gave her a puzzled look. "Lark, you hate your house that much?" he said. "Sounds like it's time to call a realtor."

"Not *that* home—I *wish*—I mean I have to go back to where I'm from originally, back to Wake County to see my father. I don't even know why I called it home. I haven't lived there since I left for college. It's a good thing we're finished with the gigs, because I have to be dropped off at the airport to catch a commercial flight this evening. And if there isn't one, I may have to charter something the size of a squirrel cage to get me there."

"You're leaving? Now?"

"Now. The phone call was a summons to Hamelin. My father may be dying. Or not. Becky panics every couple of months and calls me home, but my father always rallies. Still, he's eighty-three, so I have to take every call seriously, and I go when I can. Unless you or the front office come up with something really urgent that needs doing so that I have to postpone the trip—Will you?"

He shook his head. "Nope. You'll get no argument from me. I think you could use a rest. I've enjoyed this little jaunt on the road, seeing the music business from the performer's end for a change, but I think a steady diet of this would make me crazy. The food alone would kill me. So go. Enjoy. Although I gather you're not exactly thrilled to be going on this little vacation."

"Vacation. Oh, right. These visits are such an ordeal that I'd rather stay in Nashville and scrub the floors in the studio. This is a duty visit—not that I think it will be appreciated. I'm sure Daddy hates for me to come just as much as I hate being there. It seems like the farther apart we are, the better Daddy and I get along. When I've been away long enough, I think he almost forgets he can't stand me."

"Your father doesn't like you?"

"Nope."

"But you're rich and famous. Surely he brags about you?"

"I expect he does, but that doesn't change anything. It just means he's trying to take some credit for the success I bought with my hard work. Anyhow, back when I was poor and struggling, Daddy harped on what a failure I was, and then when I did become successful, that didn't suit him, either. Made him feel inadequate or something, I guess. We never talked about it. Talking to Daddy was always like getting somebody's voice mail, anyhow."

Jamie shook his head. "You amaze me. I thought mountain families were like the Waltons—poor but happy, and thick as thieves."

"Well, the McCourrys didn't live up to that stereotype. We weren't big on reunions. The only time we ever saw kinfolks was at funerals. When I was a kid, Daddy was very conscious of being the family's first college graduate, so he stayed away from the rest of the relatives, for fear he'd end up having to support them. I have first cousins I've never met."

"I wish I did. My family considers me their inside track to show business. My cousins send demo tapes instead of Christmas cards. I wish my parents had been more reclusive, like your dad."

"It didn't start with him, even. My grandmother once ran her brothers-in-law out of the yard with a broom."

An image rose unbidden to Jamie's mind and he started to laugh. "With a broom? Was she riding it at the time?"

"Shut up. It's no use trying to cheer me up

121

with your jokes. My father is ill—at least Becky says he is—and I have been summoned to The Presence." Lark made a face. "I'll be drinking Maalox like it was Chardonnay before I get out of there. Out of there... Oh, god! Where am I going to stay while I'm there?"

"Doesn't your father have a guest room?"

"I don't know and I don't care. I wouldn't stay there if every other place in the county was radioactive. Daddy acts as if Becky is his daughter, and he treats me like a visiting social worker. No way I'm staying with them, but you should see what passes for motels in Wake County. Tourist courts, mostly, left over from the fifties. A string of little free-standing buildings the size of tool sheds all lined up around a gravel parking lot. No phones, no ice, no television. I'd rather be in jail."

"No Holiday Inn?"

"Nearest one is Johnson City. I'll have to rent a car anyhow, though. Unless you're in a small private plane, you can't actually fly into Wake County, Tennessee. Commercial flights land at Tri-Cities, which is a good twenty miles from Johnson City, and Hamelin is another twenty miles south of that. Cherokee National Forest area. It's almost as hard to get back *into* that place as it was to get out."

"I'm sure it's lovely this time of year," said Jamie in the polite tones of one who can think of nothing else in the way of consolation.

She grabbed his arm. "Jamie! You wanted to see the music business from this side. Come with me."

He eyed her warily. "As delightful as you have made the prospect sound, I absolutely cannot. I have work to do back at the studio. When the company tells me to find new songs for people, they expect me to do it in the office, for the most part. Listening to demo tapes and such. My corporate masters don't actually mean for me to be wandering around the hills of east Tennessee with a tape recorder, you know. But it sounds like an unusual sort of place. I do wish you'd tell me why your grandmother ran her in-laws off with a broom."

Lark sighed. "Well, I wasn't around to see it happen. It's a story my father tells. Happened back in the twenties, I think. My grandfather had nine brothers, and they all used to get together to play fiddle and banjo, but apparently they also did quite a bit of drinking to limber up their playing. Granny did not approve of drinking or idleness, and she thought the brothers were leading her husband into wicked ways, so she put a stop to it. One summer evening, they were all sitting out beside the smokehouse in straight-backed kitchen chairs, playing their tunes and passing the fruit jar, when she lit out the back door with that broom and chased them off the place, telling them not to come back."

"Did they? Come back?"

"Yeah. About fifty years later. Their long absence wasn't all because of her, you understand. Some of them went north during World War II to work in the car factories, and some of them ended up in the army and then settled elsewhere, but what with one thing and another they stayed gone for the next half a century. They all went back home when they retired, though. Then…my grandmother died. We went back for the funeral—I must have been about twelve at the time, and I was just learning to play folk guitar. When we walked into the house to see my grandfather, we found all the female relatives sitting around in the front room—not a man in sight. So we walked through the dining room and kitchen—which was all of about twenty paces—and there were all the menfolk sitting in straight-backed kitchen chairs in the dark on the screened-in back porch, singing old country tunes. It was Grandaddy and his brothers. Great-uncle Henry had a beat-up Martin guitar, and he was playing chords while the others joined him on the vocals. I remember thinking that they were picking up where they left off forty years before." Her voice trailed off, and then she murmured, "I wonder…"

"What is it?"

"I've been trying to think of a song I heard once. I think it was an old ballad but I never heard it before or since. I've been thinking that if I can track it down, it would be perfect for the album. I wonder if that's when I heard it—from one of the uncles on the screened-in porch after Granny died."

"Can you ask them?"

Lark shrugged. "We're not what you'd call a close family. I haven't seen any of them in twenty years, and my grandfather was the youngest of the brothers, so they'd all be fairly ancient by now. I wonder if any of them are still alive."

Jamie smiled. "So go home and find out."

LeDonne was walking up a trail that must have once been a logging road. It was a steep path, overgrown in spots with weed trees and bramble bushes, but it was headed in the direction he wanted to go—straight up. He wanted to reach the summit of this mountain, to get his bearings from what he saw from up there, he told himself, but mostly he was in search of a breathtaking view. Mountain vistas gave him a feeling of peace that he supposed other people got from prayer—a sense of being in the presence of an all-encompassing being, and feeling its benevolence toward him. This was never something he would have discussed with anyone, not even Martha. When she accompanied him on hikes, he always took a camera so that he could disguise his yearning for high places as a quest for good photographs, but for this outing, he had not even packed his camera.

LeDonne looked at the pines and poplars that grew near the path, and tried to determine how long ago the mountain had been timbered. Maybe thirty years, he thought. These trees were tall now, but they were fast growing. The oaks were still the size of goal posts—still half a century away from grandeur. He heard a sound in the underbrush—a cross between a cough and a snort—and he froze in mid stride, took a deep breath, and turned his head slowly in the direction of the sound, knowing what was watching him.

Under a canopy of birches a few yards up and to his right stood a white-tailed doe, as intent and motionless as he was. For long minutes LeDonne and the deer stared at each other in perfect stillness, and in the strained silence he could hear the buzzing of flies and the drone of a distant jet far overhead. She was a yearling, he thought, judging from her size and the coltlike way that her long legs seemed a bit too large for her body. He could barely detect the twitching of the deer's velvet nose as she stood poised for flight, and he knew that she was reading his scent and not liking what it was telling her. Any second now she would make a run for it.

LeDonne kept still for as long as he could, but at last a gnat swooped too near his face, and when he raised his arm to deflect it, the deer sprang away, white tail flashing as she bounded down the slope of a ravine, and faded into the leaves of a distant laurel thicket. He stood still and watched her go, trying to record the encounter with his mind instead of on film. The idea of using a gun to "capture the moment" did not even occur to him, which might have seemed odd to anyone observing him, since he spent all of his working life in the company of firearms, but although he went hunting now and then, as a social gesture, LeDonne had no interest in killing for entertainment. He had seen enough of death to know that killing something does not make you its possessor. He only wanted the memory of this encounter—nothing more.

He was about to turn away to go on with the task of following the trail to the summit when he noticed an odd shape and a spot of incongruous color in the depths of the ravine. He could just make out bits of red and metallic gray entangled in vines at the bottom of the long gully, nearly obscured by weeds and the branches of a dead tree limb. Whatever was down there was not a natural part of the forest, he thought. Trash, maybe, discarded by some hiker, but even as that possibility occurred to him, LeDonne dismissed it. Years ago in combat he had learned not to discount his intuition, and now his nerves were telling him that something was wrong about this place. An instant later, without even a conscious thought to guide his actions, he was scrambling down the steep slope, thrashing his way through branches of thorns, and in other places slipping on bits of loose soil as he plunged toward the vine-covered mound below.

Idly, in the back of his mind, LeDonne began to wonder which side of the mountain he was on, and he realized that before he even reached whatever-it-was he was already thinking about jurisdictions.

Joe LeDonne stood at the bottom of the ravine, tugging at the branches and vines covering a mound of debris. A few yards away he noticed a sudden movement in the grass and froze, wondering for an instant if the place could be a nesting pit for rattlesnakes, but then he saw that the scurrying creature heading for another clump of underbrush was only a chipmunk. He let out his breath in a long sigh. The fact that the thing in the grass was a chipmunk was no guarantee that there weren't any snakes, only that he hadn't seen any evidence of one. Forewarned now, he worked more slowly, warily eyeing each vine before he pulled it aside. He thought his boots might be thick enough to protect him from anything he accidentally stepped on, but since the mound was taller than he was, he had to be careful of his hands and upper body. He had brought a long-bladed hunting knife with him, and now he took it out of his pack and began to hack away at the undergrowth. It didn't work as well as a hatchet or a machete might have, but it was better than using his bare hands, especially if—as he suspected—some of the plants entwined around the brush pile were tendrils of poison oak.

Judging by the thickness of the vines and the size of the bushes grown up around the site, LeDonne judged that it had lain undisturbed for at least a decade, perhaps more. He may have been the first person to find it, but whatever it contained was surely past salvaging now, so there was no urgency to the excavation. He was beginning to think he knew what he was going to find.

Another twenty minutes' work proved that his expectations had been wrong, which was just as well, considering that he had taken no precautions in approaching the site.

LeDonne thought he had stumbled on an illicit moonshine operation, with the still carefully camouflaged by the dense foliage. Bootleggers often liked to locate their operations on national forest land, because the current laws called for the confiscation of any property used in the commission of a felony. Often lately you'd hear about a marijuana grower or a bootlegger losing his house or his car to the feds after his operation had been raided by the authorities. If you located your still or your marijuana patch on federal land, the ownership would be harder to trace, and even if the owner were caught, he would not forfeit his personal property if convicted.

One problem, though, with illegal outfits operating on public land: They were as vulnerable to thieves as they were to law enforcement. To protect the goods from intruders, the owners booby-trapped the surrounding area with an assortment of deadly snares, ranging from small land mines to open pits. LeDonne was thinking that he had been both stupid and lucky in his approach of the vine-covered mound. Stupid, because he had forgotten to

129

check for traps before he ventured into the ravine, and lucky because nothing had exploded in his face as he attempted to excavate the buried object. Stupid, too, because he had been wrong about what lay beneath the tangle of vines and underbrush, and lucky that it had not been a booby-trapped moonshine still.

When he had torn away enough of the foliage to get a clearer look at what lay beneath, he saw the crumpled hull of a small single-engine prop plane. The red and white heap of fiberglass and metal seemed to have slammed into the ground at high speed, burying the plane a few inches into the soil of the ravine and breaking off the wheels and landing gear. Bits of metal and plastic were scattered about the clearing. Both wings of the plane had broken off at the juncture with the hull, and one hung in the vines, twisted and splintered, perpendicular to the ground. The other wing was nowhere to be seen.

LeDonne wasn't sure what make of plane it was, and in its present state of decay, even an expert might be hard-pressed to do more than speculate. The plane had obviously crash-landed on the mountain a good while ago. It would have sheared off branches and even treetops in its plunge to the earth, but as LeDonne looked around him he could discern no damage to the surrounding area. So the plane had been where he found it long enough for the trees to recover from the impact. A decade then. Maybe two.

He wondered if the crash had ever been

reported, and whether searchers had ever located the plane. Crashes were not uncommon in the stretch of wilderness that lay between Asheville, North Carolina, and Knoxville, Tennessee. Much of the land was national forest, and the high peaks made for turbulent winds and uncertain weather conditions. LeDonne knew that Audie Murphy, the most decorated soldier in World War II and later a cowboy star in western movies, had died in a plane crash in the Virginia Blue Ridge. Murphy's body had been recovered, but then he was a celebrity, and his plane was missed almost as soon as it went down. The occupants of this small craft might not have been so fortunate. This plane might never have been located by searchers or stumbled upon later by hunters, and if that were the case, then the bodies might still be trapped inside the wreckage. LeDonne knew that he would have to find out.

It took Lark McCourry five minutes of rooting around in her purse to find the little slip of Ritz-Carlton memo pad with her father's new phone number on it. She refused to memorize it. Her parents had owned the lake house for nearly fifteen years, and she thought her father would stay there for the rest of his life, or at least until infirmity forced him into an upscale managed-care facility. The fact that he had given up the beautiful glass and cedar lake house to live in a backwoods bungalow with Becky Tilden made his daughter cringe. Memorizing the telephone number would be an admission that the situation was permanent, and Lark was unwilling to concede that. She did, however, have to call there from time to time, and so the number was squirreled away in a leather zip bag along with her Visa, American Express, and Frequent Flyer cards, receipts, and tip money, sandwiched among a tattered collection of business cards from people she had met along the tour. Here were the names of fans to be added to the mailing list, radio disc jockeys to be kept in touch with, and helpful service people/hotel personnel in various cities. The scrap of paper with the area code 423 number scrawled across it was simply labeled "Scotch"—the family's private joke for her father's name: Scotch as in Johnny Walker.

Lark sat down on the wooden bench outside the hangar and pulled out her cell phone. She dialed the number and stuffed the scrap of paper back into the leather bag with the rest of the paper hoard. As she listened to the burr of a ringing phone, she looked out at the runway, frowning at a collection of small prop planes parked a few yards away.

The ringing stopped and a drawling voice said, "Uh-lo."

Becky. She never said, "Walker residence," or "Becky Tilden speaking," or anything remotely official. Lark unclenched her teeth and endeavored to sound pleasant. "Becky, this is Lark again. How is he?"

"About the same. He's watching TV now, eating his lunch on a tray in the den. You wanna speak at him?"

"No. I'm on the cell phone again, and I have to go in a minute. I just wanted to let you know that I've made it back from Colorado. We landed in Nashville about an hour ago. I didn't even go home to repack. The problem now is that nothing is going to Knoxville or to Tri-Cities today, and of course there are no direct flights to either one anyhow. You have to go through Atlanta or Charlotte to go two hundred miles up the road."

"Car would be faster."

"Well, it probably would be faster than a commercial flight, but not by much, and anyhow I'm too tired to try. So I've chartered a plane. I found a guy here who's willing to fly me from Nashville to the Wake County airstrip, and he thinks it'll only take an hour and a half or so. I'll need to be picked up there, though, so I wanted to make sure you'd be around this evening to come and get me."

There was a pause. Then Becky said, "I don't know where the airstrip is."

"Well, can't you ask somebody? You've got two hours to find out." Lark sighed. "Are there any taxies in Hamelin, Becky? If you could just look in the yellow pages and give me the phone number of a cab company, I'll just call when I get there."

"A cab company," Becky repeated as if the words were foreign.

Lark resisted the urge to spell it for her. She

133

said patiently, "The pilot who agreed to fly me there says that the Wake County airstrip is just a concrete runway. There won't be a terminal, or anywhere that I could call from or sit and wait. It's just a long strip of concrete. That's why I wanted to call and let you know when and where I'd be. Did you find the number yet?"

"What number?"

"The taxi company!"

"Oh. No. The cord won't reach to where the phone book is. Why don't you wait and call back when you get here? I'll work something out by then. I don't think we have any cabs in the county, but I might have a friend who would pick you up for twenty dollars."

"All right, Becky." Becky always had a "friend" who would do something cheaper—and less reliably—than professionals, but Lark decided that it was easier to agree than to prolong this torturous conversation. "I'll call again in a couple of hours. Tell my father I'm on my way to Hamelin, please."

"Don't you want to surprise him?"

"No, Becky. I want him to know I'm coming. I have to go now. I'll see you soon." Lark switched off the phone so that Becky couldn't call her back to argue.

Malcolm McCourry—1776

If the sum total of the practice of law were the making of pretty speeches to the court and figuring out the wherefores of legal conundrums by research and pure reason, I think I should have been a successful attorney and perhaps even a happy man, but long before my years of apprenticeship in Morristown had been completed I learned that the profession of law requires the practitioner to engage in the business of politics—not an endeavor that comes easily to me. It costs me a good deal of effort to smile and engage in idle banter with nodding acquaintances when I care nothing for their opinions and would rather be about my business. Idle pleasantries seem to me a great waste of time and breath, though I have seen enough of the practice to know that such encounters are the grease that make the wheels of civilization turn smoothly. A large circle of benevolent acquaintances take it in turn to open doors for an ambitious young man, and often will send a client his way, if they can do so without inconveniencing themselves.

Politics may be social as well as governmental. One need not run for office to dabble in local affairs—though many do—but it was nevertheless necessary to keep on the good side of those in power, to tack one's sails with the wind of prevailing opinion, and to become adept at *seeming*. On a ship you obeyed the orders of the officers and in turn gave orders to the men beneath you. Here the ranks were more difficult to discern—though I had no doubt that they were still there. To me village life seemed a long and tedious chess game to be played without ever knowing the rules.

In the ordinary scheme of things, playing at politics might mean only that one must take care to befriend the men in power locally, friendships that might cost me only a few dinners and some hours of social tedium invested toward keeping one's place in the social ranks. But these were no ordinary times. Decisions made now might well mean life or death for oneself and one's family. Life itself had become a game of chance.

I finished my apprenticeship in 1766, and on December 21 of that year I married the prim and serious Rachel Freeman, the daughter of my master and benefactor. I went to the altar willingly, partly in gratitude for the Freemans' kindness toward me and partly because I perceived that such a union would benefit me in my new station in life, though I found myself thinking more than once of the pretty and spirited young Elizabeth, who had died too young. Still, a man must have a proper wife if he is to take his place in the constellation of local society. Perhaps our marriage was politics on Rachel's part as well, for she was a plain lass, and she saw no other takers in the offing. I, with my new profession of law, was now a man of prospects. Something might be made of me by a determined and ambitious woman. Anyhow Rachel meant to try.

Our daughter Phebe was born on the eighteenth of October 1768, a hale and lusty little lassie, who much favored her mother in temperament, but I flatter myself that her handsome features came from me. A second daughter, Jane, arrived two years later, followed by our only son, Benjamin, and then three more girls: Elizabeth—I insisted upon the name, and sometimes yet I feel a pang whenever I say it— then Rachel and Sarah. It seemed strange to be so much in the company of women after having spent my youth at sea in a man's world. With such a large brood now in my care, it became even more imperative for me to succeed in the profession of law. I was able enough in the mechanics of litigation, but the social side sorely tried my patience, and it was there that Rachel took a firm hand, insisting that I should not be as solitary as my nature inclined me to be.

I let myself be led into the thick of Morris County society, and I did my best to say and do all the things that Rachel advised me to, but although the phrases of polite society were easy enough to learn, I confess that I never got the "tune" of them, so that I never did even the smallest thing without conscious thought and effort, and I was never sure if I had put my foot right or not until a smile or a civil answer from the person I was speaking to reassured me that all had gone well. Such courtly behavior never came naturally to me, and I plodded through dinners and social gatherings like one who is trying to perform a complicated dance step from memory. Always a part of me hung back, watching my other self nodding and smiling to people, thinking how silly it all seemed and wishing that I were elsewhere.

I suppose I did well enough. I had a ready smile and a quick wit, and I fancy I was as good company as the next man, and if I felt like a changeling playing the role of country lawyer, then it seemed that no one but myself was the wiser. People came to me with wills to be written and deeds to be drawn up, and so by diligence I prospered. In an effort to speed my success, we left Morristown and settled a few miles away in the little community of Black River, where Rachel supposed there would be fewer lawyers vying for clients, and I in turn hoped that there would be fewer people to be charmed.

I liked the smaller village. People here were not so ambitious, and there was less pomp in the ordinary business of living. For Rachel it was not enough to live in a town; she must be one of its lions of social prominence. In Black River I felt equal to the task of providing her with an acceptable house and adequate coach horses and carriage, as here there were no dizzying heights to aspire to. We settled in to the backwater of village life, befriending the right people and attending the right church, so that our children should have the legacy of a lofty place in the social order, and so that our girls could marry well and want for nothing.

I had been practicing law for nearly ten years when the war broke out. In April of 1775 shots were exchanged at Concord and elsewhere, between Massachusetts citizens and British soldiers, and we knew that the conflict would spread southward and threaten us, too, sooner or later. On June 3, the Provincial Congress of New Jersey passed into law a plan for regulating the militia of the colony. This act called for each township to form militia companies of eighty men each, comprising the village's male inhabitants aged sixteen to fifty.

Back in Scotland the boys of our island used to talk longingly of the Rising of '45, wishing that they had been old enough to fight in the rebellion against King George, for the glory of it, as the politics meant nothing to us then. I was quite grown before I understood the rights of it—how the English Parliament had passed over the rightful heir, James III, on account of his Catholicism, and plumped instead for a German prince, George of Hanover, who knew little of England and cared less, but whose catechism suited them. Now that I understand the legal points of sovereignty, I think that Scotland's position was the right one in the politics of the rebellion, but I'm sure the matter was never as simple as that. The people who did the dying in that war would not have profited in any measure no matter which side carried the day, and that is why I distrust the call of patriotism. They say now that some of the highland lairds on the losing side of the '45 have been restored to their estates with all forgiven, but the poor sods who died in their cause lie forgotten in the earth.

In my youthful ignorance I had wished for a glorious war as loudly as any of my young companions. *Be careful what you wish for. There are some prayers that the devil answers.*

Another George of Hanover was sitting now on the throne of England, and the talk around Morristown was that the powerful men in the colonies were tired of this land belonging to a little island an ocean away. They objected to the taxes and to the attitude that we should pay the rates of citizens while having none of the privileges. In Morris County prominent men like Jacob Ford and William Winds were saying that since the struggle for independence had come to war, we would soon be in the thick of it, and so the troops were being recruited and drilled in preparation for the coming conflict.

The idea of war no longer filled me with elation and excitement. A rapturous imagining for an eight-year-old boy may fill the heart of a thirty-five-year-old man with dismay. When Rachel's dear little sister lay dying, making such a brave showing of her passing while the rest of us wept, the minister at her bedside remarked on her courage, saying that old people fear dying more than the young, for the old have become too tied to the earth and to material possessions, while the young go back home to heaven with a gladdened heart. Perhaps it was my age and my material comfort that made me now dread war: more to lose.

The fortunate location of Morris County suddenly seemed to me a monstrous liability. The very source of the county's prosperity might now become the cause of its destruction. Here we were, on the stage road between Philadelphia and New York, prospering from inns and taverns and goods sold to the traveling public, and now, with war on the horizon, the county lay like a fatted calf waiting for slaughter in the very path of an invading army, and equally liable to destruction from the defenders.

When the American colonies united to form a new country, the great cities of New York or Philadelphia would be centers of supply and crucial seats of government, and, given the size and importance of both places, they would soon be objects of conquest for the invading British army. Here were my home, my children, and the town in which I had established my law practice—all threatened with devastation—and I knew better than most just what sort of horrors lay in store for us. In my youth in Scotland I had heard stories aplenty about the ravages of the Duke of Cumberland and his troops after the defeat of the Jacobite Army. He had laid waste to the Highlands, people said, and indeed one of the prophecies of the Brahan Seer had been that not a lum would reek nor a cock crow in the lands that lay in his path. The British Army was the greatest fighting force on earth, and now I found myself living in its path, while the villagers boasted about their prowess as marksmen and set about recruiting volunteers for a Continental Army.

I knew the prudent course of action, the sensible thing to do—stay out of harm's way and let others do the fighting—but the political answer, as always, eluded me.

"Of course you must join the Morris Militia," said Rachel, when I broached the subject at our fireside late one evening. "It is the law. The county's best men have put themselves forward to be officers, so I'm sure it is the wisest course."

Our dinner guests had departed, and now my wife and I sat alone watching the fire burn low, while we talked again of the evening's conversation, which had been full of fire and vinegar in praise of revolution. I had said little while the others waxed eloquent on the glories of independence. I could see that freeing ourselves from the ruling lords in England would create a political opening for men of wealth and power on this side of the ocean, but I did not see much benefit to the ordinary man from such a transition. I was sure that taxes would continue to be required, and that sooner or later the new government would hem us in as readily as the old one did. As we sat before the parlor fire I said as much to Rachel.

She sighed heavily, as she always does when

one of the servants has misunderstood a simple command. "There may be some truth in what you say, Husband," she said. "I know that you have seen rebellion against England before, and it cannot have left you unscathed. There will certainly be a new government over the colonies and powerful men will no doubt be in charge of it, but I see no reason why you could not be one of those new leaders."

"Because I am not a joiner," I said with a sigh of resignation. "I do not know how to make myself 'one of the company,' as it were. I always stand apart. In my own estimation, at least, I do not belong in the thick of anything. Besides, to join a rebellion might well get me hanged and bring ruin to you and the children." We had heard tales in Scotland...the Duke of Cumberland's soldiers going from house to house, in search of the fleeing Jacobites: cottages burned, livestock slaughtered, and families shot, or turned out into the road with nothing, which was only a slower means of dying. I could well imagine it happening here. It was after all the same army, and many of the people who had settled *here* had fled from *there*.

Besides, I was a lawyer, and if the law is about anything, it is dedicated to the orderly resolution of conflict, without resorting to violence. Well, wiser men than I swore that we colonists had tried that route, and had failed, so that the war was now the only recourse to reasonable men of honor.

"If the rebellion is put down, it will go hard on the rebels," I told Rachel.

"And if it succeeds, it will go hard on those who hung back and did not join," she replied.

"Very well," I said. "I will speak to Nathan Drake about joining his battalion. He has been made colonel of the Western Battalion of the Militia, and I shall offer him my service. I doubt if the regular army would think much of me, though, old as I am. War is a young man's game, unless of course one is made a general, and I have no hopes of that."

"It is enough to stand up and be counted," said Rachel placidly. "The militia's duty, as I understand it, is to guard the village itself, and surely you would wish to do that anyhow. I see little danger in the prospect, unless the war comes to our doors, and then no one here would be safe, in the ranks or out of it. Besides, I do not think that this campaign for independence will be lost. The British may find it very difficult to wage war when they are an ocean away from home. Naturally you hesitate because you are thinking of the troubles in Scotland, but that land lies a good deal closer to London than the Americas. I think, with an eye to the future, that joining the militia is a risk worth taking."

Since the risk we were taking was my life, I am sure she did think so. Nevertheless I did enlist in the Morris Militia, which, as Rachel noted, was not a part of the Continental Army, but more of a local guard entrusted with the safety of our home county and providing what help we could to the army should it ever come this way. We privates were enrolled for a term of one year's service, for which we were paid five dollars per month and issued clothing—a felt hat, a pair of shoes, and yarn stockings—but we had to provide our own weapons: a musket and bayonet, a sword, flints, cartridges, a ramrod and priming wire, and a knapsack in which to keep these supplies. We drilled on the village green, making ready for a war that was edging toward us from north and south. I was made quartermaster of our little band of soldiers, responsible for supplies and record keeping, a fitting occupation for a lawyer-soldier, I thought.

We drilled and practiced our marksmanship to make ourselves battle ready, and we took what precautions we could to ensure the protection of the women and children in case we should be called away by the fighting. The old people of the community remembered the days of Indian attacks, and many of the same defensive measures were adopted now to safeguard our loved ones from enemy troops. Three stone houses in the area were designated as fortified places of safety so that in the event of fighting in the area, the women and children might seek shelter there. The militia also set up a system of signal fires from a succession of hilltops to warn of the approach of British troops. When I heard about this, I thought to myself, *There's a Scotsman in back of this plan,* for the hilltop signal fires had been a tradition in my homeland for a good thousand years and more. When the watchman on a hill spotted advancing enemy troops, he lit his signal fire—a barrel of tar set on top of a tall pole. Seeing the blaze, the watcher a few miles away on the next hill lit his own signal fire in turn, and so on, until by a line of sight, the warning could be carried for many miles. We also had "Old Sow" to warn us of trouble— an eighteen-pounder cannon atop the Beacon Hill that was fired to alert the local militia to assemble and be ready to fight, should the war ever come this way.

Should the war ever come this way. Oh, it came all right. It arrived with the new year of 1777. The Continental Army had been driven out of New York by the forces of General Sir William Howe, and they had retreated to the south of us, finally crossing the Delaware River into Pennsylvania. General Washington was still alive and in command of the forces of the rebellion, but our brilliant Major General Charles Lee had been captured, and it began to seem as if the Rising of '75 would last little longer than the terrible one I remembered from thirty years back. The British seemed intent upon dividing the colonies at the midpoint to weaken both halves. With Howe's army advancing from the south and Burgoyne's sweeping down from the north, the might of the British forces would be centered between New England and the Southern colonies—in our backyard, that is. They would seek to control the Hudson, open supply lines to Canada via Lake Champlain and Lake George, and put an end to the uprising—for they never considered it a war. All seemed lost, but no one would say so, and our troops persevered despite the overwhelming odds against us. In December 1776, while Washington's forces camped to the south of us near Philadelphia, the Morris Militia was called out to stop a tide of Tories and Hessians who came over from Staten Island into Springfield, and we stopped the advance and took prisoner a goodly number of Hessians.

General Washington's determination was equal to our own. On Christmas night he again crossed the Delaware with an army nine thousand strong, and at dawn the next day he attacked the enemy in Trenton, winning a decisive victory over an army six times the size of his own. From there he moved his forces north to Princeton, and on January 3, he defeated the British yet again, causing them to retreat to New Brunswick, where their main stores of supplies and ammunition were kept. Had the Continental Army moved on to New Brunswick and attacked there, they might have ended the war, but Cornwallis had attacked the departing army at Princeton, leaving Washington's forces too exhausted for further assaults, after forty-eight hours of marching and fighting without rest. So instead of attacking New Brunswick, they destroyed the bridge over the Millstone River and marched northwest, arriving on the snowy evening of Epiphany—in Morristown.

The army camped in the snow-covered woods just outside Morristown, and General Washington himself took lodging in the Arnold Tavern. I wished the soldiers well, but even more I wished them gone, for they would draw the enemy forces like flies to dung, and then, I thought, the battle would rage here, and everything I loved would be in peril.

"Why can't the army find somewhere else to roost?" I grumbled to Captain Horton, who was my friend as well as an officer in the battalion. "Surely there are other villages the general might grace with his presence."

"There is no place better suited to his purposes than this," said Nathan Horton with a grim smile. "Consider it from a soldier's point of view. There are farms enough hereabouts to feed the general's troops, and in the hills west of here there are forges to provide more weaponry. The county is protected on the east by Long Hill and the Watchung Ridges. There is swampland on either side of the main road from Bottle Hill. And we are nearly at midpoint between the main centers of British activity at Newark, Perth Amboy, and New Brunswick, so that the army may counterstrike any offensive from an ideal central position. Why, General Washington must think that God made Morristown for just this very purpose. The place is an answer to prayer."

Prayers the devil answers, I thought.

So we fought. Old men and boys, farmers and blacksmiths and lawyers took up arms against regiment after regiment of professional soldiers. There is a rush in the blood that comes to a man in battle, and if he can swallow his fear and feel only the exhilaration of combat, he may grow fonder of war than he is of the tedium of ordinary life. If fighting were all there was to having a war, we might be able to bear it, but the twin scourges of famine and pestilence make cowards of even the bravest of us. They are enemies that you cannot fight. You can only endure, and hope that your strength is greater than theirs.

By the time Washington's army had reached Morristown, his troops were already ridden with fever and flux, and while his concern was that his army would be weakened by the infirmities of his troops, the citizens of Morris County feared that their deliverers would instead become their destroyers, spreading disease to the villagers and leaving death in their wake as surely as those who killed with musket and bayonet. It is one thing to risk your life in battle with an enemy soldier, but quite another to be absent from home and wonder what pestilence might carry away your children while you are gone.

General Washington insisted that his army be protected against the smallpox, for in every war disease killed more soldiers than the enemy did, and in the winter of '76 there was a great round of fever and pestilence cutting a swath through the Continental Army. The doctors' advice on combating this scourge struck fear into all of us. "Give everyone a mild form of the sickness," they said. "This will prevent them from acquiring the more virulent form of the disease." By the time his troops had settled in Morristown, the general had been persuaded to proceed with this course of action. Dr. Nathaniel Bond was given charge of the procedure, and he began setting up stations in Morristown and in the surrounding villages, wherein the "inoculation" as it was called could be given to the soldiers. Guards were posted at these medical posts, to prevent the spread of infection it was said, but I think it might have been to prevent the more timorous from fleeing before they could be treated. Every five days or so, the soldiers of a particular division would be marched up to the treatment stations, and each one would be pricked with a needle bearing a weakened strain of the pox. It was the army's hope that the men would be stronger than the weakened pox germs, and that they would recover without any ill effects.

When it came our turn to join the ranks of the inoculated, I found myself full of misgivings. "Has anyone not been strong enough to fight off the pestilence?" I asked the doctor, as he advanced on me with a large and bloodied needle.

He stopped in mid stride and frowned at me,

or perhaps at the impertinence of my question, for he was used to obedient men-at-arms. I met his gaze, though, and he saw that I was no young boy in the ranks, but a militia man of mature years, serving in my home county. At last he shrugged and said simply, "Most recover. Some die—but not as many as if we did nothing."

Most.

I held out my arm then and submitted to this bizarre attempt to cheat death of plague victims. Another thought struck me, though, and before I could be pushed aside in favor of the next victim, I asked another question. "What about all the people of the villages here where the troops are encamped? If all these men have a mild form of the pox, might they not spread it among the townspeople unawares?"

"That thought had occurred to us," said the doctor, with the dry irony of one whose confidence in his own ability is absolute.

"Am I not correct?" I demanded.

"Perhaps," he said calmly, turning toward the next patient. "And to prevent just such an eventuality, we have taken steps to inoculate the civilian population as well."

"The civilian—" I froze in my tracks. "But there are old people! Children! Many of the villagers have not the strength and youth of your young soldiers here. The pox may kill them, full strength or no!"

"So it may," he muttered. "But war is terrible, and many die. It is God's will."

If that was God's will, then I wonder what it was the devil wanted, for the effect could hardly have been more terrible. I was ill and feverish for more than a week, I think, and in my delirium I roundly cursed every war and every general from Washington to St. Michael the Archangel, but in truth I was one of the fortunate ones.

Some of the people took sick from pox before the treatment could be administered to all, and some caught contagion from those who were given the milder pox, and their own cases became severe. In Morristown both the Baptist Church and the Presbyterian Church were turned into hospitals for those stricken with the disease, and more than sixty parishioners died in the Presbyterian Church that had once been my family's spiritual home.

This was the price we paid for our freedom from the Crown. The war dragged on for a good few years past that winter, and there were other skirmishes, and Washington camped there for yet another winter in '79, but for the most part we were spared the ravages of battle. I had a clerk's war of forms to fill out and records to keep, and no fine tales to tell my children about my days as a soldier. Perhaps the bravest thing that I did as a warrior was to bare my arm and invite death to come into my body, and then to go home and risk spreading the pox to my wife and my little ones.

And when I've come back home, I will be changed—oh!—Indeed.

Chapter Five

Jenna Leigh Gentry was alone in the sheriff's office when the call came through, which was just her luck, she figured. You could sit in that office for a solid month with nothing more exciting coming in than a domestic call at the trailer court, and then the one time everybody else was gone, something earthshaking would happen and you'd be the one that had to deal with it. At least Sheriff Arrowood wasn't the kind to yell at people if they made mistakes.

Deputy Martha Ayers had just left on patrol and Sheriff Arrowood was off at some county meeting with a scowl on his face and orders not to be disturbed, which probably meant that the department budget was under review. Deputy LeDonne had the weekend off. That left Jenna Leigh, Wake County's new dispatcher, nominally in charge, but with orders to radio Martha for any calls more urgent than a tourist asking for directions. Martha had trouble delegating authority, probably because the dispatcher's job had been hers for umpteen years before she went off to Walters State and took the training to become a deputy. Jenna Leigh hadn't anticipated having to call for help, though. It was going to be a slow evening in Hamelin. It always was.

Jenna Leigh had been on the job for eight months now, and the prospect of running the Wake County sheriff's department for the evening shift did not faze her. In fact, law enforcement had definitely lost its luster as far as she was concerned. She was the envy of her friends for having landed such a glamorous and exciting job just three weeks after graduation from the community college, and she never corrected their mistaken impression of her work, but any resemblance between her current position and the cop shows on TV was strictly in the imagination of the beholder. Jenna Leigh knew better the week after she was hired. Perhaps she was disappointed that her life lacked the drama of *Law and Order,* but the pay was all right, and she didn't really want to leave the area to find a job. She came from a close family, one in which mothers and daughters saw each other every day of their lives. Well, even if she did want to move somewhere with more opportunity—like Knoxville—she didn't know anybody there, and with her community college degree and no experience, she doubted if she could get much more than a waitress job. Maybe in a few years, when she was older and had some job experience, she would give the big city a try, especially when it was time to do some serious looking for husband material.

What mystified her in the meantime was how many people from the big city were moving in to give her hometown a try.

Hamelin was an unincorporated village in a county whose land was mostly national forest, and the low crime rate reflected the nature of the population: churchgoing farm folk and a steadily increasing number of college-educated new people, attracted by low land prices and beautiful views. Burglary was rare; vandalism usually traceable, and the county murder rate was a steady three a year—usually an alcohol-fueled quarrel between drinking buddies or a domestic case, in which the husband took the divorce decree or the restraining order as an affront to his manhood, and, as Sheriff Arrowood put it, "decided to take the matter to a higher court." Usually the arrest was made before the pistol cooled off.

Jenna Leigh didn't really mind being alone in the office, because she was the new employee. The peace officers had all known each other forever—or at least since Jimmy Carter was president, which amounted to the same thing as far as Jenna Leigh was concerned, because Carter was in the White House when she was born. This meant that her ability to make small talk with her older colleagues was severely limited. Oh, they communicated well enough with her on a professional basis. Jenna Leigh was bright and competent. She had been an honor student, and she worked hard at whatever task she was given. But a large part of an office environment is the social pleasantries that grease the wheels of communication, and that was where she found it hard to participate. She practically had to read *Newsweek* to find something to say over coffee, because culturally speaking they were from a different world.

She was reading the social page of the *Hamelin Record,* eyeing the brides she knew from school with a mixture of envy and contempt, when the phone rang. She reached for it and said, "Wake County Sheriff's Department," in a voice of practiced calm.

"It's Jenna Leigh, isn't it?" Without waiting for a reply, the caller went on, "This is Ben Hawkins over at 911. We just got a distress call, and I thought I'd better notify you folks right away. Sheriff there?"

"Sheriff Arrowood is in a meeting. I can try to reach him, though. *Ben Hawkins!* Jenna Leigh kept her voice carefully neutral. Just when you got to thinking that everybody in Wake County was older than God, somebody like Ben Hawkins turned up and made staying home seem like a good idea. He was maybe twenty-eight, tall and blond with a runner's body and a serious expression behind wire-rimmed glasses. Just once, though, she wished that he would call when it wasn't a thundering emergency, so that she could have a conversation with him about something besides fires, wrecks, and accidents. She'd see him in the coffee shop sometimes, but it seemed too forward to invite herself to join him. Sometime, though, she wanted to talk to him long enough to ask why somebody with a degree in physics from SUNY-Binghamton was making raku pottery and working part-time fielding 911 calls in the hills of east Tennessee. "Before I page the sheriff, can you tell me what this is about? He'll want to know."

"Report of a plane crash. The caller is on a cell phone, reporting that a small private plane has gone down somewhere in the mountains."

"Okay," said Jenna Leigh. "I'm writing this down. On a cell phone?"

"Roger that."

"Okay...cell phone... Did the caller see where the plane went down?"

After a pause, Ben said, "Apparently, the caller is *in* the plane."

"The *pilot* called you? Called 911? On a *cell phone*?"

"No. The caller thinks the pilot is dead. Unconscious anyhow. The person who phoned in is a passenger, and she says she's trapped in the wreckage."

"*She*..." Jenna Leigh almost lost the thread of the conversation, but she reminded herself that if she allowed herself to become distracted, someone could die. "Did the caller give the plane's position?"

"She has no clue. Even if the instrument panel was intact, I doubt if she could make anything of it, and she says she wasn't looking out the window so she doesn't know where they went down. She may be in shock as well, of course."

"Yes, but she thinks she's in Wake County?"

Ben Hawkins sighed. "She just called 911,

and the call was routed by a receiving tower which in turn rang at my office, so I guess that means she's around here. Somewhere. I'm going to maintain contact with the caller as long as possible, but right now I have to call the Civil Air Patrol and get the rescue team mobilized. Could you see that the sheriff gets the message? Your department coordinates the search."

"I'll call him right now," Jenna Leigh promised. Before she could add "Nice talking to you," the connection was broken.

Spencer Arrowood was not altogether unhappy to be hauled out of a county board meeting by Jenna Leigh's summons, but when the details of the emergency became apparent his good humor vanished. To the county commissioners, he murmured something about an emergency situation as he excused himself from the meeting, promising to get back to them within the next few days.

When he reached the local headquarters of the Civil Air Patrol, eleven volunteer members were assembled, many of them still in work clothes from their day jobs. Now they sat in alert silence in the small conference room, listening to a tape recording Ben Hawkins had made of the 911 call. On the cinder block wall in front of them was a large topographical map of the area.

The sheriff sat down in one of the metal folding chairs, waved away an offer of coffee, and pulled out his notebook to record details of the call. "Start it again for me, Steve, will you?" he asked the man at the tape recorder.

Steve Ashley, an earnest-looking young man still in his brown UPS uniform, nodded and rewound the cassette. "I've got the volume up as high as it will go," he said, "but it's still hard to catch, so listen closely."

"Right."

"Hello... Is this 911?" The words were slurred, and the voice indistinct, perhaps from injury to the caller, or from interference with the signal. He couldn't tell. "Plane crash," the caller was saying. "We left Knoxville...flew awhile... *What time is it?*... Never mind. Then we hit the mountain..."

Ben Hawkins's voice came on then, clearer than the caller's, and calm but tinged with urgency to extract information as quickly as possibly before the connection was broken. "You witnessed a plane crash?"

"No. Lived it." Spencer thought he heard a note of irony in the response.

"Your plane crashed?"

"Not my plane. This is my cell phone, though. Come and get us, will you?"

"Can you give me your location."

"In the back...of the...damn...plane..." A sleepy slurring to the words, characteristic of drunks and people in shock.

Get the name, thought Spencer. *You have to keep her talking, and you have to get her to start giving you useful answers. Her name will help.*

As if on cue, Ben's voice on the tape was saying, "Tell me your name please."

The reply was muffled, followed by Ben's attempt to clarify the response, "Laura? Did you say that your name is Laura?"

"Look, Operator—or whoever you are—" The voice was louder now, but the caller was not in a cooperative mood. "I'm stuck out here...wrecked plane. Pilot's dead. Surely. Blood all over... Look, all I can see from here is trees." Anger crept back into her voice and seemed to strengthen her. "I wasn't looking out the window when we hit, so I can't tell you if there's a McDonald's over the hill or not. *Okay?* Now, you trace this call, you moron, or whatever it is you do to track cell phone calls, and you get me out of here. *Right now!*"

The tape ended abruptly, leaving the room in strained silence. Finally one of the men whistled softly. "Whew-ee! That is one tough lady. Sounds like she could chew her way out of the wreckage."

Spencer bit back a smile and stopped writing in his notepad. "Was the connection deliberately broken or did the caller run out of power—or did she lose consciousness?"

Steve Ashley shrugged. "We're not sure, but judging from her evident annoyance with Ben's questioning, we are assuming that she hung up."

Spencer nodded. "That would be my guess, too. Maybe she wants to conserve the batteries in that phone, too, which is certainly a good idea. It might take days to find her. I hope she calls again. Now, next time, we need to concentrate on getting her full name so that we can check airport flight logs, and above all: *Trace the call*... Can you do that?"

"We can call a cell phone company and ask them. My guess is no. We know the caller is close enough to bounce her signal off a relay tower in our area, but that may be all we can determine."

"She mentioned *Knoxville*," said one of the volunteers.

"So the plane took off from Knoxville." Spencer Arrowood walked up to the map at the front of the room and put his finger on the position of the Knoxville airport. "We know it's a small private plane that crashed somewhere in our vicinity—or at least within range of the cell phone relay tower serving our 911 number." He looked at the ring of faces around him. "Okay, where is that tower?"

After an uncomfortable silence, one of the men said, "We think we can find that out."

"Right," Spencer nodded. "That's good news. Then we can phone the Knoxville airport and get a flight plan for the aircraft."

The volunteers looked at each other and shrugged. Finally one of them said, "We can try, Sheriff. We *will* try, of course: Miracles have been known to happen. But we know that asking for a flight plan probably won't do us any good. These little private crates don't have to file flight plans. They fly too low to interfere with any of the commercial flight paths. They're like...well... cars. You take off in your vehicle, and you don't have to tell anybody where you're going or why."

Spencer took a deep breath, and swallowed

his frustration. "Well okay. So what do we know then? We know that a small plane is down somewhere between here and Knoxville."

Steve Ashley gestured for the sheriff to stop again. He sighed. "Maybe not, Sheriff. The cell phone towers bounce signals in strange directions because of the mountains. We don't know where the plane was headed. Maybe Charlotte. Or Pittsburgh. Probably not Atlanta, because that would have taken them south toward Chattanooga, but they could still be east of here, or north."

"East?" Spencer scowled at the map. "*East of here?* That would put the crash site in North Carolina. Are you sure?"

"Well, no. We're not sure of anything right now, but we have to get this search up and running while we still have a chance of finding survivors. With any luck someone on the ground will phone in a sighting of the plane as it went down. Anyhow, jurisdiction isn't a problem for us. We just call the Civil Air Patrol in North Carolina and work both sides of the mountains."

"And, Sheriff, I guess you call their law enforcement people to coordinate that end of it."

Spencer Arrowood sighed. "I was afraid you'd say that."

"Something wrong, Sheriff?"

He shook his head. "Some of the people over on that side of the mountain are strange, that's all. The last time I went over there, a waiter in the French Broad Bistro called me a *cosmic possum*. I'm still trying to figure out what he meant by that."

On the North Carolina side of the mountain, Baird Christopher was shelling peas and shucking corn for a vegetarian supper for twenty.

The Cosmic Possum Hikers Hostel was a white Victorian mansion dating from the late nineteenth century. Three miles from the Tennessee state line and a mile outside town, the house stood on a hillock overlooking the French Broad River, surrounded by mani-cured lawns and tall rhododendron bushes, and shaded by oaks and poplars. The mountain mansion had been built in the 1870s when the western North Carolina highlands became fashionable for summer vacationing, because, in a world without air-conditioning, the cool mountain air made southern summers toler-able. When the last of the original owners' family had died or moved out of the county, the farmland was sold at auction, and Baird Christopher bought the remaining acre of land and the big white house. Then, with the carpentry skills he had perfected in the Peace Corps, he set about renovating the elegant old mansion into a dormitory for transient Trail folk. Wallboard partitions split the spacious upstairs bedrooms into two smaller rooms, and the chestnut-paneled dining room with its bronze chandelier and ten-foot ceiling was now crammed with homemade pine tables and

163

metal folding chairs set close together to accommodate the twenty or thirty hikers who would turn up for dinner.

Baird usually let one of the hikers do the kitchen scutwork in exchange for a meal, but when he had asked around at lunch today no one seemed to need a free dinner bad enough to work for it, so Baird was doing his own culinary prep work. He took care to station himself in the most conspicuous spot in the garden, however, and he kept another chair close at hand in case a volunteer happened along. Baird wasn't much on chopping vegetables, but he was glad of an excuse to sit out in the shade of the oaks and watch the world go by—migrating monarch butterflies or investment bankers in hiking boots: it was all one to him. With the white plastic colander balanced on his knees, Baird Christopher snapped open pea pods to the steady beat of a tune in his head.

"Need any help?"

A stout middle-aged man with a red face and a Cornell sweatshirt stood over him, glistening with sweat. "This is the hostel, isn't it?" he asked, wiping his forehead with his sleeve. "That potato farmer in the old green truck said it was."

"Potato farmer?"

"Yeah. Guy in overalls hauling bushel baskets of potatoes in the bed of his pickup. He offered me a ride, but I told him I just needed directions to a place to stay. Said to tell you hello. Gordon Somebody, I think he said."

"Oh. *Gordon*," said Baird with a bemused smile. "Potato farmer in an old green truck. Right. I'll tell him you said so. He'll be tickled to death." He chuckled. "*Potato farmer.*"

"Well, weren't they potatoes? Or yams, maybe?"

"Well, they might have been yams, but old Gordon is no potato farmer. He's a cardiologist from Charlotte. Likes to come up here to his summer place and play farmer whenever he can. He'll be thrilled that you mistook him for the genuine article. It'll make his day. Now, what can I do for you?"

The man mopped his face with a grubby bandana. "I need a bath. Can I get a room for tonight?"

Baird nodded. "Welcome to the Cosmic Possum Hostel," he said. "I'm just getting the vegetables ready for tonight's dinner. You can help if you're so inclined." He removed the paper bag of corn from the second lawn chair and indicated that the man could sit down. "I'm Baird Christopher. I run this place."

"By yourself?"

"More or less. Every so often one of the Trail puppies will take a break for a couple of weeks or months, either to recuperate from an injury or to earn some cash to take them the rest of the way, and I give them a job helping out around the place, but sooner or later, everybody but me moves along. You should have been here *last* month: The guy working here then had been trained as a chef. Used to work at the Four Seasons. He headed out when

165

the weather broke. While it lasted, though, we were eating like kings around here. He even made us call the grits *polenta*."

The hiker sat down in the extra lawn chair, loosened his boot laces, and sighed. "Feels good to sit," he said. "I'm Stan, but my Trail name is Eeyore. Nice place," he added, looking approvingly at the gingerbread trim on the covered porch, wreathed by the branches of shade trees. He wasn't sure what kind of trees they were. Trees had never played a big part in Stan's life up until now, but in his last few weeks on the Trail he had begun to feel that they were old friends. "It's peaceful here."

Baird held a pea pod up to the light and inspected it with the eye of an artist. "There's a serenity about the whole mechanical process of opening pea pods, you know? I was watching the butterflies a little while ago, and I thought: *They know what it's like to be inside a pod, only no one helps them break out. They have to do it on their own.* Now, with people, some folks break their own pods, and some have to be broken out by others, but it doesn't matter which way you're set free. The important thing is that you emerge—get out there into the great world and seek your destiny."

The man blinked. He looked from the colander of peas to the amiable face of his host and back again. After a moment's pause he ventured a guess: "Are you a poet?"

Baird smiled. "Well, we're all poets, aren't we?"

Eeyore shrugged. "I'm a mechanical engineer."

"Yeah," said Baird, "but the way I see it, just planting those hiking boots of yours on the Trail is a poem to the unspoiled glory of nature. Where are you headed, friend?"

"All the way." Eeyore's face shone with pride. "This is my first time on the southern end of the Trail. I've done short hikes in New England for years now, but this time I'm going to try to make it all the way from Springer to Katahdin."

"Georgia to Maine. Sounds like you're breaking out of the pod, friend." Baird dumped another handful of peas into the strainer. "More power to you."

"Ever hiked it yourself?"

Baird nodded. "Bits and pieces. Mostly North Carolina and Tennessee, and up into Virginia. Pennsylvania is tough going—rocky and steep. Mostly it's a question of time for me—I can't find anybody who'll stay and look after this place for six months while I take off to hike. But you know what Milton said: *They also serve who only stand and wait.*"

The stockbroker, to whom English literature was a never-opened book, nodded politely, wondering if Milton was another local doctor turned potato farmer. He said, "Hiking the Trail is a great experience. I've already lost eighteen pounds. Feel better than I have in years."

Baird smiled and went on shelling peas. He had this conversation three times a week, but with every hiker who told him this he tried to share the joy of it as if he were hearing it for the first time. "It's a magical place," he

167

said. "The Trail through these eastern mountains follows a chain of a green mineral called serpentine that leads from Alabama all the way to New Brunswick, Canada. The chain breaks off at the Atlantic coast, skips the ocean, and then picks up again in Ireland and snakes its way through Cornwall, Wales, and Scotland, till it finally ends in the Arctic Circle. These mountains here once fit on to the tail end of the mountains over there like pieces of a giant continental jigsaw puzzle. The chain of serpentine is a remnant of that togetherness, and it still links us to the mountains of Celtic Britain, where most of our ancestors came from when they settled here. *Will the circle be unbroken.*"

"Pretty country," Eeyore said. "Great views. I hope my photos turn out."

"Oh, this country is more than pretty. It's elemental. You know, a hiker from Queensland once told me that the aborigine people of Australia believe that their ancestors sang the world into being, and that there are special song paths that those first people took while they were doing it. Singing up the world from out of nothingness. That hiker said he thought this trail was one of them. That wouldn't surprise me at all. If this was one of the creation roads. *A song path.*"

Eeyore shrugged. "I didn't think the AT was that old," he said carefully. "Government built it. Maybe forty years ago, something like that?"

"Yes, that's the official word on it, but

parts of it follow a much older trail called the Warriors Path. The Indians made that one centuries ago, and they used it for everything from raids on other tribes to trading expeditions." Baird smiled. "And before that the Ice Age animals made trails over the mountains to the salt pools. Who knows how far back this northbound path stretches? All the way to the serpentine chain, I reckon—and that would make it 250 million years old."

"Interesting part of the country. Lots of stories."

"Lots of Celtic bloodlines in the people here. Stories is what we do."

"Well, I'll be interested to hear some stories. This is my first visit to *Appa-lay-chia*."

Baird said gently, "Well, folks in these parts call it *Appa-latch-a*."

Eeyore shrugged, as if the information did not interest him. "In New York we say *Appa-lay-chia*."

Baird had this conversation rather often, too, and in this round he was less inclined to be charitable. The statement *We say it that way back home* sounded like a reasonable argument unless you realized that it was not a privilege Easterners granted to anyone other than themselves. If a Texan visiting New York pronounced "Houston Street" the same way that Texans pronounce the name of their city *back home,* he would be instantly corrected by a New Yorker, and probably derided for his provincial ignorance. But here in rural America, the privilege of local pronunciation was revoked. Here, if there was any difference of opinion about a pronunciation, Eastern urbanites felt that their way was the correct one, or at least an equally acceptable option. One of Baird Christopher's missions in life was to set arrogant tourists straight about matters like this.

"You know," he said to Eeyore, gearing up to his lecture in genial conversational tones. "Over in Northern Ireland once I visited a beautiful walled city that lies east of Donegal and west of Belfast. Now, for the last thousand years or so the Irish people who built that city have called it *Derry,* a name from *darach,* which is the Gaelic word for 'oak tree.' But the British, who conquered Ireland a few hundred years back, they refer to that same city as *Londonderry.* One place: two names.

"If you go to Ireland, and you ask for directions to that city, you can call it by either name you choose. Whichever name you say, folks will know where it is you're headed and most likely they'll help you get there. But you need to understand this: When you choose what name you call that city—*Derry* or *Londonderry*—you are making a *political* decision. You are telling the people you're talking to which side you're on, what cultural values you hold, and maybe even your religious preference. You are telling some people that they can trust you and other people that they can't. All in one word. One word with a load of signifiers built right in.

"Now, I reckon *Appalachia* is a word like that. The way people say it tells us a lot about how they think about us. When we hear somebody say *Appa-lay-chia,* we know right away that the person we're listening to is not on our side, and we hear a whole lot of cultural nuances about stereotyping and condescension and ethnic bigotry, just built right in. So you go on and call this place *Appa-lay-chia* if you want to. But you need to know that by doing that you have made a po-li-ti-cal decision, and you'd better be prepared to live with the consequences. Friend."

Eeyore blinked at him and took a deep breath. "*Ap-pa...latch-ah?*" he said.

"That's right," said Baird. "Appa-latch-ah. Say it a time or two and you'll get the hang of it. Pretty soon any other way of saying it will grate on your ears."

Another long pause. Eeyore peered at his smiling host, who had gone back to shelling peas and humming an Irish dance tune. "Who *are* you?"

Baird Christopher smiled. "Why, I'm a Cosmic Possum."

The best road from upper east Tennessee into North Carolina was 19-23, which was now four-lane all the way to Asheville, enabling you to see beautiful mountain scenery without feeling that you were about to become part of it. Unfortunately, the caravan of Civil Air Patrol search party people were not headed as far south as Asheville, which meant that they would be taking one of the older two-lane roads over the mountains and through the gap into western North Carolina. That road had originally been a drovers' trail, dating back to the era when the cattle drives headed east over these mountains were bigger than the ones in Texas. The road had long since been paved, but neither state government thought there was any town in its path big enough to warrant the expense of a highway expansion project, and so the little trail meandered along the same route it always had, following the natural gaps and curves of the landscape.

Sheriff Arrowood had taken the patrol car, but Steve Ashley was riding along with him so that they could discuss the upcoming search. Plane crashes had not happened often in the vicinity of the county, and Spencer thought that the technology of search and rescue might have improved since their last effort, back in the mid-nineties.

Steve Ashley looked thoughtful. After a few minutes' silence, he finally said, "So, Sheriff, what were you saying when that waiter over in Bluff Mountain called you a cosmic possum?"

Spencer shrugged. "Well, nothing much. I was ordering my food, and he asked me what kind of salad I wanted, and I said spinach. Then I said something about iceberg lettuce not being fit for anything but rabbit fodder, and that's when he grinned and said, 'Sir, you are a cosmic possum, for sure.' "

Steve shook his head. "Doesn't make any sense to me. Maybe you can ask one of the Bluff Mountain people when we get there."

"I'm not sure I want to know."

"It's a nice little town, though, Bluff Mountain," said Steve.

"It has its good points," said the sheriff, sounding as if he'd be hard-pressed to think of any.

Bluff Mountain was not a typical North Carolina highland village, but no one could say that its unique character was a recent phenomenon. Bluff Mountain had been a haven for outlanders for more than a hundred years. Like its fellow western North Carolina communities Blowing Rock and Hot Springs, Bluff Mountain had become a popular resort area in the middle of the nineteenth century, when the cool climate of high altitudes was the only air-conditioning there was. Wealthy city dwellers from the flatlands to the east would flee the fevers and discomfort of humid southern summers by retreating to hotels or second homes in the hills. In villages throughout the mountains genteel ladies ran boarding houses for the summer visitors, and elegant hotels like the Grove Park Inn in Asheville housed a succession of wealthy travelers. Bluff Mountain had boasted two stately Victorian houses for paying guests, each with gingerbread trim over long covered porches and high ceilings adorned with intricate plaster moldings in the elegant sitting rooms within. The town now contained a number of modest-sized homes belonging to people who worked in the local businesses or who commuted to larger towns nearby for factory jobs, but the core of the village was a two street area of old white clapboard houses that had once been the summer homes of wealthy flatlanders. For a few decades in the mid twentieth century most of these homes had become vacant, falling into disrepair and heading toward decay, but the 1980s saw the trend reverse, and city people were once again flocking to the mountains—this time in search of less traffic, low crime rates, and clean air and water. One by one the grand old homes had been bought up and refurbished, so that the village looked much as it had in its first heyday. The new people professed to want simple country living, but soon they found that they also wanted portobello mushrooms, *The Wall Street Journal,* computer technicians, nouvelle cuisine, and a wine shop. By the 1990s all of these things were available in Bluff Mountain. People from Charlotte and Atlanta and Washington quit their jobs in the city and migrated to the hills to sell real estate or open a bed and breakfast or to become a craftsperson. Investment bankers ran bistros, corporate lawyers learned woodworking, and retired professors turned into bluegrass fiddlers. The shops, the music festivals, and the excellent restaurants made Bluff Mountain a fine place to visit. Spencer Arrowood was pretty sure he didn't want to live there.

"Portable wireless phones are a wonderful

invention, aren't they?" said Steve Ashley. "Just a few years ago that poor woman would have been stuck up there on the mountain with no way to let anybody know she was out there. Now no place is as remote as it once was."

The sheriff shook his head. "That's a dangerous illusion," he said. "People think that because they can make a phone call the wilderness is somehow less wild, but I'm not sure that's true. A couple of years ago a climber was caught in a killer snowstorm near the summit of Mount Everest, and he used his cell phone to call his wife back home while he huddled in an overhang inside the blizzard."

"Did he get rescued?"

"No. That's just it. He was so high up that helicopters couldn't even reach him, and the weather was too bad and the air too thin for a rescue party to reach him. So he died of exposure, just as he would have eighty years ago when the first explorers started trying to climb Everest. Did it help that he could talk to people in other countries while he waited to die, or did he think that nature can't kill people in *modern times*? Because it can. And we're fooling ourselves if we think our gadgets prove otherwise."

Steve Ashley nodded. "Well, Sheriff, maybe we can save this one. At least we don't have to worry about blizzards."

"No," said the sheriff. "I wonder what else will be sent to try us."

Malcolm McCourry—1794

There was once a man who became so tired of the sea that he put an oar upon his shoulder and vowed to walk inland until he met someone who asked him what it was. I read that tale long ago—in the works of Homer, I think—and now, in my fifty-second year, I find that I am determined to become that man.

Lately I have come to feel that I have lived all my life among strangers, never belonging, and never knowing what is expected of me. I have managed well enough here, I suppose. A quarter of a century has passed since I left my ship and came to settle in a New Jersey village. I have a profession and a respected position in the church. I married well. I did all the things that one must do to be counted successful in this world, and yet I feel an emptiness.

By observation and practice I have learned to say and do the proper thing in most any situation, but I never know what it is I am supposed to *feel*. I pass the time of day with my neighbors in a welter of impatience for the inconsequence of their chatter, or else, if it is a person of rank to whom I speak, I must concentrate on keeping up the banter as if it were a chess game to be won at all costs. In any case there isn't an ounce of pleasure in my dealings with my fellow man.

My Rachel is a good wife by all accounts, though she never forgets that she is a Freeman of Morristown, and I am mere flotsam from a passing ship. We have been twenty-five years together, and she is grown stout and gray, but perhaps I would not mind that so much if she would ever laugh or show me for even an hour the spirit of the young girl I married, for though she was stiff and prim in her youth, she was not the cold, dour woman I live with now. I know that I was besotted with the idea of marrying the daughter of a prominent man, but whether that was the same as loving Rachel herself, I cannot say. If Elizabeth had lived, things would have been different for me, but as it was, I had to make the best of a bad bargain. Rachel and I are as content as anyone, though, after so many years yoked together, but I am weary of this town, this life.

My wife is vigilant about our social position, and I suppose that our children are a credit to her upbringing, and no doubt to her fine bloodlines as well. They got little enough from me. Now that they are all grown, I look into their faces, and I see more strangers. All, that is, except my Jane, who is my light of love, and every inch her father's daughter, though not for want of Rachel's trying to make a Freeman of her.

Even the children's names are Rachel's doing: Phebe, Jane, Elizabeth, Benjamin, Rachel, and Sarah. Good Congregationalist names, without any taint of "Irishness" to make people here think less of them, and though I chose Elizabeth's name to honor Rachel's dear, lost sister, it made the name no less foreign to me. All our daughters were christened staunch English names, none of the sibilant Highland ones I knew in my youth… *Sine, Mairi, Morag, Ealasaid*…names that slide off your tongue like springwater gliding past rocks and over green rushes.

Benjamin was called after Rachel's father: a bit of diplomacy, there, for I owed the old man much for my start in this third life of mine. We have a daughter named for Rachel, but none of our children is called after me or anyone in my family. I always meant to name our next son Malcolm, but there was no second boy, which is a great pity because there's little love lost between me and the first one.

He stood over me, glowering, and I marveled anew at the speed at which bad news travels. "Surely you're not serious, Father?" Benjamin said in that hectoring tone of his. Sometimes I think that my son was born old, with Latin verbs rolling off his Congregational tongue. He became a lawyer as a tadpole becomes a frog, apparently without any conscious effort, simply a preordained transformation. He was here now to confront me on his mother's behalf. Rachel had gone off to visit our eldest daughter, professing herself too distraught to speak to me. Obviously she had sent Benjamin here to argue her case for her. He was standing over my chair, scowling at me as if he were the parent and I were the errant offspring.

I did not get up, but kept my eyes fixed on the parlor window. I had pulled back Rachel's heavy lace curtains so that I could look out at the green lawn and the massive oaks that shaded it, trying to imagine the scene untrammeled by clusters of neighboring houses.

They say that there is a great wilderness lying to the southwest of here. A land of endless forests, teeming with deer and buffalo and a hundred kinds of fowl, a fertile land to be had for pennies an acre, but best of all: The rivers are so narrow that you can step across them, and there are Indians, but as yet no lawyers.

I smiled at the inward jest, knowing better than to share it with sour-faced Benjamin.

"Father, are you attending to me?" He tapped my shoulder. "I say: You cannot be serious."

There was no point in prolonging the discussion by asking him what he meant, since I very well knew. The family had spoken of little else for weeks. "I mean to go," I said, as sullenly as a schoolboy. "Your sister Jane is going, and I intend to go with her."

Benjamin drew himself up to full height and favored me with his most magisterial glare. "Yes, Jane is going. Jane, who has been Mrs. Zephaniah Horton these past five years, is heading to the back country at the bidding of her husband, who may be a rash and headstrong fool, but at least he is a *young* fool. While you, sir, have passed the half-century mark, and you have a wife and business aplenty to keep you tied here to Black River. Mother thinks you have gone mad to propose giving it all up for a cabin in some godforsaken wilderness. She asked me to reason with you."

179

I could not help but smile. "And this is your idea of reason, Benjamin?"

He flushed. I find too much pleasure in taking the wind from his sails, I know, but sometimes I think that a few years before the mast would do wonders for his town-bred arrogance. *Try reciting your pedigree to a nor'easter, me lad,* I thought.

"Your life is here, Father," said Benjamin. *What little there is left of it* he meant, but that barb went unspoken, hanging in the air between us, the young bullock facing down the old bull. I wished he would stop pacing. He was addressing me as if I were a jury. "See here, Father! The family could understand if you wanted to go back to Scotland to see your family there, but to strike out for the backcountry— the dangers! the privation!—at your age— well, the folly of it beggars description!"

I sighed. Had I not said all this to Rachel days ago? "I have no family in Scotland, Benjamin. Forty years have passed since I was taken from there. My parents are dead, and if they are not, then they have long ago come to terms with the loss of their child, and after all this time seeing an old man come back in his stead would do nothing to comfort them or assuage their loss—or mine."

"What about your responsibilities to the family here?"

"I asked your mother if she wanted to go," I pointed out. "She would not hear of it. She says that she is too old to begin anew. Besides, she likes her comfort, and her social standing in this village. As for you children, all of you are grown and gone. The girls are settled into marriage, and you are twenty-one this year, and newly made a lawyer. I judge you are well able to assume my role as head of the family."

Benjamin hesitated—his pride was warring with his sense of propriety, I thought. Of course he thought he could look after the family interests, especially with all his sisters safely married. No doubt in time he would find some suitably well-connected Black River maiden to further his prospects even more. I surmised that his distress at the thought of my leaving had little to do with his grief at parting with a parent and much to do with his anxiety over the scandal it might cause.

"But what will people think, sir?" he burst out as if in answer to my thoughts.

"They will think what this family's demeanor tells them to think," I said. I may not feel like a part of this community, but after all this time damn me if I don't know how their minds work. "If you all go about hangdog and ashamed at this base desertion, the village will take you at your word. But after all, I am only going on a journey with family, Benjamin. I will travel to the Carolina back-country with Jane and Zephaniah. No doubt they will be glad of help in setting up a homestead in the wilderness, and it will give me pleasure to see them safely settled in their new home. There will be fences to build and trees to fell. I grew accustomed to hard work in my youth. I miss it. Put it about that I am going as a favor to the young Hortons, and that you all admire my heroic self-sacrifice."

Benjamin sighed at the folly of it all. "Hard work on a backcountry homestead—from a lawyer who is past his fiftieth year! Buy them a slave if you want to help them with their farmwork. It would do them more good."

I doubt that there will be many slaves in the backcountry—though there are plenty of them in Black River, New Jersey. Pointless to have that argument again with Benjamin. Slaves are wealth, he would say, as Rachel did. All the best people must have one. Instead I said, "They say there are fortunes to be made in this new land, Benjamin. Fertile farmland. Timber and furs, perhaps even gold. I shall go and see for myself. Perhaps I can do the family more good by going west than by staying here and eking out a few more dollars writing up deeds and wills for the townsfolk."

He was silent for a moment, and I could see him trying out the phrases in his mind. When he began to look accustomed to the thought of my departure, I played my ace. "And when I go, Benjamin, I will give you my power of attorney, of course."

My son took a deep breath. Power of attorney! My abandonment of his mother weighed in his mind against the thought of his gaining control over my three parcels of land—113 acres all told—and the idea of his taking over my law practice, no junior partner but sole proprietor, at the age of twenty-one. If the neighbors could be bluffed into seeing this as a family sojourn, he would stand to gain a great deal by my absence—and he set little enough store by my presence, I well knew. He could not be more thoroughly a Freeman if he had been the product of a virgin birth. He had my surname, and that was all the McCourry I ever saw in him.

"Very well, Father," he said at last. He could not bring himself to smile. "Go along to the backcountry with Zephaniah Horton, and I wish you joy of your adventure. If you are scalped by Indians or dead of fever within the year, you cannot say that you weren't warned."

"I will miss you, too, Benjamin," I said gravely. "Good-bye."

They call it the Wilderness Road, but there was little enough solitude to be had on it in Pennsylvania, at least as far as I could see. Just west of Philadelphia a great river of canvas-covered wagons flowed south-southwest toward the backcountry where tall mountains and trackless forests walled out the fainthearted. The wagons headed off to their promised land in a procession like that of the children of Israel on their journey in the Book of Exodus, led by Moses and escorted by the cloud of Jehovah—only the cloud that escorted this exodus was much less exalted in origin: It was Pennsylvania dust, stirred up by hoofs and wheels and the running feet of the restless children. I could barely hear myself think for all the commotion on that well-worn track: Dogs barking as they dodged the dinner-plate hoofs of lowing oxen, babies wailing, wagons creaking, a cacophony of chickens, cattle, goats, and sheep, and above it all, like a grace note in a howling gale, the sound of a lone fife, piping out a spritely tune to cheer us on our way. Why, the road itself was a village.

While Zeph's brother Nathan took a turn at driving my rig, and Jane slept within with her three little ones, I sat in the front of the Horton wagon, beside my son-in-law, marveling at the sea of creatures around us. "How will all these people fit into the backcountry?" I mused aloud.

Zephaniah laughed. "With miles to spare between them, Father McCourry," he said. "Remember, I have been to those mountains, and I promise you that there is more land in them than there are souls brave enough to settle it. Even the Indians do not live where we are going, though they do make raids of the settlements now and again. They are devils for horse stealing, so be warned. The mountains were Indian land until the War for Independence freed it for homesteading, but even before that the tribes lived elsewhere, and only used the mountains as a common hunting ground for the Catawba, the Shawnee, and the Cherokee. You will have solitude aplenty once we get there."

"That will make a nice change," I told him sourly, planting my boot on the rump of a cow who strayed too near our wagon.

It was to be a spartan life in the wilderness. We had come to get away from villages, not to make new ones. I had left most of my money and belongings back in Black River, taking only enough cash to outfit the wagon and buy supplies for a homestead, plus a little left over for later provisions. With the sale of my law books I bought a long rifle—the symbolism of that was not lost on me.

As we mounted up to leave the village, Rachel had come to bid us a stiff farewell. She stood there at the roadside—iron-faced, stout, and gray—but wearing her dignity at full sail, with her best bonnet and a shiny black dress that put me in mind of widow's weeds. Perhaps it would help her to think of me as dead, I decided. It would give the village less to gossip over, anyhow. Rachel could never bear to be talked about, and she could never understand why I was left undaunted by the village scandalmongers. Perhaps the reason for her concern and my indifference was that she belonged there, and I never did. She had spent the best part of her life trying to teach me to fear the wagging tongues of the neighbors, and to civilize me, but it didn't take, and she knew it. Now she gave me a baleful glance before turning to embrace Jane, tearfully wishing her Godspeed.

"Now, you must write to me, dear Jane. You know how I will worry about you." She shook

Zephaniah by the hand. "Now, see that you take care of my grandchildren, sir, and mind you look after my daughter, for she was raised to be a lady, not a backcountry slattern." Jane's traveling clothes were of simple calico, practical, but not sufficiently grand for her mother's liking.

"My wife will be a lady," Zeph Horton said. "I mean to make my fortune in Carolina, and Jane and the little ones will lose nothing in this venture. I promise you that."

This satisfied the doting mother. Brushing away a tear, she turned to me. "Well, Husband," she said, tight-lipped and stern of countenance. "If your mind is set on going, there's no more to be said. I bid you farewell. You know the way back."

Dutifully I kissed her rice-powdered cheek. "Be well, my dear," I said. "Benjamin will see that you are provided for, and I will see that no harm comes to our Jane and the babies."

She sniffed at that, seeing it for the poor excuse it was. She did not ask for any correspondence from me, and I did not offer any. There was nothing left for us to say to one another. Best to make a clean break with the past, I thought. Each time my life had changed, it had always been a clean break—not always by choice but, I realized, all for the best nonetheless. With a quick wave of her hand, Rachel turned away and walked back up the street to our white frame house, back to the safety and respectability of the village. Without a backward glance, she consigned me to perdition—or at least to the wilderness, which in her eyes amounted to the same thing.

So we set off, stern pioneers setting our faces toward the unknown, but secretly exulting to be done with the tedium of village society. After a few days on the journey, the road became our village, and though the landscape changed from day to day, the neighbors remained constant, their wagons keeping pace with ours as we followed the ridges to the southwest. We came to know the folk in the wagons nearest us by name, and we learned which dog and child went with each wagon, and their names as well. At night we sat together around campfires, exchanging stories about our pasts and pooling our knowledge of the territory ahead. Late at night, when the food had been eaten and the children bedded down for the night, someone would bring out a fife or a fiddle, and after a bit someone else would begin a song.

One night after we had heard "Greensleeves" and "Barbry Ellen" sung a time too many by a great toad of a woman with a corncrake voice, Jane said to me, "Father, can you give us a song?"

I had thought to sing "Heart of Oak," from my seafaring days, but that tune had been conscripted into the War for Independence, and I could not remember its new American words, other than the fact that now it was called "Chester." Besides I didn't want the talk to get round to politics, for that is the surest way to start a quarrel brewing in a company of strangers. I was casting about for a tune that would serve when Jane touched my arm and whispered, "How about that old one you used to sing when I was little? I haven't heard it in so long that I've nearly forgotten it. The one about the ghost and the shepherd girl?"

" 'The Rowan Stave'?" I asked.

"That's it. Please, Father?"

The others at the campfire took up the cry—anything to silence that infernal woman, I suppose—and so, though I hold no brief for my singing voice, I closed my eyes and summoned the words from memory, though I had not thought of that song myself for many a year.

"Upon the hill above the kirk at moon rise
she did stand
To tend her sheep that Samhain eve, with
rowan stave in hand.
And where she's been and what she's seen,
no living soul may know,
And when she's come back home, she will
be changed—oh!"

I was surprised to find that I had remembered all of the verses, and I sang it straight through, faltering only once or twice to sort out what came next. When I had finished, there was a little hush in the firelight, and then they all said what a bonny song it was, and that they had not heard it before.

Then the fiddler, a Pennsylvanian Dutchman, asked me to sing it through again, because no one else had ever heard it and he wanted to learn the tune. I took him through it yet again, while he picked out the tune note by note.

"It's a devilish hard tune to play," he said. His accent was so thick that I had to lean forward to catch the words. "I have to change the tuning on the fiddle to make the notes fit."

"What makes it hard?" I asked him. It seemed to me that I had no trouble reaching the notes with my voice.

He waved his hand impatiently. "I don't know the words so good. Different mode maybe. You sing scale with different notes. Ionian, I think."

I smiled. "Well, I come from there—from pretty near Iona, anyhow," I said.

He let out a deep sigh then, and rolled his eyes, and he muttered, "It is an Irish sound." His shrug seemed to say that my ignorance was too vast to be tackled with his meager supply of English, so I never did learn why my song was so different from the other tunes he played that night. In truth he never did get the tune quite right, but he seemed to think that his way of playing it improved the song.

After a bit a woman asked for the story behind the song, and I told the tale of the shepherd girl of the MacKenzies and her son Kenneth who was given the Sight. I even remembered one or two of his prophecies, and folk marveled over that for a bit. I thought then of my own magic stone, but that was a story I did not tell, then or ever. The story of Kenneth Mackenzie satisfied the listeners, and then the fiddler commenced to play a livelier air, and a few of the young people got up to dance in darkness under the canopy of stars.

After we had finished singing, Jane was quiet for a bit, gazing into the fire, and then she said, "I suppose we will be like that, too, Father, won't we? Like the shepherd girl in the song, I mean. After we have been in the back-country awhile, then where we've been and what we've seen will change us, too, won't it?"

"I hope so," I said.

We were many weeks on the trail, for we followed the rivers, and they do not go in a straight line. We went west from Easton into the Pennsylvania hill country, and from there we followed the great valley down into Maryland and crossed the rocky, wide Potomac into Virginia, where the wide valley between ridges of mountains led us southwest toward our destinations. Not everyone was headed to the same place, though. There is a point deep in Virginia where the trail splits, and many of our wagon neighbors turned their teams toward the west, heading for the Cumberland Gap that would lead them through the mountains and into Kentucky. Some twenty years ago Colonel Daniel Boone and his followers had founded a settlement there at Boonesborough. Kentucky was said to be good land, and flat beyond the first fifty miles or so of mountains, but Zephaniah knew the

Carolina territory, and his heart was set to go back there. "It's wild country," he had said again and again. "No neighbors for miles around, and none that you can see." I liked the sound of that.

"Our way lies through Indian country, though," he warned me. "There has been talk among the wagons of raids by the Cherokee along the Holston River in Virginia. More than thirty raids this year, they tell me. We must pass through there on the way to Carolina."

This was disquieting news. I had been in my share of battles, between my sailing days and my years with the militia in the War for Independence, but I feared for the safety of the young people. The Indians did not often spare women and children when they raided a farmstead. "We might buy more powder and shot at the next settlement," I said. "Do the Indians claim the land that we aim to settle?"

Zephaniah shook his head. "The Cherokees gave up their claim to the Carolina mountains two years ago in a treaty, but that may not stop the odd renegade war party from attacking a settlement for horses or goods."

When the trail divided in Virginia, the Hortons and I headed west, following the valley into the new state of Tennessee, but when most of the other wagons headed off to the Cumberland Gap, we turned south toward Jonesborough, which had been a state capital of the mountain territory while "Franklin" had existed as a state. That was finished six years ago, owing to some political chicanery in the legislature, and having to do with money, like as not, and so the governments had left the mountains and packed all their politicians into the flatlands, in Nashville and in Raleigh, and I was glad of it. Living too close to politicians does not make for a peaceful life. I hoped they would take their wars and their laws elsewhere. I'd sooner contend with the Indians.

There was good land around Jonesborough, but it was already spoken for, and a deal too civilized for my liking, besides, so from there we headed east, back over into Carolina, where the mountains rose highest and there were tracts of wilderness still to be had for pennies an acre. Strange to think that I could buy a tract of land bigger than all of Black River for less than the price of a saddle horse.

I was all for finding the wildest land to be had, a place so remote that even the sun would have trouble finding it, but there was more talk of Indian raids when we reached a stockade, and Zephaniah feared for his family's safety. I could not advocate a course of action that would put my daughter and her babes in danger, so I agreed to go along for a while down the mountains into the rolling hills of Wilkes County, where there were a few settlements and neighboring farms to give aid in time of trouble. I never meant to stay there, though, for I'd had my fill of neighbors back in Black River. Besides, I had seen the great mountains beyond the piedmont, and I meant to go back there before long, Indians or no. Something about the place called me home, and put me in mind of far-off Scotland, not the place as it would be now, but the golden country of my childhood.

Still I cannot regret our sojourn in the foothills of Wilkes, for it changed my life yet again. In July Zeph and I bought a few adjoining acres near the farm of a family called Lynn, and we set about clearing land for fields and putting up makeshift cabins to see us through the winter. The neighbors came and helped us with the cabin raisings. The men gathered and stacked the stones for the foundations and fashioned the stone chimney, which we could not have managed on our own. They dovetailed notches into the chestnut logs so that they would fit together snugly, and they showed us how to chink the spaces between logs with red clay and lime to keep the wind out. While we worked, the women spent the day cooking a big supper over an open fire. They wouldn't take money for it, so I reckoned we would have to stay long enough to do them a favor in return.

The cabins weren't a patch on the white frame houses back in Black River. There, such rude dwellings as these would have been slave quarters at best: just one large room with a fireplace at one end and a loft at the other. Had they been made of whitewashed stone instead of chestnut logs, and thatched with straw instead of shingled, I'd have thought myself back on Islay. Still, we were proud of them, for we all had a hand in their making, and I for one wanted no fine house to tie me to these foothills.

We had only a few weeks for planting, but we reckoned that the crops added to the money we had brought with us would see us through the winter, plus what more we could earn by hunting and selling the pelts at a trading post. While we worked, Jane tended the livestock and saw to the cooking and the garden. Little Nathan, who was five, helped by looking after his little sisters Rachel and baby Sarah. Jane worked from sunup to dusk without complaint, but I knew that Zephaniah would have help for her soon, even if he had to go hungry to get it.

Hunting with a musket was an unaccustomed experience for a village lawyer. I had done little enough shooting in the Revolution, and I confess that my eyes were too old to be much use to me in shooting objects at any great distance anymore, but after I'd spent many an evening shooting pinecones from fence posts, I managed to make myself into a tolerable marksman—for an old man, that is.

One evening as I was setting up a row of pinecones for another round of target practice, Jane came out to watch my efforts and to take a turn or two of her own at precision shooting. It is not a bad thing for a woman on the frontier to know how to use a gun, though I'm sure her mother would have objected loud and long to such unladylike behavior from a genteel Black River matron. She would not hear of it from me.

Jane knocked more pinecones off the fence rail than I did.

"The light is bad," I said. "The trees cast shadows on the fence."

Jane nodded, trying to banish the smile from her lips. "Well, Father," she said, "I'm sure you shot a good many more targets this evening than you would have done three months ago. Why, our Black River neighbors would hardly know you these days!"

I took this for a criticism of my unkempt appearance. "The clothes I wore for lawyering in the village would scarcely serve me here in the backcountry," I told her.

"It isn't only the fringed buckskin, though," she said, looking me up and down as if I were a horse. "You may not be dressed like a gentleman anymore, but you are the better for it. You are leaner now, and your face is brown from working in the fields all day. You look stronger, too. Sometimes in the twilight until you are quite close to the house, I cannot tell you from Zephaniah, for even your walk is that of a young man nowadays. I think this journey has done you a world of good."

"A change is as good as a rest," I said, taking aim again at the dark shapes on the fence post.

Jane walked away then to see to the cattle, and in the dusk I heard her singing, *"And when she's come back home, she will be changed—oh!"*

I wondered if she had picked the song at random out of her memory, or if its words were an indication of the way her thoughts were running. I hoped not. Did my daughter suppose that I had come on this journey to the wilderness as a rest cure, to regain my strength and vigor before returning to my wife and my law practice in New Jersey? I hoped that this was not the case. Jane would be sorely disappointed if her expectations were running that way, for I could no more return to Black River than a butterfly could crawl back into its cocoon.

My life was here now, and it was just beginning.

A few weeks after our arrival, our neighbor James Lynn, being a conscientious man, asked us all over to his farm to take Sunday dinner with his family. We were glad to accept his offer of hospitality, having grown weary of one another's company for so many weeks on end. Here was a chance of news from the outside world, and the hope of a better cook than Jane to give us our dinner.

Zeph and Jane and I walked the few miles to the Lynn home place, each of us carrying one of the children, to give the horses a well-earned day of rest. It was a fine September day, not too hot for a walk, and though we carried weapons with us in case of a surprise attack, we saw nothing more menacing than a pair of rabbits, chasing each other through the underbrush, and we did not care to break the peace of the Sabbath by shooting at them.

The Lynns' place was a likely looking homestead, a big log house constructed of oak and shingled in chestnut. It stood in an L-shape, with its long part two stories high with real glass windows, and a low short side joined to a small slant-roofed porch over the front door. At each end of the dwelling stood a fieldstone chimney. The house faced a rail-fenced pasture where the Lynns had built a log cow shed. A dozen red cows and calves were grazing there on the banks of a stony creek. The family had settled their land a good five years ago, and old James Lynn had plenty of sons to tend his livestock, build his fences, and keep the buildings in good repair. By backcountry standards he was a fortunate and prosperous man.

As we neared the gate, Zephaniah helloed the house to let those inside know that we were not marauders. Folk did the same in my youth in Scotland, where the dreaded savages were not *Redskins* but *Redcoats*. We stood our ground then and waited to be asked on.

Before the echo had died away, the cabin door opened, and a procession of Lynns hurried out to make us welcome. I recognized three of the strapping young men from our own cabin raising, but I scarcely spared a glance at them, for hanging back in the doorway like a fawn at her mother's side was the younger daughter.

Sally, they said her name was, and I took care to hear it right. Now, back in polite society, we would have addressed the young lady as *Miss Lynn* if she had been the elder daughter of the family, and *Miss Sally* if she be the younger, but here in the back of beyond we dispensed with such frippery, and so she was called plain *Sally* by one and all. Plain she was not, however.

Had I seen her before? Did she stand in cape and bonnet in a church pew when the circuit rider held a Sunday preaching, or had she been one of the slender forms in calico who dished out beans and salt pork at one of the barn raisings? I had no memory of her face, but that day on the porch, as I lingered over my handshake, I took care to memorize every curve and line of it.

She was a wraith of a girl, pale and silent, with round blue eyes like Jamaican tidal pools, and a shiny curtain of chestnut hair. She barely came up to my shoulder, and I judged her to be no more than fifteen. That was ten years younger than Jane, though a lass of that age is counted as a woman on the frontier, and many no older than she are big with child, and have another one already in tow. She met my gaze for only a moment, and then she drew back her hand and was about to turn away when I said, "Sally is a fine name. Is it a diminutive for Sarah perhaps?" I almost added, *Like my granddaughter's name,* but the words would not come.

She shook her head. "Just Sally," she murmured, casting a glance about to see where the other womenfolk were. They were in the yard, talking nineteen to the dozen and paying us no mind.

"Back in Scotland, where I come from, folk would call you Morag," I told her, smiling. "Would you like that?"

She shook her head. "It has a strange sound to it, sir. I'm partial to simple names. Sally suits me." She paused for a moment, and then added, so softly that I had to bend down to hear her. "What is Scotland like?"

I had been so long away from there that I scarcely knew, but to prolong the conversation, I searched for a reply that would please her. After a moment's reflection, I said, "Have you seen the mountains to the west of here, the tall ones in the mist, where Burke County meets Tennessee? Well, it's a bit like that, as I recall, only perhaps there aren't so many trees on the *bens* in Scotland. I grew up on a wee island, though."

I cast about for something else to say to keep her listening. "In Scotland we have a kind of sheep with four horns instead of two."

She shook her head in disbelief, and I saw that she thought I was teasing her, but what I said about Jacob's sheep was true enough, though I couldn't prove it to her. "After Scotland, I was a sailor," I said. "Seen a good bit of the world in my time. I'll tell you about it if you'll sit supper with me."

She slipped away then without giving me an answer, and before long the women trooped off into the cabin together to begin setting out the food. I went out into the yard, where the Lynns had brought out a new roan saddle horse for Zeph and me to admire, but I was still thinking about the lass who had just gone inside, and feeling a bit of a fool for the way I took to her. Young enough to be my granddaughter. Surely I was done with all that now, at my time of life: an old man come to die on the frontier. The image of my lawful wife rose unbidden to my mind—my shrill Rachel, she of the hairy chin and the pudding hips.

"He's a fine stallion, isn't he, Mr. McCourry?" said one of the Lynn sons, elbowing me in the arm. He slapped the new saddle horse on its glistening rump. "He comes of good breeding stock. We reckon he'll cover many a mare in his time."

I managed to croak, "Aye, that he will," before I turned away from them, for I was afraid to be caught blushing, an old man my age and a grandfather to boot, caught in calf love like a beardless boy.

Chapter Six

Ben Hawkins's shift on the 911 line had ended two hours earlier, but he could not bring himself to leave. He told his replacement, Mrs. Lafon, a farmer's wife from over in Dark Hollow, about the woman in the crashed plane who had called in earlier. He explained that the sheriff's department and the Civil Air

Patrols on both sides of the mountain border had begun the search, but he thought it might take hours or even days to locate the downed plane. If the caller phoned in again, Ben wanted to be around to give her moral support while she waited to be rescued. "She asked me for help," he explained. "I mean, I know it was just a coincidence that I happened to be manning the phone lines when her call came in, but I can't help feeling that it's my responsibility to see it through. I'll sit over here at the desk and stay out of your way."

He spent the next couple of hours eating take-out food and catching up on paperwork while Mrs. Lafon fielded frivolous calls: She scolded people for wanting to know what time it was or asking for a telephone area code. There was one ambulance request for a heart attack victim, and a fire truck summons for an out-of-control brush fire. All in all, it was a routine night for the Wake County 911. He supposed that his time might have been put to better use back at his place getting some pots ready to be fired for the Bluff Mountain Craft Fair next month, but he didn't want to abandon this stranger who had called him for help. He had been working for 911 about six months now, and this was his first major emergency—the first one he could do anything about, anyhow. A little boy had drowned in the Little Dove River a couple of months back, but even though Ben had dispatched the emergency crew in a matter of seconds, there was nothing to be done for the child, who had been swept to his death by the swift current before witnesses had even placed the call.

People seemed to think it strange that Ben Hawkins, a suburbanite from Maplewood, New Jersey, had opted for the life of a potter in the Tennessee Mountains after completing a physics degree at SUNY-Binghamton, but he liked the quiet, pastoral lifestyle of the southern mountains. Even before he finished his degree, he had realized that he wasn't cut out for the Borgia Court politics of a career in academics, and having removed that option, he supposed that one job was as good as another for a theoretical physicist. After all, Einstein had developed his theory of special relativity while working in a Swiss patent office. Ben knew he wasn't destined for any such breakthroughs in quantum physics. He couldn't think outside the box the way C. N. Yang or Max Planck had done. Sometimes, though, his knowledge of physics helped him to make better pots. Getting the metallic glazes right on raku pottery was as much a science as it was an art, and it helped if you understood the processes involved.

The summer after graduation, Ben had done some white-water rafting and then some hiking in the Cherokee National Forest, finally ending up at the John C. Campbell Folk School in western North Carolina, where he had taken a course in raku, mostly out of curiosity. He found that both the area and the potters' art had so captivated him that he turned an idle interest into a vocation, and he never did go home. His specialty was small vases decorated with cascades of gingko leaf prints in shining gradations of metallic blues shading into hues of green and gold. His work was exhibited in a few art galleries around the region, and he had won a few ribbons at area art shows. He wouldn't get rich practicing his art, but he found both the physical labor and the end result spiritually satisfying.

The sad truth was that equations and numbers made perfect sense to Ben; it was people he didn't understand. He never had any idea what people were thinking or feeling, and he found it impossible to predict what anyone would do in a given situation. Human behavior seemed more random to him than the path of any subatomic particle. When someone asked Ben what he considered the most difficult thing about making pottery, he replied with perfect truth that attending the craft fairs was the worst part of the whole endeavor. To an introvert like Ben, making small talk with total strangers and trying to establish a rapport with them so that they would buy his wares was an exquisite form of torture that made toiling at the potter's wheel and kiln burns pale by comparison.

He had taken the 911 job as a form of penance for his solitary nature. Ben thought that helping people was the highest calling there was—in the abstract, anyhow; he didn't much like any people he actually knew. Didn't dislike them, either. They just came and went;

it was all one to him. He also thought that a part-time job forcing him to interact with strangers might improve his social skills, which would in the long run help his business. At 911, he reasoned, he would be able to observe strangers in crisis—and after enough experience with that, he might begin to see the pattern in people's actions. So far he had made little progress, but the experiment continued to hold his interest, and the idea of helping to save a life every now and then gave him a satisfying feeling of worthiness, as if he were paying his karmic rent.

It was ironic that after a childhood of scrawny mediocrity Ben was now considered attractive. Women went out of their way to talk to him and to get his attention, and they seemed to expect him to behave in a certain way—confident, perhaps, or simply as if he belonged in their circle of friends—but as far as Ben was concerned his belated handsomeness was simply misleading. He had spent too many years as an ugly duckling to master the persona of a swan, and he found that, unlike his yearnings in high school, he now had no desire to be popular. He felt most comfortable around older people, who were kind to him without seeming to want intimacy in return.

Ben finished his paperwork and began to make up a shopping list for his next trip to Johnson City. He had a busy week coming up, now that tourist season was just ahead, and he could not afford many sleepless nights, even in a good cause. Just as he was beginning to nod off, thinking that he might want to call it a day after all, another call came in. After a few moments of monosyllabic replies, Mrs. Lafon turned around and signaled for Ben to take the headset.

"It's her!" she mouthed the words soundlessly, sliding past him as he stumbled into her place in the swivel chair. She programmed the machine to send incoming calls to the other phone line, and sat down again, ready to field the remaining crises in the county that night.

Fully awake again, Ben adjusted the headphones. "Hello...this is Ben speaking. Is this Laura in the plane crash?"

"Not *Laura*... It's Lark. L-A-R-K. Lark McCourry. I'm famous. Who do *you* listen to? Gloria Estefan?"

"Uh... I guess." Ben scribbled the name *Lark McCurry* on a message pad and motioned for Mrs. Lafon to come over and take a look at it. Underneath the name he wrote *Who?* and underlined it twice. To the caller he said, "Listen, I'm glad you called back. We were worried about you. I've reported your situation to the local Civil Air Patrol, so there are people out there right now combing these mountains for your plane. We're going to get you down. How are you?"

"Sore," she said, in the least belligerent tone he'd heard from her yet. "Scared."

"I don't blame you. A plane crash. I'd be scared, too. Are you injured, though?"

"I don't think so. Bruises maybe. We hit hard.

I'm not bleeding. I'm still in the plane, though. The door won't open."

"Good, that's very good—that you're all right, I mean. And staying in the plane isn't a bad idea, either. It will keep you warmer than you would be outside, and it will make it easier for the searchers to locate you. You just hang in there…uh…*Lark*. We're doing all we can. Tell me, are you able to see outside the plane?"

"Some. It's dark out here."

"Yeah, but the searchers will have lights. Watch for them. If you see any lights flashing all of a sudden, or if you hear anything like shouting, you need to call me, so I can let the rescue team know they're close. Okay?"

"I'm on a cell phone. I don't know how long these batteries are going to last. I just charged it, though, before I left, but I don't want the thing to go dead on me. Who knows how long I'll have to make these batteries last."

"Just a few hours, I hope," said Ben. "Help is on the way. We don't have to talk long. I just need you to check in. Let me know you're still okay."

Out of the corner of his eye Ben could see that Mrs. Lafon was scribbling furiously on the message pad. He craned his neck, trying to catch a glimpse of what she had written, but before he could make it out, she finished the reply to his query and thrust the pad under his nose. *Lark McCourry—Famous singer,* she had written. *Wrote song "Prayers the Devil Answers."*

Came from here. Celebrity! She had under-lined the last word twice and put exclamation points after it.

Ben's heart sank. Oh, great, a famous person. He couldn't even make small talk with country club types from Kingsport, and now he was supposed to talk to somebody famous? And if they didn't save her, there would be reporters crawling all over the place. Ben wanted to hand the phone back to Mrs. Lafon and make a break for it, but he took a deep breath and made himself sit still and listen.

"You never heard of me, huh?" she said, the irritation creeping back into her voice.

Ben glanced at the message pad in front of him. "Uh... Sure I have," he said. "I was just surprised, that's all. You sang 'Prayers the Devil Answers,' didn't you?"

"Yeah. I sang it. I wrote it, too. It's an old family saying. That was my first gold record. Funny... I guess that's what you could call the situation I'm in now: a prayer the devil answered. I prayed not to have to go home and see my dad. And here I am."

"Your dad." Ben made a note on his message pad. "Would you like us to get word to him?"

"No. No need to upset him—or *not* upset him, which is more likely. I can't see any point in it either way. But there's something else that I needed to do while I was here and this has certainly ruined my chance to do it. I can't get it out of my head. Well, maybe that's good, because I takes my mind off the situation."

207

"What did you need to do?"

"I have to find a song. An old song. Heard it once when I was kid. Are you from around here, Ben? You don't sound like it, but these days you never know."

"New Jersey," he said.

"Oh. Well, I guess you wouldn't be any help then. This song definitely didn't originate in New Jersey. In fact I think it's probably from Scotland, but I don't remember much about it. I really need to find it, though."

"Well, let's work on getting you rescued so that you can find that song," said Ben. "Where were you headed when the plane crashed?"

"Wake County. Only the guy wasn't sure if we could set it down at the local airport. Something about wind shear, maybe? Anyhow, I don't know if he was still heading for Wake County or if he was going to put down at Tri-Cities. He had his hands full with the turbulence, and he didn't say much to me." After a pause, she said, "Can you find out if Garrett McCourry is still alive?"

For a moment Ben was confused by the change of subject. "Was that the pilot?—Oh, no, sorry. McCourry, you said. Same as you. Your father?"

"*Not* same as me." He could hear a ripple of amusement in her voice. Ben looked at Mrs. Lafon for some indication of what she meant, but the other line had rung and Mrs. Lafon was busy.

"I'm sorry. I thought you said McCourry."

"I did. 'S my grandmother's name. I was born

208

a Walker. Linda Walker. Didn't have a ring to it, though." There was a long pause, and he thought the phone might have gone dead, but then she said, "I wish I could remember the pilot's name. I think it was Bill. He was a nice guy. I can't remember the rest of his name, and I can't reach him. You'll need to notify his people, too."

"We're working on it," said Ben, assuming that somebody was. "After the rescue, it's our first priority."

"And the song. I need to find that song, Ben. When I came to, I had this sudden vision that if I could find that song, I'd get out of here alive."

Ben took a deep breath. Shock did funny things to people. Do you talk them out of it, or play along? "Now that kind of thinking..."

"I know, I know. Superstitious magic. I went to college, too. Save the condescending lectures. You don't know it all, boy. Take it from me. Now, do you have a phone book there?"

"Umm...yes." A whole shelf of them. He wondered why this woman was so insistent about finding this song, in light of the fact that she might not even come down off the mountain alive. Who knew what kind of injuries she might have sustained in the crash? The victim's preoccupation with music was a form of displacement, Ben supposed. It was less painful to worry about tracking down an old song than it was to consider the possibility that she might be dying. Ben wondered if it would be a kindness to humor her in her quest, or if the rescuers' purpose might be better served by forcing her to focus on the gravity of her situation. He should try to prod her into helping them locate her. "Now, try to remember the last thing you saw out the window of the plane…"

"Sky. Look, I'm serious about this song. I need it. It's an old song about a girl and a grave. Listen—this is all of it that I remember: *And when she comes back home, she will be changed—oh!* Have you got that?"

"Well, what you just sang is on the tape now," said Ben. "We record all the 911 calls. The words don't ring a bell though."

"No, I didn't think they would." She sounded amused. "Somebody around there knows them, though. Look, they'll probably put me in the hospital when I do get down off this mountain, and then I won't be able to do anything. Right now I've got nothing but time. Let me spend it wisely."

"But I can't help you."

"Ben, I'm going to hang up soon to conserve the phone batteries, but I'll call back in an hour. Will you be there?"

"As long as you want me to be here, I'll stay."

"Good. I remembered something else that I saw from out the window of the plane. No, I won't tell you just yet. I don't think it will help you much. Have you got something to write with? Okay. Now take down these names. Garrett McCourry. Carver Jessup. Let's see…who else? Oh! Nora Bonesteel. Is she still around?"

"Is Nora Bonesteel still around?" Ben repeated the statement aloud, making it a question for Mrs. Lafon, who nodded vigorously. "Yes. Yes, she is. All right, I have the names."

"Good. I have to go now. Tell them you need a song about a girl and an open grave. And sing them that bit of the verse. That's all I remember. I'll call back in an hour."

"But—" Ben heard the click of the phone being turned off and then silence. He leaned back in the swivel chair and took a deep breath. "Did you hear that? She wants me to find a *song*. Of all the stupid—"

"Famous people get like that sometimes," said Mrs. Lafon in the tones of one who has heard it all. "They get used to ordering folks about, seems like. I heard of one stock car racer who would only use pink towels during a race 'cause he said it brought him luck. Strange notions."

"Or else it's a publicity stunt," said Ben, putting the New Jersey spin on the crash victim's behavior. "She's sure she's going to be rescued and this song quest will be an interesting angle to get the story more play in the news magazines. Should we tell the searchers about this new call?"

"Might as well," said Mrs. Lafon, shrugging. "We're always told that they need to be kept fully informed. You see if you can raise the sheriff, while I go through the phone books."

"The phone books?"

"So you can start rounding up those people she asked for."

"What, you mean we should cater to her because she's famous?"

"No. Because she's probably going to die."

LeDonne wished now that he had brought his cell phone along so that he could report the crash site. Not that anyone would come rushing up the mountain to look at decades-old debris, but maybe the Civil Air Patrol or the Rescue Squad would make a hike of it some weekend for practice. He wished he knew whether he was on the Tennessee side of the line or not. With his hunting knife he had nearly chopped away all the encircling vines that shrouded the wreckage, and now he was trying to get a look inside. He could see now that the aircraft was an old Cessna 152, dating as far back as the early seventies, he thought, though he was not expert on aircraft makes and models.

What was left of the plane was angled away from him, lying on its side where the wing should have been. The nonretractable landing gear had been torn away on impact as well, leaving only the fuselage intact in the clearing. He saw that the cockpit window had broken out, whether on impact or as a result of the elements in the ensuing years he didn't know, but he could not reach the opening to see inside.

LeDonne hoped that the bodies were gone. Any human remains within would be skeletons now, of course, but it troubled him to think of accident victims left without proper burial. He recognized this thought as an automatic reaction from his time in combat, and now he found himself wondering if it mattered. The army had been obsessed with the idea of recovering their dead and sending the bodies back stateside—halfway around the world— for an honorable funeral. Was this to appease the families, he wondered, or was there a superstitious dread about lying in unconsecrated ground, as if the angels might not be able to find you on Judgment Day? He wasn't sure that recovering bodies would serve any purpose not already taken care of by the birds and insects, but still, he needed to know if there were bodies on board, and if so, they would have to be identified, so that their families would at least have the peace of closure. He believed that the living were entitled to all the peace and closure they could get.

LeDonne found a fallen tree limb with one thick protruding branch that seemed to have enough spring in it to hold his weight. He worked it free of the underbrush and dragged it to the far side of the plane. The wings were gone, and the cockpit was closer to the ground, though still above his head. He thought that if he stood on the branch and stretched as high as he could, he might be able to reach the window. He would risk cutting his hand if he tried to grab it, but he would try to be careful.

LeDonne took off his jacket and climbed up on the tree limb, teetering for a moment until he found his balance. Then he leaned forward and stretched until his fingers reached the lower edge of the side window. He could grab the metal rod to the side of the window and try to pull himself up. He had to jump to reach it, but on the second try, his left hand grasped the rod and he hung there for an instant with his full weight on the wreckage of the plane.

Everything seemed perfectly still for an instant, even silent, as if the birds had suddenly hushed and the forest itself were holding its breath as he hung there. Then with a crack and a sigh, the battered hulk rolled back toward him and continued downward toward the earth, with nothing but his dangling body to stop its fall.

LeDonne tried to push himself away from the side of the falling plane, but it took a few seconds to untangle his hand from its grasp of the metal, and he landed back across the tree limb, not entirely clear of the falling wreckage. The body of the plane hit the ground with a shuddering thump, rocked once and settled in an upright position, pinning the lower part of his leg beneath it.

His first cry was involuntary, a protest of the shock and pain of the impact on his bones, and then he shouted in earnest, hoping that he was still close enough to the Appalachian Trail for passing hikers to hear his cries. He doubted that he was that near, however. Surely if he were within a mile of the Trail, someone would have found and reported the wreckage of the plane before now. After a few minutes' shouting, he listened for answering cries and heard nothing but the drone of gnats near his head and far in the distance the screech of a bird.

He felt dizzy. He thought his head must have smacked against the ground as he fell, but he could not focus on that sensation because the pain in his leg was worse. Fighting the spinning in his head, he began to take stock of his situation. He was trapped in a forest gully on a mountainside miles from town, with no means of calling for help, and no one to miss him until Monday. How long did people live in situations like this? At least the weather was warm, so exposure shouldn't be a factor, as long as he could manage without water.

He wondered if his leg was broken. He could still feel, then, anyhow, a dubious blessing considering how much it hurt, but at least he was fairly certain that he wasn't paralyzed. He couldn't get out, though. The full weight of the plane was bearing down on his leg just above the shin, and he was trapped where he lay. He struggled, twisting his body first to one side and then the other, trying to find an indention in the wreckage that might allow him to slide out from under it, but he was held fast.

He lay back, panting, and closed his eyes, trying to keep himself from panicking. He must stay calm in order to think his way out of this. The feeling of dizziness seemed to increase as he lay still and looked up. The trees seemed to be spinning in a slow circle around him, and then he was gone.

The patrol car radio erupted with noise, breaking the silence, and they heard Jenna Leigh's voice sounding excited. She was doing well in the job of department dispatcher, but she had yet to master the dispassionate tone of voice required in law enforcement communications.

"Wake County One to Alpha. Are y'all Code J, Sheriff?"

"Affirmative, Go ahead, Jenna," said Spencer. "Steve Ashley of the Civil Air Patrol is with me, and we're on our way over the mountain into North Carolina. You may lose contact with us as we go around a curve. Over."

"Can you pull over then? You need to hear this!"

"Ten four. Go ahead." He edged the car to the shoulder of the road, hoping that he wouldn't have to stay there for long. Two-lane mountain roads on precipices left very little room for off-road parking, and if a pickup truck came barreling around the curve, there might be yet another accident to deal with today.

"Nine-one-one just called with more information about the subject in the—um… I don't know how to encode this, Sheriff, and it's pretty urgent. Okay, you know that lady in the plane crash?"

Spencer sighed. She was new. The job didn't pay much. Maybe nobody was close enough with a scanner to eavesdrop. "Affirmative."

216

"Well, we think we know who she is!"

Steve Ashley clenched a fist and whispered "Yes!"

Spencer smiled at his own relief. There wasn't a happy ending yet, but it was something to go on. "Good work," he said into the receiver. "Give me the name."

"You are not going to believe this... Sheriff, when Ben told me the name, I immediately thought about Patsy Cline—rest her soul!— and I got all shivery..."

"Jen-na Leigh..."

"Right. Subject in downed...um...vehicle currently being sought is Lark McCourry, recording star of—"

"I know who she is. Is this identification confirmed?" *Or is it some wild guess from a country music junkie who reads too many supermarket tabloids?* he finished silently.

"Confirmed, sir."

"*How* confirmed? Over."

"Subject repeated cell phone call to Wake County 911. Caller spelled name for Ben...for 911 operator, that is. Lark McCourry. She said she's from around here..."

"Thanks, Jenna Leigh. See if you can round up Deputy Ayers. Get her to call me. Over."

She's from around here. Spencer pictured a girl with dark, curly hair and blue eyes, sitting in algebra class with the vacant expression of one whose mind had long ago strayed from the subject of mathematics. She was Linda Walker back then, but maybe even then she wasn't... They had been classmates together in high school, but not particularly close friends. Spencer thought that Linda Walker had taken up a lot of "psychic space": She was impatient, ambitious, idealistic, and mostly angry. She was angry about everything: that women were not treated as equals; that young people's opinions were dismissed by their elders; that television used Southern accents as shorthand to convey the idea of stupidity. She wanted to change the world—or at least back it into a corner and yell at it for a while.

Spencer wasn't surprised that she had gone on to become famous. People like Linda didn't take no for an answer. In her yearbook he had written, "To Linda—I wish I wanted *anything* as bad as you want *everything*." It had taken her awhile to become famous. She wasn't an overnight sensation like some of the younger country stars, but she had finally made a name for herself. He hoped it wasn't going to end on a mountainside ten miles from where she started—that was just too much irony, even for country music.

Members of the Bluff Mountain chapter of the Civil Air Patrol had assembled in the community center building that served as everything from town hall to flea market site during the Memorial Day festivities. Someone had brought over a bulletin board from the town library, and a topographical map of the area had been pinned up. This would be the headquarters for the search, with volunteers on hand around the clock to man the phones and relay information from one group of searchers to another.

Baird Christopher, who had been one of the first to arrive, was leaning against a long wooden table near the map, chatting with some of the other volunteers. Like most of the other men present, Baird was outfitted in his brush clothes, in case he was needed to join the search, but while the rest of the group had arrived in jeans and windbreakers or plaid flannel jackets, Baird was wearing a Hawes & Curtiss tweed jacket over a black T-shirt, khaki trousers, and gum boots.

"I've passed the word back at the hostel to the hikers headed south," he was saying. "We're telling everybody to keep their eyes open for signs of sheared treetops or broken branches, and of course to be as quiet as possible so that they can hear any cries for help in the distance."

"It's a long shot," said one of the volunteers.

Baird Christopher smiled. "Well, hell, Boyd, *you* were a long shot, if it comes to that. At the time of your conception, do you know how many sperm were racing to get to that one little egg that would turn out to be you? Why if one of those other ones had won the race, you could've been a six-foot redheaded brain surgeon instead of a short, balding electrician. A slim chance is better than none, Boyd."

"Sheriff's coming!" somebody called out.

The crowd parted, and as they turned and faced the doorway, another volunteer said disgustedly, "Ah, that's not the sheriff! That's a Tennessee trooper."

Spencer Arrowood smiled politely at this jibe. The speaker was one of the "natives," someone whose family had been in these mountains for two hundred years or so. The new people were always affable and polite to peace officers, in case they should have to report a burglary or a fender bender in the lawman's district someday. "I called over to Marshall," Spencer said, "but my counterpart on this side of the line is tied up this evening, and he asked me to coordinate the search on behalf of both states. We both have the same goal—finding the downed plane with survivors. I'm going to fill you in with what we know, and then you can choose a volunteer to head up the search teams here. I'll head back over the mountain to supervise the operation on the Tennessee side. Now, you know that a passenger in a private aircraft called our 911 on her cell phone to report the plane crash. She believes the pilot to be deceased. She does not know the make of the aircraft or their current position, which is why we're having to search in North Carolina and Tennessee." He surveyed the listeners, whose faces bore no surprise at this information.

"On my way over here, I received new information about the identity of the survivor, and this may further complicate the search." Now they were giving him their full attention. "The woman in the crash has identified herself as Lark McCourry—the famous folksinger who is originally from Hamelin, Tennessee."

The excited hum that began before he had even finished speaking told him that they knew who she was, and that her disappearance would be of interest to the media. Spencer waited until the buzz of voices died down. "Celebrities complicate anything they're involved in, so if word of this leaks out, we will have to contend with a swarm of reporters and television crews as well as all the usual difficulties involved in a mountain rescue operation—weather, snakes, rough terrain, communication problems, and so on. I think for the time being it would be best if we did not let word get out concerning the identity of the passenger."

A sleek silver-haired man with the face and body of a dedicated runner raised his hand. "Sheriff, have you considered the fact that the victim phoned 911 from a cell phone, and that those lines are not secure? People over a wide area could have inadvertently intercepted that transmission?"

Spencer Arrowood nodded. Engineer, he decided. California accent. Maybe Oregon had finally put out a NO VACANCY sign and they were all moving here instead. "Yes, sir," he said politely. "I'm aware of that, but it's a chance we'll have to live with, because there's nothing we can do about it. I'm just asking the members of the search and rescue team not to make it any worse."

"Maybe the reporters could help us search," said one of the locals.

Baird Christopher shuddered. "I'd rather be found by the bears," he said.

Becky Tilden looked at the kitchen clock for the third time in as many minutes. The supper dishes were dried and put away, and it was nearly time for Judge to go to bed, but still the phone had not rung. She picked up the receiver and listened to make sure there was a dial tone. Hearing the familiar buzz in her ear, she shrugged and put the receiver back into place. Lark was later than she'd expected. Maybe it took longer to fly from Nashville than she had thought. Becky had never been in an airplane herself, but she had seen enough about them on television to know that they weren't always reliable. She decided that now would be a good time to tell Judge about his daughter's visit so that he could decide whether or not he wanted to wait up. She filled a glass with tap water and took a selection of pills out of the cabinet next to the sink— Judge's nightcap, a mixture of vitamins and blood pressure medication. With one last look around the tidy kitchen, she flipped off the light and walked the few paces down the hallway to the den.

Judge was sitting in his shabby old chair, nodding off, seemingly oblivious to the blare of a car chase flickering across the screen in front of him. "Time for your medicine, Judge!"

said Becky in hearty tones designed to rouse him from his nap.

John Walker opened his eyes and gave his housekeeper a mischievous smile. "I believe a little moonshine in a fruit jar would do me more good, Becky," he said.

It was his favorite jest, and Becky answered as she always did, "You tell Dr. Banner about that the next time he's over here, and see what he says about it. Open up." She handed him the glass of water and the first of the pills, keeping the others in the palm of her hand to be given in sequence.

"Do you feel like staying up a little longer, Judge?"

As he swallowed the pill, his eyes strayed to the television. "Why?" he said. "What's on?"

"You're going to be having company tonight," said Becky, handing him another pill. "Your daughter is on her way here. She didn't want me to tell you she was coming, but I thought you ought to know." It was a habit of Becky's, so ingrained now that she hardly had to think about it, to frame any encounter in terms that made her seem to be fighting the world on your behalf. By inventing a difficulty and claiming to have overcome it, she could take the credit for anything that went right. *The pharmacist didn't want to fill the prescription with a less expensive brand, but I insisted on it. The mechanic declared himself too busy to change the oil today, but I talked him into it.* Sometimes she even tried this form of counterfeit virtue on Lark. *Your father didn't want me to call and tell you he's sick,*

223

but I thought you needed to know, she would say, despite the fact that John Walker had specifically asked her to telephone Lark with the news of his illness. Becky counted on father and daughter, walled away by pride and estrangement, not to compare notes, and indeed she was seldom caught out in her self-serving claims. Becky figured she got little enough in life, she may as well take some credit when it didn't cost anybody anything. She stored up gratitude against hard times to come.

This time, though, John Walker's reaction was not the one she expected. Instead of smiling and thanking her for her selfless devotion, he stiffened and began to shake his head. "No. She's not coming."

He said it with such certainty that Becky began to wonder if she had missed the phone ringing, and Judge had taken the call himself.

"She's not coming here," he said again.

"She said she was," said Becky, sticking to the facts as she knew them. "Did you hear different?"

"Yes. Somebody came to see me and said she would not be able to make it."

Becky was careful to keep her face expressionless. "Oh, one of your visitors, Judge? One of the ones I can't see?"

"That's right. Said not to expect her. She isn't coming, so I might as well go to bed." He began to struggle up out of his armchair, and Becky grasped his elbow to steady him as he tottered to his feet. With her other hand she touched the off button on the television's remote control. Out of the corner of her eye she watched the shadows, in case one of the mysterious visitors had lingered on in the room to keep Judge company. She was always afraid she was going to see one of them.

"Well, you're probably right, Judge," she said, keeping her voice calm and nonchalant. "No point in waiting up. I guess you can go on to bed then. I'll stay up a little while longer in case she does turn up, then I'll put the lights out and lock up. See you in the morning."

With a quick nod that meant good night, the old man limped off down the hall toward his bedroom.

If Lark turned up tonight, Becky would say that she had begged Judge to stay awake to spend time with his daughter when she arrived, but that he had insisted on going to bed regardless. She did wonder about his invisible guests, though. This was the first time they had ever said anything about what was happening here and now. Before now they just seemed to come to pass the time of day, and the conversation as Judge had reported it concerned the past: things the old man remembered anyhow, though perhaps he had not thought of them in years. She wondered what it would mean if the things the visitors told Judge about the here and now turned out to be true.

"I need your help," said the woman in the doorway.

Nora Bonesteel looked up from her loom, where threads of grays and heathers mingled on the woven cloth. She stared for a moment at the short, dark-haired woman who stood on the threshold, but she did not speak.

"May I come in?" the woman asked her, politely but with a trace of impatience in her voice.

"Is there something I can do for you?" asked Nora Bonesteel. Without waiting for an answer, she left the loom, walked over to the open door, and stepped out onto the covered porch. "Why don't we sit a spell out here? The evening is fine this time of year." She sat in one of the apple wood rocking chairs near the front window and motioned for the visitor to join her.

"I didn't mean to startle you," said the woman, settling into the chair and beginning a steady rhythm of rocking that punctuated her words. "I thought you must have heard me at the door, but the noise of the loom must have masked the sound. What is that you're making?"

"A coverlet," said Nora Bonesteel.

"I always wanted to learn weaving," the woman said. "May I go in and take a look at it?"

"I don't reckon you came here to talk about making coverlets," said Nora Bonesteel.

"No." The visitor smiled. "I was just trying to make small talk. Never was any good at it, though. Do you know who I am?"

The old woman nodded. "Yes. I recognized you as soon as I saw you."

The visitor sighed with relief, and summoned a smile. "Well, that's good," she said. "I didn't want you to think I was a trespasser or a salesman."

"No. The family resemblance is strong in you. All the Wolfes have dark curly hair and steel blue eyes. I knew your mother."

"I remember. So you know which one of the Wolfes I am, then?"

Nora Bonesteel pursed her lips. "Bonnie Wolfe," she said at last.

"Right!" The visitor smiled as if pleased to have been remembered. "Sometimes when I get back home, it's hard to keep a grip on being famous. It's like it was a dream, and I'll wake up and find that I'm waiting tables in the cafe downtown. When I come back, it doesn't seem possible that I actually got out of here and made it all happen with my music. It seems like just yesterday that I was in school here. Of course, when I get around strangers, even here, they treat me like I'm an exhibit in a museum, and that's a pretty sharp reminder of how far I've come. Sometimes I think I've forgotten how to be ordinary...which makes it difficult when you need to come back and ask for help."

Nora Bonesteel said nothing.

"It's about a song."

"I'm not one for singing."

The woman smiled. "No. The Bonesteels aren't known for their singing voices, are they? They're known for something else."

"Not all of us." Nora looked uneasy. She

didn't like to talk about the Sight. Some people thought you were cursed with the devil's sign for having it, but even worse were the folks who were fascinated by it and wanted you to tell their fortunes or give them advice. "They say it skips a generation, sometimes two," she said.

"Well, it didn't skip yours. But your kinfolks are also legendary for their memories. Bonesteels never forget anything. So I need to ask a favor of you. You see, there's this old mountain song called 'The Rowan on the Grave.' You've heard it, haven't you?"

"I may have," said Nora Bonesteel.

"I expect you have. The family used to sing it a lot when I was a girl, but fortunately none of the songcatchers ever came snooping around to collect it. As far as I know, none of those so-called music scholars ever snatched it up and copyrighted it with ASCAP or BMI, the way they did with so many mountain ballads. Imagine that—you get a song for free on the pretense of preserving it for posterity, and then you go and put your name on it and charge people to sing it."

"Well, they thought we wouldn't know any better," said Nora.

"I know better. And I've decided that I want that song for my new album."

"I can't help you."

"No, that's all right." The woman gave her a mischievous smile. "You wouldn't be much help on the tune, anyhow, would you—being a Bonesteel? No, that's not what I came back for."

"No?"

"No. I already know the song, you see. I learned it by heart before I was seven. The thing is that there's somebody else trying to track down that song as well. Somebody who has heard it, but doesn't remember much of it. She's trying to find my song. The Walker girl— calls herself Lark McCourry these days. Have you seen her?"

Nora Bonesteel shook her head. "She hasn't been here."

"Well, she may turn up. Anyhow, I'd be grateful if you would not give her any help in recovering that song. If it turns up in some-body's else's work, it will spoil my album, and it's *my* song. My family's song, that is. Maybe we didn't copyright it, but we're the ones who kept it going, and it means something to us. She has no right to use it."

"Maybe it's in her family, too," Nora Bone-steel pointed out. "If you go back far enough, all the old families around here are descended from those first few settlers."

"I don't care. It's my song. I had it first, and I'm planning to use it. I won't rest until I know that nobody else is going to get it."

Nora Bonesteel stood and opened the screen door again. "I can promise you this, Bonnie Wolfe," she said. "If you can record that song so that it won't be lost, I will not give it to any other singer."

Bonnie Wolfe smiled. "I'll be going then," she said.

Malcolm McCourry—1804, Tir Nan Og

It has been ten years since I left Rachel and Black River and my law practice. I have now spent ten years in this my fourth life, as a pioneer in the wilderness—as long as I spent in my childhood home on Islay, as long as I sailed the great Atlantic circle as a seafarer. Not yet as long as I spent in the courts and the curtained drawing rooms of Morris County, New Jersey, but I hope to outlive that record of servitude here in the freedom of the wildwood. In health and happiness I feel that I could go on here forever.

I felt that I was an old man, back in the days when I went down the Wilderness Road with my Jane and her husband. I was hoping to see a bit of the new country before I died, traveling west, as I had since I was a boy, still searching, perhaps, for Tir Nan Og, the golden land where the Fianna live in eternal health and youth.

And, do you know, I have found it?

Here in these bright, green mountains, I felt time stop. When I came here in 1794, I was old and tired, but something about this place brought me back again, and I grew stronger and leaner and less weary as time went on. There was so much work needed here, and none of it to do with books and courts. The Carolina backcountry is a beautiful land, with wild steep mountains floating in a haze of cloud. Covering everything is a green sea of trees, swallowing the hills and valleys, and curling around the trails and rivers with the wind in the leaves for its tide. *The sea will take him,* the old woman said of me when she birthed me. Perhaps it has, this sea of wilderness, but I have gone under willingly, and I mean never to emerge again.

Still, there is much work to be done, for, unlike the Tir Nan Og of my boyhood legends, in this paradise one must work to survive, but at least I am not alone.

I tarried in Wilkes County long enough to get the hang of frontier life, and long enough to be sure that Miss Sally Lynn shared my feelings of affection, though our courtship was not a happy time for me. It is hard enough to court a girl of fifteen when you are three times that age; it is harder still to manage it when your grown daughter watches you at it, tight-lipped and silent, like a thundercloud of disapproval. Sometimes I thought I could see in Jane's cold eyes a look of scorn for her old father's weakness, and I thought that she had never looked more like her mother than she did then.

I began to be uneasy in my daughter's presence, and I worried that she would explode in anger one day and end the idyll. Worse yet, she might write a letter to her mother, complaining of my behavior, and while I did not think that anything would induce Rachel to leave her comfortable home to brave the wilderness, I had no desire to wager my happiness on it.

Jane watched me like a shepherd watches a stray dog. Any time she saw me within three feet of James Lynn's daughter, she scowled and flounced off, but so far she had kept her peace about the situation. Any day now, I thought, Jane would draw Sally aside and have a few sharp words with her "for her own good," and to my everlasting ruin. I did not even want to imagine my predicament if James Lynn should learn that his daughter's suitor was a widower by distance and not by death. Visions of this calamity troubled me waking and sleeping for days on end, and at last I decided that I could endure it no longer. I would tell Sally Lynn the truth about myself, and put an end to my agony one way or the other.

The next Sunday after meeting, as we all walked back to the Lynns' farm for dinner, I fell in step beside Sally, and took care to slow our pace so that we should fall behind the rest of the party. We walked for a while in companionable silence, listening to the crunch of leaves beneath our feet, and watching our breath mingle to make little clouds in the air before us. Sally wore a blue dress that day beneath her homespun cloak, and I thought she was as beautiful as any woman I had ever seen.

"I have something to tell you," I said when I judged that we were out of earshot of the others.

I heard her gasp, and she turned to look at me with a shy smile and an expression of expectant innocence in her blue eyes. You can never propose to a woman unexpectedly, I thought—only sooner than she thought you would.

"I want to marry you, Sally," I told her. "If you'll have me, that is. But there's something about the matter that I must make plain to you before we proceed with this. You know I've had a wife before—Jane's mother?"

Sally nodded, and then looked away quick, for not even the most victorious woman cares to hear mention of a rival.

"The fact is that Jane's mother is still alive. Back in New Jersey."

Sally's face went whiter than river ice, and she gasped again. I looked around for the rest of the party, fearing that one of them had seen her stricken look, but they were plodding ahead unaware of what went on between us. Sally, too, was looking toward the others, and I laid my hand on her arm to keep her from running to them.

"Sally," I said, "New Jersey is five hundred miles or more away from here. I don't ever mean to go back there. Ever. My life is here."

She shivered. "But what if your wife should come here?"

"She will not. She is old. She may die soon anyhow." I was babbling. I would have said anything to wipe that stricken look from Sally Lynn's pretty face. "We are quits, my wife and I, but soon I will be going back to the mountains west of here to homestead, and I want you to go with me."

She shook her head, and whispered, "But it would be sinful to live with a man already wed."

I sighed. "Wouldn't it be a crime to leave me alone and friendless because of an old woman far away that I will never see again? Will you go?"

"I don't know. Pa would never let me go off not married."

"We will marry then. We will start a new life here on the frontier."

She looked doubtful, but she no longer looked as if she would bolt, and I knew that at least she was considering my proposal. "What will your daughter—Mrs. Horton—say about it?"

"She can take it or leave it," I said. "She has her own family now. But I will speak to her and make it plain that this will be done with her blessing or without it. Now, what is your answer, Sally Lynn?"

She ducked her head, but I could see the blush spreading across her cheeks. "I reckon if Pa lets me, I'll go."

Late that night, when we returned to our farm, I told Zeph and Jane what I had done. Jane had left her china plates back in Black River, which was just as well, for the wooden one she hove at me did not break when it bounced off the log wall.

At that, Zephaniah got up, yawning and stretching like a man who is ready to retire after a dull evening. "I believe I'll check on the calves before I bed down," he said offhandedly. He did not look at either of us as he said it, and without waiting for an answer, he hurried out the door.

"I won't have it!" said Jane, stamping her foot. "I won't have you make fools of us all! I have held my peace, and bit my tongue, and looked the other way when a child of three could have told what was happening, but I'll have no more of it. You have a live and lawful wife in Black River, and three grandchildren in yonder loft there, and I'll thank you to remember it, sir!"

I sighed. Of all my children, I was fondest of Jane. She had the brains and the spirit that I saw in myself, and I had no wish to quarrel with her now, but she could not have her Black River gentility here in the backcountry, and I meant to tell her so. My mind was made up. "Your mother and I are done now," I told her. "We will never see one another again. Nothing you do or say can change that, and I cannot believe that your mother would wish it. You know that she will not come south with us. She made that plain. And you must know that I will never go back there."

She sniffed. "What Benjamin would say to all this I cannot imagine."

"It is none of Benjamin's affair," I said. "Though perhaps he might come closer to understanding than a woman would. Nevertheless, he is there, and we are here. I came to the backcountry to begin again."

"But, Father, why? I mean, you're so *old*." She caught her breath, and looked as if she meant to beg my pardon, but her anger won out, and she tossed her head and went on talking. "I had thought you were tired of the rigors of a law practice, and that you'd come to live with us in your old age. I thought you might play with your grandchildren, teach them a bit of Latin, perhaps, and help Zeph with some of the lighter tasks around the farm. I even thought you might tire of this harsh life on the frontier, and that another hard winter would see you on your way home to Black River by the next stagecoach."

I shook my head. "No hardship here could make me go back to Black River. If I had to sleep in the snow and eat dirt clods, I'd rather be here than there. And I'm not ready to be a doddering old man yet, thank you. Whether it suits you or not, I mean to marry Sally."

Jane set her jaw and gave me the Freeman look of withering scorn. "*Marry* Sally Lynn! Hardly that, I think, whatever you choose to call it. And I suppose you will abandon that poor girl when it suits you, too?"

"No," I said. "I'll stand by her as long as she wants me to. I think I did the same for your mother, Jane, whether she will admit to that or not. Anyhow, Sally and I will be heading back to the mountains come spring. But before we go, she wants a church wedding here among her kinfolks, and I wanted to ask you— not on my account, but as a favor to her—not to spoil it."

"I'll not lie for you, Father," said Jane, turning away. "I will not pretend my mother is dead when she isn't, and I'll not watch you betray her in a church before God and everybody. Don't ask it."

"I guess we're done then," I said.

I will say this for my Jane: She may be stubborn, but she has a generous heart, and she is no holder of grudges. The air was chilly between us for many a day after that outburst of hers, but I took care to be civil to her at mealtimes and to be helpful with the children, and gradually she thawed out to the point that we could converse again almost like old times. I had not changed my intentions one iota, but out of respect for my daughter's feelings I did not make a show of my plans.

A few days after my quarrel with Jane, I went to see James Lynn on my own to tell him that I wanted to marry Sally. I felt a bit of a fool going to man younger than I was to ask for his daughter's hand, but I was determined to see the business done right, for Sally wished to be in good graces with her family—and if possible with mine—before we left.

The disparity in age between myself and Sally was not mentioned in our discussion, for it was not an uncommon situation, for all that the ladies carp about it, and some—the oldest, plainest ones—even call it unseemly.

I think James Lynn must have taken me for a widower, for childbirth and fevers take a toll on our womenfolk, so that many of them die young. At my age many a man has had a succession of wives, and I did not enlighten him about the truth of my situation. Or perhaps Lynn was a practical man like myself, and he realized that here in the backcountry a piece of paper from the government had little bearing on people's lives. Most of the people who came to the frontier hated having other folk tell them what to do and how to act.

Sally and I would be living far enough from courthouses and polite society. Perhaps the formality of legal recognition mattered as little to the Lynns as it did to me, as long as Sally was well and happy. He did set a store by the fact that I was a lawyer and could read and write, and also that I had a bit of money put by to purchase land in the mountains.

"Well, you'd better take her, then" was all her father said to my profession of love for his daughter and my promise to treat her well.

Word about the wedding went round our little community faster than a brushfire, and within a day of my meeting with James Lynn, Jane got to hear of it, though not from my lips. She froze up again for a day or so after that, but at last, when she saw that my mind was made up past changing, she gave in, and even said that she would accompany Zeph to the wedding, though she wanted no part of the preparations. It would make her feel like a traitor to her mother, she told me.

"I don't know what they would say in Black

River about this," she sighed. "A child for a wife, and not even a lawful one! The shame of it would kill Mother and Benjamin."

"We'd best not tell them for a while, then," I said, but in truth I doubted that it would matter as much to them as she supposed. So long as their neighbors never got wind of it, I'm sure that neither Rachel nor Benjamin cared what would become of me. When our wagon rolled out of sight of Main Street, I was as good as dead to them, and I saw no reason to steer my life by the stars of their inclinations.

It wasn't much of a wedding by the standards of New Jersey society, but the women of the Wilkes settlement took on as if it were a coronation, as women always do. I suppose that courtship is to women what warfare is to men, and the marriage ceremony to them was the surrender at Yorktown. At least we had it in the meeting house with a minister to pray for our union. Some couples in the back-country jump over a broomstick together and call themselves married. I reckoned Sally and I were at least as married as *that*.

We went back to the farm after that, and got on with the business of building a life for ourselves, and before the week was out, Jane turned up at the door with a loaf of fresh-baked bread and some newly churned butter. Sally ran and hugged her, and as I thanked her for the bread, I think she knew that my gratitude went deeper than that.

"We're family" was all she said.

I'd had enough of Wilkes County by then.

Counting my new in-laws, I had almost as many relatives there as I did in New Jersey. I set out to sell my parcel of land and to move farther out into the backcountry. Most folks reckoned that mountain land was steep and rocky, with poor soil—not good for much—so the land up there went cheaper. I reckoned I could buy twice as much mountain land with the cash I made from selling my holdings in Wilkes.

We headed out a few weeks after the wedding, bound for the high country. Jane and Zephaniah promised to follow as soon as their land sold and the babies were ready to travel. I do not know if Sally minded leaving her kinfolk. She never said. But I kept my vow to treat her well and see that she never wanted for anything. Rich we would never be, but there was always food and warmth and joy. And every day the mountains changed in color or shadow, so that the year was a succession of tapestries, never twice the same.

We homesteaded a sheltered cove on Jack's Creek, and settled in to an American Eden, safe from the winter drifts, the Indian raiders— and from all those self-righteous hypocrites in Black River, New Jersey. I was home at last.

I have three new sons now. My Sally is a strong young woman, a good worker, and not one to complain. She has lost that first bloom of youth that made her a flower in the forest, but she is still pretty enough by my lights, and I'd not trade her for all the powdered, silk-gowned city wenches in Jersey, by God I wouldn't. We've built this farm together, her and me, with our own hands, and no slaves to do the fetching and carrying for us, either, mind you. She has hoed Indian corn in the blazing heat and trudged through snow up to her knees to feed the oxen, and never a word of complaint from her. We have been together ten years now, and in that time I've pulled up stakes and moved the family three times, homesteading three parcels of land, abandoning one and going on to the next, and each time settling farther from civilization. Sally has stuck by me through all this, accepting my decisions with unquestioning loyalty.

Our first son, James, was named after his mother's father, as custom will have it. He is a fair lad, light-haired and big-boned, with the clear blue eyes of a McCourry right enough. There won't be much likeness between him and his half brother in New Jersey, I'll wager. The two of them started life differently enough. Young Master Benjamin was cradled in lace and linen, with a nursemaid to tend him and a silver cup waiting for him to drink from when he grew older—a gift from his Freeman grandparents, that was. Jim had none of that, but I'm sure he'll think himself none the worse for it.

Jim was born in a log cabin on a mountainside in Tennessee, a state only six years older than he is. I did not send word to the family back in Black River about their new little kinsman, for I did not think that silver cups or words of congratulations would be forth-coming from that quarter. Jane wished us well, but even she said that it didn't seem fair for men to have two lives and two chances of a family while women were lucky even to get one. As I could think of no reply that would not compound the injury, I let her have the last word.

I wonder how Benjamin is doing these days. Well enough, I'm sure. He'd be close to thirty by now, married well, and prospering. I wonder if he will name his second son for me. He needn't bother. I took care of that myself.

Chapter Seven

Lark McCourry clicked on her cell phone, and then shut it off again. How long had it been since she had called that fellow at 911? Twenty minutes? An hour? She must conserve the batteries in the phone in case the search stretched into days and she might need to report hearing planes overhead or the sounds of a ground search—anything that might help them to locate her. Right now she had nothing new to report. She was cold and sore, hungry and frightened—they could take all that as a given, though.

The 911 guy probably thought she was

crazy as well. *Find a ballad for me.* What was that about? Did she really think that having half the county out hunting for an old song would make any difference in whether she lived or died? Intellectually, of course not. She would have derided that superstition as firmly as any skeptic. But emotionally, she felt that somehow this search for the song was a lifeline, and that while it held, she would not be allowed to die. So let them look.

The song about the girl in the graveyard. She remembered sitting in the dark, listening to the words of that song. But whose voice had it been? She couldn't have been older than twelve when it happened, and she had never heard the song again. It wasn't a happy song, but she had dredged it up from a better time, maybe the last good time there had ever been between her and her father. When she turned thirteen—a puppy-fat wallflower of a teenager—the connection between them had been severed for good, kinship replaced on both sides by civility and stony obligation. She wondered if things might have been different if she had been a pretty little princess of a girl, or if the rift had been inevitable.

She knew that there would be no reconciliation, not after all these years, but at least she could look across the chasm and remember some of the good times: a bedtime story, a book read aloud to the still-pretty toddler, the echoes of a song. Perhaps the song was all she could salvage of that distant time. The snapshots faded and the love was lost, but there was still the song. If she could find it. If she got out alive...

She wondered if being a celebrity was going to help her odds of survival. Would there be search planes sent out on her behalf, or tabloid reporters combing the woods for the downed plane? Or should the wording on the inevitable bronze marker read: "Not Famous Enough"?

It was beginning to get cold out on the mountain now that the sun had gone down, and her legs were cramping from the hours she had spent trapped in a confined space with little freedom of movement. She was afraid to try anything drastic, though, like rocking the plane, for fear of making the situation worse. She decided that for now she would hunker down, try to keep warm, and wait to be found.

The next hour came and went, but Lark McCourry, who had finally succumbed to sleep, did not call back.

Spencer Arrowood wondered if he was doing the right thing. He maneuvered the patrol car through the dark streets of Hamelin, not bothering to look at the numbers on the road-side mailboxes. He knew where he was headed; he just wasn't quite sure why. It was late; he had driven back from the searchers' meeting in Bluff Mountain with no definite information, and no words of comfort to offer the family of the crash victim. Since the object of his visit was an elderly man, the sheriff was tempted to leave the errand until morning, especially

244

since Ben at 911 had told him that Linda Walker herself had asked that her father not be notified. Obeying her wish would be the easiest course of action, which was why Spencer wasn't going to do it that way. As a matter of principle, he distrusted the easiest course of action.

You had an accident: you notified the family. It was that simple. He figured John Walker had a right to know. Spencer remembered John Walker: Back in the days when the sheriff had been a quiet loner in high school, John Walker had been one of the town leaders, occasionally appearing in the crowd at football games or school plays, and always introducing himself as "Linda's dad." He had been an able, genial man, but you always felt that the warmth was a little forced, a gesture of politeness with no real feeling behind it at all. Linda and her dad had never been close, as far as he could remember, and it had been years since Spencer had seen the man. He didn't suppose he would even recognize him after all these years. Funny how people tended to stay the same age in your mind when you went a long time without seeing them. They became frozen in memory at the age when you knew them best.

Spencer parked the patrol car in the gravel driveway of the shabby frame house. This was the sort of neighborhood where the clients of a small town criminal lawyer might live, but not the lawyer himself. It certainly wasn't where the Walkers had lived when John still practiced law here, and it wasn't what you expected of someone who had once retired to a lakefront resort, or of one whose offspring was a well-known singer. He wondered what the story was behind it, and figured—as with most of the little domestic dramas he encountered in the course of his work—he wasn't likely ever to find out.

He hurried up to the concrete stoop that served as a front porch for the little house. The porch light was on, and the four steps leading up to it were covered with a green plastic runner, made to look like grass. As Spencer knocked, he wondered if John Walker had chosen either the house or its working-class fixtures.

After a few minutes' wait, the front door opened wide enough for a plain, scowling face to peer out at him. The woman's narrowed eyes took in his badge and uniform, and she opened the door a few inches wider, waiting for him to speak.

Spencer introduced himself, smiling and trying to sound both official and nonthreatening. Uneducated people tended to distrust peace officers and to regard any encounter with them as a confrontation, so over the years the sheriff had learned a succession of soothing words and facial expressions designed to put wary constituents at their ease. Privately he referred to these mannerisms as his "Andy Griffith rap," an homage to the Mayberry sheriff of sixties television. "I'd like to see John Walker if I may. He's an old friend of mine," said Spencer, stretching a point. "I don't believe I've met you, though, ma'am."

"Becky Tilden," said the sullen woman. "You don't remember me. I grew up around here. Went to school with you—though I was a few years back. When I was in second grade, you were a crossing guard. You used to help me across the street to school."

Crossing guard... Spencer had been in ninth grade that year. He wondered if she really expected him to remember her from that far back, or if she was only expressing a general resentment because nobody ever did. Plain women were invisible all their lives. It wasn't his fault, but he wasn't blameless, either. He said, "Well, nice to see you again after all these years. Is Mr. Walker still up? He *does* live here, doesn't he?" It had just occurred to Spencer that he might have come to the wrong house.

"Oh, this is Judge's house, all right, but he's gone to bed for the night."

"This is important, though. I have news about his daughter, and I need to see him." Spencer supposed that this woman was some form of live-in help for the old man, and he had infused his words with a shade more authority, designed to make her obey him.

The woman did not seem impressed by what he said. Her truculent expression did not change and she did not ask him to come inside. "Judge's daughter was supposed to come see him tonight, but then he told me she wasn't coming after all."

"Did she phone him, too?"

Becky Tilden hesitated a shade too long before she said, "I don't know."

"Does he know what's happened?"

She shrugged. "It's hard to tell what Judge knows. I wouldn't wake him up, though. He's not been well. I'll give him the message in the morning."

"But this is important," said Spencer. "His daughter Lark—well, I guess she's Linda to him—anyhow, according to our information, she has been in a plane crash, and she has not yet been located. We've got search teams out now on both sides of the mountain trying to find her." That would teach her to treat him like a bill collector. A note of satisfaction crept into Spencer's voice as he anticipated the shock and surprise with which this announcement would be received.

He was wrong about that, though. Becky Tilden merely nodded, as calmly as if he had told her that Lark was stuck in traffic on the interstate. "Okay," she said. "I'll tell him in the morning. Thanks for stopping by, Sheriff. Good night." With a curt nod of dismissal, she softly closed the door.

And that was that.

It had been daylight for perhaps half an hour, and Baird Christopher was ready to hit the mountain. He had left the hostel in the care of a part-time employee, and now he was heading out to take part in the search for the missing aircraft. In his knapsack, Baird had packed a cell phone, a liter of Evian, a topo map of the area, a flashlight, two sticks of ostrich jerky, and four Stayman apples from the Curtis Fosters' orchard. He and the other searchers had met at the community center for a hurried meeting over coffee and day-old cinnamon buns donated by the local grocery. The previous night's search had yielded no trace of the downed plane, and now they must mark off the areas already covered and decide where to look today. Spencer Arrowood had gone back to the Tennessee side of the mountain, where the Wake County Civil Air Patrol was conducting its own search.

The searchers were setting off in pairs, and Baird was teamed with one of the new people, Anne McNeill, who had relocated her small animal veterinary practice from greater Atlanta to Bluff Mountain, North Carolina. Baird had seen her around, knew who she was, of course, but since he hadn't needed the service of a vet in a while, he hadn't become acquainted with her. She seemed like a bright and capable young woman, though. She lived in a glass and cedar A-frame partway up the ridge that overlooked the town. He heard that she did whitewater rafting in her spare time, so she ought to be physically capable of conducting an extensive search over rough terrain.

They had been assigned to cover a few mountaintop acres at the end of a dirt road near the Tennessee line, and they were driving to the road's end in Baird's battered old Land

Rover, which he liked to tell people was just like one the Queen used to drive a few years back.

Anne McNeill settled back in the passenger seat with the map spread out on her lap. "This is my first search for a downed plane," she said.

"You didn't have plane crashes around Atlanta?"

She smiled. "Scads of them, for all I know, but I didn't belong to the Civil Air Patrol when I lived there. I didn't feel qualified somehow."

"Qualified?" Baird raised his eyebrows. "Dr. McNeill, we take thirteen-year-olds."

"Well, I know, but you see in Atlanta there were so many experts that I suppose I felt intimidated. Down there they have so many resource people: retired commercial pilots, firefighters, ER physicians. Being found by me might have been the worst thing that could have happened to a Georgia crash survivor. Then I came here... Bluff Mountain is such a small place, and I *do* have medical training, so I thought that I might be of some use here. And I enjoy hiking and outdoor sports, so I'm in good shape. I thought it might be a good way to get involved in the community. You know, a way to meet the people whose dogs *aren't* sick."

Baird laughed at that. "Glad to have you aboard," he said.

They had left the town limits of Bluff Mountain in less than two minutes, and now they were heading west along the two-lane main road that led over the mountain into Tennessee. Fields and stretches of woodland flashed past them, punctuated by small white frame houses, modest brick houses with carports, and here and there a larger angular structure of stone and glass perched high above the valley. You didn't have to ask where the new people lived.

Anne McNeill broke the silence. "Have you been a member long?"

"Couple of years. They're a good bunch of people up here. Hard workers. They don't call off a search in any hurry. You just about have to drag them back off a mountain."

She nodded. "I did wonder about this search, though. I'm mean, it strikes me as being very low-tech. Can't we afford modern equipment up here?"

Baird thought of launching into his lecture on the number of millionaires residing in the county, but he shelved it and merely asked, "How do you mean?"

"Well, I was thinking about infrared, for example. I read about the search planes they use to search for marijuana crops, and I thought that technology would be useful for plane crashes."

Baird kept his eyes on the blacktop, watching for the four-digit road marker that would indicate their turnoff. "It sounds like a good idea," he said, "but it wouldn't be much of a help. Infrared is a heat-seeking system, you know. By the time the search begins, the plane's engine is cold."

"What about the survivors?"

"What about the deer out there? And the pastures full of Holsteins? How are you going to tell what's human and what isn't?"

"Okay. What about helicopters?"

"Well, they might be more help, but remember there's a lot of territory to cover out there. Usually we call in a chopper when we've narrowed the search, but it's not my call. The fellow who directs the operation can get help from the National Guard or anybody else if he thinks we need it, but all that takes some time, and time is what we don't have, so we leave the strategy to the bureaucrats, you and I, and this morning we'll make tracks up on this mountain. Sometimes the old ways work the best."

"Do you think we'll find her?"

"Well, sooner or later. Of course, we all hope it's sooner. And I hope it's *real* soon—for her sake and mine. I have to get back to the Cosmic Possum this evening, so that my helper can get to his other job." He slowed the Land Rover and turned right onto a graveled road that wound its way up the mountain. "We're almost there," he said. "We go to the end of this, and then walk up an old logging road as far as we can."

"Should we search together or split up?"

"Split up. Cover more ground that way. But stay within hollering distance if you can. In case we find something. If the lady's still alive, she may need medical attention. You can do first aid, surely?"

"Yeah, sure I can," Anne muttered, "but I wish she was a golden retriever."

Baird Christopher grinned. "Naw. She's a cosmic possum, same as you and me."

Nora Bonesteel had been up for hours, she was not used to having visitors before nine. The dark-haired young man on the porch had the rumpled and hollow-eyed look of one who has not slept at all. He was a good-looking fellow, but she did not recognize him. One of the new people then. She hoped he wasn't one of those foolish souls who had heard the talk about her having the Sight and came to have their palms read, or some such nonsense. Or a reporter looking to write a story about her. She had no patience with folks like that. They never got past the front door. She did wonder, though, why he was holding a pot in his hands.

Ten minutes later, Ben Hawkins was sitting at the old chestnut table admiring the view from the bay window in Nora Bonesteel's sunny kitchen. In front of him was a mug of steaming black coffee, a loaf of homemade bread, and a pot of Nora Bonesteel's own raspberry preserves.

He had apologized twice for calling on her so early in the morning, but he explained that working two jobs didn't leave him much free time, but that this errand was an important one.

Nora Bonesteel turned the metallic blue and gold pot around in her hands, studying the fern patterns embedded in the glazed clay. "It's a fine piece of work," she said. "And I thank you for it. You have the gift for working with clay. But I don't reckon that's what you've come about—just to bring me this."

He blushed. "I came to ask a favor. And so I thought I'd bring this along as a thank-you in advance."

Nora nodded, recognizing the mountain people's fear of being "beholden" to anyone. They hated to be in anyone's debt for even so much as a small kindness. The young man was one of the new people, but his instincts were good: He would fit in well, she thought. She didn't think there'd be any imposing on her from him. He wouldn't want his fortune told. "How can I help you?" she asked.

Haltingly at first, because he realized how foolish it sounded, Ben told the old woman about the caller on the downed plane, and how the searchers were out even now on the mountain trying to locate the wreckage.

Nora Bonesteel said nothing, but her expression told him that she misunderstood the purpose of his visit. Ben knew what she must be thinking. Before he'd left, Mrs. Lafon had warned him about Nora Bonesteel and her way of knowing things.

"I don't want you to locate the plane by... um...any unusual means," he said quickly. He didn't believe in such things, of course, and it would have embarrassed him to watch her try any hocus-pocus. He pictured her with a dousing rod, walking up the mountain with her eyes shut, trying to catch the plane's "vibrations." No. Even if the old woman offered to help with the search, he couldn't allow that. Hurriedly he told her who was in the missing plane, and about the calls to 911, and his own attempt to humor the crash victim by focusing on her quest for a song, so that she could ignore the fact that she might be dying.

He blushed. "It sounds stupid, doesn't it?" he said at last. "I mean, it won't help us find her."

Nora Bonesteel thought about it. "Well, it will occupy her mind, and that may keep her alive until they do find her."

Ben nodded. "That's what I thought—hoped, anyhow. She said it was a song about a girl and a grave. And about going home different. That's all she remembers, but she says it's an old song that used to be sung around here. She gave us three names—people she thought might remember the song. The first one is Garrett McCourry..."

Nora Bonesteel nodded. "He died two years back."

"Carver Jessup. I called him, but he's somewhere in Florida this week, going deep sea fishing with his son-in-law. That leaves you."

She nodded. "I see that."

Ben took a sip of cold coffee and set the mug down again. "Well, I hope you can give me the song, because I have to get to work, and I don't have any more time to look for it." He reached into the pocket of his jacket and pulled out a palm-sized tape recorder. "She sang a line of it over the phone last night, and I taped that much onto here so you could hear it." Ben pressed the play knob, and the faint voice of a woman sang, *"And when she comes back home, she will be changed—oh!"*

Ben leaned back and looked at the old woman triumphantly. "There!" he said. "That's the song we need. So if you could just sing it into here, I'll take it back with me to the office, and play it for her when she calls." When Nora Bonesteel made no reply, he looked uneasy. "You do know the song she's talking about, don't you?"

"No," said Nora Bonesteel. "My family isn't what you'd call musical. I think she just wanted me to help you look for it. Because I know all the old families from around here. I wish you could give me more to go on. That scrap of a tune and a few words isn't much help. Lots of songs have similar words, you know. Tunes, too, if it comes to that."

Ben Hawkins sighed. "I'm out of time," he said. "I have to go in. I'm on duty at eight. If I go tracking down this song all over creation, then I won't be there if she calls nine-one-one again." There was a note of desperation in his voice, frustration that something that had seemed like an easy task had now become so complex and time-consuming. He was ready to call it quits. He wanted it to be someone else's problem.

"You go on back to your office then," Nora Bonesteel told him. "Let me look for the song for you. I'm too old to go traipsing up the moun-

256

tain with the search party, but I'd like to do something to help out, so I'll try to track down this song. She mentioned Garrett McCourry and Carver Jessup. That tells me where to start asking. They were second cousins through their mothers. Let me see what I can do. If I find it, I'll come down to Hamelin and tell you."

Ben thanked her profusely as he hurried to the door, glad to be rid of an obligation he had taken too lightly. Now he could forget all about that song nonsense, and get back to the serious business of manning the emergency phone line.

When the young man had gone, Nora Bonesteel settled back in her chair and stared out the window with a thoughtful expression. This song that Ben Hawkins was looking for was the song that Bonnie Wolfe had forbidden Nora to give to her rival. The old woman wondered if Bonnie Wolfe had known about the plane crash when she issued her command, and whether that would make any difference. She also wondered when Bonnie Wolfe had learned the song.

It took Joe LeDonne a moment to wonder what he was lying on that made his neck itch. Oh, yes, twigs and dry leaves. He had gone out alone on the mountain, but now his head was throbbing and his muscles ached, and he decided to forget the whole thing and go home. He started to get up, so that he could brush the leaves from his clothing, but when he tried, he found that his leg would not move. All this took only a few seconds—the time it took to come to full consciousness. He opened his eyes, saw the wreckage of the fuselage a few feet from his face, and remembered where he was and what had happened. He had tried to fall back clear of the rolling plane, and he had nearly succeeded, but his leg was still pinned beneath the wreckage, trapped between knee and ankle, and he could not work it free.

He peered upward toward the fading light. Above him he could see pewter colored patches of evening sky wreathed in oak branches. Soon it would be cold out on the mountain, but it was still summer, and temperature was the least of his worries, far surpassed by thoughts of gangrene, sepsis, wild animals, and dehydration. There were many ways to die out in the wilderness, and as he raised his head up to survey his predicament, he could not think of one single way to escape. Where was his pack? Had he taken it off when he started to examine the plane? He tried to shrug, feeling as he did so the pull of the straps against his shoulders. He was still wearing the pack, which meant that water, food, and extra clothing for warmth were all within reach—if, in fact, he could manage the gyrations it might take to retrieve anything from behind him while he lay pinned to the ground.

LeDonne wished his head would stop hurting so that he could think more clearly. Surely if only his leg was pinned beneath the metal hulk, he could manage some degree of maneuverability with his upper body. It was just a question of balance, really. If he could get himself up into a sitting position so that his shoulders were not pinned back against the ground, he could ease the straps of the knapsack off his back and retrieve supplies from it. The problem was that the pack itself was heavy, and its weight was making it harder for him to move. If he could manage to sit up, then perhaps from a more upright position he could do something to work his foot free of the wreckage—get a large stick perhaps and try pushing the fuselage away from him. He wasn't sure that he could reach it with his bare hands. His fingertips might touch it, but such tenuous contact would not give him enough force to move a heavy object. The stick idea did not strike him as practical, but at least he was beginning to formulate plans, and once he was upright, something better would surely occur to him.

"Looks to me like you're stuck," said a voice behind him.

Malcolm McCourry—1829, Tir Nan Og

It has been many years since I left my wife, my adopted home, and my law practice in New Jersey. More years than I care to count. I believe that now I have been gone longer than I was ever there, but the memory of it has not left me entirely. Your old men shall dream dreams, as it says in the Book of Joel—I have come to that. Sometimes I can summon from memory the faces of my lost daughters or the sound of a great hymn rising forth to the rafters of the Congregational Church, and I miss those fleeting joys, but even if I had the strength to make the journey north again I would not go back.

Black River sits in my mind unchanged, although I know that in the years since I left it, the village must have grown beyond recognition. The world has moved from one century to the next since my time there, and in one sense the town I knew is gone forever: It ceased to be called Black River back in 1799, and began the new century with the name of Chester. Jane told me this bit of news, gleaned from her letters from her mother, but apart from such impersonal nuggets of information, she says little about the family back in New Jersey. I was told when my daughter Elizabeth died nearly twenty years back. Though she was a grown and married woman by then, settled with her husband Sam Carnes in Mississippi, I found myself mourning the little girl she had been to me all those years ago. Now in my thoughts Elizabeth is no more dead to me than the others I left behind. They live in my memory, unchanged since I saw them last, and that is enough.

I have never asked Jane why she is silent on family matters. Perhaps I am afraid she will tell me. My guess is that either she thinks me not interested in the welfare of those I abandoned, or she hopes that I do care and will be curious enough to go back there to see for myself, or else she is mortified that her wicked father has two families and she thinks it improper to mention the one while I live unrepentant with the other. I think the latter explanation is the most likely one. Poor Jane: Not even the backcountry can take the starch out of her petticoats. She will be a lady or die trying.

She should know by now that I will never return to Rachel and Black River. My life is here in the Carolina mountains now, and of all the lives I have had, I think this one has suited me best.

In far-off Islay I had my kin and my heritage and what joy there is to be found in childhood. Later at the sea I had youth and freedom, and then as a lawyer in New Jersey I had wealth and a respected social position. Here I have none of those things, and yet now I am happiest of all. When I try to put into words what it is that makes me love this place, I feel as if I am under some enchantment—a man who has gone into the fairy hill and lives happily in his illusions, eating earth and ashes for bread and meat without ever knowing the difference.

"The shining folk are in these hills," an old trapper told me once. By the sound of him, he was an Irishman, and I knew at once what he meant, for I had heard those self-same stories in my youth. The Shining Folk, the Seelie Court, the *Daoine Sidhe*—we have many flowery names for them, and we always spoke of them politely, for fear that one might be in earshot, for they are quick to take offense.

The trapper had settled a claim of land near us, and we had got into the way of being friends, on account of both of us being from over the water and remembering the old ways like we did. One gray afternoon he and I were hunting elk together deep in the wooded hills toward Tennessee, and when the cloudburst came, we waited it out under an overhang of rock high above the Cane River. Sitting under the shelter of the ledge, we watched the river swirl over rocks beneath us with a froth like ale. I balanced my musket on my knee and leaned back against the cliff wall, knowing from the curtain of rain that we would be there a good while.

"Have you seen these Shining Ones, then?" I asked him to pass the time.

"I have not," he said. "Nor am I wanting to. But my trading takes me to the Cherokee

Nation now and again, down to their main village of Chota, and there I hear their tales."

"Indian tales? What are they like?"

"Same as ours," he said, glancing behind him as if he feared the rock itself would open at his words. "They tell of a race of little brown-skinned people who live inside the hills. Magic creatures, who have cat eyes, and who dress in fur and feathers, same as folk would say of them back home. The Indians say that sometimes these little people help travelers along, but that they do mischief sometimes, too. My people said the same. Here they call them the Nunnehi."

I felt the rising of the old fear from my childhood days, seeing the stone circle on the hill at Cultoon and fearing that the Fairy Queen would step out and take me with her into the earth, but that had been many years ago, and newer ways had worn down the path of my old beliefs. Now the lawyer in me rose up to cross-examine the witness. "Those are only stories," I told the trapper. "It is not proof. Did you ever meet anyone who had seen them firsthand?"

He shook his head. "People who see them don't come back. They go to live inside the hills in the fairy kingdom—just as they did back over the water. They never grow old."

I mused on that for a while, watching the rain make a waterfall from the overhang of rock.

"It's odd, isn't it?" I said at last. "These mountains have the same look about them as those I knew in Scotland—"

"And some of ours in Ireland," he said.

"—and the people here tell the same stories of wee magic folk living inside the hills. Now, I wonder why that is."

"Well, perhaps because it's true," he said. "Maybe this is where they went, the Shining Folk, when the blessed saint cast them out of Ireland. To the land in the west."

"Well, it is a good story to tell the children," I said. I would have been ashamed to say that I believed his tale, for I had once been both an elder of the church and an officer of the court, but more than once I have caught myself thinking along the same lines, and wondering if there is magic in this place. I had been here more than a decade then, and if anything I felt younger than when I came. The spell would not last forever, of course, for the lines were growing deeper about my mouth, and already my eyes needed a strong light to read by, but to me the Indian summer of my youth was a miracle all the same.

We sat there another half hour or so, smelling wet leaves and sodden earth, and listening to the drumming of the river. When the rainstorm stopped, the afternoon sun came out from behind a dark woolly cloud and cast a rainbow over the farthest mountain, but we did not follow it.

The years have passed peacefully in these unchanging mountains. Sally and I had hardship enough, and our share of mortal sorrow:

cold winters, sick babies, blighted crops, and even now and then the rumor of an Indian raid, but we managed to live through it all, and we never wished ourselves elsewhere. The seasons came and went, and decades slipped by, but I stayed a man in vigorous middle age, on and on. We built a cabin and hacked every foot of farmland out of the woodland. I hunted elk and bear, braved the winters, worked through the blazing summer suns. Sally Lynn and I raised up a brood of fine sons...young James, called after Sally's father, then Malcolm, and Zephaniah after Jane's husband, and last our baby lass Harriet. All grown now.

Just lately I have begun to feel time slipping back into my bones. I am tired again, as I was in Black River, all those years ago, and my eyes fail me except in the strongest sunlight. I do not cut trees anymore or plow the fields. My boys can do that. Now I sit on a log bench on the open porch beside the door, looking out at the green mountains, misty in my vision but beautiful still. It is a good place, and I am content to stay here forever.

I suppose that of the seasons of my life I am now in Indian summer—that time of summer warmth and clarity that comes in late autumn just before the cold death of winter. Perhaps it is all the more precious to me for knowing that my days grow short.

"What are you doing, Gran-dah?"

It is my grandson Eldridge, first child of my namesake Malcolm. He is my first grandchild of my Carolina family, and I find that it is pleasant to have children about again. As a young man in New Jersey I was so busy with my law practice and my business ventures that I had little time for my offspring there, but on the frontier, when I became a farmer, I had time to spend with my brood of sons, and I found that I liked the company of children. They do not judge you by wealth and position, as their elders do.

I know that I will never see the descendants of the New Jersey children, except for those of Jane and Zephaniah. They had a fine family—three boys, one of them named Malcolm in my honor, and five girls, including an inevitable "Rachel," but they are grown and gone. Phebe the youngest of the Horton brood, is nearly twenty now, and none of them have much time to spend with a tired old man. The eldest are all married with children of their own. I've lost count of the great-grandchildren now, and the names confuse me—so many Sarahs and Zephaniahs. The little ones seem to answer to whatever I call them, though. I don't see them often enough to keep them straight, I suppose. Even a short distance is a long journey to one as old as I am, and their visits are few and far between.

Young Eldridge is here often, though, for his father lives just over the ridge, and he seems to like to sit with me instead of being tended to by the womenfolk, so we see a good bit of one another. The lad and I seem to get along well with our shared infirmities—the feebleness of youth and the infirmity of old age give us something in common. Eldridge is two years old now, a big-eyed, solemn child with hair as white as mine, and a quick brain that may lead him either to mischief or greatness. He thinks himself too big to be tended by the women with the little ones, for all that Eldridge himself still wears a lap-baby's sacking dress. He can fetch and carry small things and feed the chickens, but he is not yet allowed out where the axes are being used to split the rails for fencing. "Why, I am just passing the time of day with that butterfly yonder," I told him, and he turned to look where I pointed. We watched a wisp of blue wings dip and soar among the coltsfoot blossoms until a breeze tilted it away from us and bore it aloft toward the pasture.

The boy sat down beside my bench and looked up at me with grave concern. "Butterfly gone."

I nodded. "He has work to get on with, as does everyone except you and me, lad. What shall we talk about now, then?"

He looked up hopefully. "Story?"

I considered it. "I could read to you out of the Bible," I told him.

He shrugged, which I took for a polite decline of my offer. "Play fiddle?"

"I never learned. I could sing you a song, though." He indicated that this plan was acceptable, and crawled into my lap at once. I smoothed his grubby little dress over his wee pudgy knees, and cast about for a song to

267

amuse such a little lad. *"The Frog he went a courtin'. He did ride, umm-hmmm..."*

Eldridge clapped his hands with glee, and when I sang *"He did ride,"* I dandled my leg up and down to shake him as if he were riding a horse. By the last verse he was warbling along, his reedy little voice making quavering circles around the deep notes of my singing.

No sooner were we done with that song than he cried, "Sing Eld'idge 'nother!"

I tried a hymn or two, but the boy didn't take to those, so at last I remembered the old song that had been Jane's favorite. "Shall I sing you one about a ghost, then?" I asked.

He nodded eagerly.

I settled on the tune in my mind—it had been years since I sang it—and I began, *"Upon the hill above the kirk—"*

He tugged on my sleeve. " 'S a kirk?"

"Over the sea where I come from 'tis an old word for church...*above the kirk...at moon rise she did stand / to tend her sheep that Samhain eve, with rowan staff in hand...*"

"A *what* staff?"

"Hush!" I hugged him tighter and whispered, "Let me finish, boy, and then I'll tell you the story behind the song. It's told for true back in Scotland."

For some reason the lad seemed partial to that song, even before he understood the sense of it. After he had the words down, I wondered what Patty, his mother, would think of me teaching a wee bairn a tale of dead people walking out of their graves. If she had to get up with him of a night for his bad dreams, I'd be getting the rough side of her tongue, and no mistake, but in the bright sunshine he seemed happy enough to talk of wandering spirits. Perhaps young Eldridge would grow up to be as brave as he was bright.

It struck me then, looking down at this small red-cheeked descendant of mine, that I would surely not live to see him grown to manhood, and that this one day, this song, might be all that he would ever have to remember me by. Perhaps he would forget even this moment, but I hoped not. A song is a small legacy to leave a grandson, but it must serve, for it is all I have.

We sat there together in the bright July sunshine in companionable silence, until at length little Eldridge said in a drowsy voice, "And do people go home when they die, Grandfather?"

"Some do," I told him, looking out at the haze of mountains in the distance. "Those that are not already there."

August 31, 1829

My dear sister Phebe:

I hope that this letter reaches you before I return home, but as there is no way in or out of this benighted hill country except over steep mountains, who knows how long it takes a letter to wend its way to civilization? Winter must make this place

*well nigh inaccessible. At least it is
summer now, although here it is as cool as
an autumn in Chester, and a cloud bank
hangs forever among the lofty peaks—the*
Smokies, *these mountains are called, and
aptly so.*

*I am writing the somber news to you, in
hopes that you will convey this message
more gently than I might to our mother
and sisters. Our father, old Malcolm, has
died at last. Indeed, he had lost consciousness by the time I arrived, so that I was
not even able to speak with him and offer
him our blessings and our Christian forgiveness for the wrongs he did us. This is
just as well. Such great lies might have
stuck in my throat and choked me. My
only consolation is to compare what he
had here with what he threw away in
Chester.*

*I came to try to understand what he had
done, and to find an end to my bitterness,
but I cannot say that I have had much
success at either endeavor. I saw him
dead, and I felt nothing, nothing at all.
But as I stood there contemplating the
waxen face of a shrunken old man who
was a stranger to me, the thought rose
unbidden to my mind: "Now he cannot
hurt or humiliate us ever again."*

*Let me tell it from the beginning,
though. When the letter came from Magistrate Baker, I opened it with trembling
fingers, half daring to hope that it was a*

message from Father himself, old and feeble and declaring himself ready to come home. But of course it was not. It was only the news that old Malcolm was blind and failing fast, and that I might wish to come to Carolina to make my peace with him. The letter made no mention of Mother. I wonder if the writer knew that "old Malcolm" still had a legal wife back in New Jersey. Anyhow, I thought it my duty to go, and I cheered myself with the thought of seeing our sister Jane and her husband once more. They have prospered in the backcountry, and are a credit to the family. As I was making preparations for the journey, a letter arrived from Jane herself, telling me that Father was poorly, and offering her hospitality to any of us who should wish to make the journey to see him. I went alone, of course, for I would not dream of exposing any lady in our family to the distasteful sight of Father's sinful household. I have resolved to be civil to his concubine, but I would not dream of permitting my mother or sisters to meet her.

I took our own McCourry & Drake stage south from Morristown and across the Delaware by ferry to Easton. I must say that our wagon compares favorably with the rigs I was forced to endure on the other legs of my journey. From Easton, I made my way farther south still on the "Pittsburgh Pike," which took so many

westward during the "Great Migration."
From there I traveled in a succession of
ever smaller and shabbier conveyances,
until at last I reached Morganton, North
Carolina, the county seat of the region
Father settled in. It is a pleasant little
town, quite like Chester with its neat
frame houses, steepled churches, and
thriving inns catering to travelers. Father
might have done well to settle here, for it is
the county town, whose business supports
half a dozen lawyers, but he did not.
Instead he is holed up in a remote mountain cove forty miles to the west of here
where there are no roads to speak of, much
less towns or courthouses. This last forty
miles of my journey would be harder than
all the rest put together.

In Morganton I met briefly with some
fellow attorneys in my quest for maps and
advice on how best to brave the
mountains. Mr. Burgess Gaither, the
young clerk of court, was most helpful to
me, and would have taken me home to
dinner at Belvoir, the plantation
belonging to his father-in-law, but I
begged off, explaining the urgency of my
journey, and he agreed that I could not
spare the time to visit. Dying old men wait
for no one.

I was surprised to find that the name
Malcolm McCourry was not known to the
attorneys of Morganton, for I did think
that Father would practice law in the

backcountry, where learned men are scarce, but apparently he did not. He seems to have shed all vestiges of his former life, as a snake sheds its skin. I was treated kindly and accepted as an equal by the attorneys of Morganton only on account of my own profession of law and my rank of colonel in the militia, and not because of any respect engendered by the name of "McCourry" in these parts. You may be sure that I said very little about the family circumstances that brought me to Carolina.

I found Father's property listed on the Burke County tax books, and with that description of its location I was able to make plans to journey there, a distance of some forty miles. At McIntyre's Tavern I arranged to hire both a horse and a wizened old bear hunter named Honeycutt to guide me up into the hills. There is no stage past Morganton. We set out early the next morning on the Yellow Mountain Road, a drovers' trail for the cattle markets in the east. The state of Tennessee lay only a few miles past our destination of Jack's Creek, which is not a village but merely a geographic designation for the acres surrounding a stream in that upland valley. Honeycutt, who lives in that area himself, put our provisions on a packhorse, along with extra food and blankets in case we should find the family in need of supplies once we got there. Travel is hard here even in summer, and I was glad enough to leave the stifling heat of the plains for the cool mountain fastness. More than once I regretted my decision to come, but death offers us no second chances, and I decided that I would prefer present discomfort to future regret.

It was only on that hot and monotonous trek up into the mountains that I began to wonder what I had come to say. The urgency of the journey had thus far prevented me from concentrating on what would transpire after my arrival. My guide, a hairy and disheveled fellow who smelled of ale and bear grease, was determined to pass the time by making conversation.

"H'it's your daddy that's a-dying, ain't it?" he inquired, mopping his brow with a dirty calico bandana.

"Yes," I said, wondering if I should assume an attitude of grief. "Malcolm McCourry."

"I know old Malcolm," he said, peering at me as if to divine some family resemblance. "He has right many sons up to the home place. Don't none of them favor you, though."

"I am the son of his first marriage," I said repressively, not wishing to explain the matter further. "I have not seen my father in some time, though."

Thirty-five years, to be exact. When Father left Chester, vesting me with his power of attorney, I was only twenty-one years old. Now I am fifty-six, older than Father was when he left, though in truth I do not feel much older than I did then. Fifty-six—and yet I feel none of Father's longing to get away and begin a new life, only a foolish desire to receive his blessing, or his approval; or even his apology, per- haps—anything but this long silence from him that might mean anything.

At twenty-one I had felt strange to be suddenly head of the family, without an illness or a death to make it necessary, though the war had made orphans of many a lad younger than I. My Freeman grandparents were dead, and of course the Scotch McCourry ones over the water we were never to know, so it was left to me to take care of Mother and my sisters, and to see that the family did not fall into poverty and disgrace. I felt that Father trusted me to look after his interests in Chester, and I worked as hard as I could to show that his trust was not misplaced. I suppose I thought of myself like the servant in the Book of St. Matthew who is given ten talents by the master and told to use them wisely, so that when the master returns he can be proud of the servant's industrious- ness. Only for me the "master" never did return, nor did he seem to care if his tal- ents prospered or not.

I did prosper, though, whether he cared about it or not. As we rode along at a *snail's pace up that wilderness road, I found myself numbering my achievements, as if to recite them to Father on his deathbed. I am a civic leader in Chester, and more than once I have been elected to the State Assembly to represent our citizens' interests in government. I am a colonel in the militia, and director of the Morris County Agricultural Society. I own the Crossroads Inn, plots of land along both sides of Main Street and up Hillside, and I am a partner in the stagecoach line that runs from Easton to New York. When General Lafayette returned to America four years ago in July, to receive again the thanks of a grateful new country for his help in the Revolution, I was one of the two Chester men to serve on the committee preparing the parade and banquet in his honor. I dined with Lafayette at Sansay's and had the honor of making his acquaintance.* (Though I was not such a fool about it as my colleague Nathan Cooper, who still greets people to this day by saying, "Shake the hand that shook the hand of the Marquis de Lafayette." What rubbish!)

I am a respected citizen. I married well, did I not? Catherine Brown, whose father owned the tavern and all the land from the Crossroads to the river, is as fine a lady as one could ever hope to meet: well-read, well-spoken, and every inch a gentlewoman. Father could not be bothered to

*come to the wedding, of course. He wrote
that he hoped my bride's wealth and position would bring me joy. I did not reply to
his baiting, nor did I succumb to the temp-
tation to compare my union with his own
adulterous ménage. I didn't suppose I
could make Father understand that I did
not marry Catherine for gain. David
Brown's wealth meant nothing to me. We
did not inherit any of it, anyhow, and we
knew that would be the case all along, for
Catherine had brothers to be provided for,
and we had neither the need nor the expectation of his money. What mattered to us
then, and matters still, is that Catherine
and I are happy together, knowing each
other to be of the same world, not
strangers. We have worked hard for our
prosperity and our position in the township, and we thank God for His blessings
in bestowing it. Our friends are lifelong,
and they can respect us and rely upon us,
as can our children, who will grow up well
educated, rooted in the church of their
forefathers, and rich in their heritage and
community. I will not abandon my town,
my wife, my children, or my church for my
own selfish desires.* "I will fight the good
fight," *as the apostle says.* "I will stay
the course."*

*Perhaps I had journeyed all this way
through the wilderness to hear Father say,
"Well done, thy good and faithful servant," as the Scripture records. I would*

*like to think that he would have said so,
had he been aware of my coming, but in
my heart of hearts, I know that in my
yearning for his approval, I was deceiving
myself. He would have sneered, as he
always did at my achievements, and then
he would have countered my news of the
Lafayette banquet with some tale of a bear
shot or a wrestling match won by one of
his new sons.*

*It took my guide and me a day and a
half of hot and dusty traveling to reach
that part of the wilderness known as Jack's
Creek, and although Honeycutt assured me
several times that Indians had ceased to be
a danger in these parts, I still kept a sharp
watch on the thickets and underbrush
along the trail. By the end of the journey
we had killed three snakes along the path,
and once I saw a black bear peering out at
us from a berry thicket, though it chose not
to attack us. Nevertheless, I saw no
human marauders, so perhaps Honeycutt
was right about the absence of Indians. It
is no less perilous country, though, for
there are wild beasts and snakes, and
fevers aplenty to carry one off to the here-
after. It is a wonder that Father has lasted
to such a great age in this wilderness.
Eighty-eight years of age. Do you suppose
he realized when he went off in 1794 that
barely half his life was over?*

*It was late on a hot, still afternoon when
we reached the McCourry home place in a*

woodland clearing near the creek. Honeycutt helloed the house, to warn the inhabitants of our approach, so that we should not be shot for our troubles. At first I did not realize that it was *the house we had come upon. The rude log and wattle structure was small and squat, with a stone chimney and a chestnut shingled roof, more suited to use as a barn or a smokehouse than a human habitation, I thought. The clearing in which the dwelling stood was flanked by a stand of towering hardwood trees—oak, poplar, and chestnut, I noted as we passed—and three scrawny red cows grazed on the bank of a stony creek. Surely no one has ever felt more a stranger than I did at that place and time. The collar of my linen shirt seemed to tighten about my throat, and I felt that the very shine of my boots mocked the simplicity of this rustic setting. Perhaps I should have outfitted myself in buckskin trousers, like the ones old Honeycutt wore, soft moccasins, and a leather hunting jacket instead of my black broadcloth, but I have never worn such garb, and I would have felt a fool in it. The Bible says:* "Train up a child in the way he should go and he will not depart from it." *"Well, Father," I thought as we neared the cabin, "I was trained up to be a lawyer and a gentleman in an eastern township, not a backcountry farmer. It is too late to change the rules on me now."*

I was advancing toward the house when a gaunt woman appeared on the cabin threshold, shielding her eyes from the sun as she peered out at us. I saw that her hair was iron gray, and she wore a brown dress of coarse homespun material such as servants wear back home. In height she would scarcely have reached my shoulder, though she stood straight, and not stooped and bent as people often do in great age. Her skeletal thinness made her dark eyes and sharp features even more prominent. She continued to stare at us with an expression of fierce pride, or perhaps resentment, and as I hastened forward to allay her fears and introduce myself, I suddenly realized who she was.

This was Sally Lynn.

The concubine.

I must have stopped in my tracks, to stare in openmouthed amazement at this revelation. This...was...Sally Lynn. For years we had gossiped about her and pictured her as a lithe young beauty, tempting my father away from his home and his duty with her feminine wiles. Now, after all my tawdry imaginings, to be confronted with this weather-beaten old woman, rooted me to the spot, unable to utter a word. I stood there thinking: "He left Mother for—this!"

Well, I suppose she must have been pretty once. I reminded myself that thirty-five years had passed since Father began his frontier idyll, and that the shrunken old woman before me had borne many children and weathered many seasons of toil on the farm since then. She had little enough to show for her labors: a few acres in a forest clearing and a dying old man with no worldly goods to leave her. At least she had sons to take care of her in her widowhood.

Suddenly another elderly woman emerged from the cabin. She stood in the shadow of the covered porch and took our measure for a long moment, and then to my amazement she hurried toward me with open arms, calling out my name. "Oh, Benjamin!" she cried, looking up at me with glistening eyes. "You have come at last!"

It was our sister, Jane. She, too, had aged so much that I scarcely would have known her. In my mind, neither she nor Father had ever changed with the passing of the years. Since I never saw them, to me they remained forever as they had looked at our last meeting.

"You are looking well, Jane," I said after a bit, when I trusted myself to speak, and what I said was true. Indeed, she was hale and handsome for her age and situation. Her face is brown and creased from the harsh southern sun, but her clothes are those of a gentlewoman, and she has about her that calm and gracious air of one who has both breeding and material worth.

Zephaniah has done well for himself here in the backcountry. The Hortons always had a good head for business back in Chester, and Zeph has obviously made the most of his talents in his new community. "Unlike Father," *I thought bitterly,* "who did not go west to seek prosperity but to retreat from it."

During the arduous journey upland from Morganton, my guide, old Honeycutt, could find little to say about the McCourrys of Jack's Creek, but he was voluble on the subject of Zephaniah Horton, esquire, who is accounted a man of substance in these parts. For years he has served as a magistrate, and he represented Buncombe County in the state legislature some years back. How strange it is to think of Zephaniah as a man nearing seventy, but he must be, though to me he is still a lean and brown young man, waving good-bye to us all from his saddle horse on the day that he and Jane—and Father—left the village.

Father.

"Well, Jane, I have come," I said, stepping gently back from my sister's embrace. I glanced toward the open door of the cabin, half expecting to see Father scowling at me from the threshold. I realized then that in my mind he was the same age that I am now, and I wondered if I would find any trace of my father in the withered old man on his deathbed.

"I am glad to see you again," she said,

linking my arm in hers and drawing me toward the unpainted lean-to porch. She dabbed at her eyes with the hem of her apron. "You were noble and brave to make the long journey, but, Benjamin, you have come too late. We lost Father this morning."

I thought that I had lost him a long time ago, but I said nothing, and seeing the look on my face, she took a deep breath and hurried on with her news: "Father went peacefully, Benjamin. He was so very old, you see, that he was half out of this world already. He slept most of the last few days, and we could get him to eat almost nothing. His last words, murmured as if in a dream, were something about a turning hawk. 'A turning hawk'—we are all at a loss to know what that means."

"Turning hawk..." I shook my head, examining the phrase in my mind. "Nothing occurs to me."

"No," Jane sighed. "Well, our half brother James—the eldest—says that what Father actually said was, 'Turn Ann's hog,' but that makes no sense to me, either, and there is no one of that name in the family. I thought Father said 'hawk.' Well, perhaps he was dreaming of hunting. It may be that he was wandering in his mind back to other days, and that he had no strength left for words of wisdom or comfort to leave us. Still, he had lived a long, full life, and he was reconciled to

death, I think." She took me by the arm. "You must come and meet his widow now. She is shy with strangers, and she has just gone back inside."

I stiffened and stood my ground. "I know his widow quite well," I said coldly. "I left her in good health back in Chester only a few weeks ago."

Jane shook her head. "No, Benjamin," she said softly. "It is too late for any of that. You must not be so hard on us. Father is dead now, and all the turmoil is over, regardless of the legal points you lawyers are so fond of. Or perhaps you have come in your legal capacity to claim this *as our mother's rightful inheritance?*" She gestured toward the small log house in the clearing, and to the gaggle of bony red cattle ambling across a field of long grass, and I felt ashamed of myself for having said what I did. I shook my head and turned away, too embarrassed to speak.

Jane sighed. "I fear that poor Sally thinks the real reason for your visit is to confiscate her few possessions and to turn her out of the family home."

I looked around me and shuddered at the thought of it. Surely these people could not think that the McCourrys of Chester needed or wanted any of their meager belongings. Why, the sale of their entire goods and property could not keep our family for even a year back in Morris County. I thought of Mother's pale silk

*dresses, the carved walnut parlor furniture
ordered all the way from Philadelphia,
and the soft sheen of the pewter dishes on
the mahogany sideboard. Why, this backcountry widow's mite would not keep my
mother's household in candles.* "Sally
Lynn flatters herself to think that anything she has here is worth taking," *I
thought.*

"I did not come for money or goods," *I
told Jane.* "I came only to see Father one
last time. Perhaps I might be permitted
that?"

"Yes, of course." *She pushed open the
cabin door and motioned for me to follow
her inside.* "We have laid him out in his
coffin next to the fireplace. Malcolm and
Zephaniah built it for him yesterday."

"Zephaniah? *But surely...*"

"I'm Zephaniah," *said a sullen voice
from the darkness.*

*After a few minutes my eyes grew accus-
tomed to the dim light in that windowless
cabin, and I could make out the form of a
dark-haired young man standing at the
head of the coffin. He scowled back at me
with a face that resembled my own, and
an expression that smoldered with fierce
pride. I knew it well: From my mirror, I
knew it well.*

"Zeph was named for my husband,"
*Jane whispered, just as I had reached that
conclusion on my own.* "Benjamin, he is
your youngest brother."

285

I could think of nothing to say to this truculent fellow, except "Sorry that your father has passed away," and I was damned if I'd say that. My half brother seemed equally lost for words, and so we stared at each other with frank curiosity until at last Jane touched my arm and led me toward the wooden casket set up on stools by the dark fireplace. I caught my breath in anticipation and took a few steps closer so that I could see inside.

There he lay—waxen and shrunken, his face as pale as the winding sheet they had wrapped him in, and his eyes closed. His nose seemed more hawklike than I remembered it, and the hands clasped primly on his chest were bony talons. I would not have known him. How odd that I had fought and raged all my life against this frail old creature as if he were a worthy opponent. The loss I felt was not that of a son for his father, but that of a general suddenly bereft of an enemy.

I stood there at a loss, casting about for something to say to this stranger who shared my blood and bone, when he said to me, "We are glad to know you. Would you sit with us a spell? It is the custom in these parts to play and sing in a house where someone has passed on—a wake, they call it. We would be proud to have you join us."

I felt that I could hardly refuse such a gallant invitation from one who had every right to resent me as much as I did him. So I seated myself upon a rough wooden stool a little way from the open coffin, and I listened respectfully while my father's other sons sang and played a fiddle to honor his passing. They played well, and sang better than any of us—a skill that must have come from their mother's side, I thought. More than once they asked me to sing with them, but I am not much of a singer, and besides I scarcely knew their tunes—rough, mournful songs whose melodies would not stay in my head once the notes had died away. One of the airs seemed a bit familiar—something about a shepherd girl in a churchyard. I fancy I have heard it somewhere, but it is a rough Irish tune, and I did not care to charge it to memory.

Well, I have gone on at too great a length in giving you my account of our father's passing, but I have little to do while waiting for the stage to take me away again, and I thought I would record these thoughts while they were still fresh. I trust that you are all in good health and that I shall soon be back in civilization and will see you thereupon.

Your devoted brother,
Benjamin McCourry

Chapter Eight

After Ben Hawkins had gone, Nora Bonesteel sat for a long time at her kitchen table, lost in thought. *How do you go about finding a song?* she thought. Music was not one of the gifts her family had been given. They were skilled in other ways. Nora could look at a Wake County homemade quilt and tell which local woman had made it by the pattern and by taking a close look at the stitching. She could see the ruins of an old log cabin out in an abandoned field and tell you by the architecture whether the settlers who built it had been English, Irish, or German. But music was a closed book to her. She could not play an instrument, and the nuances of mode and tone eluded her. She liked listening to music well enough, but she heard a song as a whole, without being able to analyze the sum of its parts. Where do you look for a song? Ask a musician.

After she had consulted the family Bible, and thought some more about the problem posed by the scrap of an old song, she changed into her walking shoes and left the house. She had put on her woolen shawl, for although the day was fine, she was old, and she still felt a bit of a chill in the air. Fall was apt to arrive suddenly and without warning in the Tennessee mountains. Already the slant of the light and patches of brown locust trees on the ridges heralded the coming of autumn. Nights would be cold soon. The searchers needed to bring that woman off the mountain before another night had passed, but she could not help them with that. She wasn't sure she could help with the song, either, but she thought it might be her duty to try.

Nora Bonesteel walked down the winding road that snaked its way down Ashe Mountain, overlooking green and gold vistas of field and forest in the valley below. Yellow wildflowers, growing on stalks nearly as tall as she was, fringed the road, and dark butterflies with a dot of cobalt blue on each wing danced among the purple thistles. As Nora walked, she hummed the bit of tune to Lark McCourry's song so that she could keep it fixed in her mind, and she thought about the dying summer. Somehow the song fit that mood of loss, and it seemed apt to her that the song should be remembered and sung in the waning days of August. She knew that there was more to finding the song than satisfying the whim of a famous folksinger: The song has been buried too long. It needed to be brought to life again. At this thought, she wondered with an uncharacteristic trace of uneasiness what Bonnie Wolfe could do about it.

Why did they want the old songs anyway? she wondered. She didn't think it had anything to do with making money from the recording, for she didn't suppose it would amount to much. People wrote ten thousand new songs every year, and some of them sounded just as ancient as the traditional tunes. Why set such a store by one old, lost song? She supposed that it was a touchstone with the past—a remembrance of all the singers who had ever kept a story alive on the strength of their music, and that singing the ballad was a chance to join that chain of voices stretching all the way back to across the ocean, to the place where the families began. Or perhaps it was simpler than that. Humans had a desire to own things, even things they couldn't really take possession of. In her mail-order catalogues Nora had read about a company that sold stars. You sent them a check and they'd send you back a certificate and a star chart, telling you which one of the pinpricks in the vast night sky had just been named after you, so that for one instant of the star's billion-year existence, a self-important little primate on a small planet could strut about and say he "owned" it. If people could try to buy stars, then they might easily come to think they could own a song they didn't write. She didn't suppose it mattered any to the song, though, nor to the people who did fashion it long ago. Songs were like seeds: They wanted to be scattered so that things would grow far from where they started. They didn't care who took them where, or why.

Less than a mile down the ridge from her own white frame house, Nora came to her destination: the log cabin home of her nearest neighbor, Virgil Swift. In a few more decades, the cabin might weather enough to be mistaken for an authentic pioneer dwelling—Virgil hoped so—but now its newly hewn logs, set in white chinking that still gleamed in the sun, proclaimed the structure to be of recent vintage. Virgil Swift had built it himself five years back, with some help from the local sawmill for the plank floors, and with heavy machinery brought in to level the site, and dig the well and the septic system, but he had felled the trees himself. Working the weekends and holidays he could spare from his job in a Research Triangle biopharmaceutical lab, Virgil Swift had built most of the cabin with his own hands. The house had modern plumbing, enough electricity to power a backup generator and a state-of-the-art computer system, and a two-hundred-channel satellite television, but to look at it from the outside, one might think it was a relic from the days of the early settlers. No vestige of the current century was allowed to show: Virgil was adamant about that. He even parked his Volvo in a shed in the back so as not to spoil the illusion.

Two years back, Virgil and his stock portfolio had left the humidity and the traffic jams of Raleigh and retired to the ridge on Ashe Mountain, where he began his second career. Using his hard-won skills in woodworking, he fashioned custom-made dulcimers and fiddles by hand. With no advertisement except word of mouth, Virgil now had an eighteen-month backlog of orders for his instruments, and his list of customers sounded like the ballot for the Country Music Awards. Signed press kit photos with inscriptions like "Love from

Naomi" and "Your are my Sunshine—Allison" dotted the walls of his workshop out back.

Besides making instruments, Virgil also made music whenever he had the opportunity, although by mountain standards he wasn't much good at it. It wasn't from ignorance or from lack of trying. Virgil knew all the music theory you could get out of a book, and he'd just as soon talk music as play it. He always practiced diligently, and every summer he took a week off to study playing technique in classes at Hindman or Brasstown. Virgil was as good a musician as you could will yourself to be, if you hadn't been born with talent coming out your fingertips. Folks said that Virgil played well enough for backyard jamborees, but that his true gift was in making the instruments, not playing them: The dulcimers and fiddles and psalteries he carved out of native walnut and cherry wood were second to none.

Nora Bonesteel was a few feet shy of the front porch when the door was flung open, and Virgil Swift himself hurried out, waving a garden catalogue, and calling out, "I found it!"

Nora Bonesteel smiled, ambled over to the oak bench next to the door, and patted the space beside her for him to join her. "Well, let me have a look," she said. "The light's better out here."

"Page thirty-two," he said, flipping the pages. "Green-fringed orchid. Isn't it beautiful? Well, not beautiful, I suppose. The blooms and the leaves are all green, so it isn't what you'd call a showy specimen, but, boy, is it rare! And now I can get one to plant here in the yard. I was thinking about putting it over there under the mountain ash. See where the Dutchman's Pipe vine is growing up the oak's trunk? To the right of that. The Dutchman's Pipe is doing well, by the way. The mailman left it in my box in a plastic bag last month. Said he'd noticed all the gardening catalogues I get, and he figured I might want one of his old vines... So what do you think of this one?"

Nora Bonesteel sighed and closed the catalogue. "Well, it's a fine plant, Virgil," she said gently, "but you know the point of having a yard filled with all native plants is that they're supposed to grow here naturally. It's supposed to be easy to let the natural plants take over your yard, because you won't have to work so hard to keep them alive. I have a notion that the pioneers would just fall on the floor at the thought of you spending that amount of money on something that most of the world considers a weed."

He grinned. "I know it, Nora, but don't begrudge the nursery people here their money. You have no idea how expensive it is to conjure up the past. I had to root out all the timothy grass and the kudzu and the ditch lilies and all the rest of those little green foreigners that had moved in over the years, and I installed a water filter to make sure that what I was drinking was as pure as what the pioneers took for granted. I'm telling you: Alice in Wonderland had it right when she said it takes all the running you can do just to stay in the same place. The past doesn't come cheap."

"Sometimes it doesn't come at all," said Nora. "That's what I came to talk to you about."

Dr. Anne McNeill let out a sigh of exasperation. "All right," she said. "I've been puzzling over it all morning. I have to know. *What* is a cosmic possum? And don't tell me I am, and leave it at that, because I'll...I'll throw leaves at you!"

Anne McNeill and Baird Christopher had been searching for more than two hours through the woods and underbrush on the mountain. By nine the sun had broken through the morning mists so that picking their way through briar thickets and moving fallen branches out of their path had become a hot and sweaty proposition. Finally the strain of looking for a scrap of color or a glint of metal that wasn't there, coupled with the need to watch for sunning copperheads and dodge wasps, had taken its toll on their nerves. In order to keep up their spirits for the long hours of tedium ahead, they had agreed on a ten-minute break, long enough to eat a granola bar and drink some water.

Baird Christopher took a swig of his Evian, set the bottle down, and smiled. "*The Cosmic Possum!* It's a wonderful term, isn't it? I didn't think it up. Jane Hicks, who is a poet over in east Tennessee, is the one who coined the term. Me, I just latched on to it, the way you do when you hear the truth spoken in perfect eloquence. What is a cosmic possum? Well, according to the definition of Jane Hicks herself, it's the child who was born to the first generation out of the holler or off the ridge. Grew up in touch with those past generations who settled these mountains. As a young'un, the Possum learned the old songs, the old stories, knew how to hand-tie tobacco and kill hogs, but he did not live in that world. Grew up in town. Went to college. Now the Possum is a grown-up citizen of the world. He may eat penne pasta instead of fatback and vacation in Aruba instead of Gatlinburg; he has a stockbroker and a cell phone, but he can still tell you how to make poke salad. He lives in the modern world, but he knows what has been lost."

Anne McNeill looked thoughtful. "My grandparents had a farm near Burnsville," she said softly. "I used to spend a week there in the summers."

Baird nodded. "Yancey County. Know it well," he said.

"What about you? Did you come back to the mountains in search of a simpler life?"

He laughed. "*Simpler?* When I lived in Manhattan I had no car, I ate out all the time; the building maintenance people took care of all the repairs; and I had the luxury of ignoring ninety-nine percent of all the people I met every day, knowing that they neither knew nor cared who I was, and that my life did not intertwine with theirs in any way. That was the simple life. Living in a village is *hard*."

"Well, I meant...there's no traffic jams, or crime, or long lines of people. It's peaceful here."

"I'd be here even if it wasn't peaceful," said Baird. "I belong here in these mountains. Never felt at home anywhere else. Oh, I did my share of traveling, and loved every minute of it. But sooner or later, after a week or a month...I'd find myself searching the horizon of wherever I was, looking for the curve of mountains in the distance. And if I didn't find them, I'd start to get restless, just an uneasy feeling, the sort a claustrophobic might get in a waiting room with the door shut. Finally I gave up fighting my nature and came back. Gave myself up to the call of the bloodline, I guess you could say. But I gave it a good run while I was out there. Been on every continent except Antarctica."

"And you don't travel anymore?"

He shrugged. "Nothing much. London in January for the sales and to catch a show or two. And I try to volunteer a week or two a year at an archaeological dig of Inca ruins in southern Ecuador—friend of mine is short on grant money, and needs help with the excavation work. And then every other year, I go to see old running buddies in New Zealand, or else they'll meet me somewhere, like Virgin Gorda. Here and there. Just short jaunts, you know, when I can get away. The

Cosmic Possum takes up most of my time. So my traveling these days is nothing to speak of."

"Nothing to speak of." Anne McNeill sighed and shook her head. "Do the guests at your hostel ever mistake you for a local?"

"Well, I am a local," said Baird. "I'm not even unusual in these parts nowadays. If the tourists come here looking for an 1895 hillbilly, then they're the ones who are backward, and that's their problem. Lord, there's nothing more provincial than city people. I had one the other day trying to tell me about Pilates. It was all I could do to keep a straight face."

"Are you in the class at the community center?" asked Anne. "I've been meaning to sign up."

"It's done wonders for me," said Baird. "You haven't had to carry me off this mountain, have you?" He stood up and stretched. "Now, I think we'd better get back to hunting for this plane. This heat won't make it any easier for somebody trapped inside a wreck."

Virgil Swift sat on a hickory stool in his sunny kitchen, bent over his dulcimer with an expression of rapt concentration. He plucked a single note, listened until the echoes died away into silence, and then tried a different one. "You want me to help you find a lost song," he said again to Nora Bonesteel. "But...don't you just *know*?" Usually Virgil would be too courteous to refer to his neighbor having the

Sight, but her request had so bewildered him that he spoke without thinking.

Nora Bonesteel frowned at him. Then she sighed. "I *don't* know," she told him. "The Sight doesn't work like that. The best way to understand it is to think of someone tuning a radio at night: Sometimes you can get far-off stations that you never thought you'd hear, and sometimes you get nothing at all but static. You can't control your reception, though. You just have to take what is given."

Virgil Swift shook his head. "All right. I'll do what I can with it. Sing it again."

"I never was much of a singer," Nora said. "And my pipes haven't improved with age."

Virgil nodded. "You'll do fine," he said. "Sing the line again and I'll play it back to you. Just tell me if the note you hear me play sounds like the one that's in your head."

She took a deep breath and began again. *"And when she comes back home, she will be chang-ed—oh!"*

"Changed—oh," Virgil muttered to himself. "Archaic phrasing. Hmmm." He plucked another string. "That's all you have? Just that one line?"

"That's all. Apparently, it's an old song that existed around here sometime in the last fifty years or so. Lark McCourry must have heard it once when she was a child—sung by some men with musical instruments out on a covered porch."

"Can't she ask her father then? If it was some of his people, he'd be likely to know."

"No," said Nora Bonesteel. "John Walker never was much interested in music. Never played an instrument, and didn't have the voice for singing in public. He's a fine man in some ways, but he's likely to tell folks that he taught Lark all the songs she knows so that he can get a little gilt off the gingerbread of her fame. Truth is, though, she never learned her music at home. We need to know where she picked up this one."

"The fragment you have is not much to go on. Let me sing it back to you." He suited his action to his words, plucking notes on the dulcimer to punctuate the tune. "Is that it?"

"Yes."

"All right. Well, I can tell you the mode. Hear those intervals? The flattened third and sixth. That's how I know. Aeolian: minor scale, Shady Grove tuning." Seeing her blank look, he smiled. "Well, never mind. This bit of tune is written in a minor mode called Aeolian—the word comes form the Greek for wind."

"It's a sorrowful sound," Nora agreed.

"The wind mode... Here it puts me in mind of lambs in an open pasture in late winter, huddled together, trying to shelter from the cold. It's that minor key mournfulness you're hearing. Is it an old song? Well, that's a tough call. You know people have been collecting songs from these mountains for close to a hundred years now. We're supposed to be the last repository of English ballads. You've heard of Cecil Sharp?"

"Yes. He was an Englishman. He came collecting in my grandmother's time."

"Right. *Folk Songs of the Southern Appalachians.* Coauthored with Olive Dame Campbell. Putnam. 1917. Two hundred and fifty bucks if you're lucky enough to find one. I have one here. Let me look in my ballad books while you make us a pot of tea. Maybe one of the collectors found this song and put it in his book."

Half an hour later, Nora Bonesteel sat at the kitchen counter sipping green tea out of a craft fair mug, while Virgil sat on the floor surrounded by a pile of well-worn books that were bristling with page markers. "Well, if that song was up here, the ballad collectors didn't get it," he announced. "I have gone through Sharp, Niles, Lomax, Ritchie, Betty Smith, Lunsford, and a dozen more—basically, the dream team of musicologists, and nobody has any song that fits your description. So if the thing does exist, and if it is an authentic old ballad, it would be quite a find."

"Valuable?"

"Well, maybe, if you were wanting a topic for an article for the *Journal of Popular Culture* or *Sing out!* Or some scholarly publication. I mean, it would look good on your charge sheet for a tenured professorship, but outside of that, I can't see any money in it. That's not to say that some of the later collectors didn't make money off these songs."

"Did they?"

"Oh, yes. I think of it as intellectual strip mining. A collector would come into the mountains, interview all the old-timers and get them to sing for him. Then he'd write the songs down, take them away, and copyright them. That means that any time somebody sings one of those songs, they have to pay the fellow who holds the copyright."

"But the collector didn't write the song."

"Doesn't matter. As far as the law is concerned, whoever copyrights the song owns it."

"Selling stars," said Nora Bonesteel.

"What was that?"

"Never mind. Go on."

"Well, that's about it, really. Except that it stinks. Imagine: Eighty years ago your great-grandmother sings a song for a ballad collector—doesn't get a dime for it. You learn the old song from your grandmother who learned it from hers—family song, been in the family for two hundred years—and when you go to make a recording of it, they tell you that *you* have to pay the ballad collector a royalty in order to sing *your* family's song. A song that your family gave the ballad collector for free."

The old woman shook her head. "It doesn't seem right, Virgil."

"Well, I know. It's the law, but it ain't justice. And it isn't helping us find your old song."

"If it *is* an old song."

"Good point. That brings us back to the

granddaddy of the collectors, Cecil Sharp, who incidentally was a decent fellow and not out to make a killing by music rustling. He claimed that authentically old songs will conform to the Pentatonic scale. You're probably wondering if this one does."

Nora Bonesteel smiled. "Well, Virgil, I might, if I'd ever heard of a such a thing." The trouble with asking Virgil Swift a music question was that he got so carried away with the subject that he told you lots of things you never wanted to know, explaining all the difficult parts in terms that didn't help much toward understanding it, and finally he digressed so much that he was likely to forget the original question.

"The Pentatonic Scale?" Virgil's eyes lit up, and he took a deep breath to launch himself into lecture mode. "It's a scale containing only five notes instead of the usual seven. The way I explain it is to tell people to go to the piano and play only the black keys. You know: C-sharp, D-sharp, F-sharp, G-sharp, A-sharp. A lot of the old Scots-Irish ballads conform to that scale. The only problem is that I don't have enough of the tune here to make that call. Anyhow, I'm not sure I agree with Sharp about that test for authenticity."

The old woman sighed. "But, Virgil—"

"Now, I know what you're thinking!" cried Virgil, and his visitor nearly laughed, because never in his life had Virgil Swift had any idea what another human being was thinking. He plunged on into his obsession, wanting nothing more than an attentive audience. "You're thinking that songs change, and you're exactly right. A folk song might have come to this country centuries ago in a simple Pentatonic scale form, but after people sang it for a few decades, they'd start filling in the gaps between those notes, sort of flattening out the tune so that it would sound like the sort of music they liked to hear. Normalizing the sound, you might say. Songs had to be changed to accommodate our musical instruments, too. People wanted tunes that you could pick out on a guitar or a fiddle. Our musical instruments are not suited for those primitive songs. Except the dulcimer, which is a modal instrument. You can tune a dulcimer to Aeolian or Dorian or whatever. Now, a lot of people just keep their dulcimer tuned to Mixolidian mode—old folks call it *Old Joe Clark* tuning because it's got a flattened seventh note. Nowadays they put an extra fret on the dulcimer so that it can have a major scale. Some people get in that tuning and just leave it there, but I call that just plain indolence."

Nora Bonesteel's head was spinning with unfamiliar words and concepts, and Virgil seemed poised to hold forth again. Before he could plunge deeper into this unenlightening explanation, Nora Bonesteel said, "Virgil, just hold on. Will any of what you just said help me track down this song?"

He opened his mouth and closed it again. After a few moments of silence, he said sadly, "Well, no. Probably not. Most of the musicians around here just do things by instinct, and they don't bother with theory. But it *is* interesting."

"I just wanted to know if you'd ever heard anybody singing that song before. Does it sound familiar?"

Virgil Swift closed his eyes and hummed the tune, nodding his head in time to the rhythm. After a few moments, he opened his eyes and sighed. "No," he said. "It's a nice tune, and I could compare it to some other Aeolian pieces they play around here, but—no. I've never heard anybody sing this one."

"How would you go about finding that song, then?"

"Well, the words are in English, and since most of the early settlers up here came from Scotland or the north of England, I'd say the song comes from there as well, but that doesn't help much, does it?"

"No. Not when everybody has the same heritage."

"Well, all the old families around here have the same heritage, pretty much, don't they? I mean, if you go back two hundred years, don't you find the same twenty families or so?"

Nora Bonesteel looked thoughtful. "That's so," she said. "The Arrowoods. The Honeycutts. The Millers. The Banners. Yes, I see what you mean. So, to find someone else who knows a local song, you must learn which family brought the song over from England, and then follow it through the kinfolks."

"I suppose you could," said Virgil. He wrinkled his nose. "But that's not music. That's just genealogy."

"Well, I reckon I can do that," said Nora Bonesteel. "I have one more thing to go on. Bonnie Wolfe had that song."

"No," said Virgil. "I have every album she ever made, and there's nothing like that on any of them."

Nora Bonesteel was silent for a moment. Then she said, "I didn't say she had recorded the song. I said she *knew* it."

"But how would you— Oh. *Oh*. Bonnie Wolfe. Oh, my god. But she's..."

"Yes." The old woman stood up and set her mug of herbal tea on Virgil's granite countertop. "I have to go now, Virgil, but I thank you. You've been a great help."

"I have not."

She blushed. "Well, you told me where not to look. That's a help. I'll come back one day next week and help you weed the garden." Her eyes twinkled, and she added, "That is, I'll tell you what is a weed and what isn't."

"Now, that's a silly way to die," the voice said. "To be messing with an old wrecked airplane and get yourself caught under it. *Silly* way to die."

Joe LeDonne strained to see the man who was speaking, but he could not turn his head far enough back to catch a glimpse of him. He struggled to turn his body, but the weight of the plane held him fast. "I'm not going to die," he said hoarsely. "Can you get this thing off me?" He waited for a reply, but there was none.

LeDonne lay back, straining to hear the sound of footsteps receding in the distance, but he heard no sign that anyone was near. The leaves made the back of his neck itch, and he could feel the sweat beading on his forehead, but he lay perfectly still, listening.

I'm hallucinating, he thought. It had happened to him before—a long time ago, also when he was wounded and lying out alone in a wilderness. He had been feverish then, and suffering from blood loss—much worse off than he was now. He had only been out on the mountain for one night, and there didn't seem to be much wrong with him except that he couldn't extricate himself from the wreckage. He saw no blood and felt no throbbing from his trapped leg. He wondered if the delusions meant that he was worse off than he had thought.

Much to his relief, LeDonne did not recognize the voice he thought he had heard. To have his mind conjure up the cries of buddies from that long-ago war would have been more terrible than the prospect of dying. In all the nightmares that he had suffered in the years since combat, the one thing he had always hoped to be spared was images of the men he had seen die. He thought that if he had ever awakened from a battlefield nightmare to see the shattered face of an old friend gazing back at him, he would have put a bullet through his head then and there.

Or else someone really was there.

After a few more moments of sweat and silence, he called out, "Hello! Are you still there?"

"Yes. I'm still here." The voice was nearer now. "No place else to go."

"Where are you? I can't see you. I need help!"

"I can see that." The voice had a wry note to it—not amusement, exactly, but a certain detachment, as if the predicament LeDonne was in was of no particular interest to him, perhaps even of no importance.

LeDonne tried to concentrate on the voice. By the sound of it, the speaker was not a teenager. A hiker, maybe. Somebody who hated cops—no, LeDonne thought, he wasn't in uniform. There was no way this guy could know who he was. He decided to keep talking so that the man wouldn't leave.

"Do you think you could push this thing off my leg?"

"No. I just thought I'd keep you company. Looks like you're going to be here awhile. Thought I'd come say hello. But it *is* a silly way to die. Like the man who was hit by Robert Kennedy's funeral train. I had to laugh. Some people couldn't see the irony of that—getting hit by a funeral train—but I laughed till I cried."

"Look, I can't see you."

"Sure you can. Just have to know how to look, that's all. I'm over here on the wing."

LeDonne raised up on his elbows and managed to catch a glimpse of the wing half hidden in the underbrush. The canopy of leaves above them made the shade so thick that it seemed like twilight here in the clearing. LeDonne wondered if it had been a clearing before the plane crashed there. He thought perhaps it hadn't. In the shadows he could just make out the figure of a slender man in a leather flight jacket, watching him with interest.

"Can you go for help?" asked LeDonne.

The man considered it. "You'd think so, wouldn't you? I mean, *she* left. Of course, she does anything she damn well pleases, always did. Guess you never get over being famous. But I just hang around here. Name's Fred. She calls me Fly-Boy."

So there was someone else. Maybe the other person would be saner than this odd fellow perched on the wing. "When is she coming back?" he asked. His voice was becoming hoarse, he noticed.

"Oh, I don't know. When the spirit moves her, I guess." Fly-Boy seemed to think this remark was extremely funny. He slapped his leg, and nearly rolled off the wing.

Demented, thought LeDonne. *Better keep him talking so he doesn't wander off.* "How long have you been out here, Fred?"

"I dunno. Ever since I crashed this plane into the mountain."

Pinckney McCourry—1865, Hart's Island Prison, New York City

I'm afraid to go home.

That's the pure truth of it.

Now I know there's some old boys in my outfit who ran away, and others who'd press their faces close to the blanket late at night and say their prayers, "wishing for the war to cease," like the song says. Some soldiers I knew were so afraid of dying that they'd look for signs and portents before they'd turn a hand to anything. *Are there crows on the road?* Death is a-waiting round the bend. Hang back. *Did three drops of cold blood fall from your nose?* Then one of your close comrades has seen his last sunrise. *Are the two ends of yonder rainbow touching ground up ahead?* Someone standing now betwixt them is bound to die. Now my great-granddaddy and my brother's namesake, old Malcolm the Irishman, was a great one for seeing omens, they say, but I never set much store by such things. I didn't figure I was important enough for the angels to send me out any warnings when my time was up. Why, I thought I'd be lucky just to get a grave all to myself if I didn't last out the war. Maybe lucky to get a grave at all.

It seems like I've been at war all my life. I was fifteen when it started, but we didn't hardly pay no attention to it back then. "Wait and see what comes of it," my daddy Eldridge would say when people asked him what he thought about it. He said it wasn't any of our business what them rich people in Raleigh did in the way of politics. There weren't two dozen men in the whole of our county who owned so much as one slave. My people sure didn't own any and we didn't buy high-taxed goods from England, either, so we didn't figure we owed anything to them that did. Daddy said he didn't reckon the war would affect us one way or the other, living back up in these hills the way we do.

He was wrong about that, but then so were the rest of the folks in these mountains. We managed to stick it out for nigh on to two years, though. The bureaucrats would send out a call for volunteers, and we'd all make ourselves scarce. It's the nature of mountain folk to wait and be cautious about a new thing. We thought that if we waited, the war might go away or get won quick up in Virginia like folks said it would, but that didn't happen. In the spring of '62, they passed what they called a conscription act, saying that any man between the ages of eighteen and thirty-five had to join the army. Oh, some folks could get out of it: mill workers, college teachers, government men, and those that could afford to pay somebody to go in their stead. That wouldn't save a soul I knew. We knew it would go hard with the families who didn't have men in the war. Some folks were going over the mountain into Tennessee to join up with the Union troops over there, but that would mean leaving the farm and the family to the mercy of the Secessionists, and it seemed to me that war ought to be about protecting your home and family, not seeing it torn up on account of you.

My brother Malcolm and I told Daddy that we'd go serve in the war so that the government would leave the farm alone, and that he could stop off home and keep the place going as best he could with the help of Momma and John, who's only twelve. Daddy was just thirty-five himself, but he was sickly, and we all hoped for the family's sake that they wouldn't take him, too, and they didn't. They said that Malcolm and me volunteering to fight for the Cause was enough—for now.

I was eighteen and Malcolm a year younger when we signed up in March of '62. When it was time to leave, Daddy walked with us down to the settlement where we was to join the other volunteers. By the calendar it was the first day of spring, but it was still a cold, bitter day, and flakes of snow driven by the wind spiraled past us as we made our way down the ridge. When we reached the muddy square where the men were gathered, Daddy shook my hand and wished me Godspeed, telling me to do my duty and make the family proud. Mama had cried so much that morning that she couldn't come with us, but Daddy didn't seem fazed much that I was going. I told him

311

I'd do my level best to be a good soldier, and then I walked on off a ways, intending to go over and talk to John McLaughlin, who was also taking the oath that day. Daddy turned to say good-bye to Malcolm then, and I could hear the break in his voice turn into a sob as he hugged my little brother, wishing him God's protection, and saying how he hated to see Malcolm go. Just Malcolm. Tears for Malcolm; for me only a lecture about doing my duty. I felt like I'd been shot through the heart then, but I never let on that I'd overheard. After that I figured there was nothing the Federals could do to me that would hurt any worse.

They told the both of us that we were now privates in Company C of the 16th North Carolina, and they give us ten dollars apiece for joining up, most of which we left with Daddy so that he could buy food and provisions for the home place. We had brought knapsacks from home with such things as we could think of that a soldier might need to carry with him: a tin cup and plate, socks, a comb, a few pieces of writing paper, and some deer jerky in case we got hungry on the journey.

They sent us off to a camp to train for the war—a couple of weeks we had in North Carolina's east flatlands. There they give us .69-caliber muzzle-loaded Springfield muskets and paper cartridges of powder and shot to keep in leather pouches on our belts. They taught us how to march and all the wherefores of soldiering. They didn't have to teach us how to shoot. Seems like we was born knowing that, but it took awhile to get used to a new weapon.

We had old flintlocks up home for hunting game in the hills, but learning how to shoot in a war is a different matter, because now the quarry is shooting back at you. It takes maybe half a minute to fire off one shot: You take the paper cartridge out of your belt pouch, tear it open with your teeth, and pour the powder and shot, paper and all, down the barrel of the weapon. Then you take the ramrod out of its housing on the underside of the gun barrel and poke the powder down to the bottom of the barrel, stick the ramrod down in the dirt—it takes too long to put it back in the slot—take out a percussion cap and set it on the little peg under the arc of the hammer, cock, and fire. One shot. Just one. Then you must begin again, and while you are fumbling with powder and ramrod and percussion cap, a swarm of enemy soldiers are running at you, shooting their weapons, and you must keep your calm in a storm of smoke and screams and explosions, with bullets flying past you and men falling everywhere you look. Half a minute doesn't sound like a long time to someone sitting peacefully at home, but when you are in the heat of battle, it can seem longer than any hour spent elsewhere. Some men became so flustered that they dropped their shot or the ramrod, and lost even more time. You got used to the kick of the gun quick enough. In training camp you bruised your shoulder, but then your hide toughened up until you hardly noticed it anymore, but one thing I never did get used to was the metal gun barrel heating up after the weapons had been fired two or three times. After you had fired off two or three rounds in quick succession, that barrel would get so hot that you'd burn your fingers trying to aim the weapon. I wrapped a rag around my hand so I could keep on shooting, but the blisters came up all the same.

When the training period was over and summer was on its way, they loaded us up on a train and sent us north into Virginia, where the fighting was. We ended up under the command of a Virginia general, name of A. P. Hill, and he wasn't one to run away from a fight. We hadn't been ten days in the field before we found ourselves pitched into a campaign called the Seven Days Battle, trying to stop McClellan's army. He had sailed his troops down the Potomac into the Chesapeake Bay, landed on the Yorktown Peninsula, and was fixing to sneak up through the swamps and march on Richmond.

That's when I learned the worst part of being an infantryman on the field of battle. It isn't the slow loading of the Springfield, or the noise and smoke, or the gun's kick, or even the red-hot barrel you had to touch to aim. No— the worst part was before the shooting started, when the sergeant doles out your forty rounds of ammunition and you pack it away carefully in the leather cartridge box on your belt. You have forty shots. Forty. To last you the entire battle. Now, there might be five thousand bluecoats running at you in a hail of smoke and shot—but you can only shoot back forty times. And the gun will be too hot to aim before you have done half that much. Each time you fire it, the inside of the barrel gets dirtier from the powder residue, so that sooner or later it will not fire at all unless you clean out the barrel— and all the while bullets whizz past you like wasps in an apple orchard.

After a while you learned to hope that someone near you in the ranks would die early on. Then you could pick up his weapon, and rifle through his belongings for his supply of unused cartridges—anything to buy you a few more minutes of breathing time. Sometimes when we ran out of bullets, we threw rocks at the enemy. It was better than sitting helpless, waiting to be shot: We threw rocks.

If the Angel of Death had walked abroad during the war, he surely would have marched with the 16th North Carolina, for we lived through it all. We endured the Seven Days Battle; tragedy at Chancellorsville; the carnage of Antietam, where the very air turned red; fighting atop corpses in the Wilderness Campaign; a welcome taste of victory and Yankee provisions at Second Manassas; and finally the ragged and useless march to Gettysburg, where so many died.

After Gettysburg, when Lee pulled the army back into North Virginny, most of us figured we had seen all the horror we could stomach—enough to last six lifetimes—and the murmured talk when the officers couldn't hear you was that it was all for nothing anyhow, because we were out of supplies, short on ammunition, stealing shoes off the feet of dead men, and growing weaker from starvation rations. John McLaughlin from up home, who had enlisted the same day as Malcolm and me, had died raving with fever back in January near Fredericksburg. The Confederacy was losing men by the thousand, while the Federals kept their army up to strength by swearing in immigrants right off the boat and sending them into battle. Fighting this war began to feel like trying to dam up a river with just your two hands—you'd drown before you stopped the river. They just kept coming. I was just a corporal in the 16th, so I never understood the big ideas behind the war: why we did what we did or went where we went, and why one hill was so important that a hundred men had to die trying to take it. I just did what they told me, and I tried to keep myself alive so that I could keep on doing it. But the futility of it began to sap everybody's will, not just mine.

In the late summer after Gettysburg, when we were encamped in Virginia, near a town called Culpeper, some of the soldiers began to slip away. It was harvest time back home, and the letters from the womenfolk would make your stomach knot, talking about making coffee out of weeds, feeding the young'uns nothing but dandelion greens and water— watching them waste away. You couldn't blame a man for feeling like he owed his family more than he owed the government, and so when the cries for help came in the mailbag, some of the men lit out for home. Others left because they couldn't stand the war any-more—the nightmares, the shaking hands, and the sudden terrors. My brother Malcolm deserted on August 2. He was on picket duty the night before, and in the darkness after mid-night while the camp settled into sleep, he simply walked away without a word to anyone. They questioned me long and hard after roll call the next morning, wanting to know if I knew he was going, and if I gave him any supplies or aid in deserting, but I told them no. They didn't ask me why he went. It didn't matter. He had been wounded at Seven Pines, back in May of '62, and he spent most of last winter trying to come back from that, with the cold and the meager rations not helping him none. Still, if they caught him they'd shoot him, reasons or no.

I hoped they wouldn't find him. He is my little brother, and I'm kind of in the way of looking out for him, even if I do have to stand in his shadow up home. I didn't reckon Mal-colm left on account of cowardice, but only because he was so sick that he knew he was no use to the army. I figured Mama and John could use help back home on the farm if he made it that far and his strength held out. I knew I would be staying with the army, though. When I joined up, Daddy had told me to do my duty and make the family proud, and I was too stubborn to go back on my word. There would be some consolation in dying, I thought, knowing that I had done it to spite Daddy. He would never say a word against Malcolm for deserting, though. He'd say it was the smart thing to do. But if I had done it, he'd have called me a coward in a heartbeat.

So I went on marching hungry, wrapping rags around my bleeding feet, and keeping warm by the fire in my gut—I was going to show Daddy who the brave one was. I made it to a place called Hatcher's Run. I was captured on the thirty-first of March. The 16th was strung out in skirmishes all the way from Five Forks to Petersburg, and when half the regiment was cut off from our lines and captured, I was one of their number. I had run through my allowance of cartridges, firing until my hands throbbed from burns from the gun barrel, and still the Federals kept coming. Before I could take ammunition off a dead man, we were overrun, and so I laid down my gun and let them take me prisoner. Dying in battle is one thing, but only a damn fool would fight on with an empty weapon.

Later in the prison camp I learned that our commander, General A. P. Hill, had been killed in a skirmish on the road, and I felt better then about my captivity. I had not let the general down. I stayed in the war as long as he did. Now it was over for both of us.

They rounded up all the prisoners in the holding camp at City Point near the coast, and they put us on board a steamer ship to transport us to an official prison camp somewhere up north. The name of the transport steamer was the *Robert E. Lee,* and I thought it queer that the Federals were using a ship with that name, instead of changing it, but perhaps they relished the irony of using it to transport Lee's army as prisoners.

Charlie McPeters, who is also from home and is a sergeant now, was captured same time as me, when his gun barrel clogged up from repeated firing. Before he could clean the barrel or take another weapon off a corpse, he was taken prisoner. We tried to stick together on the march to the ship, sharing our rations and keeping up one another's spirits by talking about home. Sometimes all that keeps me going is the thought that if I let myself die, I'll never see the mountains again.

It took about five days on that great noisy steamer to reach the prison. It was hard to keep track of time. I'd never been on board a ship before, and I don't intend ever to get on one again. The hold where they kept us was a dark, stinking pit filled with the sick and the wounded, and their cries came close to drowning out the thunder of the engine. "I just want to live through this," I told Charlie McPeters. "Because I don't want this to be my last sight on earth."

"Prison will be better than this," he said. But he was wrong.

We knew that the Union had plenty of supplies, and all the food they needed. The war had hardly touched their farms or factories at all. But having and giving is two different things, and whatever they had, they didn't mean to share it with enemy prisoners.

The prison they took us to was just up from the city of New York, a place called Hart's Island, for it was an island, shaped like a pair of eyeglasses: about a mile long and a third again as narrow. It sat at a point where the East River meets a grander spread of water—the ocean, I thought at the time, though Charlie allowed as how there were not waves enough for it to be the ocean. That island might have been a peaceful spot, for there were fields and some woods, and a sandy beach, but the place had become consecrated to misery, and we were not to spend a happy hour on its shores. We were the first prisoners to reach the place, for it had only just been opened to accommodate the hordes of troops taken in the new assault on Richmond.

Our jailers had closed off about four acres on the northern part of Hart's Island, turning it into a hog pen for four thousand men. The barracks held a hundred men each, quartered in three rows of wooden bunks, sleeping two to a bunk, but there was no bedding for it, except the dirty blankets we had brought with us. First the guards stripped and searched us, and took whatever they wanted from our belongings, especially anything that we might make mischief with, like a barlow knife. Then they turned us into the pen to while away the rest of the war.

For a day's rations, they give each of us four

hardtacks, a cup of watery soup, and a small piece of pickled meat—beef or mule. We was used to starving, though, so it didn't make any difference to our bellies. Sometimes I'd just gulp down my day's worth of food to keep the camp thieves from getting it, and then I'd fill my belly with water and wait until the next drawing of provisions. Other men gambled for pieces of hardtack in a game called keno, or else they would swap one of their crackers for a chaw of tobacco. It passed the time, and it was better to smoke or gamble like men than to scrabble around in the cookhouse waste barrels like wild dogs, looking for slop and garbage to fill your gullet. Hunger is a harsh master, though, and if you want to survive you do what you must. We'd gather up old beef bones, grind them against two rocks, and boil them in a kettle of water for hours to make a weak broth—anything to stop the cramping of an empty belly. The weather was wet and cold in April, and the rags we were wearing were not enough to keep us warm, but we tried not to think of the cold and hunger. We told tales to pass the time, or trapped rats for sport. They went into the stew pot along with the beef bones.

One of the Georgia boys had a French harp in his belongings, and he would sit up against the barracks wall and play tunes by the hour. Sometimes a group would gather around him and sing "Aura Lee" or "Barbry Ellen." I didn't sing much, but I liked to listen to the music. Every now and again they'd sing a song I knew from home, and I'd shut my eyes and pretend I was back there on the porch, surrounded by kinfolks. As long as we didn't sing any rebel songs, like "The Bonnie Blue Flag," the guards left us alone.

Three days after we reached Hart's Island, a new shipload of prisoners arrived, men captured in New Bern, North Carolina, they told us. Some of them must have been too sick to fight there at the last, or else they had taken some wasting fever on the boat: Gaunt faces stared out at us through sunken eyes. At the sight of them, Charlie McPeters—I remember to call him "sergeant," mostly—nudged me in the ribs, and, nodding toward the emaciated prisoners staggering toward us, he said, "The Wilderness."

I knew what he meant. Back in east Virginia we had fought twice over mostly the same ground: in '63 at Chancellorsville, when General Jackson was killed in the confusion of the night battle by a soldier from our sister regiment, the 18th North Carolina, and then a year later in an engagement called The Wilderness. If I live to be a hundred, I will still see that stretch of ground before me when I close my eyes, for when we returned to that battlefield to fight again, we found that some of the dead had been left to rot where they had fallen. Perhaps their bodies had been hidden by the thickets, or perhaps the local people were afraid of contagion if they went too near a decaying corpse. Some of the buried soldiers, shoveled quick into shallow graves, had been dug up by wild animals or uncovered by the elements, so that now leg bones jutted up out of the earth, and here and there in the underbrush a white skull grinned at its former comrades in arms. Seeing these walking skeletons in Hart Prison made Charlie and me think of the bones of The Wilderness, except that those poor souls on the battlefield had passed out of their misery, while the poor devils before us suffered still. The sight of the filth and the ragged, starving men sobered us: We knew that they were not likely to get better on the food and doctoring given here. They would not see home again.

They say the war is over, and that Lee has surrendered. We have not been here on Hart's Island for more than two weeks, and since we were used to going hungry it has not taken much getting used to, but now a guard has come along and read us a proclamation that says the war is over. He told us that any man who will take an oath of allegiance to the United States will be paroled and turned out to make his way home. Charlie is my sergeant so I turn to him with this news.

"They lie," he said, spitting in the direction of the barred door.

I thought about it some more. "It might be true," I said. "We was bad off toward the last. Supplies most gone, and losing men we couldn't replace. And General Hill getting killed like he was. It takes its toll."

"It is a trick," said Charlie. "I'll not believe

it until General Lee himself comes and tells me he's licked."

I held my peace then, for it wouldn't have been fitten to be the first soldier to take the oath of allegiance, and I reckon most everybody felt like that, for there was no rush to do it. A few days after that announcement, though, another officer marched in looking sick and angry at the same time. He told us, quietlike, but every word falling like a hot coal, that President Lincoln had been assassinated on the orders of Jefferson Davis, and that when Davis was captured, some of us prisoners would be made to act as the firing squad to execute him for this crime of murder. Before we could ask the officer any questions about this thunder strike of news, he turned on his heel and left, but he told the guards to open fire on any man who cheered or shouted approval of the death of the president. We were all too shocked to react, though. Things were happening too fast for us to take it in.

I found Charlie leaning up against the fence, staring out at the gray sky. "You heard?" I asked him.

He nodded without turning back to look at me.

"They wouldn't lie about a thing like that," I said.

"No. Maybe they'll get mad enough about it to hang us all."

"Or maybe they'll just let us go home. The guards don't want to be here, no more than we do."

I started thinking about going home then, and wondering if Malcolm had made it back from Culpeper, where he deserted, and if he'd ever be the same again after all he'd suffered in the war. Wondering if anything had happened to the farm. There were no great battles fought in the Carolina mountains, not like in Virginia, but there were skirmishes right enough, and plenty of hate to fuel more. Things were bad back home—in some ways maybe worse than in the flatlands where we fought. Charlie and I had talked about what we heard was happening back home, and we were glad we hadn't been there to see it.

In most parts of the country, whatever side you were on, all your friends and neighbors were on that side, too, and so they supported you in the time of trouble and shared your sorrows. But the folks in the mountains never were much on agreeing with anybody about anything, and they were used to acting alone, so they chose up sides according to how they felt about the matter, and they didn't care what the neighbors thought or the preacher or the county officials. That meant that the battle lines went from farm to farm, and neighbor to neighbor. Back home you'd know who stole your horse or shot your father. There'd be harder feelings from that war than from the grand army engagements on the hay fields of Virginia. Back home the war would be personal, and no declaration of peace could make you forgive.

I wondered who would run my home county

now, and whether they would make it hard for those who fought on the wrong side. I wondered if I would go back hating people who had been my neighbors and my schoolmates. I was almost too afraid to go back. I didn't want the war to taint the land I had dreamed of for nigh on to three years of war. Still, I wanted to go back to that place. I ached for the sight of those dark mountains swirling in the mist, and for the smell of pines and clean cold air. I didn't belong anywhere else. I'd find myself humming a scrap of a tune my daddy used to sing about a girl in a graveyard: *"And where she's gone and what she's seen, no human soul can know, / And when she comes back home, she will be changed so."* That was my story all right. I reckon I had seen things that would haunt me all the rest of my days, and I had been changed by them right enough. I had left Yancey County a boy, but I reckoned I was going back an old man, as if each day of the war had lasted a month, for it felt that way to live through them.

On June 17 at Hart's Island our jailers administered the oath of allegiance to all those who had not taken it before, for they were tired of us—ghosts of a war that was two months past—and they wanted us gone so that the war could be consigned to history.

They turned us out of the prison pen, to march us down to the beach where a ship was waiting. I wondered how far it would take us—back to Virginia or just to the mainland so that we could begin a long walk home, and maybe die trying to get there. As we filed out, some of the starving men fell to gathering scraps of moldy bread thrown out by the guards' tents and then to fighting over them, but I swallowed my hunger and walked down to the beach with my head held high, for the mountain was a-waiting, and I meant to go home.

Chapter Nine

John Walker sat propped up in his chair in front of the television, staring at it as if it were on. "I'm not feeling too well this morning, Becky," he whispered.

Becky Tilden nodded. She didn't doubt it. He looked like somebody who ought to be in an oxygen tent. His skin was blue-veined and transparent, and his eyes seemed sunken into hollows, burning out of his face as if they were the only part of him still alive.

"Well, Judge, I can call the rescue squad," she said calmly.

"No. I don't want a bunch of strangers poking and prodding me and calling me John, when they're one fourth my age. No hospital. I'm ready to go, and I'll go right here."

Becky Tilden took the news calmly. To her mind, there was no point in getting upset about the death of a man over eighty. He'd had a long life, and a better one than she was likely to get, and if he was ready to turn loose of it, it wasn't her place to talk him out of it.

"Who was that at the door a little while ago? I thought I heard knocking."

"Just somebody from the trailer court, Judge. Wanting to pick mint in the garden for their iced tea." Becky didn't think it would do any good to tell Judge about the reporters camped out in Hamelin and snooping around the house in hopes of getting a quote from Lark McCourry's daddy for their sob stories. She had sent them packing without any comment. No point in worrying Judge with details about his missing daughter. If he was going to go, let him go peaceful, she thought. It wasn't as if he could do anything to help Lark now, and as much as he hated people, there was no point in tormenting him in his last hours with a bunch of useless strangers fussing over him.

"Can I get you anything, Judge?" She said at last. "Your medicine?"

He tried to shake his head. "No." It was the barest whisper.

Becky nodded. "I'll see to the dishes," she said. She went into the kitchen and began to wash the breakfast dishes that had already been cleaned and were drying in the dish drainer. Methodically, staring out the little window over the sink at the wisps of clouds scudding past, she washed and dried each dish again. Presently, when it had stayed quiet for half an hour, she went back into the den and looked at Judge. His eyes were closed and his mouth hung open a little, as if he were sleeping, but when she leaned close she saw that he did not draw breath.

She stood up. It was over now. Time to telephone the strangers. She wondered if his invisible visitors had returned at the end.

In the 911 office Ben Hawkins was waiting. He had brought granola bars and bottled water to see him through the vigil, because he planned to stay at his desk until the call came in. The regular 911 calls, which were few in number this time of year, were all routed to the other line.

A little before nine, Mrs. Lafon had answered a call and said to him, "Rescue squad call. Not an emergency, patient is already deceased, but I thought you'd like to know. That was John Walker's housekeeper on the line. Lark McCourry's dad just passed away."

Ben took a deep breath while he digested the news. "Shock?"

"Seems not. He's been ill for some time. Are you going to tell her?"

"If she calls? I don't think so. I don't think she needs any more to worry about while she's waiting to be rescued."

Surely she would call again. If she weren't badly injured, a few hours out on a mountain should not prove fatal. There was shock, of course, but Lark McCourry had not sounded like someone in shock. She had sounded like someone inconvenienced. He hoped the batteries on her cell phone would hold out until they found her.

Everybody hoped that would be soon—except possibly the proprietor of Dent's Cafe, who was doing a land-office business in burgers and diet soda since the media came to town. As the searchers had predicted, news of the identity of the crash survivor had leaked out, possibly to the tune of money changing hands, and since it was apparently a slow news week, reporters representing every segment of the media had converged on Hamelin—though most of them were careful to arrange accommodations in Johnson City. A few of the network types ventured no closer than Knoxville, perhaps believing in the inaccessibility of east Tennessee as reported in the 1890 travel guide which most of America seemed to think was the latest word on the state of things in Appalachia. So far Ben had managed to dodge the minicams and the microphones, and he knew that the reporters had been forbidden to enter the building, but they swarmed everywhere else in town, hunting up anybody who had ever sat next to "Linda Walker" in class or had her baby-sit their children once upon a time. The word was that one of the wealthier programs had even chartered a helicopter and intended to conduct their own search, reasoning that the ultimate scoop would be to make the news yourself. Everybody would be glad when the media circus was over.

He hoped no one would mention the fact that

he had spent a few futile hours trying to track down a folk song. That story was just silly enough to get him cornered by a howling pack of journalists, eager to make him into a hopeful lover or a crazed fan, or whatever they thought would make the best copy that week. The fact that he photographed well wouldn't help, either. Pretty people always got more coverage, whether they deserved it or wanted it—or not.

The phone rang and he lunged at it.

"Good morning, Ben," said a weary voice. "I'm still out here on this mountain."

"The search parties have been out all night. Have you heard a helicopter go over?"

"No. Have they got one of those out, too?"

"No. That's one of the television shows. They're hoping to find you first—show all us rubes how it's done, I guess."

She snorted. "With my luck they'll crash on top of me. Listen I can't count on this phone for much longer. It's beeping—"

"I know, and—"

"Don't talk. I have to get this out. When I told you I saw something shortly before we crashed...well, it's rather silly. It may even have been my imagination or just a trick of the light, but if there's a chance it will help. Okay—I saw a turtle."

"A...turtle?"

"Right."

Whatever he had been expecting, it was not this. He discarded the thoughts that ran through his head: that she could see a small animal on the ground, that she was describing a cloud formation, that there was an odd-shaped building...

"It was a field, and there was a brown design cut in the shape of a huge turtle surrounded by ordinary greenery. A turtle. At least it looked that way from the air. I probably imagined it, but I thought I'd tell you. Did you find my song?"

"Well, I found the person you told me to ask, and—hello? Hello?" Ben felt like slamming the earpiece against the desk. The line had gone dead.

A turtle?

He picked up the phone again.

Nora Bonesteel sat at her polished oak table in a circle of lamplight, with the family Bible open in front of her and a scattering of papers and newspaper clippings covering the rest of the table's surface. Beside the Bible lay an old loose-leaf notebook, its pages covered with charts and notations in Nora's graceful italic script. For many years she had kept track of the families in the valleys, faithfully recording the births, the deaths, and who married who. Even in her youth, the young people of Wake County had been moving away, called out of the hills by the war or colleges, or the promise of better jobs in the cities. She knew that someday they or their children would be coming back, perhaps only briefly, but returning to look for the pieces of the puzzle of who they were. Sometimes they came to see her—these well-dressed strangers bearing in their faces the echoes of their bloodline. They would ask her about their roots, and she would always do her best to sort it out for them.

Now she needed to find a connection. She should have thought of this method earlier, but she had been so certain that Virgil Swift with all his skill and musical knowledge would find the song for her, and she had hoped to be spared the necessity of spending hours poring over the fine print of these brittle yellowed pages. On one page she had written "Lark McCourry" and on the facing page was printed the name "Bonnie Wolfe." All she had to do was find the place where the lines crossed—unless, of course, Lark had heard the song at a Sunday school outing or some other event with people who were not kin to her.

She ran her finger down the tree of names: Lark McCourry (Linda Walker), John Walker–Luanne Taylor. Luanne's people were from the other end of North Carolina, though. John had met her during the war and brought her home afterward when he came back to practice law. So it must be on John's side. That made it simpler to follow. John Walker, son of Wesley Walker and Ellender McCourry. She looked up from the page, lost in thought. Ellender McCourry...from over on the North Carolina side of the mountain. The McCourrys...

The knocking startled her so much that she slammed the book. She sat very still and waited, and presently a voice from the front porch called out, "Nora Bonesteel! Hello!"

After another moment of waiting, Nora Bonesteel went to the door and regarded her visitor with a solemn stare. "Hello, Bonnie Wolfe," she said.

The visitor stood a few feet back from the screen door, apparently reluctant to come closer. "Did you know that somebody has spilled sugar all over the threshold to your front door here? You'll have every ant on the mountain traipsing into your house, Miz Bonesteel."

The old woman did not open the screen door. She stood a few inches back from the line of white granules that covered the threshold and stared out at the visitor. "It's salt," she said.

"Salt. I see." Bonnie Wolfe shrugged, and then summoned a smile. "Well, perhaps I won't come in this time. I just wanted to come talk to you again, because something tells me you aren't keeping that promise you made me. You've been trying to hunt that song, haven't you?"

Nora Bonesteel set her jaw. "That song needs to be saved," she said. "I said I wouldn't give it out while there was a chance of you recording it. But there isn't a chance of that, is there?"

The visitor looked away. "Well, I—"

"There isn't much chance of that on account of you being dead, Bonnie. You went in a plane crash on the mountain some twenty years back."

"It's *my* song."

Nora Bonesteel met the cold stare with her own steady gaze. "No," she said. "A song like that belongs to everybody. Not just to you or your family. That song was left to all of us, and I reckon it's up to the living to keep it going. You can't make that song dead just because you are. I reckon it must be a McCourry song, because that's the only common blood I can find between you and Linda Walker. I'll find it. So you go on back to wherever it is you stay, because I can't help you."

Nora Bonesteel took a step back and closed the front door, knowing that when she opened it again her front porch would be empty.

"A turtle?" said Spencer Arrowood. He glanced through the open door of his office to make sure that none of the reporters had followed him over to eavesdrop. They hadn't. They were still sitting in the chairs near Jenna Leigh's desk, talking among themselves, and apparently content to wait for the story to come to them. All they wanted from him was a sound bite, and he would make it as bland as he possibly could. If Lark McCourry were giving a concert in the area, not one of them would be here, but the prospect of her violent death brought them out in force.

"A turtle," said Ben Hawkins. "Some kind of design that can be seen from the air, apparently, like the Nazca lines in South America. From her description, it seems to have been shaped by planting crops in patterns. Does this sound familiar to you?"

Spencer Arrowood grunted. "It sounds like Bluff Mountain," he said. "There's no telling what sort of stunts they'll get up to over there. Crop art. What next?"

"Well, I hope this piece of information helps, because it may be all we have to go on. I don't think she can call in again. The cell phone batteries have given out."

"Okay, Ben." The sheriff was staring at his topographical map of the surrounding mountains. "Let me call North Carolina. Unless they've all gone turtle-happy over there, that little detail should tell us where to look."

The searchers had been tramping through the underbrush for most of the morning, and Baird Christopher could see that after hours of contending with sweat bees and the heat of the late summer sun, his companion was beginning to falter. He supposed it was the tedium more than the physical exertion that was making her weary, so he began to try bits of entertaining conversation to keep her mind occupied while her feet plodded on over the rest of the mountain.

"How would you describe your decorating style?" he demanded as he helped her clamber over the trunk of a fallen oak. "Be creative!"

Dr. Anne McNeill thought about it. "I don't know," she said. "Pier One and Goodwill? I still have a lot of the stuff that was in my apartment while I was going to vet school. They're shabby but perfectly serviceable so I don't throw them away. Besides when you live with two cats, a Lab, and a ferret, there's no point in even *having* a decorating style. What about you?"

Baird smiled. "I call mine: *If the Shakers Had Made It to Santa Fe.*"

"Okay," she said, shrugging, and then suddenly she got it. Rustic Southwest simplicity: white upholstery, coral and turquoise accents—throw pillows maybe. Sand paintings or a Kokopelli statue, and then for the wood pieces, like side tables and chairs: the clean-lined Shaker furniture from back east. It was a perfect picture of a room. "That's pretty good," she said at last. "Did you think it up?"

"Nope, a couple of weekend Trail hikers from Dyersburg, Tennessee, stopped by last fall, and the wife took one look at my living quarters and came out with it. She was dead right, too. After that I started looking at my friends' houses to see if I could come up with as good a summation of their decor. Our minister, who is big into antiques and spends his spare time chasing his Scottish roots—I have christened his style: *The Duke of Argyll had a yard sale*. And my friend Gordon, the cardiologist who impersonates potato farmers, has his house decorated in *Early American Cliché*. He's a mail-order catalogue junkie, is Gordon."

Baird's cell phone rang. He took off his

knapsack and rummaged through the granola bars and rolled-up pairs of socks until he
found it, still ringing, and flipped open the
cover.

"Bluff Mountain Search Team," he said, and
waited to hear what the news was. "A new piece
of information?... Well, what is it?... A
turtle?... What do you mean, a turtle? That's
the most damn fool— Oh, I see. Landscape
art. Hmm... Okay, give me a minute. I have
to figure out which one of the new people
has architecture *and* contour plowing in his
DNA. And a turtle fixation." He thought for
a moment, shutting his eyes while he sifted
through a mental file of local landowners.

Anne McNeill, who couldn't help over-
hearing, tugged at his sleeve. "Turtles?" she
said. "Try Bob Martin. He raises Devon
Closewools."

Baird frowned. "Those are sheep."

"Yes, but when he bought his farm he
changed its name to Turtle Creek. And he did
his own renovations on the barn."

Baird nodded. "Must be. Okay." He turned
back to the phone. "We think we've got it, Steve.
We think that was Bob Martin's field. Can you
have somebody call him to make sure? Bob
Martin. It's a Bluff Mountain exchange. They
must have just flown over that field—coming
from the west, right? I thought so, and they'd
hit a mountain...there!" He had stood up
and extended his arm, index finger pointing
at the line of mountains on the other side of
the valley. "Now I'm pretty certain where to

look. Steve, verify this as fast as you can, and then send the searchers to Bob Martin's farm, and tell them to climb the hill out of his back pasture. Dr. McNeill and I will get there first. We're almost within sight of it."

He ended the call and turned to his search partner. "Now we're getting somewhere!" he said, his eyes sparkling.

Joe LeDonne was alone again on the mountain. He had been alone all along, he told himself, but now he could feel the emptiness of the place. The insects had ceased to swarm near his face, and the birds were still. The pain in his leg was still there, but it seemed to be coming at him from far away. He found himself viewing his situation from the detached point of view of someone who no longer takes his predicament personally. He had done a stupid thing, alone in a wilderness that too many people underestimated, and now he was going to die.

So that was it, he thought. His life, now that he could see an end to it, had suddenly taken on a shape, so that he could put his experiences into perspective. Suddenly he knew the answers to those chatty questions that women always liked to ask. Who was your best friend? What was your favorite Christmas present? The most wonderful vacation you ever took?— Now he knew because all the data was in. There wouldn't be any more friends, or Christmases, or vacations, so he was free to evaluate all the ones he had experienced. *These were my friends...this was my house...this was my happiest moment.* It seemed strange to think that there wouldn't be any more.

He wondered if having time to critique one's life was a blessing. How many people would have wanted to add little footnotes to their grave markers: "I meant to get a better job... I hadn't finished redecorating the place... I would have made it to Paris..." He had once read a news article about people going down in a crashing commercial airliner. For perhaps three minutes before impact, the passengers knew that they were not going to survive. In that slow, terrible descent some of them had scribbled notes to their families to be found when their personal effects were recovered. "I love you. Good-bye." It all seemed to come down to that, in the end.

Should he try to leave a message? He had no paper with him. He was never one for journal keeping. It always made him feel like an exhibitionist to record his deepest thoughts, and then to imagine some stranger reading them. What would he say to Martha, anyhow? *I'm sorry* ought to cover it. It ought to cover everything.

He found himself wishing that Fred-the-Hallucination would reappear. He wasn't afraid of dying, but he didn't want to have a lot of time to think about it.

Anne McNeill and Baird Christopher were taking turns calling, then waiting for the echoes to die away, and listening for a reply. "As soon as the other searchers get here, we have to quit this," Baird remarked. "If we're all up here yelling, we'll never hear the person we're hunting for."

"I don't see why we couldn't spot a plane crash by just looking at the mountain," said Anne, whose feet were beginning to ache.

"Topography," said Baird. "The mountain only looks smooth because it's covered with trees, but all that foliage hides a maze of gullies and ravines and outcroppings of rock. Maybe if it were January we'd have a chance of spotting something amiss—just a chance— but not in late summer. Are you tired? You can turn back if you need to."

"No. If I were stuck in a plane wreck out here, I wouldn't want somebody to give up on me just because they were uncomfortable."

He touched her shoulder. "Look down there—where we just came from. You have to look over those pine trees and between the white oaks. The field down there. See?"

She stood on tiptoe, twisting her body this way and that in an effort to catch a glimpse of the field below. Finally she saw it. "It *does* look like a turtle," she said with awe in her voice. "Or at least like a Navajo pictograph of one. It's huge. How did Bob do that?"

Baird studied the design for a moment. "Well, I think the brown part—the outline of the turtle—is some grass that goes brown earlier than the surrounding vegetation. Like rye, for example. And then he plants something that stays green outside the outline of the turtle. The tricky part was getting his pattern right from ground level while he was doing the planting."

"Wow. Crop art. What a...cosmic possum... thing to do."

"Shhh! I think I heard something."

Anne listened. There was some noise from farther up the mountain, but she could not make it out. "What is it?"

"Singing."

They clambered over roots and through thickets of thorny shrubs, following the sound, which became clearer as they ascended. They picked their way carefully, maintaining silence, so that the voice would lead them on. They were within ten yards of the plane before they could see it. The little prop plane had plunged into the side of the mountain above Bob Martin's farm, shearing off tree branches high up in the oaks, and finally coming to rest in a tangle of rhododendron. It seemed to have hit nose first, and the forward part of the cockpit was crumpled, but the back part of the aircraft seemed completely intact. The passenger had been lucky.

They could hear her plainly now. She was singing "Take My Hand, Precious Lord, Lead Me On," an old gospel hymn far removed from the usual repertoire of a modern folksinger, but a song that she probably had learned as a child in Wake County. Her voice was strong, and she sang as if she thought someone could hear her.

Anne felt tears spring to her eyes. She was all right then. They had come in time.

When they were near enough to speak without shouting, Baird Christopher called out, "Ms. McCourry! Help has arrived."

They heard the singing stop, and then a gasp. And then sobbing.

Zeb McCourry—1882

My Uncle Pinck used to say that there comes a time in a man's life when he either has to go to hell—or Texas. I never could see much point in saying that, though, because with the timber business booming, the mica and copper mines starting to run full tilt, the big hotel bringing in summer folks from the flatlands, and now talk of a railroad coming through the Carolina mountains, it seemed to me like Texas was coming to us.

I wasn't but twelve, so I didn't have much chance of getting hired on with any of these outfits, but there was a feeling like a gold rush in the hills back then and even the young'uns felt it. Cheap liquor and gambling in the mica mines and the logging camps made a Wild West out of the place for sure. I'd go down to the mill to get some cornmeal ground for Aunt Till, and I'd see fellers no more'n five years older than me, a-swaggering around in shiny leather boots and broad-brimmed hats, nickel-plated pistols on their hips, same as the cowpoke fellows we read about in the story papers. I thought it would be a fine thing to get me a hat and boots and a six-shooter, and I asked up home if I might hire out to the loggers or the mining company so that I could earn me some ready money. I even thought about seeing if the Cloudland Hotel up on Roan Mountain might have work for me what with all those out-lander people a-turning up to enjoy a cool mountain summer and needing shoes shined and meals cooked and bedsheets changed. Uncle Pinck told me the farm was as much work as I was going to get just yet, though, and then he sent me out to the pasture to tend the mules.

You might say that those mules are my friends and family, but that's all right by me. They're a fine pair. They'll work all day plowing furrows in the hot sun without balking once, and they come when I call in the morning as if they was puppies. Dolly is a little roan jenny, not much taller than my shoulder at her withers. Her mother was a fine blood mare, and I reckon she's about as smart as a person. The stallion, Stonewall, is a big razor-backed chestnut with hoofs like dinner plates, strong as two oxen. I reckon I could earn my living with them if the railroad ever comes, and if Uncle Pinck would let me hire out with them to haul cross ties, but he says those mules stay on the farm and so do I. I reckon I will have to bide my time awhile yet until I grow up some more, and meanwhile I treat those mules like kinfolks so that when the day comes, I'll know how to work as a team with my animals and make them do their best at my bidding.

I like animals a sight better'n people anyhow. They don't put on false faces nor talk behind your back, nor act your friend one day and turn away the next. You know where you are with beasts. I never could figure people out, and I've just about quit trying. I've been alone most of my life, and lord knows I'm used to it now.

I guess that's what comes of being an orphan. I don't remember my folks. They say my daddy Malcolm—Uncle Pinck's younger brother—came home sick from the War, and that he never was strong again. He fought with the 16th North Carolina Regiment, Confederate, like my Uncle Pinck, who says my daddy was the bravest man in the outfit and led every charge they had, a-carrying the flag and dodging bullets like they was horseflies. My daddy and mama died of the typhoid when I was just a babe in arms, so I was on my own for as long as I can remember. My folks must have had high hopes for me, for they named me "Zebulon," after a governor of North Carolina who had come from these mountains. Maybe they thought that if Zebulon Vance could come out of the hills and make good, why, I might, too. That's all they left me, though: a fancy name and a dream that I might make something of myself to honor them after they were gone. How they thought

I was going to manage that with no money and no prosperous kinfolks to help me along, I do not know. I figure that about all I have going for me is the will to work hard, so that's what I do, but—to conjure with—I reckon I'd rather have Zebulon Vance's bloodlines than his name.

Uncle Pinckney took me to raise after my folks died, so I was mostly brought up by his wife, Aunt Till, on their hardscrabble farm up in Hollow Poplar, which is just a name for the land that lies there in the shadow of Flat Top Mountain. On the other side of Flat Top lies Tennessee. It was a small place, nestled there between the peaks, but it was pretty country and a paradise for boys. I had to work on the farm, but I always had enough to eat, and Pinck and Till were good to me. They'd had a young'un of their own, and of course they set a store by it, but it took sick and died. Having me never made up for the baby that they lost, but I reckon it was kind of Till to keep me at all after my folks died. I wasn't no blood of hers.

That day I rushed through my chores as quick as I could, knowing that my last task of the day was the best one. After I had fed the stock, milked the cow, mucked out the barn, and weeded the corn patch, I was to take the wagon over to Cloudland and deliver to the kitchens there two deer me and Pinck had shot out hunting on Flat Top yesterday evening.

I was mighty partial to hunting. Since I was twelve and most nigh grown, Pinck let me take his second-best hog rifle out, provided

I brought it back clean and didn't waste too many bullets by missing what I aimed at. Pinck always said that hunting on the mountain wasn't really shirking our farm chores, because if we managed to bring down a deer or even a wild turkey, we would have put dinner on the table, and surely that was worth as much as hoeing corn. Sometimes, too, when we had more than we could eat, we would sell an extra deer or a bushel of corn to Cloudland, the hotel up on Roan Mountain, for cash money to spend in the store.

Pinck knew how much I liked taking the road up to the Cloudland, which is why he let me deliver the deer by myself. As you rode along the trace on the way to the Gap and from your vantage point atop the wagon seat you looked out across the hills, all you could see was trees and fields and smoke-like clouds hanging over the valleys. It could be any time at all up here. Once you passed into the cool shadows of the thickets farther up the mountain, where the deer sleep in the daytime, you could no longer see the cabins in the valley, and your mind was free to wander to another time and place.

If I were a young'un still, I could play Indian up here on the mountain, looking to ambush the farms down below, or be Daniel Boone a-fixing to fight them. I could even make believe I was Robin Hood from Mr. Walter Scott's story *Ivanhoe,* for I supposed from reading it that the fields and forests of England looked much the same as the ones here.

One thing I would never play was War Between the States—the one my daddy almost died in. People up here still cry when they talk about that war, with the menfolk going off and never coming back, and the home folks going hungry, with Kirk's Legion a-rampaging through the mountains, killing hogs and stealing horses. No, that was not a game I'd play, even alone. The War was still a fresh wound up here, not scabbed over with enough time, so that no matter which side your people had been on, there were dark tales told about bushwhackers and home guard troops torturing lone women and shooting down old men and young boys just for being on the wrong side.

I've heard Aunt Till tell what happened to a woman whose husband was a Union soldier, but the home guard thought he had come home and was laying out around his farm. So one day they caught his wife and asked her where he was. When she said she didn't know, except he was gone off to war and had not come back, they put her fingers between two close-set rails of a fence post and took turns walking on the top one to make the rail mash down on her fingers and break the bones. When she still didn't tell, they tried to make her little boy talk by forcing him to kill his own dog with an ax on the flagstone in front of the cabin door. You can't tell what you don't know. I think if I had lived back then, I would a sight rather have been a soldier in the army than have stayed home to suffer at the hands of my neighbors.

The soldiers who went off to war seem to have got over it better than the ones who stayed here. I asked Uncle Pinck about that, and he said it was one thing to see your comrades shot by a faceless army, and know that you had shot a few of them to even up the score, but it is a whole other story to have your cows killed and your menfolk shot by people whose names and faces you know. General Lee and U. S. Grant could sign all the truce papers in the world and they couldn't make that kind of war go away.

"Don't you never mention the War up to Cloudland!" Aunt Till had warned me, shaking her finger in my face. "We need the money from selling provisions to them, so don't you talk about it. Especially not to Mr. John Wilder if he's up there, you hear?"

General John T. Wilder was the man who built the Cloudland Hotel about four years back, but he wasn't from around here. He had come south soon after the war was over, and I never heard anybody around here say a word against him. Aunt Till never would call him "General" Wilder, though, in spite of the fact that most everybody else did. Back in the war he had been an officer in the Union Army, and Till never forgot that my Uncle Pinck had been near starved to death in a Union prison and never had regained all his strength. Pinck don't seem to hold a grudge against the Yankees, but Aunt Till won't never forgive or forget.

I hitched Stonewall the mule to the wagon and started off north toward Roan Mountain with the deer carcasses wrapped in wet grass and laid out in the wagon bed. The peak of the Roan wouldn't be more than a couple of miles as the crow flies, but it added up to most of a day's journey when you had to drive a wagon down roads that snaked their way through the valleys, through Carver's Gap, along the Doe Rover, and then up the steep woodland track to where the trees end, and the top of the Roan sprawls out before you like the dome of the world. I was glad of a few hours of breathing room to let summer sink into my skin before it was gone for another year. I had stuck a book in my pocket, too, to read on the slow parts of the journey and also in case I had to wait awhile to see somebody about selling the venison. The preacher had lent me a book by Sir Walter Scott, for I loved to go out into the woods and sit a spell and read when it got too warm for exploring. That Mr. Scott tells a good story, though I would rather have a yarn about Indian fighting out west, but Preacher Barnett does not have any books about that. I reckon I am lucky he didn't give me a book of sermons to pass the time with.

Stonewall was in no hurry on that hot afternoon, so despite the jolting of that old wagon, I must have read fifty pages by the time we rolled up to the summit of Roan Mountain and onto the grounds of the Cloudland Hotel. It's a big place, built out of spruce logs in a T-shape with a low covered front porch and a big chimney on the right side of the building. Almost two dozen rooms accommodate the summer people, who come to stay for a month at a time, getting away from the heat of the flatlands. They arrive three times a week on a hack line built up the mountain from the East Tennessee, Virginia, and Georgia Railroad line, and they spend their time up there drawing pictures of the scenery or a-hunting wildflowers or taking walks in the area. Folks say that the hotel is built astraddle the border between North Carolina and Tennessee, so that you might have dinner in one state and go to sleep in t'other.

I went to the kitchen and told a white-coated fellow there that I had two deer to deliver to the cook, and he told me to leave the carcasses in the wagon and wait around outside while they found somebody to inspect the deer for spoilage and then give me the money for them. I strolled out on the lawn to wait and to stretch my legs before the long drive back.

Roan Mountain isn't like any other mountain in these parts. Instead of being covered with trees, its summit is one long sloping pasture studded with rocks and laurel bushes—what the new people call "rhododendron." The winds can be fierce up here on the bald, so that even as sturdy a structure as the hotel sometimes shakes with the force of it, but you can see for miles all around up here on the summit, and it is as pretty and peaceful a place as you could hope to find.

While I was walking around waiting for my pay and watching a thunderstorm happen over one of the valleys to the east of us, two ladies in white linen dresses caught sight of me and started pointing and exclaiming to one another. "Oh, look, Geneva, it's one of the natives! Isn't he quaint! Let's go and speak to him!" The stout older woman with dark hair piled upon the top of her head like a cow pat marched over to me with her parasol held out in front of her like a broadsword.

I had heard them talking about me, of course, but I pretended that I hadn't heard them, since it wasn't polite to overhear other people's conversations. I steered clear of that parasol, and said politely, "Yes, ma'am, can I help you?"

"Boy! I say...are you a servant here?"

"No'm," I said. "I live over to Hollow Poplar. I'm just a-waiting to get paid for the deer beeves I brung in for the cook."

The lady who spoke to me gave her sallow-faced friend a satisfied look. "There, Geneva, I told you! Such an interesting accent. Rather Irish in cadence, don't you find?"

Geneva nodded and peered at me through her little round spectacles. "They say that the folk up here speak a primitive form of Shakespearean English. Fascinating." Then without waiting for an answer, she rounded on me and demanded: "Say something in your native dialect, boy."

After careful consideration, I said slowly, *"Be wise as thou art cruel: Do not press my tongue-tied patience with too much disdain, lest sorrow lend me words."*

I had meant to warn them off with that, but

they didn't pay a bit of attention to what I meant. They just exclaimed and clapped their hands. "Why, Cora, it's true!" cried the stout one. "I declare—they do speak every bit as quaint as Shakespeare."

Well, that *was* Shakespeare. We had read the sonnets last winter in school, and since I couldn't own the book, I learned off by heart a few of the bits that pleased me most. I didn't like to mention that fact to the ladies, though, for fear of confounding them with their ignorance. If I was to be caught being rude up to Cloudland, Aunt Till would have my hide.

"Oh, I must put this in the journal I am keeping of our travels to the Tennessee highlands! So interesting. Look, boy, would you sit down and talk with us for a bit?" She opened a little reticule hung from her belt and peered inside. "We will give you— Oh, dear, Geneva, what do you think? Is a nickel too much?"

A colored fellow in a white jacket walked by just then carrying a tray of filled glasses, and he must have overheard that, for he gave me a knowing look and then he winked, and I understood him to mean that folks treated him thataway all the livelong day. I smiled back at him, sharing his opinion of the two noisy guests. I didn't see how he stood it all the time, though. Still, I had to wait around for my deer money, so I said to the pair of them, "I'd as lief talk to you ladies as anything, ma'am. And in these parts we don't make folk pay us for talking to them."

That answer delighted them even more, and they led me to one of the little tables set out on the grass near the hotel and sat me down, one on each side of me, and proceeded to pepper me with questions, while the skinny one wrote down some of what I said, misspelling some of the words. I tried to set her straight on that once, but she said she was doing it on purpose so she'd remember how my pronunciation sounded to her.

I told them my name was Zebulon, and they thought that was "quite biblical" so I didn't mention the North Carolina governor who'd had the same name, for fear of disillusioning the ladies. They said they were from Boston, and tried to explain to me where that was, so I let 'em. They seemed to think they were the only people from Boston I was ever likely to meet, and I didn't like to mention Mr. Malloy down at the mica mine who studied engineering at Harvard, nor Miss Adams at the school. I was glad I knew them two and liked 'em both fine, because I wouldn't have wanted to think everybody from Boston was like those two ladies at Cloudland. It's not wise to judge a place by only one person you've met from there, because if I'd have judged Boston going by the questions those ladies asked me about Mitchell County, I'd have thought it was a sorry place indeed. They wanted to know did Pinck marry his sister or his aunt, and did we keep the hogs in the house, and were there bands of robbers on the roads a-waiting to scalp travelers, or would they be safe on a buggy ride down to Bakersville.

Summer people are fanciful.

I told them that we were just ordinary folk, living on a little farm up near the Flat Top Mountain, and that we raised corn and vegetables, and that we went to church same as everybody, but I could tell they didn't believe me.

The big biddy called Cora said, "Rubbish! We have been told differently. Why, a boy we met out walking in the valley yesterday said that his parents drowned all the girl babies that were born to them so that they would have only sons. His name was Carver, I believe. You wrote it down, didn't you, Geneva?"

"Jim Carver, I expect," I said. He has eight sisters. I know wishful thinking when I hear it.

"And he told us that as a baby he was given whiskey instead of milk to make him strong, and that the only milk he ever drank was bear's milk. We gave *him* a dime, didn't we, Geneva?"

Her companion nodded fiercely. "A whole dime."

I reckoned Jim Carver was still laughing fit to kill, and thinking up new tales to try out on the summer people.

"Do you know any music, boy? What was your name again? Ezekiel?"

"Zebulon."

"Yes. Well, we hear that the people up here are quite musical—like the Welsh, and we were interested in hearing some singing. Do you know any traditional songs?"

" 'Adeste Fidelis,' " I said.

"Nonsense," said Cora. "We mean old tunes. We pay a quarter for really good ones."

Well, a quarter. I could buy me a good skinning knife and some bullets with that kind of cash. It seemed easy enough. "Just a song?" I said.

"One we haven't heard before," the older lady warned me.

I was ready to come up with one. We had a couple of false starts. They cut me off on "Barbry Ellen" before I finished the first line, and they knew "John Riley" and "Little Margaret," besides. I was just about to try one of Walter Scott's poems out of *The Lay of the Last Minstrel,* when I thought about one I'd never heard sung by anybody but Pinck—and not often by him. It made him sad to sing, he said. I thought I remembered it, though, so I set off on the first verse:

> *"Upon the hill above the church come*
> *   moon rise she did stand*
> *A-tending sheep that summer eve, a round*
> *   staff in her hand.*
> *And where she's been and what she's seen,*
> *   no living soul may know,*
> *And when she's come back home, she will*
> *   be changed so.*

> *"When midnight came, the hoot owls called, that shepherd girl did hide;*
> *She saw the churchyard dead come out,*
> *   from graves laid open wide.*

And where she's been and what she's seen,
  no living soul may know,
And when she's come back home, she will
  be changed so.

"When all the dead but one returned she
  neared that empty grave,
And 'cross its narrow earthen sides she
  laid her rounded stave,
And where she's been and what she's seen,
  no living soul may know,
And when she's come back home, she will
  be changed so.

" 'Who keeps me from this lonesome grave
  I left this summer night?
I've journeyed to the ocean shore; I left
  there as a bride;
And where I've been and what I've seen,
  no living soul may know,
And when I get back home, I will be
  changed so.' "

I stopped then to see if that tune fit the bill. "Is that a new one to you?"

They nodded. "It is a ghost story, isn't it? Do you believe in ghosts?"

"You asked for a song," I said. There were limits to what a quarter entitled them to. "Did that one suit you?"

The one called Cora was scribbling the words down on a page of her sketchbook. "It's a fine one," she said. "I wonder what the story is behind it."

I told them the part where the ghost lady gives a stone to the shepherd girl so that her son will have the Sight, and right away I regretted it, for I could see them winding up to ask me if I believed in magic stones, but before we could have a set-to about that, a stone-faced gentleman with a white beard approached the table. After bowing to the ladies, he said, "Please pardon this intrusion, dear ladies, but I think this young man was wanting to see someone about the deer in the wagon yonder?"

The ladies bridled and twittered, "Certainly, General Wilder," and then I knowed it was the man himself, and I got up like a shot and found myself standing to attention with my breath held. "You must excuse me, ma'am," I said to the big biddy, "I must be getting back."

"There is no hurry," said the general, fixing the ladies with a pointed stare. Cora blushed and fished a quarter out of her reticule, which she handed over to me with bad grace. The general turned to walk away, and I hurried after him.

"See you don't spend it on drink!" she called after me.

"No, ma'am," I said as we walked away. When we were out of earshot, I thanked the general for fetching me out of there.

"I judged you had suffered enough," he said with a twinkle in his eye. "And I meant to see that you got your combat pay."

I pocketed my quarter. "I'm grateful to you," I said again. "I didn't expect such a kindness from...from..."

He nodded. "From a Yankee? An enemy?"

I nodded, shamefaced, thinking that my trips to the mountain were at an end. "The war's over," I mumbled, thinking that Aunt Till would skin me alive.

General Wilder sighed. "Well, son," he said, "sometimes an enemy can be more use to you than a friend, if he is an honorable man."

Well, that made no sense to me, and he must have seen the bewilderment in my eyes, because he motioned me to sit down on the steps of the kitchen. "If you will indulge an old soldier while he tells a war story, I'll explain what I mean, son," he said. "Do you know about the Green River Bridge?" he asked.

I shook my head. "I don't even know where the river is, sir."

"Well, it's in Kentucky," he said, smiling. "But I was referring to the battle of that name. Back in 1862 I was a newly minted colonel with no military experience. I had owned a foundry in Indiana, and suddenly I found myself in a battle near Mumfordville, Kentucky, and even I could tell that our forces were gravely outnumbered. Now, I understood that my duty was to engage the enemy in battle, but it seemed to me that if I did so, I would only succeed in annihilating my own troops." With a rueful smile he said, "The only thing worse than a Pyrrhic victory is a Pyrrhic defeat."

"Yes, sir," I said, to show I understood the term.

"I didn't know what to do. I needed the counsel of a wiser and more experienced military man, and the only one available to me in that time and place was the commander of the opposing forces."

I stared at him openmouthed, but I think he had forgotten I was there.

"So I set out under a flag of truce to ask for his advice." He sighed. "They thought I was mad. Oh, when I was ushered into the presence of Major General Buckner and told him the nature of my errand, he stared as if he thought I had taken leave of my senses. He would not give me any answer, except to say I had no business asking. But so many lives depended upon me. I...I have always been a *thrifty* man."

"Thrifty..."

"Yes. If I would not waste a penny, still less would I waste lives for no other purpose than to stoke my pride. No. Well, in the end the exasperated Buckner handed me over to his commander, General Braxton Bragg, and I put the question to him. I think he was bemused. Yes, I think he was. He smiled. An enemy asking for advice on the eve of battle. But Bragg was an honorable man. I counted on that."

"What did he do, sir?"

"Why, he walked me out on a precipice and invited me to count the cannons." He smiled at the memory. "He stood there, waiting politely in silence, while I stood there on the hill, pointing my forefinger at cannon after cannon after cannon."

"How many were there?"

"I don't know. I stopped at forty-six. And I knew that my own troops had—ten. Then I knew that if we proceeded with this engagement many—if not most—of my men would surely die. It seemed a useless endeavor. A career soldier might not have thought so, but I did."

"You surrendered?"

He nodded slowly. "Yes, I gave up 4,267 men, 5,000 rifles, and all our supplies. We were taken prisoner—myself included."

"Prisoners!" I shuddered. "My Uncle Pinck was at Hart's Island," I said. "He's never been right since."

He waved away that consideration. "There were no prison camps in '62, son. The army just paroled each man on his word to stay out of the war for six months and sent them all home. I'll warrant most of them were glad enough to go. I could not go, of course. Some of my superiors wished I had. There were many in the high command who deplored what I did at Mumfordville. They left me a prisoner for a few months. But I don't know that I mind that. A lot of men did not die, because I asked an enemy for help—and because Braxton Bragg dealt with me honorably. There are worse ways to make your mark in war."

I nodded, knowing that it was not for me to judge a soldier's decisions. He seemed to come to himself then, and he smiled at me. "It seems I have saved another man from uneven battle today," he said, nodding toward the two ladies at their table near the laurel. "Be more careful in future, won't you? I suppose they think they are your benefactors for having given you a quarter, but judging from what I heard, I do not think they are your friends."

"No, sir," I said. "But I told them the truth, sir. From what I heard, other folks in these parts have been telling them tall tales just to impress them."

General Wilder smiled. "Truth is a virtue against an honorable enemy," he said, "But as for those two old gossips. I see their like quite often here at Cloudland, more's the pity. Son, I'll tell you what I told Jim Carver. It has served him well. When you are dealing with that kind of condescending bigot, you take your text from the book of Matthew. Chapter twenty-five, verse thirty-five. Yes, you do that."

He paid me for the deer then, and I thanked him and headed home. That night before I went to bed I looked up the verse he commended to me for dealing with summer people who think we are savages and pay to hear lies. Verse 35: *"I was a stranger, and you took me in."*

The next summer I made steady pocket money telling flatlanders all about the dragon up on Celo Mountain.

Chapter Ten

"I don't hold with talking to dead people," said the voice.

When Joe LeDonne's eyes opened, he saw a wizened old man in dirty hunting clothes standing before him, hands on hips, wearing an expression of stern disapproval. Another hallucination, LeDonne thought. He decided to ignore it. His trapped ankle throbbed, his back itched, and his hair was matted with leaves and sweat. He probably looked like a derelict gone to ground to die. Not that the hallucination looked much better, he noted.

"No...dead...people. Period. I reckon in today's world that makes me po-li-ti-cal-ly incorrect, being prejudiced against 'em like I am, but there it is," the man went on cheerfully, as if LeDonne were taking part in the conversation. "Name's Rattler. The way I see it, that's the big difference between me and Miss Nora Bonesteel. I reckon she'd forgive anybody anything, being bighearted like she is, and she won't hold a thing like being dead against a poor soul that has come to see her, but I wasn't raised that way, and I'll tell you it just makes my insides cold being around them. So like as not I'll just look right through them until they go away."

"I'm not dead," LeDonne whispered. His voice was no more than a croak now—he had run out of water, and the shouting had taken its toll.

"Shoot, I know you're not dead, son. I'm talking to you, ain't I? Reckon you would'a been if I hadn't come up this mountain hunting you."

"You were looking for me? But nobody knows—" Now he was arguing with the apparition. LeDonne knew he should save his strength.

"*I-have-the-Sight, Cowboy,*" said the old man. "I don't like dead people hanging around, but that's not to say that I'm not bighearted otherwise. Shoot, if I had charged people for all the good I done 'em over the years, I could be sitting pretty. When people come to me for root medicine to ease their aches and pains, why, I charge a dollar or two. A man's got to live. Miss Nora won't take money, but then maybe she don't need much. She don't drink. Anyhow, the both of us help the sick, especially the poor folk what can't afford the clinics, or the city people who've been turned away because there's nothing more can be done for them by the doctoring tribe in Knoxville. Maybe Miss Nora and I even use some of the same tonics and poultices every now and again to minister to the sick, but people don't speak of us in the same breath."

The man had come closer to him now. He knelt down and pressed a water bottle up to LeDonne's lips. The water seemed real enough. He gulped at it so hard, he choked on the second swallow. The scruffy apparition went right on talking through his coughing fit.

"There's other things, too, of course, setting us apart. Nora Bonesteel lives in that paint-smart white house up on Ashe Mountain, and I live in an old tin shack that looks like a tool shed. She's a reader and a churchgoer, but that's small potatoes to my way of thinking. I'll pray for a miracle just as fast as she does when I'm doctoring, and like as not I'll get one, too. And I reckon just as many families owe a loved one's life to me as do to her, not that I keep track of such things. Folks that hold it against me for living in a shack and keeping to myself ain't worth helping nohow, I reckon. They used to take against me because of my Indian blood, but I believe that's considered a cul-tu-ral asset nowadays."

Now he had put his hands on his hips and was mimicking an educated accent. *"That old Rattler! Living in his hovel down by the river. Living on Pepsis and Twinkies. Poor as Job's turkey. What does he know?*

"What do I know? I know a lot. Why, I can tell more by looking at a person's fingernails than them boy doctors in town can divine with all their fancy X-ray machines. I look at the eyes. Smell the breath. Sometimes you can just feel death all around the person. Mostly, though, I look at the light. There's a half circle of light around a person's head, and if you can see that, why you'll know more about the state of that person's body and soul than a whole hospital could find out in a month of testing. If you're one of the ones who can

365

see that light, why you know in an instant whether you ought to fight for the patient or not."

"My foot is caught under the wreckage," LeDonne whispered.

"Yes, I twigged to that," drawled Rattler. He put his face inches away from LeDonne's and peered into his eyes. "You'll make it," he announced. "But I'm not real partial to the company you keep."

LeDonne considered it. Was he objecting to the other hallucination? "Who? Fred the Fly Boy? You know him?"

"No, he wasn't from around here, and since he's been dead about twenty years, I don't care to make his acquaintance."

LeDonne shook his head weakly. "Not dead. I was just...just...talking to him."

"I know. There's no accounting for taste." As Rattler spoke, he walked up and down the length of the plane wreckage, stepping over LeDonne's trapped leg as he went. After a few more minutes' examination he pressed his hands low against the fuselage and pushed. The plane moved slightly, and then came back to rest again on LeDonne's ankle. LeDonne screamed.

"Don't take on about it," said Rattler. "I meant well. Bones must be broken. This isn't a one-man job. I see I'll have to get some help up here. You're in luck, though. There was a plane crash somewhere in these parts and half the county is out hunting it. I'll go find the nearest search party and get them to pry you out."

"A plane crash?" murmured LeDonne. "This one?"

"You are slow on the uptake, boy. I told you: *This* here crate has been a lawn ornament since Mr. Peanut was in the White House. *Another* plane went down a day or so ago, and they're a-hunting it."

"What plane?" As if to clarify his professional interest in the matter, LeDonne added, "I'm a deputy sheriff."

"Well, you know, Hoss, considering the shape you are in, I believe they're just going to have to muddle through on this one without your valuable assistance. I know your boss, by the way. Taught him everything he knows. I'll let him know we found you."

"He doesn't know I'm missing."

Rattler snorted. "More fool you." He picked up LeDonne's knapsack and peered inside. "And no cell phone, neither. Don't they teach you nothin' nowadays?"

"Wanted to be alone."

"Well, you're about to get your wish awhile longer. I'm going to go find one of those Trail bunnies who does have a cell phone and get you some help up here."

LeDonne nodded. He had been holding his breath to stay quiet until the pain subsided. Finally he gasped out, "Get them to bring body bags. There must be bodies in that old wreck."

"Who, Fred? Naw. They got them two off the mountain right after it happened. Him and Bonnie Wolfe. That's whose plane this was. Bonnie Wolfe—the singer? Oh, she's buried in style over near Johnson City, but that don't keep her from meddling in other folks' business still. Some people just don't take being dead *seriously*." He gave LeDonne an appraising look and added, "Then there's other folks who don't take being alive seriously enough. I reckon you're one of them. Now, you stay put while I get the Rescue Rangers."

LeDonne leaned his head back against the leaf-packed earth and closed his eyes. Somehow he had thought that dying alone in the wilderness would be more peaceful than this.

Ben Hawkins stood on the threshold of the hospital room, holding a $5.99 spring bouquet from Kroger's. It had been an afterthought on his drive over, because he had suddenly remembered—perhaps as a scene from an old movie—that one should not go visiting the sick empty-handed. He felt a bit diffident about going: Surely there would be crowds of people—perhaps even famous ones—at her bedside, but Ben felt a responsibility to go himself, because for a few hours he had been her link with life, and he thought that this obligated him to see it through to one perfunctory face-to-face meeting at the finish line, as it were. He told himself that if he walked into that hospital room and saw Garth Brooks or Faith Hill standing there, he could just turn around and run.

She was alone.

In all the scenarios Ben had pictured (*Can*

I get you a chair, Mr. Cash?), he had never envisioned seeing Lark McCourry alone in the hospital room. She was sitting up in bed, wearing the green hospital gown that's guaranteed to make anybody look sick, talking earnestly into the bedside phone. She looked solemn and tired after her ordeal, but otherwise uninjured. There were no tubes or machines hooked up around her, no bandages that he could see. And she was alone. Riotous beribboned flower arrangements, mostly roses and baby's breath, covered every flat surface of furniture, but there were no people in attendance, not even a nurse. He had been afraid that the place would be knee-deep in reporters, but perhaps the hospital had forbidden them to come in. Or maybe visiting hours were over, and he would be seized and dragged from the building. He was backing away when she replaced the receiver, looked up, and saw him.

"I'm Ben," he said quickly, and when she looked blank he added, "I'm not a reporter. I'm from 911. I just came to say I'm glad—well, I'm glad you made it."

"My lifeline," she said, mustering a smile. "I was going to come and thank you."

"Mr. Christopher and Dr. O'Neill deserve the thanks," said Ben. "I just talked on the phone."

She nodded. "You never did find my song, but at least you found me, and I'm grateful. That's the important part."

"Well, it's a good thing you noticed the

369

turtle. That told them where to look. As for the song—I really did try to locate it," he said. He looked around nervously. "I thought this place would be packed."

She nodded. "Phone's been ringing off the hook. And a couple of cameramen sneaked in here and had to be forcibly removed. I told everybody else to stay away, because I'm going back to Nashville tomorrow. They're sending a car for me, and I'll have to give a press conference when I get back. I thought I'd rest tonight instead of socialize."

"Oh, rest. Of course." Ben edged forward holding the flowers in front of him as one might offer a steak to a snarling dog. "Listen, I'm sorry I barged in. I don't mean to bother you. I guess I should have just sent these."

"No. It's all right." She managed a wan smile. "I'm sorry for being so distant. I'm still kind of out of it, and I'm always afraid the next visitor will turn out to be an interviewer. They're relentless. Listen, I'm really grateful for all you did, and I swear I was going to hunt you up to thank you. Take you to dinner, even. You were great. It's just that... It's just that—" She gestured toward the phone. "My father has died."

"Yes," said Ben. "I know. We thought it best not to tell you while you were out there on the mountain. The shock, and all. Well, we thought you had enough to deal with as it was."

She nodded, half listening. "That was the funeral home. The viewing is at seven. He... um...he made all the arrangements himself a couple of months ago. Bought the burial plan, picked out the casket—everything. A do-it-yourself funeral." She made a noise that was probably intended to be a laugh. "I guess I'm lucky I got invited."

"Oh, I expect he wanted to spare you the trouble, with you being so busy—"

"Busy. Yeah, he'd have said that. Ben, what time is it?"

He looked at his watch. "Um...little after six. Would you like me to call a nurse, or—"

She peeled back the covers and climbed out of bed, backing toward the dresser where her clothes were. "Stay right there," she said, holding up a hand, palm out, like a crossing guard. "In fact, could you collect all those cards from the flower arrangements? I'll need to thank them. Then sit down. I'll be out in five minutes."

Ben Hawkins gathered up the assortment of white florist's envelopes, and then he sat. He twirled the bouquet of slightly damp flowers, wondering if he ought to stick them into the water carafe or ring for a nurse, or both. Lark McCourry was not said to be seriously injured, but she was a celebrity, and therefore capricious, and he did not want to be an accessory before the fact to whatever was coming next. Still, he had been ordered to stay. He sat there, watching *The Waltons* on the muted television, and glancing nervously over his shoulder from time to time to see if anyone else was going to turn up—someone who might relieve him of his duty as escort. Anybody. The sheriff. Alan Jackson. Anybody.

She emerged, fully dressed in a dark sheath dress that did not look like a costume, and she seemed a little less pale. With one last glance at the room, she tossed the green hospital gown on the bed and retrieved her purse from the closet. "Ben, I have a wake to go to. Could I put myself further into your debt by bumming a ride to the funeral home?"

Ellender McCourry—1916

I wasn't going to let on that I was scared. I was, though. When the teacher called me out of the schoolroom that morning and said there was a foreign gentleman a-wanting to talk to me, it was all I could do to keep from running right on past her to the open door and lighting out for home.

I was afraid the stranger might want to take me away, now that I had turned fourteen. I had made good grades last year in school—best in the class—and this might be my punishment for getting above myself. I had been singled out.

Maybe the stranger would offer money to my mama and daddy and tell them he could get me a job as a maid at one of the hotels hereabouts that cater to the summer people, or maybe he'd want to take me somewhere out of the hills altogether. They would never take any money for Esther or Zack, but I am the oldest and the plainest of the brood, and I reckon they could spare me, if they thought I was being given honest work and a chance to better myself—if you could call cleaning up after other people "bettering yourself."

Well, I wouldn't go. I never heard of anybody who was glad to leave these mountains, and the ones that do always come back sooner or later. I kept telling myself that: *They always come back*. And sooner or later, so will John. Besides, I'd heard the teacher tell about some girls up in New York who went to work in a big factory, and how the place had caught fire with all the outside doors locked, so the girls just burned up, along with all the factory goods they had been making. After she told us that, I dreamed about them, a multitude of pretty young girls in long white dresses, pounding on the locked door while the flames crept closer and the smoke snuffed out their screams. No, I would not go away from here. They could not make me.

Anyhow I never was much good at talking to strangers. I never know what to say to them, and I don't reckon I'm pretty enough to say nothing at all. I'm skinny and pale and my hair won't curl no matter what I do. So mostly I keep to myself. I reckon the hardest part of school is all the other people. Reading and writing are dead easy. Teacher even said I was good enough to go on to a mission school down in the town after I finished all the grades they had up here, but I don't reckon a girl needs that much schooling unless she wants to be a teacher herself, which I did not. Teaching would be a whole life full of strangers, new pupils every year. I don't ever want to leave the holler, unless Wesley Walker says we have to, if I do end up marrying him one day, like he's planning. And maybe I will, since John Miller went off to lord knows where on the railroad and broke my heart.

Maybe I wouldn't even be here in the school-room if John hadn't lit out, for we had an under-standing—leastways I thought we did. He sat supper with me at the church picnic, and a time or two he'd turn up to walk me home or help me bring the cows in for milking. Sometimes on late summer evenings we'd sit by the river and he'd talk to me like I was a grown girl as old as him, and not just a kid of thirteen. When he took off one day without a word to anybody, I felt like somebody had just buried me in snow until I was too numb to feel anything anymore. I didn't talk about it, of course, because they would have just laughed and said I was a silly young'un, but I minded John leaving most dreadful. I reckon he took off to see something of the world, but he could of at least sent a postcard to let us know. He could of took me with him. I'd have gone into the wide world with John—but he didn't ask me, and now I hated it, because it took him away from me.

I was standing there in the doorway, shifting from one foot to the other, and thinking about all this, trying to come up with a polite way to get out of meeting the foreign fellow, when the teacher says, "It's nothing to be afraid of, Ellender. This gentleman just needs some help from the folks in our community, that's all. He's staying over at Reverend Barnett's house in Hollow Poplar, and Preacher says we're to be helpful to the gentleman, for he's a learned professor, Ellender. He'll be talking to several of the children in this class, but since you have the best memory I am sending you first."

Well, I went, then, because she made it sound like I was the best one, as if going first was a prize, so I made up my mind to be the most helpful pupil he met, stranger or no.

Although the day was fine and not a bit cold, I put on my homespun shawl, mostly to cover my dress of faded calico, a hand-me-down that was Mama's once. When I went out into the schoolyard, I saw a tall, lanky stranger a-waiting for me, standing there squinting in the September sunshine in a gray suit and a fine straw hat, like a rich man's scarecrow. He was pale as a frog's belly, and sweating from the heat, and he was no young man, either, like I had thought. This fellow looked like he might have children about my age, if he had children at all, which didn't seem likely. He looked sickly to me, and I wondered whether wandering through these mountains on mule back in the summer heat made him sicker or just the opposite.

"You are Ellender McCourry?" he said, giving me a stiff little smile.

I ducked my head. "Yessir." He talked odd, too. I had never heard nobody pronounce my name the way he said it, and I knew I would have to listen hard to catch his meaning.

"*Ellender*," he said. "I wonder if you know why you are called that?"

I shrugged. "It's just a name."

"Oh, no. It's far more than that. In fact, it is part and parcel of why I am here. I come from England. Do you know where that is?"

Of course I did! We had to memorize all the kings and queens right up through Victoria and now her grandson George Five, and we read Shakespeare and Milton. But that wasn't any of his concern, so I just said, "Yes, sir."

"It's a long way from here. But in some ways it isn't far at all. When I look in those blue eyes of yours, I see a girl who could have come from any village between Kent and the Orkneys. And so many customs and phrases— and even dance steps—here remind me of how near I am to Britain."

I blinked. "You have square dancing, sir? And clogging?"

"Under a different name, we do. The Irish call clogging *step dancing*, but there isn't a hair's breadth between them. Are you a dancer?"

I shook my head. "We're Baptist," I told him, but he didn't seem to cotton on to the fact that we're forbidden to dance, and I didn't want to get into talking religion with a stranger, so I said, "What brings you here?"

"The people in these mountains call me a songcatcher, which is a very poetic term for the work I do. I'm quite fond of that term. Do you know what a songcatcher is?"

"No, sir," I said.

"Well, I'm looking for songs," he said. "I have come to these beautiful mountains in search of a piece of the past that has been lost where I come from."

We sat down on the split-rail bench under the chestnut tree, and he kept on talking, with me nodding every now and then when he looked like he was running out of steam. I could tell he had said this piece often before, because he hardly had to stop to draw breath while he was getting it said. I still felt a little odd about talking to a man dressed up like a camp meeting preacher, but he didn't take any notice of me hanging back. He just went on talking away.

"Britain has a rich heritage of folk music," he told me, dabbing at his brow with a white handkerchief. "Over the centuries hundreds of ballads were sung by quite ordinary folk. They are beautiful songs, telling wonderful stories, but gradually, as people moved to the cities and learned new tunes from the music halls, those old songs began to be lost. People forgot them. I thought that someone ought to track down the old songs and write them in a book before they disappear forever. Don't you think that is a worthy cause, Ellender?"

"Depends on the songs," I said, and he laughed.

"Well, some of them are rather tedious," he said. "But many of them are quite wonderful, and it would be a shame to lose even the dullest of them, for once a song is lost, we can never recover it again. As it is, I had begun to think I was too late."

"Too late?"

"Yes. I thought the songs were already lost. In England no one remembered them. The old people had died without passing the songs on to the next generation, or perhaps the young people did not care for yesterday's tunes. Anyhow the ballads were lost. And then—just when I despaired of completing my task, I received a wonderful letter from America. The wife of a missionary serving in these mountains wrote to me to say that she had heard of my work, and that she believed the songs I sought could be found in the mountains of North Carolina. Indeed she had heard such ballads sung by the people she visited."

"How did they get here?" I wondered if he was going to accuse us of stealing his old songs, but he didn't. He looked happy about it.

"Well, the people who settled these mountains in the late eighteenth century came from the British Isles—mainly from Scotland and the north of England, I am told. And they brought the songs with them—in their heads. In Britain the songs have been lost through new fashions in music, but up here in the mountains, you had no music halls or concert houses to put new music into people's heads, and so you kept the old music—much as you keep old bits of cloth from which you make quilts. People here sometimes "quilted" new words or altered tunes to the old ballads, but at any rate they still remembered them in some form, and so I have come here to western North Carolina to ask you—the descendants of those first pioneers—please to share your music with your distant cousins back in Britain."

"What are you going to do with the songs?" I asked.

He smiled. "I'm going to write them down and put them in a book so that no one will ever lose them again. But I need your help."

Well, I liked that. Most of the time strangers came here feeling all superior to the folks in the mountains, and trying to teach us things and change us so we'll be more like them. This was the first outlander who ever asked *us* to help *him*. So I reckoned I would.

"What are you a-wanting me to do?" I asked, still trying to make sense of what he had said.

The gentleman smiled. "Why, I want you to sing for me."

Well, I laughed at that. "Sing!" I said. "In England?"

"No. Right here. So that I can write down the songs you know and take them back with me."

I shook my head. "A-lord, sir. When I sing, people mostly ask me to stop."

"Oh, your voice doesn't matter," he said. He picked up a little leather satchel off the ground and took out a black leather note-book and a silver writing pen. "As long as I can make out the words and the tune, it will serve. If you will sing me a ballad, I'll write down the words and make musical notations of the tune."

"But how do you know that I know any of the songs you're a-wanting?" I asked.

"Well, I don't. I just have to ask everybody and hope that a few of them know an old ballad or two. I ask everyone I can. The sheriff himself has promised to sing for me this evening."

I laughed at that, for I could not imagine that big gravel-voiced fellow a-warbling ballads to a skinny old foreigner. The stranger laughed, too. "Well, he may know a tune worth hearing. Stranger things have happened. But I want to hear you first. Your name is a good sign, I think. Surely, if anyone knows the old songs it should be you."

"What about my name?"

"Ellender is a most unusual name. I do not recall ever hearing of an English girl called that, and I'll warrant that there are very few Ellenders in New York or Boston, either. The only one I ever knew lived only in the words to an old song. "Lord Thomas and Fair Ellender." You have heard it, perhaps?"

I shook my head.

"Yet they do sing it in these hills. I heard it myself in Georgia a few years back."

"I don't know it, though."

"Well, then," he said, smiling. "It seems I

must first sing for you." He set down the notebook, stared off at the mountains, as if he was calling something to mind, and then he commenced to sing in a reedy voice that was tuneful without being good:

"Or shall I marry fair Ellender now
Or bring you the brown girl home?
Or shall I marry fair Ellender now
Or bring the brown girl home?

"The brown girl she has house and land,
Fair Ellender she has none.
My request is to you, my son,
Go bring the brown girl home.

"Fair Ellender dressed herself in white,
And trimmed her merry maidens green,
And in every town that she rode through
They took her for a queen.

"She rode up to Lord Thomas' hall.
And tingled on the ring;
No one so ordered but Lord Thomas him-
*   self*
for to rise and let her come in.

"He took her by her lily-white hand,
He led her through the hall.
He sat her down at the head of the table
Amongst those ladies all.

"Is this your bride?—fair Ellender says—
What makes her so wonderful brown?

381

When you could have married as fair a
    maid
As ever the sun shone on.

"Go hold your tongue, you fair young
    maid,
And tell no tales on me,
For I love your little fingernail
Better than her whole body.

"The brown girl had a pen knife
Which just lately had been ground,
She pierced it through fair Ellender's side,
The blood come tumbling down.

"He took her by her little hand,
He led her to a room;
He took his sword and cut off her head
And kicked it against the wall.

"He put the hilt against the wall
The point against his breast,
Here is the endings of three lovers dear.
Pray take their souls to rest.

"Go dig my grave both wide and deep
And drape my coffin black,
Bury fair Ellender in my arms
And the brown girl at my back."

He sang all those verses about Fair Ellender
right out of his memory, just like folks do up
in these parts, and I allowed as how it was a
pretty good song, though I reckon I would have

liked it better if the dark girl hadn't of killed poor Ellender. Still, it was nice to know that my name came from somewhere.

"How did you like the song?" he said when he'd caught his breath again.

"It was a good story," I said, not wanting to hurt his feelings. "Is it true?"

"I've always thought there was a grain of truth in every old ballad, but I cannot tell you more than that."

I thought it over. "I reckon the brown girl was an Indian," I said. "There's still people around here who are dead set against them."

The songcatcher shook his head. "That song came from another part of the world, quite a long time ago. There were no red Indians there. She may have been a gypsy or a Moorish lady."

"Well, that Ellender had no call to go busting in on the wedding and insulting the bride. I'd have took a knife to her, too!"

He raised his eyebrows and looked alarmed. "Surely not?"

"Well...no. But my daddy and my brothers wouldn't stand for it. That stuck-up fair girl should have had better manners, if not better sense."

"Ah, but if she had, there would have been no ballad," said the stranger, and I could tell he was teasing. "Now it is your turn," he said. He picked up his notebook again, and he wrote the date at the top of the page, and under it my name: Ellender McCourry.

My throat felt so dry I could have spit cotton. "But what shall I sing?"

He must have heard that question a hundred times, because as soon as I asked, he came back with, "Sing the oldest song you know. Something you heard from a grandparent perhaps. A song that tells a story. Not any songs they sing in church, though. I'm sure your hymns are fine tunes, but I must limit my study to a very small section of music, so let us try to find a ballad. I mean: a song which tells a story."

Now, if my people were birds, they'd be owls, not nightingales, but we do sing our share of songs up home. My daddy Zebulon likes to hold forth with a lively tune when he's wood chopping or plowing with the mules, and Mama sings hymns to keep time with the dasher when she churns. Sometimes in the evenings we sit before the fire and sing just for the pleasure of it, not caring a whit about whether we are tuneful or not. We make a joyful noise, Daddy says. There must have been a hundred songs that I had heard over the years, but right then, with the stranger staring at me and his silver pen poised over that blank sheet of paper, I could not call to mind a single one, except "Lost John," and I wouldn't sing that, for it made me think of John Miller gone on the railroad, and it would not be fitten to cry in front of this stranger.

Then I thought about songs that tell a story, and about the songcatcher singing about a murder done, and I thought up a tune that might serve. There was a girl in Brummett's Creek killed two years back, and they never caught whoever did it, but people sang about it in memory of the poor dead girl. Her name was Carrie Rose Howell, and I hadn't known her, so I figured it wouldn't be disrespectful to sing the song. I took a deep breath, shut my eyes and balled my fists, and commenced to sing before my throat took dry from fright:

"There's many a flower of womanhood
In the land where the wild thyme grows,
But the the fairest maid in all these hills
Was the blue-eyed Miss Carrie Rose."

I opened my eyes to see what the stranger thought of my song. I had started off too low and was having trouble keeping the tune going without croaking like a frog. He was smiling politely, but he wasn't writing anything down. When my voice trailed off, he nodded for me to go on, so I did.

"She walked along the river's edge
And gaily was she dressed,
But someone waited in those woods
And stabbed her in her breast.

"Oh, do not take my life, she cried,
For it is all I have
And I will keep our secret, sir,
I'll take it to my grave.

"Then take it to your grave today,
For you are bound to die,
For I'll not marry a barefoot girl
Ta-da-da-d-adee-dee-dee-die."

I forgot that line. But the songcatcher didn't stop me, and I remembered what came after, so I kept on going.

> "He put the knife into her heart;
> He thrust and she did fall;
> The dearest girl in all these hills
> Lay lifeless as a doll.
>
> "He took the earrings from her ears
> And let down her golden hair,
> He tore her red-stained petticoat
> To cover her face so fair.
>
> "A hunter found her at river side
> At the closing of the day,
> But the man who murdered Carrie Rose
> Had gotten clean away.
>
> "They buried her in the old churchyard
> And over her did pray,
> But we'll not rest till the killer, too,
> Lies moldering in the clay."

"That's it," I said. I was satisfied that I had got all the way through it, only a little wobbly on the tune. "That one tells a story, and it's a true one, too. Carrie Rose Howell was found stabbed through the heart by the Toe River. I reckon she was a brown girl, too, for they said she had Indian blood in her. She had black hair like a waterfall, and her skin was dusky. They never did bring the killer to justice."

"A local tragedy," said the songcatcher. "Yes, that is how ballads begin, but you know since that murder took place here in America, your song is not one of the old English ballads I am looking for. It is a fine song, though," he added, seeing the disappointment on my face.

"You didn't write it down."

He coughed. "Well, I confess I have heard it before. In fact, nearly every singer in this county has sung me the sad tale of Miss Carrie Rose, and all the versions are identical in tune and lyrics. Who wrote it, do you know?"

"No. People just started singing it. Maybe folks added a verse or two as it went along." I looked wistfully at the blank sheet of paper on his lap. "And mine was just the same as everybody's?"

"Well...there was something different. What was it? Just a word, but I remember thinking that it wasn't quite right..." He stared up at the sky for a moment, and nodded his head back and forth, so I knew he was singing the tune in his head. Then he said, "I have it! It was the line about the girl's petticoat. You said *red-stained*. But it should be *red-striped*. A red-striped petticoat. It isn't important. Songs always change a bit over the years, as singers adapt them for one reason or another."

"Red-stained is how I heard it, sir," I said. "Because I remember thinking it odd that her petticoat was stained if she had been stabbed in the heart."

He smiled. "It would seem that in ballads poetry always triumphs over truth. You may find that the golden-haired maiden shot through the heart was in reality a plump woman of mature years who was in fact shot in the head. But the former makes a better story, and helps the song to be remembered. So I shouldn't worry about a word or two of difference."

After that I relaxed a bit, and remembered some more tunes. I sang him "Little Margaret" and "The Two Sisters," and he already had them both, but he said that some of the verses I had in "The Two Sisters" were different ones, too, so he made a note of those. Then he thanked me for my time and shook my hand, and I went back to the schoolroom, thinking I'd not see the songcatcher again.

I did, though.

The very next morning when we were back in school, doing sums on our slates while the little ones had reading circle, the songcatcher appeared in the doorway, asking Miss Banner if he might have another word with me. I didn't hardly have time to think what he might be a-wanting with me now. I just put down my slate and hurried out into the yard, and that's when I saw that the songcatcher hadn't come alone.

At the foot of the steps stood the sheriff, hat in hand, looking up at me with a stern face that turned my backbone into an icicle. The first thing I thought was that he was the bringer of bad tidings—the way folks do when they come sudden upon a lawman. I wondered who at home had met with an accident or worse, and I reckon the dread must have been written on my face, for High Sheriff smiled at me and shook his head. "I've not brought you bad news, Ellender McCourry," he said in a calm rumbling voice. "You're Zebulon McCourry's oldest girl, ain't you? I thought so. We just came to sit a spell and talk to you."

I didn't feel much better about that, for only a graven fool would think that a gentleman and a lawman would come to pass the time of day with a girl of fourteen. I commenced to wonder if Daddy had been up to something I ought to know about, but I was sure certain not. He was not given to making liquor out in the woods. Sometimes he and my mother's brother, Uncle Jim, would take the train to Bristol, Virginia, where it's legal to buy whiskey, and they'd bring some back to Tennessee, where it isn't, but I thought the law had better things to do than talk to young girls about a thing like that. Sheriff himself took a train ride or two a year to Bristol, like as not.

So I sat down on the split-rail bench with my hands folded in my lap, and looked up at the two men as blank and wide-eyed as a pansy. "Yes, sir?" I said.

The sheriff came and put his foot on the other end of the bench so he could lean over and talk to me without actually sitting down. "Now, Ellender McCourry," he says, all serious and formal, like church, "this gentleman here came to see me about some old songs last

389

night, and he was telling me that you sang him 'The Ballad of Carrie Rose,' about the Howell girl who was killed three years back."

I nodded, wondering where the harm was in that.

The songcatcher put his hand on my shoulder. "Don't be frightened, young lady," he said softly. "You are not in trouble. In fact, you may prove to be most helpful. I'm afraid our imposition upon you today is my doing. You see, I happened to mention to Mr. Yelton here that you had sung me the Carrie Rose ballad, and that one of your verses differed from the version sung by everyone else."

"The petticoat," I said. "I remember."

"I always heard it red-striped," said the sheriff. "But what was it you said?"

I swallowed hard. "Well, I said *red-stained*, but I didn't mean no harm by it, and I'll sing it your way from now on if you set such a store by it."

They looked at one another and smiled. "No, hon, you don't have to take on about it," said the sheriff. "We're just interested to know where you learned that song."

I shrugged. "But everybody's been singing it. You hear it every time there's a gathering."

"Yes, but nobody sings that one verse like you did." The sheriff sighed. "I suppose you just misheard it."

"No. That's how they sang it. Why does it matter, though?" I pointed to the stranger. "*He* said it didn't matter."

"Well, I reckon he was wrong about that," said the sheriff, softly, like he was talking to himself.

"How come?"

I think he swore under his breath, but after a second he heaved a great sigh and muttered, "I see I'll have to tell you about this, but you must swear not to tell anybody what I'm going to say. The verse matters because you were right. When the hunter—that was the Honeycutt boy—led us to the riverside where the body lay, I examined it myself, and then stood by while the doctor examined it again. The girl had been stabbed through the heart, all right—at close range—and there was precious little blood from it—not as much as you might think. And yet the petticoat was stained red. We thought it was— Well..."

"I know," I said quickly, 'cause I thought he'd choke if he had to talk about a woman's time of the month. I could feel the blush start at my neck and creep up toward my ears.

"We never said anything about that. It wasn't fitten to be talked about. The petticoat was red-striped. She had made it herself from some kind of flour sack cloth or some such, and the people at the farm where she worked knew that, for they'd seen it a-drying on the clothesline, but they didn't know—the other. Carrie Howell was put in her coffin, and nobody else ever saw her. Her folks were dead, and the people she worked for at the farm...well, they didn't care to see the body. So nobody knew except me and that doctor.

He didn't mention it to a soul. I asked him this morning, and he like to took my head off for suggesting such a thing. And I didn't even tell my wife."

The songcatcher had turned away when the sheriff started talking about women's trouble, but now he sat down by me on the bench, still red in the face, but determined to be helpful. "Fair Ellender," he said softly, "what we are trying to say is that the only other person who would know those petticoats were stained is the man who killed her."

Well, that was just foolish, I thought. Maybe the doctor had told somebody and just forgot about it, or maybe the Honeycutt boy had looked at the body that day before he ran for help. There were all kinds of ways that people could have found out about the stained petticoat. That John could have found out.

I remembered walking through the woods with him last fall, a-hunting the one-horned cow that had strayed off, and he started singing that song. I had heard it once by then, I think, for it had just started to be sung, but I didn't know the words. After John sang it for me, I remembered them, for I always remembered everything John ever said. *Red-stained petticoat.* He had said it, plain as day. But the song didn't seem to bother him none. He never sang it sorrowful, not like he minded that Carrie Howell had been a real girl who had died by the river a few months back. And now John was gone, too.

Sheriff Yelton was talking to me. "So, you

see, Ellender, we need to know where you learned that verse of the song. Who sang it for you?"

I hesitated for a long time, and then I took a deep breath and said, "I don't rightly remember. I believe I heard it at a quilting bee."

They went away then, before I could tell the songcatcher that I remembered another ballad he might be wanting—one about a shepherd girl in a graveyard and the ghost of a poor, sad princess. My daddy used to sing that one. But I never saw the songcatcher again.

And at Christmastime I married up with Wesley Walker.

Chapter Eleven

"Someone to see you, Sheriff," said Jenna Leigh. From the look of disappointment on her face, Spencer knew that his visitor was not Mr. Hawkins from the 911 office.

"Show 'im in," he said, repressing the urge to smile.

When he looked up and saw the straight, spare frame of Miss Nora Bonesteel standing on his threshold, he jumped to his feet. She had been his Sunday school teacher years ago, with a sternness that gave renewed meaning to the term *Christian soldiers*. In all the years that followed he had never quite lost his awe of her. She was well past seventy by now—maybe older than that—but there was nothing frail about her. She still walked the few miles to church every Sunday, and she worked as hard as people half her age in that vegetable garden of hers up on Ashe Mountain. Her hair was not yet all gray, and she had the smooth, chiseled features that made people wonder if she had Cherokee blood somewhere in her family tree. What did she want? Spencer doubted if she needed his help with anything.

Now he wondered if she had come about the Lark McCourry plane crash. He knew the stories people told about Nora Bonesteel, but he thought those tales should be taken with a grain of salt. That's all he needed: for reporters to be told that a psychic had offered to help with the rescue operation. It didn't bear thinking about.

"How can I help you, Miss Nora?" he said, pulling out a chair for her.

The old woman shook her head. "I can't stay long, Spencer. Maybe you can't, either." She held up the small woven basket she was carrying. It was lined with what looked like a hand-woven cloth of napkin size, and resting on that were a couple of apples and a jar of preserves. "These are my special blackberry preserves," she said.

He smiled. "Well, that is mighty kind of you—"

"They're for your deputy, Mr. LeDonne."

Spencer raised his eyebrows. Joe LeDonne

was an excellent officer, but despite that—no, *because* of that—nobody ever brought him little gifts. Not even at Christmas. Besides he had the weekend off. He smiled again at the old woman. Maybe she *is* losing it, he thought. Sad day. "Miss Nora, I know he'll be honored to get this, but he's not here right now."

She nodded. "He'll be at the hospital. The county one, I think. Not Johnson City. I thought I might ride over with you."

"But—"

"There's something I need to speak to you about on the way."

"But—"

Jenna Leigh poked her head in the door again. "Rescue squad, Sheriff," she said. "But it's not about the plane crash this time. They say it's about LeDonne."

Spencer looked from his dispatcher to the old lady in front of his desk to the get-well basket of jams in her hand. "I'll get my hat," he said to nobody in particular.

John Walker had made his burial arrangements at the only funeral home in Hamelin, a firm that was fifty years old, but recently relocated into a newly built building: a long, one-story brick structure with two wings of "viewing parlors" laid out on either side.

"Couldn't they have postponed this until the doctors were happier about releasing you from the hospital?" asked Ben as they pulled into the parking lot.

Lark McCourry shrugged. "I didn't ask them to. I didn't see any point in dragging this out. He had outlived most of his friends anyhow. Or shut them out. Anyhow, it wasn't my call. I suppose Becky is running the show here."

"Your sister?" said Ben, trying to keep afloat in a conversation with a stranger.

"God, no. No relation. She was the housekeeper. Though people might find that hard to believe." She sighed. "There seems to be a curse in my father's family. It shows up in the McCourry line, as far as I could tell. He never saw the pattern, but boy I did. When I was a child, I used to watch people at the family gatherings, and of course I listened in corners, so quiet that the grown-ups forgot I was there. I heard enough over the years to piece it together."

Ben looked uneasy, wondering how much stranger the evening could get. "A curse."

"Yes. Or at least a disturbing pattern. The tradition is to slight the first child. I saw it happen over and over. Look, when my dad was young, he worked his way through college and became a lawyer—the most successful person ever in the family, I guess. But his parents just doted on his younger brother Malcolm, who was killed in World War II. My father would try to tell them about some big court case that he'd won, and they'd come back with a story about the fish his brother caught when he was ten. And I think my grandmother always resented her sisters, because she felt she'd been slighted in favor of them. I saw the trait among the cousins, too. After a while I started *looking* for it. Anyhow, I always thought I'd be spared that particular curse, being an only child, but I wasn't. By God if my father didn't go out and *recruit* somebody to be Uncle Malcolm so I could be him in the family dynamic. Oh, I was slighted all right."

They walked up the curving brick path toward the low covered porch of the funeral home. A man in a dark suit was leaning against one of the white aluminum columns, smoking a cigarette. He nodded politely to them and they went inside. The foyer was deserted and no one came out of the office area to greet them, but after a moment's awkwardness they noticed a message board posted with names spelled out in removable black letters. The second line read "John Walker—B." Below the list of viewings a permanent notice said: "Viewing rooms A–F—Left Wing; G–L—Right wing."

Lark nodded. "This way, then. Left Wing."

Ben followed her through a set of open double doors, down a wide, dark carpeted hallway to the first room on the right. They opened the door to a narrow, bright parlor, decorated in furniture store Early American with chintz-patterned wing chairs and love seats placed at intervals through the long room. No one was there—not even the corpse.

Lark looked at her watch. "I guess I'm early." With a look of patient expectance, she sat down on a love seat facing the door.

Ben wondered what he ought to do now. The

idea of sitting through a viewing for a dead man he had never met, in the company of a woman he barely knew, struck him as both bizarre and awkward, but the thought of leaving felt like a dereliction of duty. Perhaps he ought to stay. He thought ruefully of the oriental tradition that if one saves a life one is responsible for that person forever after: an unexpected hazard of 911 work—and one he did not care for at all. Ben wasn't even sure that he liked the idea of a funeral home viewing at all, regardless of whether one knew the deceased or not. *Viewing a corpse.*

"It's barbaric, isn't it?" said Lark McCourry. "The custom of visiting the body."

Her words so perfectly echoed his thought that he uttered a gasp of surprise. "I suppose it is," he murmured, softening his whole-hearted agreement. "It's probably a holdover of that morbid Victorian sentiment that made a pageant of grief—mourning rings woven from the hair of the dead loved one and so on."

Lark looked around the cheerful but empty parlor. "I wonder where he is. I don't mean that in a metaphysical sense. He won't haunt me, that's for sure. I mean where *is* the body? I didn't expect a lot of people to come, but I did think somebody would turn up. And if this is the viewing—his idea, not mine, by the way—then *where…is…he?*"

Ben shook his head. He did not know. He was decades away from becoming familiar with the culture of death. His friends were young, with parents in hearty middle age.

Barring unfortunate accidents or illness, his visits to funeral homes would not begin for some years yet, and perhaps by then the bizarre tradition would have gone out of fashion. He hoped so.

He stood midway between the love seat and the door, still debating the propriety of leaving, and resolving to give it a few more minutes—at least until *somebody* turned up. She would need a ride home—or wherever it was she was going. "Will you be all right?" he asked.

"You mean am I distraught? Not particularly." She shrugged. "I may even be relieved. My father didn't like me much. Oh, he bragged about my success, and I'm sure he took credit for it among his acquaintances, but he didn't really approve of me. He came from the generation that liked their women featherbrained, gushing, and chocolate box pretty. If I stayed away long enough, he sometimes forgot I wasn't like that, but he always remembered about two minutes after I showed up. So...I stopped showing up."

A ferret-faced man in a dark suit appeared in the doorway. He peered anxiously at them, and seemed to be debating his opening line. Finally he ventured, "Are you all here for John Walker?"

"Yes." Lark stood up and assumed her meet-the-public persona. "How good of you to come. I am his daughter. And you are...?"

"Oh, I work here," said the man, looking embarrassed. "We wondered where you were, and after a while it suddenly hit me that you might have come over here, not knowing. The viewing room was changed."

"Changed? When?"

"This evening. Around six, I think. We thought there might be a few more people than this parlor is designed for—well, Becky said there might be—so we moved your father over to H, which is our largest room. It's in the other wing. Let me walk you over."

"Why wasn't I told of the change?" asked Lark. "I spoke to someone from here about that time."

The man gave her a mournful smile, intended to convey both his bureaucratic helplessness and his infinite patience with the tantrums of the bereaved. "These things are sent to try us," he intoned.

Ben Hawkins fell in beside her and they followed the man in black across the central foyer and into the carpeted shadows of the other hall. "I'm really sorry about this," whispered Ben.

"No, it's perfect," said Lark. "In fact, it's so perfect that I'm tempted to think my father left special instructions with the funeral home to make sure this happened. This is the perfect metaphor for our relationship. The grand finale. He's off in one wing with Becky and his cronies—what's left of them—while I sit alone and forgotten in a room somewhere else—waiting on *him*. I'll bet dying was almost worth it to him for the chance to pull off this one final humiliation. One last *up yours* to me before he departs this earth."

"I'm sorry."

"Oh, it's okay. Lots of people love me. Lots of people who don't even know me love me. It's just the ones who do know me that have trouble with it." Her voice quavered, but an instant later she took a deep breath and tightened her lips.

They reached the open door of Room H and saw a crowd of people standing in line in another cheerful Early American parlor, much the same as its smaller counterpart in the other wing. Thirty voices were all talking at once, sounding too cheerful for the circumstances, oblivious to the new arrivals in the doorway. Lark did not see anyone she recognized. Most of those present were dowdy women or gaunt middle-aged men in work clothes—Becky's crowd, she thought. At one end of the room stood Becky Tilden herself, standing at the head of an open casket in which reposed the shrunken body of an old man. It was John Walker—or rather John Walker as he might have looked sculpted in wax and clad in an ill-fitting shiny polyester suit.

To get to the casket she would have to pass Becky, who seemed to be the hostess of the event. Just as well, thought Lark, who could deal with strangers well enough in her celebrity persona but was hopeless at small talk otherwise.

After greeting the latest caller in the group clustered around her, Becky looked up and gave her a tentative smile, and suddenly the room fell silent. People's expressions grew grim and they seemed to edge closer to Becky, staring at the newcomer with wary expectation. *All they need is pitchforks and torches and they'd be the villagers in a vampire movie,* she thought. *Or perhaps I've been cast as the bad fairy at the christening.* The thought made her smile.

Suddenly it dawned on her that they were expecting a confrontation. A shouting match, perhaps, between John Walker's daughter and the woman he had replaced her with. *Come on,* their expressions said. *We can take you.*

John Walker probably would have enjoyed that, too: the spectacle of two women fighting for his affections over his lifeless body. *Well, think again you old trout,* thought Lark. She put on her autograph session smile and advanced toward Becky. "They put us in the wrong room!" she said, letting the Southern accent creep back into her voice. "Can you *believe* it? Thank goodness you knew where to come. This is Ben. He saved my life, and I just won't turn him loose. And I don't believe I know you, sir," she said, turning to the first man in line with the same bright smile.

After a momentary flicker of disappointment that the confrontation had not materialized, the crowd thawed and prepared to be gracious to old Judge's famous daughter. She had been right in her original impression: Becky's crowd. She guessed that her father would have been surprised to hear any of them refer to themselves as his friends: the visiting nurse, the yard man, neighbors from the trailer park down the road. Or maybe he wouldn't have—

these days. The only John Walker that Lark really knew was the stern and proud attorney who had raised her, and she knew for a fact that when she had lived under his roof, that man would not have allowed her to associate with a soul in this room. She wondered what had changed in him, and she suspected that it was nothing so benign as tolerance. John Walker liked people he could outrank, and as he grew more frail and less prosperous, the pool of people who qualified had simply shrunken to this sad little gathering.

Dutifully, she allowed herself to be led forward to view the body, and she made the expected comments on how well he looked. If the crowd had expected outpourings of grief from John Walker's only child, they would not get it. Becky, too, was cheerful and dry-eyed, Lark noticed. She found that as she talked with the visitors on automatic pilot an old bluegrass tune was running through the back of her mind: *"Ain't nobody gonna miss me when I'm gone."*

"I have to go," murmured Ben Hawkins, still embarrassed to be here at all.

Lark looked stricken. "Of course you do! I must be your version of *no good deed goes unpunished.*" She walked him back to the doorway. "You must feel like a hostage," she said. "But as far as I'm concerned you saved my life—twice. And I'll never forget it. But I'll be fine now. I really can take it from here. Thanks."

Ben turned to go and almost collided with

the man in the doorway. "Hello, Sheriff!" he said. "Good to see you out and about!" With a smile and a brief handshake, Ben was gone.

Spencer Arrowood, still in his brown uniform, looked down at the wan face of Lark McCourry and gave her an encouraging smile. "Hello, Linda," he said.

It took her a moment to reconcile the tanned middle-aged face before her with the lanky blonde boy in her history class back in high school. "Spencer," she said at last. "Spencer Arrowood. I am so glad you came." She had said it twenty times already that evening, but this time she meant it. Finally—someone from the past, the part of her father's life that she belonged in.

"I am so glad you came," she said again. "Do you know that of all the friends my father had in the legal profession, you are the only one who showed up tonight for the viewing?"

He looked uncomfortable. "Well, the truth is, Linda...Lark...your dad had retired and left the county before I ever got elected sheriff. Nelse Miller had the job back in those days. Truth is, I came to see you."

"Well...here?"

He looked around at the chattering group of visitors and shook his head. "No, I guess not. But this visitation thing ends at eight, doesn't it? I thought I might wait. If that's all right with you?"

"Yes, of course," she murmured. "Only tell me you haven't got a demo tape tucked in your jacket."

404

"Excuse me." One of the wizened men who had come to "Becky's party," was holding up a funeral home ballpoint pen and an advertising brochure. "Lark, honey, could you just put your little old autograph on this sheet of paper. It's for my girlfriend."

Lark had never seen the man before in her life. Signing, though, was quicker than arguing about the propriety of it. "What's your girlfriend's name?" she asked.

The man looked embarrassed. "Uh...just make it out to Duane."

When she had signed the paper, and the man had thrust it in his pocket and strolled away, Spencer Arrowood said, "I don't have a demo tape, Linda. I'd rather have my job than yours."

John Walker—1945

All I could think about when that Moro pointed his pistol at my chest on Mindanao was the fact that I had a master's degree from Columbia University. All that education—more than anybody in my family ever had—was going to waste in one second for a nickel's worth of lead.

It probably wouldn't have impressed the Moro much. Certainly never did impress my mama any. I guess I could have been another

Clinchfield railroad mechanic like my dad for all she cared. Never once did she say she was proud of me. Never once did I hear her bragging to anybody about what an ambitious and accomplished son she had. Oh, she talked about her son, all right, but it wasn't me. It was always my baby brother, that sweet, sunny little towhead who made up in looks and charm what he lacked in everything else. Mam named him Malcolm, a name that runs through her family like a spark in a hay field. I reckon they pulled my name out of a hat. Or maybe from a song: "Lost John." I certainly felt lost in the shuffle in that family.

Sometimes I think I enlisted in the army mainly to get away from her—never mind the draft. Some of the old boys I met in basic training were scared of going to war, but I figured I had been at war all my life, growing up with Ellender McCourry Walker on my neck every waking minute. I think she hated people. I honestly do think that, but I never could figure out why, unless it was living in town that turned her funny. She grew up in a mountain holler about twenty miles from here, one mountain over into North Carolina, so I suppose that most of the people she associated with growing up were relatives in one degree or another. Then she married my father, and came to Hamelin so that he could work for the railroad. I came along in 1917, and Malcolm arrived ten years later. We never stopped being strangers to her.

Dad was from the same remote little farm

community as Mam, but his folks were preachers and teachers instead of solitary farmers, so maybe he was more used to mingling with folk. Anyhow the change from farmstead to railroad town never bothered him. I think she was always afraid, but I never could figure out why. She hated to let people in the house. If someone knocked, she'd go in the bedroom and hide until they went away. She seemed to think people were judging her all the time, which I suppose people always are, but I still never could see what the problem with that was. We had no pets, and the house was always clean and tidy. The furniture was not costly, but it was well kept, and the unimaginative rooms were uncluttered. Such visitors as we had were no better off materially than we were, so they would hardly be likely to scoff at her furniture or her clothes. Why did she mind company so much? I never found out.

I do know that she gets no joy from being with people. She is as self-contained as a chunk of mica. I wonder if I will become like her when I get old.

I never knew whether she was happy or not in her five-room brick house in that little railroad town or not. I wasn't. Growing up in the Depression chafed my soul. I hated the patched clothes, the meals without meat, and the bicycle I had to make from scrap parts with garden-hose tires. I wanted out of there. I wanted to feel safe, with money in the bank and a solid job that couldn't be taken away by the foreman, and I didn't ever want to have to kowtow to the bosses just because they outranked me on paper. I would be my own boss—a lawyer.

I learned to read before I ever started school, and then skipped the first and third grade in that one-room school when they saw how well I read. Graduated high school at fifteen, a grinning jug-eared boy, head and shoulders shorter than the rest of the senior boys. I worked two jobs to pay for a college education at East Tennessee State in Johnson City. I lived at home and hitchhiked back and forth, because I didn't have the money for room and board on campus. They never gave me any money for college. Not a dime. After Malcolm died, she bought a refrigerator with the money she had been saving to send him to college.

By the time Pearl Harbor was bombed in '41, I had a bachelor of science degree from East Tennessee, a master's from Columbia University in New York City, and I had been to the New York World's Fair seventy-four times, so I thought myself a man of the world. There was no trick to going to the fair so much. Admission was cheap, the train ride out to Long Island was cheap, and it was the best way to pass the time that summer—always something new to see.

When the war came, I enlisted in the army, hoping to be made an officer, and knowing I deserved to be one, but I would have left, war or no war. After Columbia I had ended up back in east Tennessee, teaching all six grades at Rock Creek School for ninety dollars a month—they say none of us can stay out of these mountains forever; that's the only explanation I have. I was living at home, but paying rent just as if I was a stranger. Well, one evening, I had gone over to Johnson City to the pictures with a girl I knew from college, and it was after eleven before I made it home. When I got to the back door, I discovered that it was locked, and the family had gone to bed. They never gave me a key. College graduate, paying rent—no key. It was Mam's house, Mam's rules. I slept on the floor of the smokehouse that night, and the next morning I packed up all my clothes and books and moved to the YMCA over in Erwin.

I never did go home again, except for visits of three days or less. We never discussed it.

I started out in the Army Air Corps, because I was determined to go through this war with as much flash as I could muster, and fly-boy just about suited my swagger, but when the regular army offered me OCS to join the artillery, I took the deal. I spent my first two years in service bouncing one from stateside base to another, getting trained. Training in Waco, Texas, where we had to crawl on our bellies while machine gun bullets whizzed over our heads, one poor devil came nose to nose with a rattlesnake and went straight up in sheer terror. That was the end of him. Tank corps at Fort Knox, Kentucky. Officer training school. It began to look like I was going to spend the whole war learning how to be a soldier, and by the time I finished, there wouldn't be any more call for one.

Finally, though, I ran out of places to train, and was on my way to the combat zone. Before I shipped out, I ended up stationed at Camp Davis, in a little village called Holly Ridge, just north of Wilmington, North Carolina. I loved the ocean. The serenity of it. The vastness. I felt I belonged there, and I was determined to head back to Wilmington if I could after the war. I married a Wilmington girl—Luanne— in September 1944, before I shipped out, which was extra insurance about getting to come back. Two hundred miles east of the North Carolina mountains was as close as I ever wanted to be to high country again. Luanne laughed at that and told me the feeling would pass. "None of y'all can ever leave for good," she said.

"Well, then, if I do end up back in those mountains, I'll live on a lake," I'd say.

Most of my outfit shipped out for Europe, and arrived just in time for the Battle of the Bulge. Most of them never made it back. For some reason I got sent the other way, and ended up in the Philippines, cleaning up after MacArthur retook it from the Japanese in October of '44. I ended up on the island of Mindanao, where the fighting was still going on. We had to contend with factions of guerrilla fighters, who were fighting the Japanese, us, each other, and just about anybody else that got in their way. The Moros were a Muslim group that made things hot for us. They'd steal gas out of our jeeps, take shots at us. I also spent some time in Luzon, north of Manila, at a place called Camp O'Donnell, where many of the victims of the Bataan Death March had died. We erected a big white concrete cross over the mass grave site, and turned the place into a POW camp for Japanese soldiers.

A few months after I enlisted, Malcolm dropped out of high school to join the navy. I guess he didn't mind going to war, as long as they didn't make him *walk* anywhere. He lied about his age. At least I don't think the government knew he was fifteen when they sent him to submarine school in New London, Connecticut. Maybe he wanted to get away from Mam, too.

She carried on something awful when Malcolm went off to war after sub school. I was in the Pacific by that time, but some of the girls back home were writing me letters, and they made sure I heard what a spectacle Mam made of herself at the depot when Malcolm went and caught the train to go off to war. The day I left Hamelin, Dad went down to see me off; she didn't. They said she hugged him and cried fit to kill, and then she gave him a charm to keep him safe. A magic rock—can you beat that? It was a fairy stone; Lord knows where she got it. I know they find them somewhere in these mountains. I thought it was over in Virginia. Fairy stones were crystallized minerals that form naturally into the shape of a cross, so they're considered lucky and magical. The Cherokees used to think they were charms that had been dropped by the little people who lived inside the hills, and that the fairy folk held them when they wanted to be invisible. Well, that might have been some use to a soldier—I could have used it a time or two myself on Mindanao—but I didn't see what good it would do a man on a submarine, unless it could make the whole boat invisible to sonar, which I doubt even the Cherokees would believe. I wasn't given a magic rock, mind you.

The irony is that little brother Malcolm made it to the war itself long before I did. He volunteered for sub school in New London, Connecticut, and after he graduated from it and completed the rest of his training, he wrote me to say that he had been assigned to a six-thousand-ton sub called the *Runner,* which had been commissioned in July of '42. Malcolm shipped out to the Pacific, just as I later would. "I don't envy you your adventures in the steaming jungle, Lieutenant Brother," he wrote in that schoolboy scrawl of his. "I'm going to be spending this war on an extended cruise, mixing whiskey sours with sick bay alcohol to make up for the bad air and the lack of scenery."

While I was at Fort Knox, running tanks through Kentucky mud holes, Malcolm's sub was patrolling the deepest part of the Pacific, looking for Japanese war ships.

I heard what happened in a letter from Dad. Not from her. She never spoke about it.

Back in Hamelin they were getting ready to

go to church one Sunday morning in early August 1943, and she came out into the parlor, dressed for church, but looking like a sleepwalker. She sat down in the rocking chair by the front window, and in a dazed voice she said, "Wesley, I just heard Malcolm's voice plain as I'm sitting here. He said: *Mother, the sub is on the bottom and we can't get it up.*" She just sat there shaking and wouldn't get up.

Well, Dad talked her around. Said it was all a waking nightmare brought on by worry, and he packed her off to church to take her mind off her troubles. He had about convinced her that the whole incident had been a dream when two weeks later the government car pulled up in front of the house and the two men in uniform got out. Mam started shaking then, but she went and let them in to her well-scrubbed front parlor, and stood there stone-faced while they said their piece about the *Runner* being missing out in the Pacific. That's all the information they had. The sub was missing, but by now—several weeks, it had been—they presumed it lost with all hands.

"We don't know if the Japanese sank it or what, ma'am," said one of the soldiers.

"*The sub is on the bottom and they can't get it up,*" she whispered.

They didn't believe her, of course. Thought she was in shock, or else being hysterical, which they probably saw as often as not in their line of work. They gave her the condolences of President Roosevelt and a grateful nation, and left, disbelieving. But when I heard about it, I believed her. As close as she was to my brother Malcolm, if he had time for any last words before life was extinguished on that sub, she would have heard them. Six feet or six thousand miles away, she would have heard them.

I don't reckon she knew when the Moro aimed a stolen pistol at my chest and pulled the trigger. I never did tell her. It didn't come to anything anyhow, except the one frozen moment of terror that seemed to last half my life. The .38-caliber revolver he aimed at us wouldn't fire. While he was pulling the trigger with the desperation of a man who knows he has seconds to live, an MP we called Tex shot him, and when we took the gun off the corpse and examined it, we found that the fool had been trying to use filed-down carbine ammo in it. On the other hand, the .45 the Moro had tucked in his belt worked *perfectly*. It is the randomness of war that ultimately terrified me. How impersonal death becomes, and how little it seems to matter. A stranger's choice of a weapon determined my entire future.

I thought about the war a long time, while I was coming home on the troop ship in '46, and I decided that the only way to forget things was to let them die in your memory. I saw things and did things that I do not want to remember. So I tell two stories about the war. One is about trying to housebreak Old Man Mose, the little pet monkey I had on Luzon. Every time he relieved himself in the house, I would slap him on the butt and throw him out the window. I never did housebreak him, but after a while when he did make a mess on the floor, he'd slap himself on the butt and jump out the window. The other is a story about a training maneuver back at Holly Ridge, North Carolina, when we were out on the beach training gunners by shooting at targets pulled behind planes out over the ocean. When the first plane came over, we fired a few rounds in front of the plane, just to spook the pilot. He radioed down: "Tell those bastards I'm pulling this target, not *pushing* it." Then he cut the towline and flew back to base, leaving the artillery class sitting on the beach for seven more hours with no planes and no targets. Just sitting.

I tell the funny war stories to Luanne and Linda, sometimes to casual acquaintances, because it would be shameful somehow to trumpet my horrors and my suffering after what happened to Malcolm. The tragic war story was his. I took what was left.

Seven years after the war ended, they held a hearing to determine what had happened to the *Runner*. Insurance money was waiting to be claimed and widows presumptive were waiting to resume their lives. By then the government had searched the Japanese war records and discovered that they made no mention of sighting or sinking a submarine in the *Runner*'s last known location. The official verdict was that the *Runner* had developed mechanical trouble somewhere between the American submarine base at Midway and the islands of Japan, rendering her unable to surface.

Which is what Malcolm had told Mam years ago: *Mother, the sub is on the bottom and we can't get it up.*

She never talked about him after the war. After they paid off the house, they used part of the insurance money to buy a flat bronze marker to put in the cemetery on the old road to Johnson City, and a time or two, if I happened to be home visiting, I'd drive her out there to tend the grave. I'd walk her up to the marker over the empty grave of Malcolm Walker, Seaman First Class, USN, and I'd go back and wait in the car. I cannot look at that stark metal marker over an empty grave without wondering what it was like to be sixteen years old, trapped in a long dark coffin six miles below the surface of the waves, and knowing that you will never come up.

But Mam stays a good while there at the cemetery, weeding and polishing, and then just kneeling there by the marker, visiting with that metal plate that is all she has left of Malcolm. Once I even thought I heard her singing to him. Some old hillbilly song. Nothing that I wanted to hear. Something about *"when he comes back home."* But he never did.

He never came back.

And Mam never forgave me for being the one who did.

Chapter Twelve

"Strange way to spend your birthday."

Joe LeDonne squirmed at the sound of the voice. He was trying to free his foot from beneath the wreckage of the plane, but to his surprise it moved easily. Then the pain of having shifted it shot up his leg and jolted him into wakefulness. He opened his eyes.

He was in a hospital room—either that or hell was a sensory deprivation chamber. That explained why his neck no longer itched. The sheets felt cool against his skin. He stared for a moment at the little holes in the acoustic tile ceiling, registering the fact that looking up and not seeing oak leaves for the first time in many hours meant that he had come back. As his consciousness came further into focus, he looked around. *Oh, yes, the voice.*

Martha Ayers was sitting in a metal chair next to his bed, regarding him with an expression that was not wholly sympathetic. Cell phones would be discussed later, he felt.

There was a needle in the crook of his elbow—another pain center checking in. He watched with distaste as a clear solution dripped down from an upended bottle and slid down the tube toward his vein.

"How do you feel?" said Martha.

He said the first word that entered his head. "Stupid."

"Ah. Then your perceptions are in working order." She was trying to speak lightly, but he could hear the undercurrent of concern in her voice, and it cheered him up immensely.

A bit of color on the dresser at the far end of the room attracted his attention. It was a basket with apples in it. "A basket?" he said. "From you?"

"From Miss Nora Bonesteel. She and the sheriff came in while you were unconscious. Spencer said he'd check back later. I need to tell the nurse you're awake."

"Not yet," he said. He didn't want to be bothered just yet. "Martha, I had the strangest hallucination out there on the mountain. This weird guy in a raggedy flannel shirt... unshaven..."

Martha was laughing. "He's a vision, all right, isn't he? That was Rattler. Root doctor, storyteller, and general colorful character. He and Spencer go way back, though why the Arrowoods let their adolescent son hang out with an old drunk who lives in a tin shack is beyond me."

"I bet you could learn a lot from that old man," said LeDonne.

"Yeah—some of it legal." She sighed. "Still, he saved your life, so I shouldn't criticize him. He rounded up a gaggle of searchers, made them rig a travois with blankets and tree limbs, and supervised your descent down the mountain. He's amazing."

LeDonne was staring at the end of the bed, at the lump under the sheets where his feet were—weren't they? "How am I?" he said softly, still watching the sheet.

Martha followed his gaze. "You're fine, Joe. Really. Bad bruising. Clean break in the metatarsal. You're on painkillers right now, or else you'd have no doubt that the foot was still there. You were lucky."

"I guess I was."

She took a deep breath. "So... Did you get it out of your system?"

This was no time to pretend he didn't know what she was talking about. LeDonne considered the question. "I think so," he said. "Not everything, of course, but one question in particular, yes, I did." He knew she wouldn't ask, but suddenly he wanted to tell her anyway. "I saved somebody's life once..."

"Joe, you're a cop. You save people's lives all the... Oh. Back in the war, you mean."

"Yeah. I didn't know him. Knew his name. Saw him around. We weren't tight, though. He was new to the outfit, so we pretty much ignored him at first. And while we were out on patrol, he stepped on a claymore. It pretty much took him out up to the thigh bone. Legs, penis...everything. He looked like hamburger from..."

"Skip that part," said Martha softly.

"Yes. Well, I picked him up and carried him to where the medevac choppers landed. He was out. Shock—pain. I was glad he didn't know what was going on. I didn't think he had much of a chance to make it, but I felt like I had to try. By the time we got to the clearing, my uniform was so soaked with blood that they tried to take *me* on board. He was still unconscious. But breathing. So they got him loaded and off he went to a nice army hospital somewhere. And I went back to the jungle to wait for the next firefight. But that night some of the guys were saying how I shouldn't have saved him. Said it would have been kinder to let him die, torn up as he was. The doctors could make him go on living, but they couldn't give him back what he'd lost.

"So all these years I've been wondering— did I do the right thing? Making him live. I didn't ask his permission. I wonder if he hated me for keeping him alive. See, I knew how messed up he was. I *knew*."

"So did you find out?"

"When I was lying there, with my foot caught under that plane, knowing I would probably die out there on the mountain, I think I knew. I think it was worth *anything* just to stay alive. If I'd had to cut my foot off myself, I would have, eventually. Just to have a shot at living. Maybe someday I'll hunt the guy up and ask him if I did the right thing for him, but it doesn't matter what he says. Living would have been the right decision for me, and that's all I had to go on." He stopped then, wondering if he ought to tell her about the other apparition—he still thought of him that way, even though Rattler had proved to be real. Fly-Boy. He decided against it. "At least I found that old wrecked plane," he said, trying to salvage some merit from the expedition.

"Found it!" scoffed Martha. "Everybody knows where that wreck is. That was Bonnie Wolfe's plane. She was a big deal around here when I was growing up. For the first few years after it happened, people used to go up there on the anniversary of the crash and leave flowers on the wreckage. Hold candle-light vigils."

"So she was killed there?"

"Oh, yes. Died instantly. They brought the bodies down off the mountain, but the wreck was in an inaccessible place. Miles from even a logging road, I think. No way to get it down, so they just removed the bodies and left it there. There were two of them killed in the wreck. Bonnie Wolfe and her pilot. I forget his name."

"Fred."

"Something like that. It's not important."

"No," said LeDonne.

The visitation time at the funeral home had ended, and Lark McCourry had gone to Dent's Cafe with Spencer Arrowood. Back in the days when franchised fast-food restaurants were no nearer than Johnson City, Dent's had been the hangout for the high school students of Hamelin. Lark found that she still knew the menu by heart; only the prices had changed. She looked around at the pine-paneled walls, still displaying photos of local football players and the banner of the Wake County High School in pride of place.

"I came here the night of the senior prom," she said, toying with the straw in her Diet Coke.

"Afterward?" said Spencer.

"More like instead of. Nobody asked me to go to the prom—my ugly duckling phase—so a couple of us girls went together and stood around like graven fools for ten minutes, before we all piled into Pat's car and came to Dent's. In tulle formals." She grimaced at the memory. "You know, at a music industry dinner one year, I was at a table afterwards with Willie Nelson and Mick Jagger, and that *still* doesn't make up for my high school prom night."

"I know," said Spencer. "I took Jenny that year."

His ex-wife's name hung in the air. They both tried to think of something else to say to deflect the conversation.

"Okay, that's enough about the past," said Lark. "The past is scary. So, tell me, why did you want to see me so particularly? Don't tell me you're giving me a subpoena or something."

"No. Nothing official. But I think I'm supposed to give you something."

Lark's expression became somber. "Look, Spencer," she said. "I can't take much more right now. I almost died out there. You're not going to tell me that Becky Tilden killed my dad, are you?"

"Good lord, no!" he said in genuine astonishment. "You don't believe she did, do you?"

She took a deep breath. "No. It doesn't

matter. He was ready, and he trusted her, and— Oh, forget I said anything. I just can't imagine what you wanted so urgently."

Spencer smiled. "I hear you're looking for a song," he said.

"Well, I'll be damned. *You* know it?"

"Yeah. 'The Rowan on the Grave.' Sure. Used to play it on the guitar when I was in college. Nora Bonesteel came in today, and after one thing and another, she asked me what my grandmother's maiden name had been. This is not the sort of conversation I usually have with Miz Bonesteel, so I was mildly astonished, but I told her. 'Esther McCourry,' I said. 'Married Spencer Arrowood, who I'm named after.'

"And she said, 'I thought so.' And then she asked if I knew this song with the phrase *'And when she's come back home she will be changed'* in it, and I said I did. Then she told me to find you and give you the words. 'Pass it on,' she said, as if it was the most important thing in the world."

"We're cousins," said Lark. "I didn't know that. And you have the song."

"Yes. I learned it when I was about twelve. They sang it at your grandmother's funeral."

"They did not!"

He smiled. "No, I don't mean at the church service. Afterward, when the family went back to the house for a cold supper and to visit, all the men went out on the back porch, and one of them had a guitar, and they sang for a couple of hours. They sang that one twice."

Lark pictured the tiny screened-in porch on the back of the Walkers' tidy box of a brick house. The men had sat out there in the dark, with only the glow from lit cigarettes relieving the blackness. And they sang. But it was only the men. Girls of twelve were not allowed to tag along after the menfolks anymore. The charmed circle was closed. But Lark had wanted to be where the music was. She had crept out of the house and sat down on the outside steps to the screened-in porch. Hidden by the storm door from the view of the guitar players, she had listened until her mother called to make her go in. She could not remember seeing Spencer there at all. But she remembered hearing the song. It had resonated somehow. It was the family's ballad. It was her song.

"Sing it for me," she whispered.

And in the darkened back booth of Dent's Cafe, Spencer Arrowood sang.

Afterword

Many writers begin their careers by writing about their own lives and families, but I wrote more than a dozen books before I ventured into family history in the course of a novel. I found Malcolm McCourry while I was doing the research for an earlier book, and I was so intrigued with him that I made him the focal point of *The Songcatcher*, mostly because I thought he had such an interesting life, and only incidentally because he was my four-times great-grandfather.

Malcolm turned up while I was researching *The Ballad of Frankie Silver*. Frankie Silver, who was hanged for her husband's murder in 1833 at age nineteen, lived in the North Carolina mountains in what is now Mitchell County, where my ancestors settled in the 1790s. In researching the early settlers of that area, I discovered that Frankie Silver was a kinswoman of mine, and I also found references to the first of my ancestors to settle in western Carolina: one Malcolm McCourry, who had been kidnaped as a child from the island of Islay off the west coast of Scotland. He had served with the crew of a sailing ship until he was nearly twenty, at which time he turned up in Morristown, New Jersey, apprenticing to become a lawyer.

My account of life on a Scottish island came from my own visits there, from historical research in scores of books about that place and time, and from conversations with Norman Kennedy, a Scotsman who is a folksinger, a weaver, and a wonderful source of legends and folklore of the Highlands.

I was able to track Malcolm's progress through his practice of law and his service as a quartermaster in the Morris Militia of New Jersey through New Jersey legal documents and Revolutionary War records. I am indebted to my mother-in-law, Nancy McCrumb, who suspended her own studies of genealogy in order to take photographs of Morris County historical sites and to guide me through the maze of documents relating to old Malcolm's life in eighteenth-century New Jersey.

In 1794, when Malcolm was past fifty and a prominent attorney in Morris County, New Jersey, he suddenly left his wife, his profession, and the place that had been his home for more than thirty years to journey down the wilderness road and homestead in western North Carolina, which was in those days a trackless wilderness. It was an odd move for a prominent lawyer who was an old man (fifty was old in 1794). Why would he do such a thing? My task was not to alter the facts but to make sense of them, given what information I could find about his life and times.

Malcolm settled first in Wilkes County, where he met Sally Lynn, and then moved on to Jack's Creek, where he and his new young "wife" raised a second family. I am descended from Malcolm Jr., one of the sons of that second union, through his son Eldridge, who fought in the Civil War in the 16th North Carolina, along with his sons Malcolm and Pinckney. Pinckney's war experiences, ending with his imprisonment on Hart's Island in New York harbor—all true.

My guide through the Civil War era in the novel was western North Carolina historian Michael Hardy, who shepherded me through the records of the 16th North Carolina, and who taught me how to load and shoot a Springfield muzzle-loader. That experience gave me an entirely new perspective on war. I had never before considered the terror that one could feel in the interval of reloading while the enemy continues to shoot at you, and the idea of being allocated only enough ammunition to shoot back forty times added insult to the injury, I thought.

I'm happy to say that General John T. Wilder, the Union commander who asked the enemy for advice, is real in every particular. I learned about his story years ago and I have always admired him tremendously. I was delighted when my research for *The Songcatcher* led me to the discovery that General Wilder had survived the war and opened a resort hotel on Roan Mountain in Mitchell County, making him eligible for a cameo in the 1880s part of the narrative.

Zebulon, the young boy who meets General Wilder at the Cloudland Hotel, was the grandson of Eldridge McCourry and my own great-grandfather. Orphaned at an early age, he was raised by his Uncle Pinckney and Aunt Till. I grew up hearing stories of Grandaddy Zeb, who helped in the building of the Clinch-field Railroad through the mountains by hiring out with his mules to lay the tracks. I have no photographs of Zeb McCourry, but I do have a small cherry wood carving of a rabbit that he gave to my mother when he first met her. She had come to the mountains as a sol-dier's bride in 1945, to meet the family of her new husband, and Old Zeb, a feisty elf of a man then in his seventies, presented her with the carving as a welcome gift. It sat on the table beside my word processor as I wrote the chapter about him.

I am grateful to Tennessee poet Jane Hicks for her permission to use the term "Cosmic Possum" from her series of poems of that name, and to her husband, Ron Hicks, for sharing his expertise in aircraft search and rescue.

"The Rowan Stave," the ballad that is the centerpiece of this novel, is not an authentic old song. It was written for this book, because I thought that I could not find a song so obscure that no reader would be familiar with it, so I composed one. However, it is true that my family did hand down authentic folk songs from one generation to the next as part of our oral tradition. It took me a while to find this out, though. My father left the mountains for World War II and never went back, so my contact with my mountain kinfolks were lim-ited to visits in the summer and sometimes at Christmas.

When I was in college, folk music was in vogue, and—in lieu of going to some of the more tedious classes at UNC—I bought a ten-dollar guitar at a pawnshop and learned to play. Then I bought a Joan Baez album of folk songs and tried to play them with the half a dozen chords I had managed to master. A few weeks later I went home for Thanksgiving, determined to impress my father with this new skill his tuition money was making possible. I summoned him into the living room and began to play (badly) my latest conquest from the Joan Baez oeuvre. I had just managed to sing the first line, "A fair young maid all in the garden..." when my father joined in. He was a little Hank Williams on the tune, but letter perfect on the words. I was aghast.

"How do you know this song?" I demanded. "It is the very latest in *college* music." I had gone down to the Record Bar on Franklin Street and paid $6.98 for that album. Parents weren't supposed to know the cool people's songs, I thought.

My father smiled. "Why, that's 'John Riley' you were singing," he said. "I had that song from my grandmother, and she had it from her grandmother."

When I got back to Chapel Hill, I read the liner notes on my Joan Baez album. "John Riley" was a Child Ballad, it said. That meant that Francis Child had collected it in the eighteenth century on the Scottish borders. So the song was at least two hundred years old. It had been brought to the North Carolina mountains by the settlers who homesteaded there after the Revolution. It had been handed down in my family from parent to child for seven generations.

And I went to the Record Bar and paid $6.98 for it.

I never forgot that lesson, because to me it symbolized the fragility of one's heritage. Each of us is the link between the past and the future, and it is up to us to pass along the legends, the stories, the songs, and the traditions of our own families. If we don't, they will be lost, and your children may not be lucky enough to find a bit of their past going for $6.98 in a store somewhere. They may never find it at all. Since then I have been mindful of seeking out my heritage and doing what I could to preserve it and celebrate it so that my children, and all the children of the Appalachian settlers, will have it as a cornerstone for the future.

The story told in the ballad "The Rowan Stave" is a Scots legend about the mother of the Brahan Seer, telling how she got the stone that gave him the Sight. I wrote the words, and my friend Shelley Stevens, a dulcimer player and a singer with the Ohio folk group Sweetwater, wrote the melody.

In a way this story of a heritage preserved in song is *Roots* with a tune. It is really a story that happened in many places: Australia, Nova Scotia, wherever the people of the British Isles settled with nothing left of home but the memories. I am chronicling the version of the story I know best: the Scots who settled the southern mountains of Appalachia. There is a kinship among all these expatriates: They are many squares of the same quilt. We are all descended from people who became strangers in a strange land. I hope that readers will pick up on the universality of the story, and not think of this book as a quaint dispatch from an alien place. It isn't. It's a distillation of the American experience. So...carry it on.

ABOUT THE AUTHOR

Sharyn McCrumb is the author of several bestselling novels, including *The Rosewood Casket*, *She Walks These Hills*, and *The Ballad of Frankie Silver*, which was nominated for a SEBA award. She has received awards for Outstanding Contribution to Appalachian Literature and Southern Writer of the Year. Her books have been named notable books of the year by both *The New York Times* and *Los Angeles Times*. She lives in Virginia.